DON'T DISAPPEAR

Part 1

A Novel by Nina Guest

Best Wishes!
Nina Guest
10.8.10

First published by Dog Ear Publishing
4010 W. 86th Street, Ste H
Indianapolis, IN 46268
www.dogearpublishing.net

dog ear
PUBLISHING

ISBN: 978-160844-191-4

"Don't Disappear" is a novel based upon true events. However, some names of people and places have been changed to protect the innocent.

This book is printed on acid-free paper.

Printed in the United States of America

Thanks to James Todd and Amanda Peart for their help and advice. And, a very special thanks to my loving husband, Bill, whose support and patience made this book possible.

—Nina Guest

Chapter 1

SHE WAS GOING on a date. Oh, how great it sounded! Just to be able to see him again and look into his eyes! It was early spring. Nature was waking up from beneath its winter frost. The sun shone brighter, attempting to warm the frozen ground with its rays. By noon, the weather was warming and the air heating up, tingled with a crispy freshness.

There had never before been such a beautiful spring day in Vika Zotova's life. Never had the sun shone so radiantly, and never had the thin ice crunched so joyfully under her feet as it did this morning, as she walked down the paved alley for a rendezvous with Sergei Nilovski.

Her heart pounded as she looked around, smiling. To her, the world around her smiled back in celebration of her fourteenth spring.

In a few more steps, she would turn the corner and catch sight of the tall clock under which they were to meet. She passed by the glittering store window and squinted in the intense sunlight as she caught a glance of her reflection. She chuckled at the sight of herself. Her checked coat with the rabbit collar hung loosely. Half the city it seemed, wore the exact same coat and they all looked perfectly alike. Her new hat fit pretty well and it was not important to her that the color did not match. Vika had knitted the accessory herself, and was very proud of it.

Sergei Nilovski stood under the clock, shivering in the fresh morning breeze, thinking thoughts of Vika, 'his sweetie,' as he loved to call her sometimes.

This was a dangerous game for him – a young but experienced specialist in the KGB. He was top-of-the-line well educated, had a perfect command of two languages, and was destined for a brilliant career.

But suddenly he found himself falling in love. He couldn't help himself. He was afraid of losing her, and, as much he tried, he could not make himself forget her.

"Okay, twenty more minutes," Sergei glanced at his watch. He looked around, peering into faces, and smiled to himself. *There is no way she'll arrive so early,* he thought. He felt he had plenty of time on his hands, and his thoughts strayed to last autumn, when he first met Vika.

* * * * *

He had first encountered her in the gym. Training sessions were required as a part of his job, and Sergei did them three days a week. But last autumn, the gym at the police force closed for repairs, so the officers were temporarily utilizing the city's public gym.

Due to the large influx of additional people at the city gym, the police force had changed their workout time to the evening, beginning at six o'clock. Vika's circus training time moved up, and training began not long afterwards, at eight o'clock.

Sergei remembered one evening after their workout when he stayed later than usual with his friend Anton Darenko. The young-sters training for the circus entered the gym. Always noisy and cheerful, the young performers jumped, rolled and flipped effort-lessly through the air to their loud music. They showed off new ideas to each other, laughing cheerfully at their innovative tricks.

This environment was a refreshing contrast to Sergei and his friend's more serious training, and the men enjoyed witnessing this event. They enjoyed the feelings 'the fresh, young air' provided them.

One late evening, as Sergei was leaving the gym, he felt someone swiftly bump into him while passing through the door-way. She was ginger-haired and laughing. He would never forget how this young girl stopped abruptly, with a quick look of guilt, and uttered, "Oh mister, I'm so sorry. It was an accident!" Then just as quickly, she continued on her way into the gym. Sergei stood enchanted, gazing at the place where her face had been just a second before – those green eyes so bright and smiling, and her red hair appearing, then vanishing like a flash of light. He smiled. Just then Anton Darenko came out of the gym.

"Let's get out of here before these crazy kids trample us," laughed Anton.

That had been their first encounter. After this, Sergei started to stay longer in the gym, especially to see her.

From Vika's point of view, just looking at him made her feel embarrassed, and she could barely get out a simple 'good evening' before shyly running into the gym.

A few days later, Sergei and Anton were riding in the car, discussing their training routine.

"What do you think, Anton? When will our gym finally be finished with the repairs?"

"Probably by the New Year, I suppose. Why?"

"You know," answered Sergei thoughtfully, "when our training schedule was set up, other groups who were training at the gym had to shift their time around, and now they have to go back home very late. It's rather dangerous for them."

"You know, Nilovski," Anton smiled slyly at his friend, "I remember how stunned you were when that redheaded girl almost knocked you off your feet." Anton chuckled, "Of course, my friend, I understand your concern for children, but now you are scaring me. She may be a big girl already, but she's still a child, so forget about her, damn it!"

* * * * *

Sergei shivered and smiled to himself at his early memories of Vika. He glanced at his watch. *Now, where is my sweetie,* he thought, as he shrugged joyfully and looked around.

"Okay...she's late!" he said aloud, and memories of the past continued to fill his mind.

* * * * *

Soon after the conversation with Anton, he saw Vika again. He stopped her after her usual, very brief "good evening."

"Good evening, good evening! And what is your name?"

"Vika," she whispered.

"Vika? Vika means Victoria. Vika is such a beautiful name!"

"Thank you," she said shyly, glancing up at him.

He stood as if an electric shock had run through him. Her youthful beauty fascinated him, her lips, her nose, and those magnetic, smiling eyes. There was something so special about them, and for a second, he was taken aback and could hardly gather his thoughts.

"How do you get home at such a late hour?" he asked.

"I run," replied Vika, and she dashed into the gym.

That night, he stood and waited for her outside the exit. "Vika!" he called, after she came out into the street with a group of friends. She turned her head towards him and stopped, staring suspiciously.

"There's no need to be afraid of me," said Sergei, approaching her. "I work for the KGB. I have been delayed by my friend, but since I'm still here, how about an escort, so you don't have to be afraid and run all the way home?"

"Our coach told us that the police were training here. He also said that it's just temporary and you'll be leaving soon," she answered quickly.

"That's true. But maybe you'll allow me to walk you home at night, until we are transferred back," Sergei responded, matching her tone.

"Hmm, I don't know." Vika gave a suspicious grin and they started to walk.

* * * * *

Sergei was so deep in memories, that at first he didn't notice Vika, who had stepped out from around the corner.

He waved to her. She smiled as she fixed her eyes upon him. Sergei gave her a hug and a quick kiss on her glowing cheeks.

"Vika, you have such a charming smile," Sergei said with admiration. "Have I told you this already?"

"Oh, thanks." She lowered her eyes.

"So, my dear little conspirator, let's get a car and go to Anton's apartment. He must be tired of waiting for us." Sergei gave her a wink and hailed a taxi.

Chapter 2

ANTON DARENKO AND Lena Somova had been friends for a long time. They worked together in the KGB. Although Vika had never met Lena, she knew from Sergei that the two had plans to get married in the autumn.

When the taxi approached the house, Sergei glanced out the window, and pointed to the second floor and laughed.

"Look, Lena is standing on the balcony waiting for us. She must be frozen to the handrails already."

He looked at Vika and elbowed her. "Don't be nervous. Lena is very friendly and she already knows about you." With these words, they got out of the car and went up to the apartment.

Lena smiled and put her hand out to Vika.

"Hello, my name is Lena!"

"I'm Vika."

"There we have finally met!" Lena went on. "Let me help you with your coat."

"Why are we taking off our coats?" Sergei broke in. "I didn't know we were staying."

"No, no, and no," Lena protested. "We can't go anywhere until you try my new cake."

"And till we get drunk on tea," added Anton.

"Stop being greedy," Lena laughed, "We're not drinking tea. I happen to know that you have your hands on some delicious, rare coffee. So we'll have to break into those bourgeois reserves. Is it a holiday today or what?"

"Of course it's a holiday," replied Anton, as he hugged her tightly, "a wonderful holiday, a Russian farewell to old man winter! Right, Vika?" he said, winking at their quiet visitor.

"R-r-right," stammered Vika.

"That's why we're going into the kitchen," continued Anton, "to sweep away those reserves and then after that, we'll say good-bye to our winter with a ride in a three-horse sleigh at the winter festival. You girls will love it!"

Sergei helped Vika off with her coat and they walked into the kitchen, where Lena was busy arranging saucers and cups. She cast a glance at Vika, and then stopped, raising her eyebrows.

"Now I understand, Sergei," she said with enthusiasm and surprise. "I also would have never given up this beauty!" And then, smiling, Lena looked her guest up and down. Embarrassed, Vika blushed to a bright red and stepped back.

"Hey, what's wrong?" Lena came up to her quickly and pulled her by the hand to the table. "Don't feel shy. You should be proud of yourself. It's great to have such a stunning figure. And these curls! Never, ever cut your hair short, young lady. The longer the better!" she concluded, and they sat down at the table.

Sergei drew his chair close to Vika, placed his hand on hers, and squeezed it slightly to reassure her. His smile was warm as he looked into her eyes. Rare were these moments when they could sit so close to each other.

This caused Vika's heart to miss a beat. He seemed to take no notice of her shyness and went on joking about everything, telling new and amusing stories.

Later, they enjoyed themselves at the holiday festival. Lena was very enthusiastic about it.

"Hey Anton, don't act like a shy kid," she laughed and elbowed him, "look at this icy pole and pair of boots at the very top. Do you see that?"

"Don't be such a pushy girl," he smiled back, "You don't need those crappy boots."

"Why not? Look at how funny those guys appear slipping down the pole over and over. Let's try."

"Okay, I'm going to do something embarrassing. Could you please hold my hat and coat?"

"Sure." Lena grabbed his clothes and they joined the crowd. Anton began his journey up the icy pole amidst the encouraging cries of the crowd. He climbed higher and higher, but the slippery pole did not yield and soon his expedition was over. He slid down, laughed, and greeted his friends, "It's your luck, Lena, to be a bare-footed beauty," Anton gave her a hug. "Now it's Nilovski's turn."

"No way!" his friend smiled back. "I'm not drunk enough yet to enjoy humiliating myself. Look at that guy," he pointed back at the pole.

A teenager, wearing just his pants, was climbing up nonstop and very fast. He quickly reached the top, tore off the prized boots, and ecstatically staggered away with them.

"Nilovski, you lost your opportunity," laughed Lena. "How will you impress Vika now?"

"On the next competition, over there," he pointed to a big log about six feet above the ground. Two men were sitting on the log and knocking the sense out of each other with bags filled with saw-dust.

Sergei waited until the battle ended and he got into position on the log. Pretty soon he knocked his opponent off the log and won a prize — a soft teddy bear, which he immediately presented to Vika.

"You got lucky, dude," laughed Anton, "next year, a rematch! Lena, please help me clean my face up, and then go ahead with Vika and kick her little ass off of that log."

"Yeah, you're right," Sergei said, holding Vika. "It's the first time they've seen each other and now let's make them fight."

"It's a real tricky idea," laughed Lena. "And I'm sure you both would love to see that. It'd be better to go to see concerts and ride on the horse."

"As you command," agreed Anton.

The sleigh rides were crowded, which made finding a free horse difficult. When an empty troika rode up, they all piled into the sleigh together. The boys climbed onto the seats with the girls perched on their knees.

More young folks jumped aboard the sleigh as well and took their seats. They were noisy and laughing as they pushed each other, but at the same time, they held each other tightly so no one would fall out. Then they all shouted to the driver, "Okay, we're full! C'mon, let's go!"

The horses trotted briskly forward, jingling with small bells. In a gesture of fun, Vika and Lena shouted, "Faster! Faster!"

Vika's hair stuck out from her hat and fluttered and brushed against Sergei's face. He moved nearer and kissed her hair. He turned and glanced at Anton, who nodded knowingly.

The conclusion of the festival was the ritual burning of a straw statue, representing the Russian winter. All together they strolled to the site to see the action. Suddenly, a young woman emerged from the crowd and approached them.

"Hello, Sergei, happy holiday!"

"Hello," he answered indifferently.

"Can I talk to you for a minute?"

Vika stood, looking first at him, then at her, not understanding why his face became so alert. Then suddenly she realized, he was a handsome man, and undoubtedly he had a lot of acquaintances. She looked carefully at this attractive girl, and a completely unknown feeling crept over her.

"Sorry," Sergei smiled back slightly at the girl. "Not now. Happy holiday. Good luck." Then he attempted to walk from the girl. But she, changing her expression, glanced at Vika contemptuously.

"Well, have you switched over to minors?" she said, staring straight at Sergei. He turned to Vika, "Please, stay with Anton and Lena for a second." Then, squeezing the girl's elbow, he drew her aside.

Vika looked at Anton and Lena, as if expecting some sort of explanation from them.

"Don't worry, Victoria," Anton said warm-heartedly. "Everything will be all right."

"Thank you." She suddenly had a sick feeling in her stomach. She turned her eyes towards Sergei. He stood, bending down to the girl, still gripping her elbow and speaking to her. Then he let go of her abruptly and walked back. The girl hung her head, and turned back towards her friends who were waiting for her in the distance.

"Sorry, guys," said Sergei, as he approached his friends. "A cloud from the past can sometimes quickly darken the sky."

"That's because we haven't burned the symbol of the past," Anton piped up, as he pointed towards the straw effigy of a woman in Russian native dress that symbolized the winter past. "Let's go help burn it and begin a new life!"

They threaded their way through the crowd to get closer to the action and caught the final concert. Sergei put his arms around Vika and whispered in her ear. "Don't worry, sweetie. I know it was a difficult winter for us, but now everything will be wonderful. I promise," and he gave her a kiss on the ear.

After listening to the concert and witnessing the winter symbol burn up into the sky, they headed towards the car. But that unpleasant feeling which came after the encounter with that strange girl continued to haunt Vika Zotova after they left.

"Thank you for such nice company, guys, but I think I'll go home," said Vika.

"Why?" Sergei looked at her, "It's just past three and we have a lot of time."

"That's right," Lena interrupted. "Let's go to Anton's to boil the ravioli we made yesterday."

"And we also have champagne and wine," added Anton. "And we'll continue the festival, but we'll call it, 'A Welcoming Spring Festival,' okay?" he turned to a wide-eyed Vika.

"I don't drink!" she blurted out.

"That's wonderful," added Sergei, helping her get into the car, "all the more for me!" Everybody laughed, even Vika.

Chapter 3

MUSIC PLAYED SOFTLY in the car, as the friends carried on their conversation. Sergei Nilovski and Vika Zotova sat in the rear seat, and as he warmed her palm with his hand, Vika melted. She couldn't think of anything else as she glanced at him out of the corner of her eye.

He was handsome, built strong and tall, with wavy chestnut hair. His large brown eyes were framed by thick, black eyelashes. He had a straight nose with a slightly rounded tip, beautiful lips, and perfect, straight teeth.

Vika stared at their hands. She enjoyed having her small palm drowning in his large, warm one. She beamed with pleasure, so at ease in his company. It was as if Sergei, Anton, and Lena were from another world; so distant and unknown to her, enigmatic and complicated, and alluring with mystery.

They finished a heavy dinner and sat in the dining room planning for their future. Vika felt comfortable with Sergei. He was so caring and strong, and he made her feel secure.

"At the end of April we'll bring the youngsters to the parachute tower to jump," Sergei shared his plans with her. "Do you want to come?"

"Yes, of course," Vika blurted out. "Would they let me go?"

"Well, we'll teach you how to use the equipment and what to do, and I don't think there will be a problem," Sergei gave a discreet smile.

"We'll probably have our periodical training on the mountain in May or a little later," Lena continued the topic. "What do you think, Nilovski? How long will they last this time?"

"I don't know for sure. I think a week or so."

"Oh! I have my tests during that time," said Vika.

"And where are you going to study after that?" Lena asked her.

"Most likely I'll go to high school."

"All right, all right, let's take our minds off of work and school," Anton said, reaching for his guitar.

He slowly plucked the strings and the room soon filled with a soft, romantic melody. Anton sang one song after another, and Lena sang with him. Then Sergei took the guitar.

"Can you play?" Vika asked with surprise and admiration.

"Yes, a little bit," he gave her a tender look. "I graduated from music school and sometimes, well...I allow myself."

He started to play and sing. This was their first such experience in each other's company...in the apartment...so close. Vika brought out old and new talents in him.

He won her over with his mind and his attention. No one had ever treated her as fondly and gently. *Sergei! The most beautiful name in the world!* She thought as she looked at him. Her thoughts rushed back, to their earlier meetings, when he began taking her home after her training sessions.

* * * * *

Together they found a common language. Vika was genuine and easily amused — so the minutes to her house flew by in an instant. As they would approach the house, he would always tell her jokingly, "Welcome home!" He would lift a hand to his chest, wave, and say, "Bye-bye, sweetie!" After she entered the house, she ran up to the third floor in one breath. He watched the staircase window until she opened her apartment door and disappeared behind it.

Sometimes, on their days off, they went to the amusement park to swing on the swings and have fun. Sometimes they went to see the museum or the art gallery.

During this time, she began to suffer problems in her studies. Then, one day her chemistry teacher said, when she hesitated with her answer, "So, you can't find time to study? You should spend less time with older guys in parks."

The class began to whisper and laugh.

"Vika has two older brothers," somebody came to her defense. But it was too late. Silly gossip was being spread. And she endured a fair share of suffering, even though the boys at school feared dealing with her. They knew she was very strong and athletic and could stand up for herself. Except at home...

Vika had two older brothers, Viktor and Maxim. Her father, a military engineer, had died when Vika was two years old. She didn't remember him. Her mother had always worked two jobs in order to make ends meet. Viktor, the eldest brother, was in charge at home.

Viktor was mean and despotic. When he was in the living room watching television, no one else was allowed to enter. It didn't even matter if his mother needed to pass through to hang clothes on the balcony. She was just thankful that the balcony was long and spanned two rooms, so that she could climb through the window in the adjacent room and hang the wash.

Their mother shouted at Viktor and cried often. Vika, together with her middle brother Maxim, took their mother's side and, as a result, were the victims of their brother's wrath. At the same time, Vika saw that their mother loved both her sons more than her. She treated the boys with awe, pride, and compassion.

She did all of the physical work herself and forced Vika to help her. Rather than tearing the boys away from their studies, she always brought Vika along to dig for potatoes, which they planted in the countryside. She said that since Vika did well at school, she would catch up quickly, and learning was more important for boys anyway. The eldest brother, aware of his elevated status, treated his younger siblings badly and often beat them. He didn't even call them by their names. Viktor gave them both nicknames — fatty and skinny. Having such a dictatorial attitude in the family taught Vika and Maxim to be unafraid of fighting back, and to support and protect each other.

Vika had a good relationship with her middle brother, and used to follow Maxim around everywhere. He taught her to do everything he could do himself. She rushed about with a gang of boys around construction sites, climbed with them into other people's gardens to gather fruits, and fished with them.

She quickly learned to ride a bicycle, a moped, and then a motorcycle. Vika would run and push the motorcycle, start the engine, jump on the moving cycle and drive away with a proud grin.

Vika was not afraid of boys, but rather, was a part of their company. It was much easier and more interesting for her to be with them than with girls. They played hockey all together in the winter, with Vika often positioned as goalie, and they went skiing on weekends.

Boys never gossiped behind each other's backs nor provoked each other to play dirty tricks. They were frank and open. If they had to fight, they fought. If they had to help, they helped each other without expecting anything in return.

* * * * *

Vika looked towards Sergei, who quietly crooned a solemn song. He was already a part of her history, a part of her life. She remembered how her oldest brother found out about Sergei.

Viktor rushed into the apartment that day, like a hurricane, and shouted from the threshold, "You, fatty, come here!"

She was sitting in the room, doing her homework. He flew up to her and forcefully struck her on the head. Their mother ran in from the kitchen at once.

"Viktor, what are you doing? Why are you beating her? She is a little girl!" He didn't let her finish, turning his face to his mother abruptly.

"Are you sure?" he shouted. "Do you know the age of the guy she is dating? He is twice as old as she is, and what does he want from her?"

"We are not dating," cried Vika.

"Shut up!" screamed Viktor. "Everyone is laughing at you. I told you," pointing at his mother, "we ought to forbid her from attending such late training sessions for the circus studio. I'm almost twenty and I come home earlier than she does. It's over," he turned to Vika. "Your circus is over. Stay home!"

"No, I will keep going," Vika cried out, turning her face to him. He struck her in the face with a swinging blow and left the room.

Their mother stood dazed, staring at her daughter. This was news to her.

"Are you dating somebody?" She tried to calm Vika's crying, even though she herself was upset.

"Listen to me, Vika. I realize that you've been involved in the circus studio for several years now. I know that you like it, but you really do come home very late. Maybe you can just do the Sunday trainings. You see, you could go all morning on Sunday. And what is Viktor talking about? What grown-up guy? Is he really twenty-eight? Who is he?"

"Nobody!"

Vika, terrified of her elder brother, told Sergei about the incident, requesting that he not come near her house anymore. Sergei agreed.

One evening, shortly after this discussion, they approached her house. Suddenly Vika stopped abruptly and peered into the darkness of the yard.

"Okay, this is far enough. We must part here. My brother is standing near the entrance. Bye, Sergei." Frightened, she ran home.

She tried to shrink past Viktor, but he grabbed her and pushed her towards the door.

"Didn't I tell you not to go out in the evening?"

Vika stumbled and fell down. Suddenly she heard Sergei's voice, "Don't touch her!" he yelled, as he approached them.

Vika jumped up to try to stop Sergei, and stood between him and Viktor. The boys were facing one another — they were of equal height, tall and strong.

"Sergei, please, don't! Don't do anything, please, go home!" Vika pleaded in a strained voice.

"Listen to me," Sergei began to speak slowly, trying to keep his anger under control as he stared straight at Viktor. "Let's talk like men. I can see you're a strong guy, so why do you abuse your little sister?"

"She knows why!" replied Viktor rudely, prepared to start a fight at any minute.

"I understand your concern," Sergei said, articulating every word. "And I promise you that I will not do anything to hurt your sister. I care about her. But you..." his voice was calm, but stern and threatening. "Do not ever raise a finger to her again. That's all," he shifted his gaze to Vika. "Sorry, baby, good-bye," he said as he turned and walked calmly away. She turned her face to her brother, who was still watching Sergei walk away.

"Go inside!" he said dryly.

Viktor never beat her again after that, and soon afterwards, he enlisted in the army, requiring their middle brother to meet her every evening after her training.

Vika wasn't aware that Sergei had begun to have problems at work. But she only knew that their meetings became rarer with each passing week, until they stopped seeing each other completely by the New Year.

Vika constantly thought about Sergei, and on occasion, she arrived early at the gym in hopes of seeing him at his training session. However, the doors were always closed, and Sergei and Vika could only see each other at the exit.

He looked at her with heavy-hearted, large eyes, and simply uttered a quiet, "Good evening," in passing. The police soon returned to their former gym, and the circus actors resumed training at six o'clock.

* * * * *

Sergei finished his guitar song and looked at Vika, passing his hand in front of her eyes, "Hello...you there! Are you with us?"

Everybody laughed.

"Oh, Nilovski, I never knew you could sing so well," Vika looked at him in surprise.

"Thank you. Thank you for your gracious compliments," said Sergei jokingly, and he made a few bows. He got up and put the guitar in the closet. "Sometimes I can even dance!"

He walked up to Vika, and knelt down next to her. He took her hands in his palms and looked into her eyes.

"Tell me, Victoria, where were you just now?"

"Back in autumn," she replied softly.

"Hmm...I like her honesty," Sergei said, getting up. "Anton, let's go out on the balcony for a smoke."

I have to go home, Vika thought, *the daylight beginning to wane.* Then she eyed Sergei in the balcony door.

"Don't even think about leaving right now," said Lena suddenly, rising from the armchair. "Did I guess your thoughts?"

"Absolutely. How did you know?"

"Not so long ago I was like you," Lena smiled. "And now you must have some champagne!" She placed a glass nearer to Vika.

"Just a little bit, otherwise I would feel guilty finishing a bottle alone." Lena winked conspiratorially.

"No, no, no. I won't...I can't," Vika resisted, pushing the glass aside.

"What are you afraid of?" Lena laughed. "Just take a couple of sips, you'll get relaxed, your head will spin a little bit..." she spun her hand in the air.

"But I feel giddy already," Vika tried to protect herself, but the glass was already in her hand.

Lena glanced back at the balcony door and said quietly, "Well, let's drink to a girl's happiness."

They clinked their glasses together in a toast, and Lena started to drink. Vika, looking at her, drank her champagne in one gulp and placed her glass on the table.

"Delicious," she said, as she reached for some chocolate.

"What a wonderful day," Lena smiled happily. "What do you think? Do you want to dance a little?" she asked Vika. And slowly sipping her champagne, without waiting for a reply, she got up and turned on the stereo.

The room filled with a beautiful, soft French melody. Lena sat down again near Vika.

"I understand your feelings, Vika, when that girl came up to Nilovski at the festival," said she softly. "That was just normal human jealousy...but don't worry. Nilovski is very fond of you, and he runs a risk, continuing to meet with you...and he doesn't take that into consideration, which is completely unusual for him." Lena smiled. "That's why, 'his friend is our friend, and our friend is your friend'," she concluded joyfully. "Let me fill your glass with more champagne."

"No thank you, Lena, I don't want any more."

"Then eat some chocolate," she pushed forward a box of chocolate and, laughing, tapped Vika on her knee in a friendly manner. "Let's relax!"

As the boys entered the room, they chuckled.

"Oh, look, our girls are chatting like old friends," Anton came up to Lena and carried her off to dance.

Vika sat on the sofa, feeling a little giddy, pleasant warmth spreading over her body. Sergei settled down close to her and looked fondly and attentively into her eyes.

"Let's dance...our first dance?!" he took her hand and pulled her up. Sergei turned her slowly to himself, put her left hand on his shoulder, and enfolded her back with his right hand. He kissed her hand, as he looked tenderly into her eyes.

Vika flushed and her head began to swim from such intimacy. She looked down, afraid to meet his eyes. She felt that such overwhelming feelings would cause her to collapse, but Sergei held her firmly in his arms and wheeled her slowly around the room.

The evening continued on, and the melodies changed from slow to fast. Vika did not skip a dance, feeling exuberant in Sergei's company. She didn't want to leave, but she knew she had to go home, so as to not to create a scandal and completely lose the opportunity to see Sergei again.

Sergei called a taxi, and after thanking Lena and Anton for their hospitality, they said their good-byes. After stopping at Vika's house, the taxi waited on the corner for Sergei, while he walked her to the door. He walked very slowly, holding her hand. He did not want to leave her at all.

"Thank you for today...for the evening," he said quietly, looking at her from the side. "I look forward to our meetings, and you know, I miss you already."

He wanted to speak as lightheartedly as possible, but hesitated, and it came out in a sad tone. They walked up to the building and he opened the door for her.

"Good-bye," said Vika softly.

He bent over slightly and gave her a peck.

"See you later, honey," he said as she ran upstairs.

Sergei waited until the door to her apartment banged shut, and he started back to the taxi. His whole body ached with desire to give her a real kiss, but he was afraid of that.

He was afraid of himself, and his masculinity, worried that he wouldn't be able to control himself...and what would happen then? Sergei shrugged, trying to banish such thoughts, as he walked faster to the waiting car.

Chapter 4

IT WAS EARLY spring. Bright sunrays were shining through the thick curtains. Semyon Severov, sitting in his office, leafed through some papers from a folder brought by the Internal Security Service.

He was a powerful, professional KGB officer. The years of work in the security services made him suspicious and distrustful. He was studying the papers carefully, trying to see and understand everything, even between the lines.

So many faces had flashed by in his life. Faces that he had sometimes drawn closer to him or pushed further away, depending on their quality or their mistakes. He taught many to work in this service. He taught them to be perfectionists.

Semyon took one big, deep breath when he looked at the large envelope in front of him. He found himself reviewing once more the package with the name of Sergei Nilovski on it. The boss knew, without opening it, what was inside.

Having drawn back from the table, he lit a cigarette. *Nilovski, Nilovski,* he thought, *what are we going to do with you? How are we going to save you?*

He liked these guys. They were two friends, two soldiers, competent, clever, always fulfilling any task efficiently and bravely. *Anton Darenko is going to get married. Good boy! He has chosen a good, young girl who works here, and has already performed missions — a time-tested winner. Everything is as it should be...but Nilovski,* Semyon Severov again took a deep breath. *So many girls are attracted to this young man. He could choose any of them. He is so handsome. But instead, he chooses to start chasing after a minor, like a young fool.*

Semyon remembered in detail the conversations he had with Nilovski last autumn. It was after he had been given a report from the service, and he learned whom the officer was dating.

* * * * *

The information about Vika Zotova had been lying in front of him. He didn't invite Nilovski to his office, but rather he went to Nilovski's office himself. He had entered without knocking and closed the door tightly behind him.

The officer had jumped up from his desk. He had been expecting the talk, and by his boss's appearance, understood that he was angry.

"Sit down!" ordered Semyon sharply, then took a seat himself, lit a cigarette, and stared straight at Nilovski.

"What are you doing, son?" he suddenly asked rather softly.

"I like her very much."

"What does that mean, 'I like her'?" Semyon asked, without changing his stare towards Sergei. "Do you know how old she is?"

"Yes, I do."

"You are disgracing this service! You have so many girls to choose from, take any and get married...any of them would jump at the chance. You were dating that doctor, what's her name...Rita...for such a long time, what happened?"

"She's not for me, sir," answered Nilovski, becoming more nervous as the conversation continued.

"Not for me-e-e..." mimicked his boss. "Do you know that we can shelve you and institute criminal proceedings against you for corrupting an underage girl? Do you know that?"

Sergei shrunk beneath the intense look of his boss. His whole body was covered with a cold sweat.

"I do know," he uttered. "But I'm not corrupting her."

"Then what are you doing with her?"

"Nothing, absolutely nothing."

"Okay. Very well." Softening his tone, Semyon went on, "Leave her alone, let her grow up, and don't destroy your own career."

He lit another cigarette.

"I need you here, Nilovski. Is that clear? Here!" pointing his finger onto the table. "Don't be foolish, son."

They sat in silence. Then Semyon got up hesitantly and made for the door, where he stopped and turned back to Nilovski—who was standing at attention by the desk. The boss walked back into the office, stood close to Nilovski, and spoke in a low voice. "Sergei, I know a little bit about this girl already. Her father and I were classmates at school. It's a small world." He gave his subordinate a concerned smile, then turned slowly and exited the room.

Every evening, the officers under Semyon Severov submitted their daily reports, including the names and times of past and future meetings. All reports were submitted to the Internal Security Service, checked, and re-checked.

Soon Semyon learned everything about Vika Zotova. He had photos of her, a list of her friends, and a list of the places where and when she spent her time, and what she was doing. He knew her grades at school, references given by the agents who questioned the people surrounding her, and a list of her relatives, back to her great grandmother, with all the pertinent information.

Semyon was an old fact checker, and Vika roused his interest. He even ventured out with another officer in the middle of a cold winter day to her school, to give a lecture in law.

Vika's class was silent and respectful. They listened quietly and some of the students asked many questions. Semyon Severov immediately recognized Vika, and when his officer talked to the class, the boss carefully studied her. He liked her. He liked her expression and smile; she made a good impression on him.

At the end of class, Semyon asked, "Who of you has a dream to work at the police department in the future?"

Almost everybody raised their hand.

"Why do you want it?" Semyon pointed to some guy.

"I always want to be the boss," was the answer. The class laughed.

"What about you?" he switched his sights to Vika.

"I'm not sure, sir," she smiled, "but police work is so romantic and powerful...I'd like for people to be scared of me."

The class busted out laughing again.

"What can you tell us?" Semyon smiled, and pointed to another student.

"I want to work for the police to protect people from bad guys."

"Whew...thanks, now I feel better." Semyon looked around the class and gave them a short, patriotic speech. When time was up, he took one last look at Vika and left the room.

He liked her very much. She was a beautiful girl with a soft voice and a very magnetic look. *She will have a lot of admirers around her,* he thought at that time. *She's just what we need, but she is too young...well, fortunately this can be resolved. Plus, she has time to learn.*

* * * * *

The telephone rang in the office of Semyon Severov, breaking his recollection, and he picked up the receiver. His boss was on the line.

"Yes, sir...okay...I'll be there in a minute," he replied briefly.

Semyon took the package with Sergei Nilovski's name on it and, leaving it unsealed, put it in the safe. After removing all the papers neatly from his desk, he left the room.

Chapter 5

VIKA ALWAYS WOKE up to a delicious aroma wafting from the kitchen. Her mother awoke very early every day to prepare something fresh for her children before running off to work, which began at eight o'clock.

Vika stretched herself drowsily in bed, and strained her ears to hear the sounds coming from the kitchen. Somebody was talking. She stood up.

"Good morning everyone," she dragged herself into the kitchen, smiling sleepily. "Oh, Granny, hi!" she shifted her gaze to her Granny, who was sitting grandly on the stool. Vika went off to the bathroom, murmuring a tune.

"It's better to say, 'God bless us all' first thing in the morning before you start singing songs," she heard her Granny's angry voice after her.

"Ha-ha-ha..." Vika said loudly, and closed the door to the bathroom.

She smiled as she got herself ready, recalling how her Granny taught her to pray in her childhood. Unfortunately, to her, it was a very dull learning experience and she didn't want to bother herself with it. So, her Granny began to use scare tactics to frighten the child into compliance.

* * * * *

"I want to tell you," her Granny had begun mysteriously, "that there are the forces of light on Earth, headed by God, and the forces of darkness, headed by the Devil. And every baptized human being has an angel, who sits on his right shoulder and sees everything the person does."

"That's not true!" the little girl had objected. "Where is he? I don't see him."

"He's invisible. All these forces cannot be seen by an ordinary man, but they can help him, if he believes in them and prays.

Likewise, they can draw him into the darkness if he doesn't believe in God, doesn't pray, or doesn't observe the rules."

"What rules?" the child asked fearfully.

"When you don't obey your mother, when you behave badly and lie, the dark forces will draw you to them. They are always around you!" Granny said, looking at little Vika, who sat shriveled and wide-eyed.

Granny went on, "There are a lot of devils around. They jump with joy, when you do something wrong...they grasp you by the hands and legs and force you to go with them!"

Vika started to cry with fear.

"But if you behave yourself," Granny continued in a didactic tone, "and grow up as a modest girl and know your prayers, the Devils will jump off...repeat after me!" And she started to pray slowly, and the crying child repeated after her in a weak voice.

* * * * *

Vika smiled, recalling this. Thanks to Granny's talent, she did learn some prayers. Nevertheless, she would not be learning any new ones. It was difficult for her to think of supernatural forces when the churches were closed and the country was ruled by the communist organizations.

One would be laughed at, disgraced, expelled from the organization, and would most assuredly be punished for saying anything like that. Besides, Vika enjoyed being a Komsomol member. To be a part of this young, communist party meant to be a part of something large and important, to be together with everyone, to be the same as everyone else.

Leaving the bathroom, Vika heard her Granny trying to convince her mother, "Larisa, you should speak with your children about God..." but her mother interrupted her, not allowing her to finish. "Mom, I don't have time to talk to them about their daily routine, let alone anything else. You know, I have two jobs and I come home late at night," her mother started to lose her temper, "...and if your God is so wonderful, does that mean that I'm a sinful person because I have such a hard life?"

"Oh, Larisa, Larisa, it's sinful to talk like this," Granny gave in, getting up from the stool. "I'll go wake up Maxim."

Vika heard these debates between them often and never interfered in their conversations on this matter. Frankly speaking, they didn't make any sense. Her mother, who claimed to be an atheist and was constantly arguing with her Granny on the topic of religion, knew how to pray. And when her children left the house, she always said, "God be with you!" No matter what their different beliefs were, Vika loved Granny.

Vika also knew that when Granny came to their house in the morning, it meant she needed help around her house. Vika's family would be expected to travel to her Granny's small home in the suburbs sometime soon, in order to help her tend her garden. But Vika had no desire to go there right now.

Granny was descended from former landowners. The 1917's revolution rolled over her family with all its mass in the Civil War, having spared the lives of only a few of them, and taking all of the family fortune.

Once, Vika learned that one of her great-grandfathers supported the communists in the Red Army, while her other great-grandfather supported the Tsar and belonged to the White Army.

Only on one occasion did Granny tearfully tell how the great-grandfather in the Red Army was whipped to death by the Whites, and the other great-grandfather in the White Army was shot by the Reds; and Granny made a casual remark, that when a person was whipped to death, he started to bark. After that, the whole subject was closed in the family, and nobody asked her about it ever again.

Vika knew only one grandmother, since none of her father's relatives kept in touch with them at all. She did not know them, and had never met them.

She simply had Granny and that was enough for her. Because all of Granny's attempts to make her eldest grandchild Viktor help her with anything failed, she didn't ask for help from Maxim either, whom she loved and cared for more than anybody else.

Vika and her mother always did most of the housework. They sawed and chopped firewood for the winter, carried coal, and piled it out in the shed. They fetched water from the well to the house and bathhouse, shoveled snow in the winter, and tended the garden in the summer.

Even though her mother was small and slim, she worked so hard that she could drive anyone to exhaustion. That's why, when Granny asked for help, Vika tried to bring Maxim with her instead. It was easier working with him. Together they fulfilled the planned tasks very quickly and got away sooner.

After putting on her school uniform, Vika ran out of her room to the kitchen, ate an egg for breakfast, gulped down some tea, and without hearing the reason for Granny's visit, said to her, "I'm sorry, but I'm so busy now preparing for my upcoming examinations. I don't have time to come to your house!" She downed her tea rapidly, kissed her mother's cheek, snagged own bag, and scurried to the front door.

"Bye-bye everyone!" she yelled from the corridor, and the front door slammed as she darted out.

Chapter 6

SERGEI NILOVSKI WENT Away on business trips rather often, but never told Vika where he was going or when he would return. She always dashed home from school as quickly as possible, and waited impatiently for his phone call, convincing herself that he must be at home by now.

She flew around the apartment as if she had wings, obediently completing all the chores her mother assigned for her. She could only think about her need to be allowed outside without an argument whenever she needed to.

This necessity crept upon her suddenly last New Year's Eve, and, since then, Vika tried to avoid arguments with her mother by being attentive and obedient.

* * * * *

That New Year's Eve, as usual, Vika's family sat at their festively adorned table and watched television as they said their goodbyes to the old year and greeted the new one. They made themselves comfortable and all watched the 'Blue Light New Year's Special' on television. Vika, wearing a nice dress, sat on the sofa with Maxim, but her thoughts were far away.

Her thoughts were only on Sergei. Ever since their separation, she had missed him. She no longer enjoyed her circus trainings, and just before Christmas, she had fallen from the trapeze and severely injured her leg.

It wasn't fractured, but the injury was serious and was wrapped tightly in a dressing, so Vika sat at home on her holiday vacation.

Sergei, Sergei, she thought sadly, sitting on the sofa. She felt depressed and wanted to cry. Vika stood up and went to her room. She approached the window and opened the curtains.

It was a beautiful evening outside. Large, slow, whirling snowflakes were falling to the ground, and the trees were covered in white, like in a fairy tale. The lamp posts lit up the street, and an occasional pedestrian could be seen walking on the freshly-fallen snow.

Then suddenly, Vika noticed that not all of the pedestrians were walking. One of them stood under the light, without moving, staring up at her window.

There were hundreds of windows around, but she knew that he was looking at her window. No, not at the window, directly at her! Vika held her breath.

"Sergei..." she breathed out, and peered down at his silhouette. He waved to her, and she enthusiastically waved back.

At this moment, as if caught up by a hurricane, Vika rushed out into the corridor, tearing the first jacket she came across from the coat hook.

"Mom, I'm going to take out the garbage!" she shouted, and rushed to the door.

"What? Right now? What garbage?" her mother's puzzled voice reached her ears.

Vika thought feverishly of what to say, but as she flew up to the front door, she suddenly remembered her friend living next door.

"I'm going to see Tanya. I'll be right back!" she said, as she jumped out of the flat without waiting for a reply.

Vika didn't notice the pain in her leg. She leaned on the railing to hop down the stairwell, thrust open the door, and dashed out onto the porch. Then, she stood motionless... There was Sergei standing directly in front of her.

"Vika..." he whispered gently. He came up to her and embraced her.

"Sergei..." echoed Vika, and pressed her cheek against his chest.

They stood silently for a minute. Then he raised his hand to her head, took her hair in his palm and, bringing it to his face, inhaled its aroma. Sergei turned Vika's face to him, and their eyes met. He wanted to say something, but telltale tears welled up in his eyes, and he could only force himself to say, "I am so happy to see you," as he cuddled her again.

Sergei quickly regained his composure and began to whirl her around on the porch. "Vika, Vika, Victoria...you are my song...you are my sunshine!" He set her onto her feet and, raising her chin, asked fondly, "Did you know that? I don't ever want to be without you!" He gave her a light kiss on her full lips. Stepping back, he looked her over.

"Oh look, you don't even have your warm coat on, and what happened to your leg?" he inquired with a worried expression. Without waiting for her reply, he lifted her up and carried her into the building.

He put Vika down onto the lighted landing on the first floor and knelt by her legs.

"So, what is that?" he tried to touch the bandaged leg.

"Nothing serious," she said quietly and hid her leg behind the other. Sergei stood up.

"Can you walk in shoes?"

"Yes," she answered, even though she hadn't yet tried to put a shoe on after the injury.

"Why are we standing here then? Let's go for a short walk, it's so wonderful outside."

"Oh, I don't know! My mom and Granny are home, and they probably won't let me go," Vika responded, unsure about what they would say.

"Okay, what can we do?" he rose to his feet and hugged her. "I want to stay with you at least for a little while...your voice...your laugh," he gave her a smacking kiss on the forehead. "What can we do?" Sergei was lost in thought for a second.

"Is Maxim home?" he asked.

"Yes, he is. He's watching TV."

"Ask him to come for a walk, and we'll take a stroll all together," offered Sergei. He had met Maxim in autumn and they were on friendly terms.

"Okay." As she started up the stairs, Sergei leaped after her and raised her in his arms, and then carried her to the third floor. He touched her cheek lightly with his lips and ran downstairs.

As she walked inside, Vika's heart was pounding. It seemed to her that everyone could hear it. She made every effort to compose herself and entered the room as calmly as possible. She took a seat on the sofa and gave her brother a nudge.

"Let's go outside...It's so nice out there!" suggested Vika.

"No-o-o!" he turned his face lazily to his sister...then froze as he noticed her wide, sparkling eyes.

"Let's go, okay?!" she pleaded. Maxim shifted his sight to Granny and their mother.

"Mom, is it okay if we go outside for a little bit?" he started to ask, although not very convincingly.

Their mother was engrossed in the television program and, without tearing herself away, replied, "Well, go ahead, take a walk, but not too long. Her leg still hurts."

Maxim and Vika crept to the corridor to put on their coats. Her brother was three years older than her, and was tall and slim. He bent over to his sister in the hallway and whispered in her ear, "What the heck is going on?"

She turned her shining face to him and said very softly, staring and pointing to the staircase, "Sergei is here!"

Maxim stood up straight and fixed his eyes on his sister.

Witnessing his reaction, she changed her expression and became scared and desperate.

"Please, please! We'll just walk for a minute."

He stood, trying to make up his mind what to do. At that moment, Granny walked into the hallway and looked at them suspiciously.

"Why are you standing here whispering?" she grumbled, "If you've decided to go then go, before your mother changes her mind."

"You're right..." Maxim muttered and began to slowly put on his coat.

They emerged outside. Sergei was waiting for them on the porch, smoking. Upon seeing them, he put out his cigarette and stepped towards them, reaching out his hand to Maxim.

"Well, good evening, Maxim! And, Happy New Year!"

"Good evening, Sergei, and Happy New Year to you, too."

"Thank you very much, Maxim."

"What for?" Maxim was puzzled. Sergei shifted his look to Vika.

"For your cooperation." Smiling, he patted Maxim's shoulder. Maxim stared at them with a very displeased look.

"Let's all take a walk," suggested Sergei.

"No guys, I don't want to walk with you. Besides, her leg hurts…, she can't take a long trip."

"Thanks, Maxim. Really, thank you," he gave him another friendly pat. "We'll just wander here a little bit."

"Well, okay…" Maxim agreed. "I'll go to my friend's apartment on the fifth floor." He shifted his look to his sister. "On your way back, pick me up." After saying good-bye to Sergei, he disappeared.

Still in disbelief, they stood, simply looking at each other. Then Sergei came up to her and hugged her tightly.

"Well, let's go?"

"Let's go!" agreed Vika.

Joining hands, they walked slowly towards the backyard. As they passed under a snow-covered tree, Vika raised her hand and tugged a branch, causing a heap of soft snow to fall onto their heads.

Vika began to laugh, and ran away from Sergei. He chased after her and had almost caught up, when they both slipped and fell down into the snowdrift. She tried to get up, but he pulled her down gently. Vika took a handful of soft snow and, giggling, threw it in his face.

He laughed, rolling in the snow with her and wiping away the snow from his face. She crawled away from him and stood up. "Look!" Vika said. She chose a clear palette of snow and fell down on her back, spreading out her arms and legs. He stood up and came over to her. She reached out her hands to him.

"Give me your hand. Help me get up!" she said joyfully. Sergei pulled her up and, laughing, she pointed to her well-marked print on the snow.

"This is me!"

He stepped back and also fell down into the snow, next to her print.

"And this is me!" he laughed, lying in the snow. "Well, now it's your turn to pull me up!"

Sergei held his hands out to her. She came up to him, grasped his hands, and started to draw him up towards her, but Sergei pulled her down instead, without much effort, and laughed.

Vika fell on top of him...then rolled down in the snow beside him. She made an attempt to get up again, but he pressed her down, and, bending over her face, said with happiness, "That's it. I've caught you. Surrender!"

"Okay, okay, I surrender at your discretion!" she cheerfully laughed.

He kissed her and then helped her to her feet. They went over to a snow-covered swing.

"A New Year..." he said dreamily, pushing the swing slightly. "This is the best and the most beautiful holiday in the world! And when it snows tonight, it's a sign of your happiness!"

"And if you, like a piglet, wallow in it," added Vika smiling, "that means you will sink in happiness."

They laughed loudly together.

"Sergei," she became quiet suddenly. "I'll have to go home soon."

"Soon?" he stopped the swing. "But...yes, of course...I understand."

They sat down on a bench. He put his arms around her and smoothed her hair, sticking out from under her hat, from her face.

"I missed you, Vika, so much. And I don't want to not see you anymore."

Vika listened to him, holding her breath and dropping her eyes.

"I know you're a smart girl, but I want to make sure you understand..." Sergei went on, trying to choose his words carefully. "I've been having some problems at work, but...I can't forget you and..." he turned her face to him, but she did not raise her eyes. "We'll figure out how we can date. Okay?" he concluded in a confident and cheerful voice, cuddling her. They were silent for some time.

"And now you're right. It's time for you to go home, or else your little leg will catch a chill." They walked to her house, holding hands.

On the porch, Vika stopped Sergei.

"Please, don't go with me any further."

"Okay," he opened the door. "Have a Happy New Year, Victoria. I'll call you tomorrow and we'll decide what to do."

"Happy New Year!" she uttered shyly, and then ran upstairs.

When she came into the apartment, she was still smiling and started to take off her coat and hat. Her mother came out of the room.

"Where's Maxim?"

Vika was startled.

"He is...he is..." she was thinking frantically, "He's on the staircase!" Vika blurted out. "I'll get him!" she rushed out the door and went upstairs to the fifth floor.

Vika was running and laughing - she had forgotten all about her brother. She felt so happy at this moment, she had forgotten about everything else.

Chapter 7

GRANNY NEVER VISITED unless there was a particular reason. The snow had disappeared already, and she wanted to set the fence straight around the garden before it was time to start planting. Vika, Maxim, and their mother decided to go there all together, when they had free time, to repair the fence.

On this particular Saturday their mother had time off only in the afternoon, and on Sunday morning Vika couldn't go because she had to go to the library. So they decided to postpone the project until the following weekend.

'A visit to the library' was what she secretly called her meetings with Sergei. They had been spending almost every Sunday in the library since New Year's Eve. If the weather was good, they walked somewhere, and if it was very cold, they stayed in the library or visited the museum.

She loved those visits. Vika immensely enjoyed history and geography. Sergei told her many interesting facts about the world. Sometimes they discovered some historical books, and he would ask a librarian to bring some maps. They read about the ancient world together, and Sergei would point out the sites on the maps.

Vika took great pleasure during their meetings. It was a time when she felt very close to him. They were together and, little by little, he filled up her life. Every moment from Monday until Sunday she thought about their time together, and often she called him up in the middle of the week.

She no longer attended the Circus Studio, and step-by-step Sergei helped her to fill her free time with studies. Vika remembered that smooth transition.

Sergei always took an active interest in her schooling and sometimes jokingly called her 'student.'

"How's your life, 'student'? Have you begun to prepare for your tests already?"

"Yes, we're writing something already…," she answered unwillingly.

"In what subjects?" Sergei wasn't giving up.

"Mathematics and Russian."

"Well, what are the results?" he asked enthusiastically.

"It's easy!" she replied in the same tone.

"And what about you're other subjects? Do you like to study those as well?"

"No," answered Vika honestly. "Sometimes the subject becomes interesting, but the teacher isn't."

"What subject in particular?"

"Well, for example, German," Vika started to explain with disappointment. "The teacher has a little baby, and she's not in school very often…basically, I don't give a damn about the German language! I don't need it!"

"What are you saying, Victoria?" Sergei was surprised. "Languages are the force," he instructed her. "They open up other countries and cultures to you. It gives you the chance to read books from other countries in their original language."

"What do I need it for?"

"So you won't be silly and foolish!" Nilovski blurted out.

Vika was taken aback and offended. She lowered her eyes and pouted her lips. She was on the verge of tears.

"Please Victoria, don't be hurt. I just really want you to love learning," he looked at her with kind and attentive eyes. "I know you could easily do well, if you just gave it some additional effort." She raised her eyes, and he continued calmly, "You should be happy that learning comes easy to you. You should take this knowledge…you should draw upon the information. The one who has the information has the power." Sergei looked seriously at Vika. "I think you should do some additional learning on your own and just ask the teachers what you don't understand."

"Why?"

"You never know when and where this knowledge will prove useful to you. But it's better to have it at the right moment."

She opened her mouth with surprise, and looked at him. Nobody had ever spoken to her so convincingly before. Sergei smiled, seeing her in that state.

"Well, well! The 'student' has been frightened to death!" he laughed. "But I'm here. Don't be afraid to learn new things. I'll help you with German." And he said something in fluent German.

Since that day, he taught her German, and she learned other subjects on her own. Physics and chemistry stopped being so awful, and learning became a little bit more interesting to her.

Vika tried to complete everything that Sergei assigned to her, to make him happy. And she was eager for him to be proud of her. He was always pleased with her and longed to spend time with her, trying as best as he could to be useful. He kept up with her life in order not to lose her.

Chapter 8

SATURDAY MORNING, MAXIM got up early, turned on some music, and went to the kitchen to make breakfast. He shouted to his sister.

"Vika, wake up! What did you and Mom decide yesterday about Granny? When are we going?"

Not a sound came in reply. He went to her room and opened the door–she was still in bed. "Hey, sister, good morning!" he shouted cheerfully. "Get up! You've had enough sleep, the house-work is yelling for you!" and he returned to the kitchen, leaving the door open.

Vika awoke. The soft music from the radio in the kitchen reached her ears. She stretched in bed, and, with her eyes closed, smiled at her thoughts. The next day was Sunday, and she would see Sergei.

She wasn't ready to leap out of bed, and she was still lying there when Maxim entered the room again. He took a seat opposite her on their mother's bed and said impatiently,

"So, what are your plans? What did Mom decide about Granny? When do we have to go?"

"Why are you so nervous?" Vika said drowsily. "She hasn't decided anything. She said she would come home after work and if she wasn't too tired, we would go to Granny's." Vika looked suspiciously at her brother. "What are your plans?"

"Right now? To have breakfast," he answered, getting up. "C'mon, get up and we'll eat together."

Vika quickly followed Maxim into the kitchen. She felt her brother had something on his mind and was trying to keep it to himself. She was good at reading people, and was sure in her ability to convince him to let her in on the secret.

They had a quick breakfast, spoke about trivial matters, and Maxim got ready to go.

"Where are you going?" Vika asked him.

"I'll be back in the afternoon."

"What from?" she looked into his eyes, with a questioning smile. "Take me with you, ah?! Please, take me, too," Vika continued to pester him. "And then I'll call Tanya for a walk tonight," she added cunningly. Vika knew how to put pressure on her brother.

"You know, sister, you have an evil side to you," he said, smiling with disapproval. "Okay, come on. Get ready to go!"

She rushed around the apartment, looking for her track suit, and put on her jacket. He stood at the door, waiting patiently.

"No, take off that jacket," he said, "and put on something old."

"Aha," she replied and started to dig quickly among the hangers in the closet. "Where are we going?"

"Promise not to tell anybody?" Maxim asked conspiratorially.

"I promise," she burned with impatience and stared at her brother.

"We found a real grenade and a trench bomb on the firing ground, and we're going with the guys to blow them up in the rock quarry today," he whispered. "Don't tell anyone about it! Is that clear?" her brother concluded in a threatening tone.

"It's clear," she replied strongly and seriously.

The sun was shining brightly, and it was warm and noisy outside. The birds were whirling in the sky, filling the yard with their songs. The trees were covered with the first soft, green, small sticky leaves of spring, still transparent, and the yard seemed to be unusually large and light.

The children's playground was under repair at full speed, and a tart paint smell filled the air. Maxim whistled to his friends' windows, and when they came down, they all went together to the garage to get their motorcycles.

Vika always liked to ride motorcycles with friends. The roar of the motorcycles deadened all the sounds around them, as they sped along the city streets, splashing through the puddles and catching disapproving looks from pedestrians.

Vika sat behind her brother, grasping his belt firmly. The crosswind struck her in the face and disarranged her long hair, which was sticking out from under the helmet.

They rushed out of the city and raced each other to see who could get there first. Vika laughed with joy and waved her hand when they managed to pass one of their friends. Then they turned off the main road, and the five roaring motorcycles scattered sleepy chickens as they drove down the road of a small village.

On the way to the rocky quarry, they slowed down and turned onto a wet, puddle-filled country road. Skidding slowly, they made their way into the forest, looking for the rocky road that led to the quarry. When they found it, they drove along the road, coughing and sneezing from the dust raised by the leading motorcycle.

Approaching the quarry, they noticed with disappointment that an excavator was working below.

"Damn it, it's our luck!" said one of the guys. "What do we do now?"

"Let's go around and look for another place," suggested someone else, and they immediately took off. Soon a place to carry out their plan was found. After leaving their motorcycles in the bushes, they went into a small clearing with a shallow ditch on one side.

"So this ravine here is a good place to hide from the explosions," said Maxim.

They all agreed and started to choose a dry place to lie down.

"Is everyone ready?" asked one of them. "Okay, I'm firing the grenade, and then everything calms down, then Maxim, throw the trench bomb."

"Yes, buddy, go ahead," Maxim gave a reply.

Vika lay down close to her brother, and pressed herself to the cold, wet ground, and looked out from the ditch, gazing intently at her friend who was holding the grenade.

He lifted his arm and threw the grenade in the clearing. Vika's eyes followed the flying weapon when her brother suddenly pressed her head to the ground, and at that moment, a deafening explosion was heard.

They had expected a bang, but not one with such great force! The ground under them shuddered, and the clearing was gone! A large column of sand, stones, and soil rose and flew in all directions, covering everything around them.

They were ecstatic, shouting and looking at each other. Still lying down and shaking off the fallen dirt, they gestured to Maxim to throw the trench bomb quickly.

Maxim raised himself up a little bit, pulled the ring off the bomb, and lifted his arm... At that very moment, his leg slipped down into the ditch and he failed to throw the trench bomb far enough. It fell down close by and deafened all of them with its explosion.

The fragments whined over their heads and tree branches started to rain down from above. Horrified, they all fell into the bottom of the ditch, and covered their heads with their hands. Soil and stones fell painfully onto their bodies, pinning them to the ground.

Vika screamed after falling down in the mud, but couldn't hear her own voice at all. Somebody took her by the collar and pulled her up. She got to her knees and crawled upward.

The dust still hadn't settled before everyone, excited and dirty, looked around in a panic to help each other to their feet, and then rushed to their motorcycles with all their might.

Vika followed them, afraid of lagging behind, and didn't even notice the branch that had struck her painfully in the face. The motors roared as the motorcycles sped furiously along the road, raising clouds of dust and casting small stones from under the wheels.

Maxim, protecting his face, bent over the windshield, and peered intensely into the road, trying not to miss the turnoff.

Vika embraced him from behind and clung to his back with her whole body, in order not to fall off on the turns. She closed her eyes tightly, and squinted into the dust.

Suddenly her brother pulled up and started to turn to the left. Sand and stones under the wheels prevented them from slowing down, and the motorcycle skidded.

Maxim, doing his best to hold the machine steady, spread his legs aside, and balancing the bar, flew out onto the wet country road, where they spun around and fell into the dirt.

"Oh, shit!" swore Maxim, "we're not alone here...damn it. Sister, are you alive?"

"Probably," she said, unsure as she rose from the puddle of mud. One of their friends was already getting up from the dirt. Swearing, he pulled his motorcycle up to a dry place.

Feverishly helping each other, they kicked the starters on their motorcycles to get them started again. They jumped on them on the run, and rushed along the country road towards the village.

They took shortcuts as they made their way to the road. They decided not to drive through the village, but rather to go around it from the right, and go behind the gardens along the narrow pass.

They had almost completed the route when three big dogs jumped out from the last house and ran through the garden to head them off.

Vika was terror-stricken. With one hand she held on to her brother's belt, and with the other one, she started to hit his back.

"Go faster! Dogs are chasing us!" she shouted and pointed towards them.

Maxim, holding the motorcycle with difficulty on the slippery road, picked up speed. The dogs leaped out of the garden and dashed towards the motorcyclists, jumping on them and trying to bite their legs. The boys kicked the dogs' faces, but the dogs continued to chase them, almost falling under the wheels.

With her eyes on the dogs, Vika screamed and seized her brother. She didn't hear him when he tried to tell her something, so he kicked her leg and, turning around to her, shouted, "The stick!"

She recalled the small club, fixed to the side of the motorcycle, which Maxim always took with him. Without looking, Vika groped for it, breaking her nails in the process, then started to unhook it.

Without choosing a lane, the motorcycles sped towards the road, with the dogs closely behind. Suddenly, one of them took a leap at Maxim's motorcycle.

Vika screamed in horror and threw her legs around her brother's waist. Trying not to fall off, she held tight to her brother with one hand, and threatened the dog with the stick in her other hand. At that very moment, they sprung out onto the paved road. The motorcycles quickly accelerated, and sped away from the dogs.

They decided not to drive together, but instead, to arrive at the city separately. After driving a little bit further, Maxim turned onto the road leading to Granny's house.

As they approached the house, they stopped the engine in advance so as not to be heard and seen by Granny in their current state of appearance. After pushing the motorcycle up to the house, they hid it in the shed.

"Well done. We'll wash it later," said Maxim nervously. He nodded his head painfully, and pushing his finger into his ear, shook it. Vika, still feeling the affects of being chased by the dogs, looked around and also shook her head.

"I can't hear you," she told him. "Something is pressing on my ears."

They looked at each other confused.

"The explosions hurt our ears and that's why we can't hear well!" Maxim guessed and laughed, glancing at Vika. "Sis, you are as dirty as a pig!"

"You'd better look at yourself!" she smiled back at him, and began to examine her clothes.

Maxim ran to the bathhouse and fetched a bucket of water. They poured water on each other, and washed themselves quickly. At that time, Granny came out onto the porch.

"Hi Grandma!" waved Maxim.

"Why are you shouting?" she asked, and, looking at them, clasped her hands. "My God, where the hell have you been? Why are you so dirty?"

"Please don't swear, really, it's nothing!" answered Vika, still washing herself.

"Yeah, I see you guys, you've had a blast!"

"We fell off the motorcycle into the mud, Granny," smiled Maxim. "We just need to clean ourselves up and then we'll repair your fence."

"Aha...that's right. Don't forget about the fence!" Granny said sharply, stepping down the three steps from the porch. "I'll fetch the tools for you right now...just in case" she went on, opening the tool cabinet with the key.

Without going inside the house, they went to work immediately. They dug out the old, rickety poles, placed and rammed in new ones, nailed the fencing wood to crossbars, and fixed the crossbars up. When their mother arrived, she didn't ask why they were so dirty, since, after all, they had been working.

Chapter 9

SERGEI NILOVSKI AND Anton Darenko lived near each other. Once, at the end of last winter, they were driving home together as usual after their training session in the gym, when the subject arose.

"Sergei, what are your plans for next weekend?"

"I have to help my family around the apartment, go shopping..., they want to buy some things. That's about it. What are your plans?"

"I've got some new music tapes. Why don't you come over and listen to them?" replied Anton. "Lena and I are having a little anniversary and want to celebrate this evening." Anton looked as if he was holding something back.

"Well, speak up, buddy!" Sergei shouted, realizing Anton was keeping something from him.

"Your Rita called and spoke with Lena." Cautiously, and choosing his words carefully, he continued, "Rita said she doesn't understand you and said that you two made up...she said you were supposed to be together on New Year's Eve." Anton looked into his friend's eyes, "I thought things had sorted themselves out. I did want to ask you where you went when you ran from us on New Year's Eve?"

Sergei looked intently out of the car window at the snow-covered streets and asked, as if he had not heard the question, "So, why did Rita call?"

"I don't know. Lena and I thought of inviting her this Saturday?"

"Then I won't come...I don't think I'm going to date her anymore," Sergei answered softly but with confidence.

"Oh, I see. Then maybe you'll tell me the reason?" Anton asked, smiling and looking at his friend. "I think I can guess."

Sergei stretched a little on the car seat and started to smile. "How quick-witted you are," he pushed his friend gently on the shoulder. "And how many people are guessing like you?"

They drove up to Sergei's house, got out of the car and lit cigarettes. Sergei looked seriously at his friend.

"I went to see Vika on New Year's Eve," he said slowly, nodding in assent. "And I don't want to change anything."

They both became silent.

"Hold on a second. If you've been meeting her all this time and our boss hasn't sent for you, that means 'approved!'" he concluded with joy.

"I'm also thinking that," said Sergei thoughtfully. "But you know, Anton, I wouldn't want Vika to work with us in the future."

"Hmm… don't think so far ahead. Live in the moment," Anton replied and patted his friend's shoulder. Raising his eyebrows, he looked at Sergei with admiration. "You really amaze me," he added in a sarcastic tone. "I feel sorry for you now. Hard times have surely come to you - no sex, underage - ha, ha, ha," he laughed jokingly, "now, just try to resist it!"

They both began to laugh and shook hands as Anton left to head home. Sergei stood near his house and took in the fresh air.

The weather was beautiful. It was snowing quietly. He looked at his yard. Everything was so painfully familiar, the noise of children's voices heard from the sledding hill. A yard-keeper was sweeping away fresh snow from the porch. Parents, slowly pulling sleds with children.

"Good evening, sir!" his thoughts were interrupted by a child's voice. Sergei turned around and, smiling, tousled the hair of a boy who had walked up to him.

"Good evening, Alex! How are you doing? How's school?"

"Good!" the little fellow answered joyfully, and went towards the house.

"I wish the best for you!" Sergei said in parting. "Give my regards to your parents!"

He stood and smiled, looking after the little boy. Just think: this was the son of a girl whom he had gone to school with.

"Yes, that's life," Sergei said, and turned to face his windows.

There was a light in one of them. That meant his 'mothers' were waiting for him in the kitchen. He called them so because all his life, as long as he could remember, he had two mothers – his mother and her elder sister. They lived together in a spacious age-old apartment.

The apartment had belonged to his grandfather who had a large and tight-knit family. He was a doctor and had five children, two of which, Sergei's mother and his aunt, followed in his foot-steps and became doctors. Of the other three, two were engineers and one was a musician.

World War II destroyed the family – three sons were killed in the very beginning of the war, and the daughters went to the front line and worked at the hospitals, where they suffered from diseases and wounds.

The younger daughter, Sergei's mother, got married shortly before the war and gave birth to a boy. Going to the front line together with her husband, she left the child with her parents.

His grandfather worked in a hospital days and nights, was often ill, and was seldom at home. His grandmother looked after the boy, went shopping with him, and stood in lines for bread for hours.

When the boy was almost four years old, he was weak, slim, and unhealthy. He died in the winter of nineteen forty-three. The grandparents were devastated by the child's death. They took it hard and blamed themselves for it. At the end of the war, the grand-father had a heart attack and passed away.

The grandmother outlived her husband by only a short time. After waiting until her daughter and son-in law came back from the front, she fell ill and died quietly.

The elder sister was never married. She was wounded at the front line, became disabled, and couldn't have children. The younger sister's husband came back from war, covered with wounds and sick.

He was often taken to health centers to restore his health, but he didn't get better. They missed their first child very much and wanted to become parents again.

And then, several years after the war, happiness again came to their home. A baby boy was born. He was named Sergei after his grandfather. They worried a lot about his health, but he grew to be a strong and bright boy, who filled up their free time completely.

When Sergei turned eight years old, his father died and all the concern for his upbringing was shifted onto the shoulders of his mother and aunt. They became very close.

Sergei went upstairs and smiled as he approached the apartment. *My energetic mom*, he thought, looking at the new door to the apartment. Some years ago his mother retired on a pension, but she didn't want to leave her normal routine.

One day, she got up very early, did her exercises, and announced, "Let's redo the apartment!"

And this is when it started. Everything was changed - even the walls were shifted around. And the living space soon began to sparkle with new windows, and was much more comfortable than ever before.

Sergei opened the door, and his nose caught the spiced aroma of a newly-baked pie. "Well! Hello everybody! You're at your best!" he shouted as he entered the apartment.

Chapter 10

DURING THE MIDDLE of the night, Vika screamed in horror and kicked her legs and hands. Her mother got up from her bed to see what was wrong.

"Wake up Vika! Wake up!" She grabbed her daughter's face, "What the heck are you seeing now in your dream?"

"I'm dying," Vika trembled and slowly sat up on her bad.

"What are you talking about?"

"Oh Mom, it was horrible," Vika looked at her shaking hands. "I was in the school's gym...and I was exercising in the far corner. Everybody ran away and turned off the light. I was screaming, but no one heard me and it was completely dark. I began to walk to try find the exit, but somebody pushed me down, and covered me with a big gym mattress. They were pressing me down so badly...I was almost smashed...and then somebody began to touch me...I fought back to try to get out, but there was no way."

"Did they continue to guard you?"

"Yes," she nodded, "I couldn't run."

"Oh God, it's all your behavior," the mother took a big breath. "Look at you! Where have you been today to scratch your face like that? You better stay at home and don't disgrace your family."

"Mama!"

"Yes, watch out, don't let anyone in your skirt! I'll kick your ass immediately from the house."

"I know."

"Go to sleep. Good night." The mother went back to her bed. Vika lay down and fell asleep again.

Sunday morning Vika woke up earlier than usual, and while still in bed, without opening her eyes, she felt her body aching. Her fingers hurt. She looked at her hands with disappointment and touched her face. Her skin was burning painfully.

Vika stood up and approached the mirror to examine herself closely. What she saw she didn't like. It was a reddened and slightly weather-beaten face, with clear abrasions, left by the tree branches. Vika threw her dressing gown over herself and slipped quietly into her brother's room so that her mother, who was in the kitchen, wouldn't see her. Maxim was still sleeping, and Vika shook him.

"What were you talking about with mom last evening?" she asked.

"Nothing."

"What did you tell her about our appearance and ears?"

"Who's ears?" Maxim looked at her surprised, understanding nothing, still half-asleep.

"Our ears, which are hearing badly now, I might add," she hissed at him.

"Ah...those ones," Maxim stretched out, making himself comfortable. "I told her that we had gotten chilled from the wind."

"Good!" Vika was satisfied with the answer.

"Why are you asking?" wondered Maxim.

"To make sure we have our stories straight," she replied, smiling, walking to the door. "The big bang yesterday was cool, wasn't it?" Vika said happily, and left the room.

Her head was buzzing when she went into the kitchen.

"Hi, Mom," said Vika, and she kissed her mother on the cheek. "Do you have anything for a headache?"

"We'll find something," she took out a box with medicine. "Take some water with this pill," she gave one to Vika. "Go to bed so your headache doesn't get worse."

"Thanks, Mom." Vika smiled and, glancing at the clock, went back to bed. *Well,* she thought, *no studying today. How will I explain everything to Sergei?* And she fell asleep with these thoughts.

After a short while, Vika woke up, feeling much better. She got up and, singing something quietly, stepped into the bathroom to tidy up.

Sergei always brought something sweet for her to the library. Chocolate, an apple, a pear, a peach, something delicious, and placed it in front of her on the table before their studies.

First she felt shy about taking these things, but he said jokingly that vitamins are good for children, and always made her eat what he had brought.

Not so long ago he brought her a small cosmetics box, shiny and smooth. Vika only had mascara in a small paper box with a small plastic brush. She had to spit on the box and rub it with the brush before putting it on her eyelashes. Vika was perfectly satisfied with her mascara, but used it rather seldom, because her own eyelashes and eyebrows were black.

And here she received such a beautiful present! It was a marvelous box and with so many things inside! She was in heaven and couldn't wait for an occasion to make use of it. But she couldn't put makeup on at school, and she decided that the most proper occasion would be to put makeup on for her meeting with Sergei. So the following Sunday, she did.

Standing under the shower spray, Vika laughed, recalling the time she wore her mother's high-heeled shoes, a mini-skirt, and a short warm jacket. She teased her hair up, and made an honest effort with her makeup, then went to meet him.

* * * * *

When Sergei saw her, he almost fell over. He stared wide-eyed with his eyebrows raised.

"The Indians have gone out hunting!" he said, hardly able to keep back his suffocating laughter. He cuddled her and led her to the ladies' room. Vika was shocked. She had expected a compliment about how grown-up and beautiful she was, but not that!

She began to cry, smearing the mascara and lipstick. Sergei comforted her, wiping her face with his handkerchief.

"Why did you give that makeup to me then?" she sobbed.

"I thought you would like it!" smiled Sergei. "And you're still incredibly beautiful without any makeup!"

Wiping her face, he went on softly but instructively. "Don't be angry with me, please. It was just really funny. Use the makeup sparingly...so it looks natural. I'll bring you a magazine with faces and you'll see," he said, touching her hair.

"Victoria, I'm crazy about your wavy ginger hair, when it just hangs naturally. Please, never do this old-womanish terrible style again, OK?" he kissed her lightly.

* * * * *

She tidied herself up quickly then, and now, standing in front of the mirror, she carefully concealed her scratches and put a little makeup on her eyes.

Sergei stood near the library, leaning on the porch railing, and, upon seeing Vika approaching him, went up at once to meet her.

"Good morning, sweetie!" he said, cuddling her.

"Good morning!"

"Where are your textbooks and notebooks?" He looked puzzled at her empty hands.

"At home," Vika replied a little bit louder than usual. Sergei looked at her intently, and she continued, "Maybe we can go for a walk...say, to the park?"

He stood opposite her, holding her shoulders, and gazed into her face. "Which park do you like?" he said quietly.

"Ah?" Vika did not catch what he said.

The feeling of some unexplainable anxiety started to sneak up on him.

"What park do you want to go to?" Sergei asked a little bit louder. And, taking her hands, he started to look them over. Vika, embarrassed, hurriedly hid her hands in her pockets.

"We repaired the fence at Granny's yesterday," she tried to explain.

"And why are you speaking so loudly? Do your ears hurt?"

"Yes, they're stuffed up a little bit."

"Oh, my poor little girl!" Sergei embraced her, pressing her head to his chest. "So, what park are we going to?"

And, after talking it over, they decided where to go.

Walking in the park, they went to the swings where they chatted about nothing.

"Let's go get some ice cream," suggested Sergei.

"OK!" she responded with joy, and, looking at his trouser pocket, asked, "When are you going to give me that apple?"

"What apple?" he didn't understand.

"That one!" she pointed to the bulge in his pocket.

Sergei was taken aback for a second, and then burst out laughing, putting his hand into his pocket.

"Well, Vika...you crack me up!"

She looked at him, without understanding the reason behind his laughter.

"C'mon, Nilovski, you always give it to me at the beginning of our studies, and now what? Have you become greedy?" and she laughed too, truly not understanding his behavior, and nudged him slightly. He roared with laughter, looking at her.

"Vika...let me sit down on the bench for a little bit while you baby go buy some ice cream."

Sergei sat down on the bench and, still smiling, watched her approach the ice cream store. It was getting warmer and people were shedding their winter clothes, so it was more difficult for a man to hide his accidental excitement.

Vika brought the ice cream and sat down near him. He watched her closely and seriously with interest. Then he asked suddenly, "Does Maxim have stuffed up ears as well?"

"Yep!" she replied, without a second thought. Then she froze up at once, shifting her anxious gaze to him.

"So," said Sergei, standing up and looking around, "where is the Ferris wheel?"

"Over there," Vika pointed and they headed for it.

There weren't a lot of people, so the ticket taker asked everyone to sit in every other cabin.

The friends sat down opposite each other, and the wheel, spinning slowly, began to take them up, lifting them higher and higher to the treetops.

Sergei moved nearer to the center of the cabin and taking Vika's hands in his, looked seriously into her eyes, "Is it true that you think of me as your close friend?"

"Yes, of course," she smiled softly.

"Vika, do you remember when I told you once, that our life is full of moments when you can't say everything openly, you can't even utter it," he looked at her attentively. Vika strained herself and lowered her eyes. He went on, "So, if something like that happened, I'd like you to simply answer 'yes' or 'no' to my questions. Okay?"

Vika was tense, but he pretended that he didn't notice her state. He thought for a moment and said quietly, but loud enough for her to hear, "I think I know exactly where you were yesterday, and I hope very much that THIS was not stolen from the military storage. Was THIS found on the explosives military range?" he asked slowly, without taking his eyes off of her.

At that moment, Vika wanted to run from him, so she didn't have to answer any questions. But how could you run at such a height? Looking unhappily at the approaching treetops, she nodded. And Sergei went on, "It's a miracle that nobody got hurt. But I want to know, whether you still have anything like that?"

She shook her head.

"You've always told me about your plans. Why didn't you tell me about this?"

"I didn't know," she whispered.

"Give me your word that you'll never ever do such a thing again."

Vika nodded. Sergei moved closer and hugged her.

"Vika, it's hard to believe, just look...thousands of people around, and it's exactly you who has been there all along," he looked at her worriedly. "I promise you, I won't tell anybody about our conversation, but I think that Maxim will have some problems with the police."

Sergei took her face and turned her chin towards him.

"Vika, do you understand that you all could have died there?" he said with horror. "It's terrifying for me to even think that I could have lost you," he cuddled her. "I want you to trust me. And I'd like to teach you everything I can. We're having shooting practice on Thursday. Will you come with me?"

"Yes, I will!" Vika blurted out immediately.

He smiled, looking at her. When their cabin came down, he helped her get out onto the landing, and, putting his arm around her waist, led her slowly along the park walkway.

Chapter 11

HER FINAL TESTS were approaching, and Vika studied for days on end. Sergei was out of town for the second week already. He was right. Maxim did have problems with the police. They had agreed before they set off the explosions not to tell anybody, but someone failed to keep it a secret, and now everyone in the huge apartment complex was buzzing about it.

The story was told and re-told, adding more details. The participants of the event felt like heroes until the police came for them. Then they all were questioned and asked where they found the military equipment and the boys showed the police the place where the bombs had been found.

The inspector in charge familiarized them with the law, and they were registered in the juvenile delinquents' room. Maxim was registered there for three months, while Vika was left alone.

But now every evening, around nine o'clock, two police assistants came and checked whether the children were at home. They took a seat and put Maxim in front of them, and every evening he repeated the explosion story and recited the Weapons Law.

"I promise never to do it again," he always said in conclusion, and the police assistants left with the feeling that they had done their duty.

"What kind of crap is this?" Maxim asked angrily. "Will it be like this every evening for three months?"

"This is good for you!" scolded his mother. "You're going to remember for the rest of your life that a person cannot break the law."

"Tomorrow Vika will have it out with them," mumbled Maxim.

But the following evening he sat down obediently on the stool opposite the police assistants and started again from the very beginning. It was a clear message and a lesson learned: do not mess with the police.

But Maxim loved weapons and he had a short-barreled gun that he assembled himself. Together with his sister, they went to the forest to try shooting. They knew now how to keep secrets.

Maxim questioned Vika with interest about her shooting practice with Sergei, and Vika showed him carefully all the possible shooting positions and told him about the types of guns that she had shot already.

He was a bit envious, but knew that soon he would go off to the army and there he would shoot plenty. Now he busied himself selflessly with the car shop, assembled and disassembled engines, brought all the scrap metal he could find from the street to Granny's, and soon her yard began to look like a metal yard.

Maxim was very smart mechanically; and adults often asked for his help repairing motorcycles and cars. He never refused to help and gladly assisted everybody.

* * * * *

Sergei came home by the end of the week and called Vika right away. He didn't want to wait until Sunday to see her and asked for a meeting that evening, even if it was just for one minute. Vika was very happy with his call, but that evening she planned to go with Maxim to plant Granny's garden.

"Let me help you with it." Sergei did not give up.

"No, thank you, we have just a little work to finish," she replied. "I think it won't take much time."

"Well, then, I'll pick you up at your Granny's," he said confidently. "Tell me the time."

It was not easy to choose the time, because Maxim was still at school, and she did not even know approximately when they would go there, not to mention when they would come back. But Vika also wanted to see Sergei and they arranged a time.

Vika did her homework quickly and jumped up to look out the window for her brother. He was late and she felt nervous, but finally he came home. She warmed up his lunch and sat down nearby, hurrying him up. Maxim glanced at her with suspicion.

"What's up? Why are you in such a hurry to work in the garden?" He hated all the spring and autumn garden chores.

"The earlier we start, the earlier we finish!" retorted Vika. Taking the plate away from him and putting it in the sink, she continued, "And we'll have more time to walk around tonight."

He was still chewing a piece of pie, but she was already pushing him gently towards the door. "Well, brother, let's go, you'll finish it on the way."

After arriving at Granny's, they fetched some water from the well to the bathhouse and heated it, so they could wash themselves after working in the soil.

They then proceeded to work in the garden. They did the work quickly, planting everything their Granny gave them, while she watched closely over the quality of their work.

Granny walked to and fro, checking every planted row, every bed and kept on grumbling, dissatisfied with something or other. Suddenly Maxim got up and came up to Granny with a face writhing in pain, and showed her his severely bent forefinger.

"Oh, Granny," he said, with his voice full of suffering. "Look at how contorted my finger is from work. I can't endure this any longer. Pull it quickly!"

Granny looked sympathetically at Maxim, and pulled his forefinger...and at that very moment he farted loudly and laughed, jumping away from her. She stepped towards him, trying to slap him on the back, but a toxic smell filled the air and Granny, fanning her face with her hand, moved away from him.

Vika burst out laughing and fell to her knees, watching the scene. Of course, she knew this joke of his, since he had played her as the sucker more than once.

Still laughing, Vika started to hurry her brother up again, and he looked at her suspiciously.

"So, has Sergei come back?" he asked.

"Yes," she answered shyly.

"Are you going on a date tonight?"

"Yes."

"He'll come over here, won't he?" wondered Maxim.

"Yes," Vika answered without any confidence and raised her fearful eyes to her brother.

Neither Granny nor their mother had seen Sergei or even knew about his existence. Vika was very afraid of what their reaction would be if they saw him and knew his age. How would they respond? One could only guess.

Her brother gave an understanding smile and said sarcastically, "How brilliant you were today – yes, yes, yes! Wonderful! But don't worry, I'll take care of Granny and distract her. What time is he going to pick you up?"

Vika answered and he glanced at his watch.

"Holy cow, we have almost no time! Let's finish this part and you can run to the bathhouse."

"Thank you, Maxim!" she chirped happily and set to work with great zeal.

However, it was not so simple to get Granny out of the front yard at the right moment. Maxim tried with all his might to distract her attention, but she said that she was tired of working at such a furious pace, and sat down on a bench in front of the house.

"I think I'll take a little rest before going to the bathhouse," said Granny to Maxim. "If you need anything in the house, go and get it yourself, you know where it is."

"You should go to the bathhouse now and rest there," suggested Maxim.

"Oh hell, thank you for your advice. I don't know how I'd survive without it."

Vika was pacing nervously from the house to the porch, drying her still wet hair after washing up. She had no idea how to get Granny out of the front yard. At that moment, Sergei drove up in a car.

He got out, handsome and smiling, and made his way towards Granny. Vika stood motionless, looking at the scene, while Sergei reached out his hand to Granny.

"Good afternoon. I am Sergei Nilovski," he introduced himself.

"Good afternoon. What do you want?"

"Vika," he replied and waved to Vika, who stood frozen on the porch.

"Give me a second!" Vika yelled to him and quickly disappeared into the house. She glanced at herself in the mirror one more time.

Granny, glowing, came in the house almost immediately. Her eyebrows were raised, and she wore a surprisingly pleased smile.

"Vika, is this that friend of yours, who your mother told me about some time ago?"

"Yes," she looked hesitatingly at Granny.

"Why am I so old? That's not right!" Granny replied jokingly, throwing up her hands. "Maxim, is it possible that such a handsome man is courting our Vika?"

Vika smiled shyly and running up to Granny, embraced her thankfully and kissed her on the cheek. Granny tapped Vika softly on her back and pushed her gently towards the front door.

"Go ahead, darling! It's your time! He must be tired of waiting on you already!" and she also headed for the door. Maxim opened the door and was the first one to walk out of the house.

"I'll go say hi to Sergei," he said.

Sergei stood near the car, watching them appear on the porch one by one. He was the first to extend his hand to Maxim. He greeted him with a smile, and then shifted his gaze to Vika.

"Hello," Sergei said to her.

"Hello."

"Is it okay if I take your grandbaby?" he jokingly asked Granny, taking Vika by her waist.

"Yes, of course!" Granny answered cheerfully. She was almost too happy about the whole situation. Sergei led Vika to the car, opened the door, and offered her a seat in the front.

"It was nice to meet you," Sergei smiled at Granny, and got into the car. Vika, leaning out of the window, waved happily to her family.

"Bye!" she cried. "Please don't say anything to Mom!" and they drove away.

Sergei drove, smiling, and looked at Vika every second.

"Look at the road!" she laughed. "We're going to hit something!"

"We'd better stop someplace now," he answered cheerfully, turning off the road to the park. He drove a little bit further and found a beautiful glade near a small pond.

Sergei stopped the car and turned to Vika. He cuddled her tenderly and, for the first time, gave her a real kiss on her lips.

She closed her eyes and didn't breathe, struck motionless from the kisses. He stopped and, letting go of her lips, pressed her head to his shoulder. Vika buried her face in his neck, gasping, choking from kisses and embarrassment.

"Vika, Victoria, my sweetheart, how much I've missed you," whispered Sergei. "It's so hard not to see you and to not hear your cute, babbling voice."

He sighed and started to kiss her cheeks and neck. Vika was suffocating with unexpected feelings. Her head began to swim as his left arm caressed her shoulder and went slowly down to her breast.

"Vika..." said Sergei slowly, and then kissed her lips again. She was trembling and becoming scared, and started to push him off.

Sergei was moving slightly backwards, still cuddling her. "My sweet girl, don't be so scared, I'd never hurt you," he said tenderly and kissed her lightly on her nose. "Oh, I've forgotten completely," he went on joyfully, "a minute of patience, honey!" and he started to get out of the car. With one leg outside, he looked back at Vika. "You are...beautiful baby!" he exclaimed and got out of the car.

Vika, still coming to her senses, glanced at her reflection in the mirror, checked her hair, and adjusted her blouse, trying carefully to breathe evenly.

Sergei opened the door and helped her to get out of the car. When she got out, he presented her with a large bunch of roses. Vika opened her mouth with astonishment, looking at the magnificent gift.

"They're amazing!" she uttered. "Thank you, Sergei!"

"You're amazing," he embraced her. "I've brought you some presents. I'll give them to you later, so you can open them at home."

"Oh, thank you!" Vika was blushing. "It's so hard to hide your presents from Mom."

"Why do you need to?"

"She doesn't like it...I mean...she doesn't know who they're from."

"You still didn't tell her about me, did you?"

"No," Vika felt very embarrassed, "my mother doesn't want to hear this and just fought it every time I tried."

Vika couldn't say how, not such a long time ago, her mother had beat her with a soldier's belt buckle, when she had found some of Sergei's presents.

"I'll think about this problem," said Sergei, "let's go to a café. We'll talk, relax, and you may tell me your news."

"Okay," answered Vika readily, eager to get away from there as quickly as possible.

"We'll put the roses on the back seat, okay?" asked Sergei.

"Sure!"

"May I kiss you one more time before we leave?" he inquired and, without waiting for the answer, pressed her tightly to him, and kissed her passionately.

A little bit later, Sergei helped her into the car and, glancing affectionately towards Vika, drove the car away from the park.

Chapter 12

SERGEI LOOKED SUSPICIOUSLY at Vika and smiled, "I can only guess how many school-guys chase you about and will try to have a chance to see you during the summer."

"You're forgetting about the guys from the house play-yard," laughed Vika, "and what about my brother's friends?"

"Ah yes...those too. So tell me the truth."

"Are you a jealous dude?"

"No, but thinking about it does make me a little nervous," Sergei returned her smile.

"Don't think too much," Vika answered in the same tone as him, "You're too smart and know better than to be worried about that."

"Oh, thank you! But anyway, before your final tests begin, you should study for your tests in the mornings, and in the afternoons, I'll teach you to drive a car and pack a parachute."

"Nilovski, are you trying to make me permanently busy?" wondered Vika. "Who needs a parachute?"

"We're taking the young cadets to jump from the tower this week. You won't need a parachute there, of course, but you'd better have some idea about it," said Sergei. "And one more thing...you can invite Maxim to come with us, if he wants. I can teach him to drive a car, too."

"Great, thank you, I'll ask him," replied Vika.

Maxim was delighted with the idea and every evening Sergei picked them up from the corner of their house, and they went to the park to learn to drive and park a car correctly.

They had practice competitions and trained to pack a real parachute. Sergei showed them and explained to them how to control the chute, and where to place their body and legs when landing. Finally, at the end of the week, they went to the airport.

A bus full of young cadets picked up Maxim and Vika at the arranged place. They got into the bus, and, talking excitedly with the rest, set out. Vika was obviously nervous and she constantly looked into her brother's eyes and asked the same question.

"Are you afraid?"

"No, this isn't an airplane, after all, it's just a tower," he replied calmly, trying to look confident.

But she kept asking again and again.

"We're not the first or the last to do this," he told her. "I think everything will be fine."

The closer they approached the airport, the more concentrated and serious the faces of the new parachutists became, and even Maxim appeared nervous after another question from his sister.

"What the heck...are you a broken record? Of course, it's scary. Am I a crazy? Who would jump from a tower and not be afraid?" he said finally.

They drove up to a small, two-story building, where the air-parachute section was based. They were measured and given flying suits, which they had to put on right away. They all looked alike in their similar suits.

"Where is Sergei?" Maxim looked around for him.

"He told me not to approach him during the jump," answered his sister, "he will be busy with the instructors and paperwork."

One of the instructors checked each cadet, "Okay, the flying ostriches, I see you've all prepared for your first catapult. That's good. Now, line up and I'll remind you once again what to do."

"After a jump," the instructor said, "You count 291, 292, 293, and then pull the ring on your chest. At that time, when the parachute opens, you'll be pulled up. Then you'll have to look and see where you're falling, and be sure to land the right way. Is this clear to everybody?"

"Yes!" the group answered, but not in unison.

"Well, then let's go, spring chickens!" the instructor smiled, and they moved to a high, metal tower nearby.

It was early morning. A cool wind was blowing slightly, but Vika felt so chilly that her teeth chattered. Before going up the stairs, she stopped and fixed her fearful eyes on her brother.

Maxim glanced around to see if Sergei was looking, then pushed her up the stairs. "Sister, don't embarrass yourself! You jumped from the diving tower, didn't you? Probably it wasn't quite so high...but, just close your eyes and fly down, you won't disappear, we'll meet on the ground!"

"Yeah, sure."

"These belts around you will keep you safe. Don't panic!"

"I'll see your bravado." Vika walked slowly, while swearing under her breath, up the stairs.

When they arrived on the highest level, everyone grasped the railing tightly and were reluctant to move. They had to jump in the same order in which they were placed on the ground. They saw iron slings reaching from the tower to the ground, and the jumpers were attached to them, fastened to the slings.

Vika stood and watched the sending-off procedure. If she hadn't been so afraid, and had not known she was going to suffer the same fate, she would have roared with laughter watching it all.

Two big instructors took a cadet by his belt and fastened the straps. If he was holding onto the railing and did not want to jump, they pushed him off by force. The air filled with screams and swearing, but the sending off didn't stop. Once one cadet landed, another 'lucky one' was fastened right away.

Vika's turn came quickly. She trembled with chattering teeth. But nothing could stop these 'hungry' instructors. She immediately was fastened to the sling and led to the edge.

"Close your mouth and clench your teeth," one of the instructors said firmly. "Count 291, 292, 293, and pull the ring. Okay, let's go!" he concluded and stepped aside, letting her jump herself.

But Vika stood, clutching at the railing from both sides and looking down horrified. Then she shouted "No-o-o!" and backed up. The instructors' hands caught her easily and pushed her off.

She was screaming, and forgot about counting or pulling the ring. Suddenly she was violently pulled up, and the speed of decline instantly decreased. Vika stopped yelling and caught hold of the belts – the ground was approaching her rapidly.

She put her legs forward, as Sergei had taught her, but failed to keep her balance upon landing. She ran forward a little bit and fell to her knees, hands, and face landing in the sand.

Two instructors, who were probably supposed to catch the cadets, but didn't just for fun, immediately came up to her. "You had an excellent jump!" they laughed, helping her stand on her shaky legs, unfastened the belts, and led her from the landing ground.

"I was awfully scared!" Vika responded, spitting out sand.

"The first time is always crappy and everyone has a sandy face. The next experience will be better."

"No way!"

Everybody who had already jumped sat on a bench and watched the others come down. Vika looked around for Sergei, and waved to him when she caught sight of him. He waved back to her, smiling, and raised a thumb up approvingly. She came up to Maxim and sat down beside him, looking at his smiling face.

"Why are you so happy, brother? How are you?"

"Chewing the same sand as you!"

When the group finished jumping, the instructor came up to them, "Okay guys, without too many compliments, you're all very good! I'm awfully glad nobody peed or pooped into their uniforms. But now get up. You have two more exciting moments."

Vika looked at Maxim. "We don't have to jump anymore, we aren't in their group," she said quietly.

"Don't cut corners! When will you have such an opportunity like this again?" he replied, trying to convince her as well as himself. "And it'll be shameful to Sergei...let's go!" He pushed her gently, and they walked together with everyone else.

It was a little bit easier the second and third time. Somebody tried counting the numbers and someone even pulled the ring and landed correctly. But nobody stepped off from the tower without screaming in fear.

Tired, but pleased and proud of themselves, they went home with Sergei in his car that afternoon.

"Okay," smiled Sergei. "Now you can jump from an airplane."

"Oh, heck no!" Vika declared at once. "You can go without me!"

"But I was hoping to take you pretty soon to our periodical trainings to the mountains for several days."

"Aha, wait!" she said in sarcastic tone. "How will I be allowed to leave home for several days?"

"We'll find a way," promised Sergei. "But for now, get some rest at home. I'll pick you up in the evening to go to the theater. Let's get familiar with the arts."

"The theater! You have tickets to the theater!" Vika excited. But just as quickly, she became unsure and shyly said, "I don't know what to wear to the theater tonight."

He laughed, took her hand, and said softly, "You can choose something pretty from one of my presents. So go, get ready for the cultural program," he concluded, approaching her house.

Chapter 13

VIKA WAS BENDING over backwards trying to please her mother. But their relationship hadn't changed and time to time again she would get a rapid beating with the soldier's belt for no good reason.

"What happened this time, sister?" Maxim said in frustration, as he looked at her, when he returned from college, "Why are your legs and hands covered with red lines again?"

"I'm a masochist and I beat myself."

"Vika, please!"

"You're lucky, dude, our mother has never touched you."

"What did you do?"

"Nothing! She just hates me."

"That's not true."

"Do you think this is love?" Vika replied very sadly. "She found some more of Sergei's presents."

"Damn, it's just ridiculous! It's completely not right." Maxim got furious, "I've already talked to her about you. What crap!"

"Thank you for your support."

"You need to tell mother about Nilovski," suggested her brother.

"Cut it out! She doesn't want to listen to me. She just wants to scream at me."

"I'll speak to her today."

"Sergei already wanted to have a conversation with her," added Vika, "but it's so embarrassing for me, and dangerous for him. Who knows what mother will do after that?"

Maxim fixed the conflict somehow, but the peace at home had already been disturbed. In the evening Sergei saw Vika's hands and, with difficulty, coaxed the truth from her about the situation at home.

"I feel guilty, Victoria," he got upset. "Maybe you wanted to hide me in your pocket for a bit longer, but since this has happened again, why don't I go meet your mother?" he took her by her waist and pulled her gently to the car.

"No, Sergei, please! Hold on!" she resisted frightfully.

"Well, all right. Not now then."

They continued with their evening, without touching upon the subject again.

But the next afternoon, Sergei went to Vika's home with flowers and a cake. He met her mother, presented her with the flowers, and before long they were sitting together and drinking tea with cake as if nothing had happened.

Sergei was a wonderful storyteller, and Vika's mother spoke to him with evident pleasure. Vika felt nervous the whole time, and couldn't wait to leave.

"Please, don't worry about your daughter," said Sergei in the end. "Everything will be fine. I'll never hurt her."

"I hope," Vika's mother smiled slightly.

"May I have an opportunity to walk with your daughter tonight?" he put his arm round Vika's waist.

"Yes, but don't be too long."

"We won't. Thank you. Good-bye," he closed the front door behind them. "Wow, we're free now!"

And after that evening, he became more affectionate with Vika when they were kissing and hugging in the car. It became more and more complicated to stop him. She was scared to death, but she also liked it. She felt like she was in heaven since someone on this earth loved her!

* * * * *

Vika passed all of her final tests successfully and, on her own, applied to high school. She met Sergei almost every evening, as long as he wasn't on a business trip.

They went to the river or the lake on the weekend, often together with Anton and Lena, and sometimes with Maxim and his friends as well. Vika didn't want to change anything in her relationship with Sergei, and for that reason, she always tried to invite someone to go with them when they went to the countryside.

They usually played volleyball there, had swimming races, and jumped from the diving tower. Lena's jumps were the most beautiful. She was shorter than Vika, slim, with short hair. Her appearance was just like a teenager, but she was adroit and very intelligent.

She and Vika found much in common very quickly, and when they met, they conversed with pleasure. Vika needed an elder sister, an advisor for relations between a man and a woman. Vika was ignorant in those matters.

One afternoon, as they were lying on the beach with Anton and Lena under the hot summer sun, Sergei, with his leg on Vika's leg, was tickling her back with a piece of grass, "What are your plans, sweetie, for this summer?"

"I'll rest up for some time, and then, probably, I'll go to work in my Mom's factory, in the landscaping department. I've already worked there the last two summers."

"Wow!" Lena was surprised. "I didn't know you could work so young."

"No, I'm not allowed to," Vika felt embarrassed. "My Mom has a friend there, he is a boss, and she talked him into hiring me. It isn't difficult at all watering and planting flowers," Vika went on. "At my age you can work for four hours a day, but you're paid as if you worked for six hours, and I'm done by noon."

Sergei stroked her hair, looking into her face.

"I never worked until I graduated from college," he said. "I always spent my summer at the Young Pioneer camps."

"I went to Young Pioneer camps every summer too!" Vika livened up. "I liked it there. It was a fun!"

"I went to those camps too," smiled Lena Somova.

"Me too!" said Anton. Everybody laughed and started to reminisce about the past.

"C'mon guys, let's go swimming," Lena offered. "I don't want to feel like my time has passed!" And she was the first one to run into the water. Everyone got up and ran whooping after her.

They all played in the water, chasing after each other. Sergei, catching Vika, playfully hugged her tightly and tried to cuddle up to her with all his body. She broke loose, squealed, and swam away from him, splashing him with water.

He caught Vika, took her in his arms in the water and swirled her around. She wrapped her arms around his neck and, laughing, tried to pull his head down under the water. He dove down in the water, carrying her with him.

Vika laughed and moved softly away from him, seeing his burning gaze and feeling his strong hands around her, as well as something else up against her body. Finally, she broke loose from his grip and swam to the shore, calling Lena to come with her.

The girls stepped out onto the sand and walked slowly to their things, leaving the guys in the water. As she lay down to sunbathe, Lena saw, out of the corner of her eye, Anton coming to the shore and Sergei swimming away rapidly.

"Nilovski isn't tired of swimming yet?" Lena asked Anton.

"Oh, shut up," he laughed. "Sergei is chopping wood!"

Lena began to laugh and turned her back to the water.

"What happened?" Vika was confused, looking back and forth at her friends.

"Ah, it's okay," replied Anton. "Sergei will tell you."

When Sergei swam back, Vika asked him, "What wood were you chopping in the water?"

"Which wood?" wondered Sergei.

"They told me." Vika turned to Lena and Anton, who were choking with laughter at her naivety.

"Well, Darenko," Sergei smiled, jumped up, and started to give Anton a sound thrashing, "I think I'll bury you in the sand right now!"

"Did I miss something?" asked Vika.

"Skip it, darling!" laughed Sergei.

"For sure!" agreed Lena. "The farther the better!"

In a short while, after lying in the sun, they had decided to go home when Anton invited all of them to dinner. Without much thought, they got up and dropped by the market on their way home to buy some groceries.

When they arrived, the girls busied themselves with the cooking while the men went out to the balcony to smoke.

"Vika, do you love your motherland?" Lena brought up the subject with an unexpectedly serious tone, as she washed the vegetables.

"Very much," answered Vika, without considering it even for a moment. "I would sacrifice my life for it!"

They were real patriots. They grew up with the feeling of victory of the Second World War. They knew the stories of the participants and of the large number of casualties of the war. They loved their motherland deeply. Every one of them was ready to defend it and considered it an honor to serve in the Soviet Army. Every young man longed to participate as soon as possible, being proud to belong to a common cause.

"Would you like to work in the Security Service in the future?" Lena went on.

"I don't know," Vika answered honestly. "It's too early to think of a career choice."

"But you can start preparing for it now," Lena said, "and by that time you'll know for sure what you like and what you need."

Vika, engrossed in thought, was looking at her when the boys entered the kitchen.

"Why are our girls so serious?" asked Anton, coming up to Lena and hugging her. "Today is a day off, so no serious talks!"

"What if we go to the camp ground by the lake next weekend, ah?" asked Lena merrily.

"That's an excellent idea!" supported Sergei. "There are water-skis and bicycles. It'll be fun to go for a ride. Only, we should call there in advance."

"I'll do it!" said Anton, taking out a bottle of wine from the cupboard. "Sergei, get the wineglasses from the other room and we'll help the girls set the table."

Everyone helped prepare dinner, and soon they sat down to it, talking excitedly and proposing a toast to the bright future.

Chapter 14

VIKA'S MOTHER, THOUGH she was acquainted with Sergei, was not pleased at her daughter's friendship, and discussed this subject with everybody else. She never spoke kindly about her daughter, just reminded Vika that she would kick her out immediately if something happened.

Vika already knew from her Granny that her mother worried about her daughter getting pregnant, and Vika was terribly afraid of Sergei's impulses. But Vika could not contain herself, running to meet him for a date. She had a longing for him with all her soul and body.

Crossing her yard, Vika would hear behind her back the whisperings of old women, who sat permanently on benches near the house. Vika drew herself up proudly and walked to her door, without even looking at them.

Sergei made fun of her shyness and always calmed her easily.

"Don't pay any attention to them," he explained, "they don't have anything else to talk about, and, for the most part, they envy you. Soon everybody will get used to it and find something else to gossip about. Just say hello and greet them with a smile."

He hugged Vika fondly, and she felt that he could solve any problem.

The next weekend, the four of them went in Anton's car to go camping. They left as early as possible to spend more time outdoors. However, Anton failed to arrange for a lodge, and they were all occupied, since it was the height of the season. So, after arriving at the site, they put up a tent in the ground.

After eating a snack and relaxing, they all went together to the dock, where many people were vacationing. Some of them were fishing from the dock, and some were sunbathing.

A motor-boat with a water-skier sped by in the lake. Sergei looked at Vika and pointed towards the skier, "Do you want to ski?"

"No, thanks," replied Vika. "I've never done that before."

"Don't floor me!" he hugged her. "You're going to correct it. Water-skiing is much easier than snow-skiing."

They swam and sunbathed, waiting for their turn in the motor-boat. Sergei's colleagues came up to them and shaking hands, looked Vika over with curiosity.

Sergei introduced her as his girlfriend, and she was very proud of that. Then, Anton leased a water bike, and all four of them, sitting on it, moved off from the shore. In the lake, they dove and fooled around, pushing each other off.

Vika sat on the seat, looking at her friends swimming, when two men started to approach them on a similar water bike. Sergei climbed back on the bicycle, smiling, greeted the men. They politely greeted him back. One of them stared intently at Vika.

"Is this Victoria?" he asked, looking into her eyes. She shifted her gaze shyly to Sergei.

"Yes, please, meet her!" he said. "This is Vika Zotova." Sergei took her by the hand.

"Hello," Vika smiled discreetly and bent her head slightly as if in a bow.

"Hi, Vika. Well, guys, we'll meet you all on the shore!" and visitors sped away. Vika sat, looking at the water.

"Honey, are you okay?" asked Sergei.

"Yes, I'm just trying to recall where I have seen that face before."

"That is our boss, Semyon Severov," he told her, pointing towards the men. Vika looked back at them thoughtfully.

"It seems to me I've seen this grey-haired grandpa already."

Lena burst out laughing on hearing this, "He is not old at all!" she said, "And he's a rather strong man."

Now Sergei laughed, "Lena, would you like to hear her perceptions of age?" He looked cunningly at Vika, stepped away from her, and went on, "Vika has the following scale of measurement, everyone over 20 is an adult, over 30 is considered old. Those over 40 are considered very old!"

Lena and Anton laughed together listening to all this, and Vika jumped out from her seat and moved to Sergei, trying to push him into the water.

"And what about those people over the age of 50?" Lena shouted.

"Oh, they are ancient...like dinosaurs!" Sergei laughed back and fell down off of the bike into the water. Vika fell down too, still trying to catch and spank him.

"Oh, Victoria," Sergei amused himself, swimming off from her. "Sorry for disclosing your secret."

Lena, smiling, climbed up the bike and took a seat, "When you are young, everything seems big and grown up!" she said sprightly. "So, old men, it's time to move to the beach. Maybe our turn for water-skiing has already come."

Minutes later they got in the motor boat and went out to the deep waters, taking turns water-skiing.

Vika sat in the boat, relaxing, and showed not the faintest desire to try water-skiing. However hard Sergei tried to persuade her, she refused this diversion. But then Darenko broke in.

"Victoria, let's try from the dock." he suggested when their lease time was coming to an end. "You saw how the water-skiers took off from there."

"Oh, I don't know!" Vika answered, biting her lower lip. "There are so many people around."

"Don't be scared," Lena encouraged her. "Maybe they have never tried water-skiing at all."

Having approached the wharf, Anton stayed in the boat and made the others get out. Vika seated herself in the middle of the wharf on a special place for water-skiers, took a rope and put her legs in the skis.

"OK!" Sergei shouted to Anton and waved. "Let's go!"

And then everything became like a movie. The motor roared, and the boat, picking up speed, raced from the shore. All the attention of the campers switched to the skier and in an instant, the rope jerked her from the dock.

Holding it, Vika immediately disappeared head first into the water. The skis were left in their place, rocked slightly on the waves. Everyone on the dock burst out laughing!

Vika came to the surface, looked around and swam back, seeing laughing faces. Somebody even clapped their hands. She smiled back, but she felt very much ashamed of her 'flight.'

"Did you hurt yourself?" Sergei helped her out of the water.

"No."

"Let's try once again!"

She stared wide eyed at him.

"One more try!" Sergei went on, "You can do it, Vika!"

Anton drove up in the boat and gave her the rope again. "Sorry, Vika, it was my fault!" He said, "Now I'll try to be more careful and go slower." He started to move quietly away from the wharf.

Vika prepared herself at the same place, and tensely watched the rope. This time, she rose up on the skis and skied off the dock slowly...very slowly.

The boat's creep caused her legs to slip forward, and she fell flat on her back. The wharf roared again with laughter, and everybody clapped their hands.

Vika swam towards the shore, choking with tears from resentment. She felt embarrassed and wanted so much to show them that she was at least good at something. She looked around and swam to the tall tower, which was nearby.

Sergei understood at once her intentions. "Come back! Vika, come back!" he shouted to her, but his voice was lost in all the noise.

She came out near the tower and started to climb it. Sergei was at the point of running to her, but stopped, seeing that he would not be able to catch up to her.

"Vika, your feet first, jump like a soldier!" he shouted to her once again.

Semyon Severov came up to him and gave him a friendly pat on his shoulder, looking towards Vika.

"This is our girl! With such character!" he said proudly, and they turned their eyes to the tower.

Vika climbed to the very top. A slight breeze blew on her wet hair. She looked at the narrow, swinging, jumping board, and she suddenly became terrified.

On clenching her teeth, Vika stared at it and unexpectedly recalled the words of her circus trainer: "Don't look down needlessly, pay attention to the thing that you're working with."

She fixed her eyes forward and stepped quickly on the board, pushed off, and on swinging around, raised her hands up and jumped head first.

This was her first jump from such a height, and it was a lucky one. Upon hitting the water, only her legs were sideways, and they struck against the water surface. Sergei ran up to the tower and dove in the water, helping Vika get out. Lena hurried up with a towel and wrapping Vika in it, hugged her tightly.

"Good girl, you got the better of them!" Lena said, and stroked Vika's back. Everybody was clapping on the dock.

Sergei got out of the water, took Vika in his arms and carried her towards the beach, where they had sunbathed before.

"Why did you do that?" he started to swear, putting her on the blanket. "Do you want me to die of a heart attack?!"

"I tried to impress them."

"Give me a break, Vika. Who needs it?"

"Me."

He reproached her for a long time for her imprudence, but she said nothing to him. She still shivered with what had happened.

After resting a little bit, they went to their tent to have a barbeque. Then they saw Semyon, who was walking along the path. They invited the boss to keep them company. He came up and patted Vika's shoulder.

"Good girl!" he smiled, "Fortune favors the brave!" Turning to the rest of them, he went on, "Thank you guys for the invitation, but I already have plans. Vika has her birthday soon," he shifted his gaze towards her, "and I think I can join you then. May I consider myself invited?" he looked at her cunningly.

Vika opened her mouth with astonishment, looking at Semyon, and then she recalled where and when she had seen him.

"So?" he was looking at the silent Vika.

"Sure Semyon," Sergei broke in. "We'll celebrate it outdoors and invite you too!"

"That's good," the boss said, "I've invited myself!" and he continued along the path. "Bye everybody, have fun!"

"How does he know about my birthday?" asked Vika.

"I think...he knows a lot about you." Sergei said thoughtfully.

"I remember where I have seen him," Vika said at once, and told them about their winter meeting in her school.

"Oh, wow!" Sergei and Anton exchanged understanding glances.

"That's it." Sergei smiled, "we'll celebrate your birthday outdoors with a barbeque and relatives." He looking at Vika's puzzled face. "Yes," he confirmed, "certainly, with your mother and brother."

Chapter 15

THESE WERE HOT, summer days. The city became much emptier. Nobody wanted to breathe in the heat coming off of the red-hot asphalt, and everybody went, at their first opportunity, as close as possible to nature and water.

Vika looked at her empty yard. All of her friends were gone. Some went to the Pioneer camp, some to summer houses or grandparents. But she didn't feel sad in the least. Sergei did not allow her to work this summer, and she was mainly at her granny's during the day, helping her in the garden. They also went for motorbike rides with Maxim, or went to the lake or river to swim and sunbathe.

Vika's appearance changed a bit. Her tanned skin acquired a very nice-looking chocolate tint, and her faded hair became straw-colored. Vika, often looking at herself in the mirror, noticed with delight that she had become thinner, rather not thinner, but more mature. And, to her pleasure, she looked older than she was.

Her birthday was pending. Fortunately, it was on a day off. Vika was very excited and worried, because never in her life was her birthday celebrated properly. She did not want at all to invite her mother, but Sergei insisted.

At first Vika refused to celebrate it, but Semyon had already been invited. And being very nervous, Vika gave up under the convincing arguments of Sergei to invite her mother and brother. Her mother at once said no.

"I have no money to celebrate your birthday on such a scale!" she stated.

"Mom, relax, nobody is asking you for money," said Vika. "Sergei is organizing everything."

Her mother sat, her lips pursed, and looked reproachfully at her daughter.

"Vika," she began, "you are only turning fifteen, you're still a baby. How should I feel in such a situation?"

"Oh, Mom, I know, I don't want anything! But Sergei's boss is coming to this celebration, he invited you, and we can't change the plans now."

"What the hell is going on?" her mother was confused.

"Mom, please! It needs to be done!"

"Okay, I'll think it over," she answered kindly.

Vika began to notice long ago that she had begun to speak in Sergei's words. And here again she told her mother, just like Sergei would say, "It needs to be done!" He taught Vika to communicate with people, explaining to her when it was better to speak up, and when it was better to hold back.

"When you start to say anything," he told her, "you should always know the ending. And don't forget that 'brevity is the soul of wit!'"

Some time ago in the circus, Vika was taught to remember what was placed where, when taking just one glance. Then children lined up before the training, stood silent for a minute, and then asked who heard what sounds, developing their attention in this way.

Sergei also taught her to train her memory, memorizing various details, like who wore what clothes, who was at which seat, how many people there were in the room, and what sat on the tables.

He would ask her unexpectedly about anything they just saw and then laugh, looking at how she let her imagination run away with her, pretending that she was recalling facts.

They always had a good time together, and somehow, every disagreement settled very quickly. Now, once again, she felt embarrassed to tell him about her talk with her mother, and asked him once again to find an opportunity not to organize anything and to cancel it with Semyon Severov, giving him some serious excuse.

"Victoria, what's up?" asked a surprised Sergei. "Please, don't worry about anything! We'll take care of it with my friends," he set her mind at ease. "Let's try to narrow down the exact number of invitees."

"Just you and me, nobody else," joked Vika.

"I want that too!" he grabbed her.

"I don't want to celebrate my fifteenth...I wish it was my eighteenth birthday. Even better if it was my twentieth!"

"Are you kidding?" Sergei laughed, "Enjoy this great time in your life and be happy."

"I'll try."

"With me?" he held her tight and didn't wait for an answer as he covered her lips with kisses.

* * * * *

Vika's birthday was coming. Sergei with friends decorated a place next to the lake and surprised Vika with plenty of different, delicious foods.

Everybody acquainted themselves with each other very quickly, and then sat around the table. Vika felt infinitely happy. The evening was just marvelous! Champagne and wine flowed like water, and Vika had her glass of champagne as well.

Nice toasts were proposed to Vika, and she was glowing, slightly flushed from everybody's attention, and smiled radiantly with tears of happiness in her eyes.

At first, Vika would cast glances at her mother, still worrying about her attitude towards what was happening. But Vika finally calmed down, seeing how merrily her mother was talking with Semyon Severov.

The evening went wonderfully well. After singing along to the guitar and dancing to a tape-recorder, they all were tired, and everyone started to say their good-byes.

"Victoria," Semyon said finally, "I'm very glad to have met your family," and he looked at her mother, smiling. "I hope we'll be good friends...once again, happy birthday dear girl! Be happy!"

He hugged Vika and kissed her on the cheek. They all thanked each other for a wonderful evening and joyfully got in their cars to go home.

Chapter 16

VERY SOON AFTER Vika's birthday, Sergei told her about his preparations to go to a summer encampment in the southern mountains.

"Of course, it'd be better to go in the spring," he said. "But it's not me who makes that decision."

"Is it less mud?" asked Vika.

"Less dust," he replied, laughing. "Have you ever been in the mountains?"

"No."

"Well, that's obvious," said Sergei. "It's so beautiful and fresh in the mountains during spring time," he started to explain. "The foothills are strewn with flowers, just imagine; everything around is green, and all of a sudden there is a red island of flowers, and then a white island of flowers not far off, and then all the colors together. And the smell..." he sighed deeply, closing his eyes a little bit.

"I believe it is," nodded his girlfriend.

"Birds, Victoria, are singing — you would listen with delight," he continued. "And the mountain's rivers are clear and full-flowing, and you can stand and listen to their sound forever. But don't even try to swim. Br-r-r..." he shrugged. "The water is always icy!"

"So," laughed Vika, "what does it matter for you in which season your training takes place? Anyway, you're supposed to be working the whole time."

"There is a difference," he answered. "It's so hot in the summer. Everything is burnt down, dry, and dusty. And why did you say 'for you'? Don't you want to go with us?"

"How can that happen?"

"So...evidently, your mother told you nothing."

Vika looked at him with raised eyebrows, not understanding what he was talking about.

"She will never let me go," said Vika quietly. "I won't even speak with her about it."

"You don't have to if you want to go," said Sergei. "Semyon has already spoken with her about you."

"And what?"

"I don't know. Ask your mother," concluded Sergei.

Sergei did not at all like such increased attention of his boss towards Vika. It was very suspicious to him and weighed on his mind. Sergei didn't want anything except Vika, but he was on security service duty, and that meant he was dependent on others.

When Vika got home, she asked her mother about the trip. "I don't want to let you go anywhere, you know that," stated her mother. "But Semyon Severov promised me that you would be near him and that nothing would happen to you."

Vika looked attentively at her mother.

"Why have you told me nothing about it before?"

"I thought their plans concerning you might be changed," she replied coolly. "But if it goes that way, then I'm even proud that you'll be a part of such a strong organization. And then..." she continued, "They can fix you up with a job right now. Well, probably just delivering some papers or something like that. But in any case, you'll be paid!" her mother finished rather emotionally.

Vika flittered like a butterfly from happiness, getting ready for the upcoming trip. *It's not important what Semyon promised my Mom, I'll always be with Sergei,* she thought. *And he'll be near me, all the time.* She smiled and packed all of her things into a suitcase.

Unfortunately, there wasn't enough room for everything. Sergei brought her a brief list of things to take for a week, along with a backpack, which was already half-filled with a few outfits and shoes.

She had a blank look on her face, as she examined the list closely. "Do you think, Nilovski, it'll be enough for me?" she looked at him, "There isn't even a swimsuit in here, and if it's hot there, what will I be sunbathing in?"

"Well," he laughed, "okay, take a swimsuit. What else is missing from your list?"

"A cosmetic case."

"Don't take that," he quipped, "you might break it or lose it. However, maybe a few cosmetics that you just can't do without are okay."

"Okay," satisfied, she stuffed the backpack with everything she considered necessary.

When Sergei picked her up with her bulging backpack ready to explode, he stood motionless for a second, and then he burst out laughing.

"Did you and your mother jump on this just so you could get it closed?"

"Yes, she helped me to get ready."

"All right, let's go!" said Sergei cheerily. He picked up the backpack and left the apartment, then hugged her tightly and kissed her.

"This is our first joint trip, and I want us to always be together!" He kissed her once again. "Let's sit down a bit before the journey. It's customary for good luck." They sat down on the stairs, held hands, and a minute later stood up and hurried to the car.

They departed from the military airport, and their group boarded a military aircraft, together with soldiers. This was Vika's first flight. She felt very nervous, as she took her seat near Sergei.

The plane was small and unusual. There were no seats in the middle for passengers. They all sat down close to each other on benches along the aircraft sides and fastened their seat belts. There were rails in the middle, where the baggage was placed, covered with a net, and fastened tightly with belts to the floor.

It was rather inconvenient to sit like that and to listen to a motor roar loudly. They had to fly for several hours, and Vika, holding on to Sergei's arm, put her head on his shoulder and fell asleep very quickly.

Chapter 17

THE PLANE WAS approaching the land, and it jolted and shook, either from a strong wind or from the pilot's 'skill'.

Vika opened her eyes and looked at the opposite side, where the soldiers were supposed to be, but nobody was there. She cast her eyes slowly downwards and saw faces below her as she hung over them. Vika closed her eyes abruptly with fear.

"Are you okay?" cried Sergei when he saw her ghost-white face.

"I don't know," she shouted back in his ear.

"Take this packet, just in case you feel sick."

The plane roared like a tractor and jumped, probably like one too. Vika opened her eyes, looking downwards this time, at the place where the soldiers had been, but nobody was there...she glanced up and shuddered — the men were dangling over them.

"Damn!" Vika's eyes snapped shut and she grabbed hold of Sergei's hand. "Does a military plane always fly like crazy?"

"Sometimes," smiled Sergei, "it's probably just a little turbulence."

"Are you sure we can land in this position?" she shouted back.

"If not, we all jump with a parachute."

"Mama!"

"It's a joke, Vika! Everything will be like candy!"

When the plane finally landed and the engines stopped, everyone tried to regain their hearing and their composure. The back door part of the plane opened for the passengers to exit, but they all remained seated for some time. Evidently, they were all suffering from air sickness. Then all at once they began to laugh, looking at the happy face of a very young pilot who appeared from out of the cabin.

Vika moved down near the exit of the plane, sat down, and breathed in the fresh air. There were no stairs, just a metallic slide running downwards to the asphalt. The unloading was started, and Sergei supported Vika and helped her get out.

After eating and resting, they got into a truck that took them and their things into the mountains. Finally, after going up far in to the mountains, the truck stopped near a river and the group started to unload.

There they saw a donkey and a man, who introduced himself as David. Semyon, seeing his tired team, decided to have a short break to get used to the mountain air.

The surroundings were marvelous! Vika looked around as if enchanted. The summer sun shone brightly. It was very hot, but a slight playful breeze rescued them from the choking heat. Every breath brought a new smell of cool water or a flower aroma.

"Look at those mountains," Vika pointed far away, "they're so beautiful, colored with thick, green foliage."

"I told you, it's a gorgeous view." Sergei held her waist.

"They look like they have knitted, shaggy hats on."

"We'll go through those mountains over there."

"Oh no Sergei, I don't think so." Vika's face changed in huge surprise.

Giant mountains, with their points hidden in fleecy white clouds, towered nobly a bit further away. Rare trees ran gingerly along the slopes among snow-covered rocks.

Vika had never seen such clear water in a river – it shimmered, reflecting sunrays and clinging, showing all the stones on its bottom as it ran deep into the valley. Vika quickly took off her shoes, rolled up her trousers, and stepped into the water.

"A-a-a..." she screamed and jumped out to the bank at once. Despite the heat, the water was ice cold.

"Hee-haw, hee-haw," brayed some excited donkeys that were standing peacefully nearby. Vika looked at them and laughed, "Can we really ride these little ones? Nilovski, you'll crush them!"

Everybody regained their energy and started to mount the donkeys. All of the animals went calmly with their riders, except for one donkey, which stood still and brayed.

No efforts could make it go. Then David, who waited them here, came up to animal and took the donkey by the lead on his muzzle. The donkey lifted its tail, dropped his load and walked peacefully after the others. Everybody burst out laughing, seeing this performance.

Very soon, the group loaded the donkeys with their things, and pulling them behind, moved to the mountains. They walked and walked without stopping, rising higher and higher. Vika became light-headed.

"It's because of the fresh air Victoria, and because we're going uphill," explained Sergei. "You'll get used to it rather quickly!"

New and amazing landscapes opened up before their eyes. They went up the gorge. A river ran below and their narrow path was lost in green. Century old trees blocked the sunlight with their crowns and did not let it fight its way to the ground. That was why the air here was rather damp. The mountains became closer to each other, sometimes being split by the narrow rivers.

They stopped for a short break during their route and then went on again, tired and quiet. Finally, completely exhausted, they climbed to a little flat part of the mountain, where a small lonely house stood.

They heard dogs barking from afar and saw two dogs running towards them. David whistled and the dogs slowed down to a trot. He called them by names and they started to peacefully approach the group.

"They are smart!" David smiled proudly. "My great-grandfather lives here. They know me."

"I have never seen anything like them," Vika looked cautiously at the dogs. "They're such big, strong dogs and look at their thick, short hair! Wow, their heads are bigger than mine!"

"These are special dogs," explained David. "They kill wolves and guard flocks of sheep."

"I have read about this breed somewhere," said Vika. "But I've never imagined such power!"

"Just look at their feet," Sergei said, and patted the back of one of the dog's necks. "You've grow up, doggy! Such a big boy now!" he kept saying proudly.

"We'll spend the night here," said Semyon, approaching the house. "Tomorrow the others will come and then we'll move to the camp."

Everybody heaved a sigh of relief.

A grey-haired, elderly man came out of the house to meet the group. David hugged and kissed him on the cheek.

"This is my great-grandfather!" he said proudly and introduced them one by one to him.

Vika examined the territory. A small fence made of stones and clay encircled the house. There were sheep behind the house in a fenced area, chickens and a large, good looking rooster walked in the yard. The pert cock cast glances in their direction, strutting itself around like a gladiator.

"Watch out! It will peck you," David said with a laugh. "Be careful."

They put up two tents: one for the two girls and another one for the boys. Then they cooked dinner. After eating, everybody rested around the campfire, and once the sun set, everyone fell asleep from exhaustion.

Chapter 18

LATE IN THE night Vika woke up to the sound of barking. She became tense, listening to the noise outside.

"Maybe fire a shot there?" a male voice said.

"Shine the light higher, to the left," she recognized Semyon's voice. The dogs became quiet.

"Have you seen anybody?" somebody asked.

"No!" answered Sergei.

"This may be an ounce or a lonely wolf," said grandfather.

Vika pulled the sleeping-bag over her head and fell asleep.

Their next morning was free, and everybody did as they chose, while adjusting to the mountain air.

"I'm going to help my grandfather about the house," said David, getting up from the fire.

"Me too," Sergei joined him. "Will you go with us?" he asked Vika. She nodded in consent. It was evident that the grandfather knew Sergei very well, and he showed them what needed to be repaired. David was older than Nilovski, and as Sergei explained to Vika, they had studied together some time ago. They had become good friends and still kept their friendship.

"I've brought everything here already," said David, "clay, shingles, and prepared lime with paint, but I can't find time to do it all. I asked grandfather to come and live with me," David went on, taking out the tools busily, "but he refuses, says it's boring there. And here it's exciting!" David smiled sarcastically and pointed to the mountains.

"I'm going to live in this house while I'm still healthy and strong," the grandfather concluded softly.

Vika liked to listen to their voices. They talked with a very pleasant accent and sometimes exchanged remarks in their native language.

"So, Sergei," asked grandfather, "is Vika your fiancée?"

Vika blushed and lowered her gaze – never before did anyone talk about her like that in Sergei's presence.

"Yes," he smiled, embracing Vika. "But we don't speak about the marriage yet."

"Why not?" The grandfather looked at her, surprised. "Very beautiful girl, the curly hair, she's so cute. What more do you need?"

"Her age, Grandpa," said Sergei.

"How old are you, baby?" the grandfather asked Vika.

"Fifteen," she replied.

"Oh, the best age for marriage!" the grandfather said joyfully.

"But not in Russia," said Sergei. "The law says eighteen. Only here in the south can you legally marry such a young girl."

"Marry her here, Sergei!" the grandfather stated cunningly, and everybody laughed.

"I'll think it over," he said, looking into Vika's happy face, and they started to work.

Vika and another girl from the group began to lime and paint inside the house. They cleaned the house and washed the small windows. The men went to work outside, and some others from the group came to help them.

After finishing the cleaning, Vika remembered the small piece of fabric her mother had given her just in case she needed it for something, like napkins for instance. She ran off to get it, and brought it back to the house.

"Grandfather, can I sew small window curtains for you?" she asked. "Look, what a cheerful fabric!" and she showed him the white cotton fabric, with small red flowers.

"Well...if you can spare it, go ahead, sew!" the grandfather smiled, looking with satisfaction at his dwelling that had been given a new look.

Soon all the work was finished and everybody left noisily to go swimming in a small pond of water near the river. Swimming sounded grand, but because the water temperature was next to freezing, the girls wanted no part of it. The boys pushed them off the bank, and the girls screamed, jumped out, and rushed back to their tent.

Some more people were expected to come after lunch, but they were late, so everybody went to play volleyball. The others finally arrived that evening, and it was decided to spend one more night there. The grandfather butchered a lamb, and together, they all barbecued the delicious, fresh meat.

When darkness fell, a fire was built, and they all sat around it and listened to everyone take turns singing along with the guitar. Sergei embraced Vika fondly and kissed her ear. Semyon, who was sitting next to them, glanced at them and smiled.

Sergei felt absolutely at ease, remembering his talk with his boss after Vika's birthday.

"You know, Nilovski," said Semyon then, standing by the window in his office, "you're almost thirty and you are still not married, and furthermore, it'll be more and more difficult for you to find a significant other."

He walked to his long table, sat down opposite Sergei, and looked into his eyes.

"You are already used to living alone, son, and if you don't find your love now or take a strong liking to somebody, you will never have anything," he became silent for a minute, lost in thoughts. "Everything is better of its on time."

"Have you ever been married, Semyon?" asked Sergei.

"Yes...I've been," the boss answered with a deep, sad sigh, and finished their talk.

The fire was burning down and the party began to break up so everyone could go to sleep, since it was agreed upon to leave the camp before sunrise. Soon, Sergei and Vika were the only ones who remained sitting near the embers. Hugging her, he combed his fingers through her hair and started to kiss her face.

It was a bright night. A large moon hung above them like a glaring sphere, illuminating everything around with its shimmer.

"Vika," said Sergei quietly, "tomorrow we'll be climbing a cliff. I think it'll be very interesting for you, and then we'll go to the cave. It's not just a cave, it's the border crossing. I hope you understand that nobody should know about it."

"Yes, of course," she confirmed seriously, looking at him.

"It's dark and dangerous in the cave, and it might be better if you don't go there. You don't need this." he stated suddenly.

"How is it I don't need this?" Vika asked, smiling playfully, still in his arms. "If you go, I'll go too."

"My little girl," he pulled her to his chest. "You're such a naïve little chickadee. Nobody trifles with the mountains, or rather the mountains don't joke around. I have already talked to you about this, and that is why you have to be extremely cautious and attentive. OK?"

He moved her face towards his and looked into her eyes anxiously.

"Please, take care!" and he kissed her passionately.

Later, Sergei took Vika to her tent and stood nearby to have a smoke. He looked thoughtfully into the dark expanse with an uneasy feeling in the pit of his stomach.

Chapter 19

AT SUNRISE, EVERYBODY huddled drowsily, had a quick snack, packed their things, and set out. Heading up the mountains, they went rather slowly, and eventually the air became much colder.

At last, they came to a high cliff. They all stopped to look at the side of this majestic beauty. It was as if somebody had cut off a part of the mountain. A small flat area of ground with several large stones were scattered around its foot, and a narrow, fast river ran on its side.

They chose the site to set up camp. After taking a rest and eating, they started to unpack their outfit, showing once again to the beginners how to fix and hold their line, and then they went to the cliff to practice. Vika climbed together with them, straddling the stones like a frog, but did not go up as high as everybody else. When she became afraid, she went down, and after a short break started to climb again.

Time flew by, and they went sight-seeing after the training.

"My grandfather goes up here to gather medicine, herbs and roots," David said, pointing to an almost invisible path leading downward.

"Look, Vika, what a smooth boulder!" Sergei pointed towards a large stone, not far from the path.

"Let's go over there," Vika suggested and the three of them walked to the stone.

It was rather high, and if a man was alone, he could climb it with a run after jumping off the smaller rock that was right up against it. But there were three of them, so they each other climb the boulder, and stood and looked afar.

Vika swooned, seeing the vast expense! The mountains lay beneath them, and they were everywhere, as far as the eye could see. A large bird was hanging high in the air, stretching its wings.

"What a beauty!" she said enthusiastically.

"Would you like to live here?" asked David.

"No-o-o!" Vika refused cheerfully after thinking a little, and everybody laughed.

They returned to camp and began to study the area on the map. Towards the evening, Semyon Severov gathered everybody and gave final instructions.

"Guys," he began quietly, "you know that we are at the border. Here we are as sportsmen and tourists, but tomorrow, before sunrise, a part of our group, headed by David, goes to the cave." He looked slowly among the people and named everybody who was going to leave tomorrow.

"I warn you once again to be extremely careful, comply with instructions from the leader, and move silently. It's dark in the cave, and as you've already been instructed, you should walk, pressing your back against the wall, stepping with one leg and sliding the other leg, and again stepping with one leg, determining accurately the stability of the surface under it, and only after that, slide the other leg. Nobody takes a flashlight, only the leader will have one. All of your movements will be transferred very quietly in a chain," Semyon said, looking seriously at the beginners. "Well, for example, to step up, the leader says 'up' and rises up, the next repeats 'up' and rises up as well, the next after him repeats and so on. I'm sure I don't have to explain that 'down' means to step downwards, and if a part of the body, back, or head is named, it means "be ready for a stone or rock in that area. Is everything clear?" he asked. Everybody nodded together.

"When you get to the other side," Semyon continued, "before you go out into the open, everybody must put on a mask. Do not show yourself. I would like to remind you once again, you all wear shoulder straps and a breach of secrecy will be punished cruelly. And now," he said, standing up, "those who set out tomorrow, go prepare your gear. Everybody goes to sleep early tonight. Those who remain in the camp, continue to practice on the mountain."

Vika was scared already. But how could she refuse going to the cave now – it would be great cowardice in everyone's eyes, and above all, in Sergei's eyes.

"So, let's go prepare?" he said, holding out a hand and help-ing her get up. "You may refuse now and stay here," he continued suddenly, "nobody will consider it cowardice."

"And what will they think?" she raised her eyes to him.

He stood confused for a second, looking at her. "Well...you are a young girl," he said softly. "And not responsible for military service...everybody will understand." He hugged Vika.

"No, Nilovski," she sighed deeply. "It's already too late to turn back, and tomorrow I'll be together with everyone. Let's go pack!" and she pulled him out from the tent.

In the morning, their part of the group got up before dawn. After dressing quickly and having a snack, they lined up in front of Semyon Severov. He came up to each of them, checking and adjusting their gear. Very soon everything was finished, and five people disappeared into the darkness.

Chapter 20

THE GROUP WALKED quietly, dodging through the mountains, going up and up along a narrow path. Around dawn they stopped; at that moment, David pointed upwards to a rock, which covered up an entry to a cave.

Everybody looked around. The main path receded further, and they had to climb the jut. Without any noise, they crept onto it one by one and began to crawl downwards, inside along a narrow crevice. Getting down on a small platform, they lined up along the wall and stood motionless for several minutes, peering into the darkness and listening carefully to the sounds.

Fear gripped Vika's heart. Light could hardly penetrate into the cave. It was very damp and stuffy, and something seemed to be dripping. Sergei was standing in front of her and whispered suddenly in her ear, "Okay, let's go!"

She shuddered from his hissing, and not yet taking a step, heard his voice again, "Don't forget to tell the next one."

And Vika repeated everything automatically in a low tone, turning her head the other way. Sergei squeezed her hand encouragingly. "Speak more quietly," he hissed. "Let's go!" and they set off.

That was it — Vika was stricken with terror! Pressing her body against the wall and feeling completely unconscious, she repeated everything Sergei told her. Groping for a firm place with her right foot, she took a step slowly and slid her left foot.

Vika opened her eyes wide, trying to see something, but it was pitch dark. Her teeth chattered, and she cursed in her mind, feeling sorry that she came here.

"Head," whispered Sergei.

"Head," she repeated as if in shock, and at that same moment, on taking a step, hit her head painfully against a stone.

"Oh-h-h..." her quiet voice was heard in the darkness and Sergei immediately hissed at her, "Calm down and be careful."

At least this blow brought her around. She had forgotten the oath, and she now began to pray in her mind.

Time seemed to stop for her. They continued in the darkness, turning around, climbing and descending, and there was the feeling that they were simply not making any headway. Then suddenly her nose caught the scent of fresh air, and after walking a bit further and turning around, her eyes began to see a flicker of grey light. She immediately wanted to dart off and run to the place from where that invisible light was coming. But now Nilovski said abruptly, "Freeze," and they stood motionless for some time.

Then, as if going upstairs, she took a few steps and, after twisting sharply, saw narrow light ahead. Sergei, pressing himself into the crevice, pulled Vika after himself. It was rather easy for Vika with her size to squeeze into this stone space.

After leaving the cave, they lay down at once on a very small stone jut. Vika was shaking and felt sick.

"If you need to, throw up in the bag," Sergei handed it to her, "try to leave no sign that you were here." He looked with compassion at her absolutely bloodless face and trembling lips. Sergei hugged her and was a thousand times sorry for having brought her here.

"Take a deep breath," he told Vika, "and try to relax. Look upward."

She lay motionless, pressing her face to a stone. David looking over all of them, whispered, "You're all very good, guys. Please, cover your face." Everybody carried out his order obediently.

"The invisible way to go downwards is on that side," David pointed to one of the edges of the platform. "It's rather high there, and we won't do it today, but instead, one by one, you should crawl there and take a careful view of the area without haste."

Taking turns, they all crawled to the edge, to where David showed them, and looked around. After coming to her senses, Vika was the last one to creep there.

A hazy expanse and barely perceptible small mountains from one side opened up before her eyes. A huge eagle was hovering in the sky nearby. Never in her life had Vika seen such a beautiful, majestic bird.

The eagle was circling smoothly, slowly and nobly, spreading its large wings, and, on approaching rather close to the rock, began to fly down. Vika watched it flying as if hypnotized and also shifted her gaze downwards...and pulled her head back.

There was an abyss under them. With an open mouth and raised eyebrows, she looked at the narrow path under her which stretched around the corner to a small platform that was somewhat hidden in the corner. Sergei began to pull her to shelter.

"If you look at an abyss for a long time," he said to her, "the abyss will start to look at you." He pressed her to himself. Vika glanced at the group, they were lying very silently.

"Vika, it'll be all right," Sergei calmed her. "The main thing is not to panic and distract your mind. Do you want some water?"

"No Sergei, thanks," and she turned her face to him, "may I go home another way?"

He stroked her cheek gently, "There are no two ways about it, Victoria," uttered Sergei slowly. "After starting down this path, we must follow it to the end. Everybody goes his own way, but you and I are together," he whispered. "I've hold your hand firmly the whole way, and whatever happens, we'll be together. But please, be a good girl," he kissed her cheek. She shifted her doomed gaze to the sky.

Somebody crawled up to the edge once again to look over the area. But soon David, glancing at his watch, told the group to pre-pare to go back. And they all began to squeeze into the crack in exactly the same order.

Vika walked back in just the same state of mind, and beseeched God to forgive her for all previous and future sins. She heard Sergei say 'head,' repeated it after him, but did not bend over enough and again bumped her head painfully against a sharp rock. She felt something warm run over her head under her thin hat.

Finally, they reached the creep-hole and scrambled out. It was misting slightly. They took off their overalls while still on the move. They went down along the path and came to the camp very quickly.

Semyon Severov met them and invited them into a tent. Vika was quivering and felt sick. Without going into the tent, she ran by the path to the rocks. Choking with tears, she climbed up a boulder and sobbed there, hiding her face on it.

She didn't hear anybody come up behind her until somebody put his hand on her back.

"Go away!" she waved her hand. "I'll be there in a second."

"Hey, Victoria," she heard Sergei's tender voice. He knelt down and clung to her shuddering back with his cheek.

"You should not walk away from the group alone out here," he said quietly. "My little girl, I so understand you, I'm such a fool to take you here. I just wanted so much to be with you."

He patted her on her back and lifted her from the rock.

"I'm so sorry," she sobbed and hid her face in his chest.

"You know, Victoria, it doesn't matter how many times you're on the verge of danger," he said softly, "it's always scary. Only someone who is crazy would not be afraid of nothing."

"I don't understand why do I need to know about this cave? Never in my life I will find it," she confused. "I feel completely lost even in the unfamiliar city...I can never find my way anywhere."

"Well, don't worry about city," he grinned, "if you want to meet someone in an unknown city and you don't know where the place of the meeting is, you should go at noon to the central square. Or, if you can't find it, to some large clock," he began to explain, "or else, to something important or famous in that city, and stand and wait there for about an hour, if you want to be found."

He lifted up her tear-stained face and looked fondly into her eyes. "I'll find you wherever you are, my little girl! I love you so much!" and he pressed her head to himself.

"I have a headache!"

"It's probably from all of the excitement of the day," Sergei took off her helmet carefully and saw the clotted blood. "You've hurt your head!" he became anxious and examined her wound. "Let's go to the camp and I'll clean it."

The next day another group went to the cave. Vika was alone in the tent when Sergei entered with a smile, "Let's get up sleepyhead, to have breakfast!" he bent towards her and looked at her bandaged head. "You are like a wounded soldier," he laughed, "but don't worry, you're not alone with that bump. Almost all novices hurt their heads this way or that way. Put on a hat so the bandages are not seen."

He knelt down, looking at her sleepy face.

"Gitchi, gitchie, goo," he said fondly as he took her hair away from her face and unfastened her sleeping bag. "You're such a warm little chickadee," Sergei went on cooing. His hand slipped into the sleeping bag and he hugged her and started to kiss her.

She took out her hands and put her arms around him, lost in his kisses. Sergei lay down upon her with all his weight, kissing her, giving her no time to gather her senses. His hand slipped under her T-shirt and he caressed her small, firm breast.

At that moment, they heard the voice of Semyon quite close to the tent, "Hey everybody, breakfast time!" Vika and Sergei gave a start and froze. Sergei pressed her strongly to himself once again.

"I'm going to kick his ass." Sergei said with a laugh. "Okay sweetie, I would rather die now than to leave this tent, but let's put your clothes on and get out." He gave her a kiss, rose unwillingly to his feet, and left the tent.

The second group came back safely as well. The next morning, after striking their camp, they set out to go back. It was much easier going down than it had been coming up, and they were much more cheerful.

They made a brief visit at the grandfather's house for lunch. Those who wished to, swam in the river. Then they hurried back up to the base following the same path, and using the same donkeys. A small, rickety, and dirty bus that smelled heavily of diesel fuel took them to the airport.

They had a snack and some rest at the airport. Vika took off her bandages, covering the small wound with her hair. While waiting to board, they sat on their bags and listened to someone from their group singing by the guitar.

On the way back, the plane was more comfortable and spacious, and in several hours they landed at the airport without any incidents.

Chapter 21

IT WAS NOT long before school, and Vika Zotova tormented herself over idleness, not knowing how to stay busy. The first days after her trip, she couldn't find any peace, burning with the desire to tell everybody about her journey. Unfortunately, she was not allowed to say anything, moreover, she would destroy her reputation. How would she explain to people that she went with her boyfriend?

Sergei had been on a business trip for a week already and Vika, with her family, became busy harvesting and preserving for the winter. She often went with her Granny and her brother to the forest for mushrooms and berries.

Granny, with curiosity, questioned her about Sergei and what was going on. She wanted to know everything, including their plan, trying obviously to get some 'hot facts.' And she was sincerely worried together with Vika, when Sergei went out of the city for a long time.

One day, it was cloudy and drizzling and all the plans to work had been cancelled. Her brother went to his friend's house, and Vika was lying on the sofa reading a new magazine, when the phone rang. On picking up the receiver, she recognized at once the voice of Semyon Severov.

"Hello, Vika, what are you doing now?"

She was at a loss at how to answer. Could she confess to him indeed that she was lying idly on the sofa? However, he noticing her stalling, and proceeded to answer himself, "I think you're playing couch-potato. Am I right?"

"Well..." she drawled, utterly confused.

She thought feverishly, trying to come up with something to tell him offhand, but he didn't let her gather her wits, "So why not do something instead of enjoying the boredom?"

"We do go out for mushrooms and berries almost every day," Vika answered, pulling herself together.

"Oh, that's fine," Semyon approved cheerfully. "Going out does one a world of good. But I would like to discuss something with you," he went on, "about life...your future plans and all. Would you mind meeting with me in an hour so we can walk and have a chat?"

And he decided the place to meet her. Vika looked blankly out the window, "But it's raining outside."

"Even better, the air is clean and dustless!" he answered cheerfully. "Just dress warm, will you? Okay, see you soon."

Vika gazed at the silent receiver for a moment. "Man, why did I answer the phone?" she said unexpectedly loud, and went to the window to study the weather.

It was wet and gloomy. She didn't feel like going out at all. She looked at the clock and lay down on the sofa again, covering herself with a blanket.

What kind of business has to do with me? she was thinking. *If he wants to offer me a job, he's a bit too late. There's just two weeks left till school begins. If it is all about going to some training muster again, Sergei didn't say a word about it...he's even out of town right now.*

And at this thought she sat up abruptly. She caught her breath at the thought that had just occurred to her, "Something must have happened to Nilovski!" she uttered in horror and quickly got up from the sofa.

* * * * *

Vika arrived at the appointed place a bit early, but Semyon had already been waiting for her. He held his umbrella, looking at the still fountain.

"Good afternoon, Semyon." Vika greeted him once more. "Is anything wrong with Sergei?"

"Hello Vika, hello." he smiled, glancing at her. "Don't worry, he's all right. Shall we take a little walk?"

"Sure," she said, relieved, and they started walking slowly to the park.

"Well, not to beat about the bush and keep you wondering, I'll get down to the brass tacks at once," Semyon began calmly, glancing at her. "I want you to work with us."

Vika raised her eyebrows and opened her mouth to say something, but he was the first to speak, "You will go on studying at your school and simultaneously study at our school. You'll have to take the courses according to a special curriculum."

She stopped and turned to him, blinking her wide-open eyes.

"Moreover, you're going to be paid for it." He took her arm gently and continued to walk on quietly. "You're already enrolled on our staff, and there is money assigned to you for the last training muster."

Vika stopped short again and looked at him in amazement.

"I've brought it to you and the envelope is already in your waistcoat pocket." He inclined his head to look at her carefully.

"How is it possible?" Vika made an attempt to feel her pocket, but he easily caught her hand.

"Please don't take anything out now," he smiling. "You'll check it out at home." And they resumed their walk.

Vika felt astonished and happy at what she considered to be a lucky strike turning up. She consented at once to his proposal. *What a surprise I have for Nilovski!* Vika thought, marching along with Semyon and only half-listening to his quiet speech. *As for Mom, she is just going to die of joy, and of course, she'll stop scowling at me at once and threatening to turn me out of the house.* Just then she remembered that she had not even thanked Semyon for the money. "Thank you, Semyon," she said abruptly.

Now it was his turn to stop short and gaze at Vika in surprise. He started smiling, obviously seeing that she had not really been listening to him.

"You're welcome, Victoria!" Semyon grinned. "And so..." he cleared his throat. "Umm...what was it that I was saying? Well...yes, indeed," he pursed his lips and glanced at her seriously. "I know, Vika, that all of your family members have always loved our motherland. And everyone is going to work as hard as ever to make it better. And I know that you, being a Komsomol member, will do your utmost to increase your well-being." He looked her closely in the eye.

"Yes, it's true." Vika said in an undertone.

"That's very good!" he smiled again. "I knew we thought the same way. I can offer you something even now," he uttered with an air of mysterious importance. "We only need to settle some little formalities and get you a passport. You have no passport, have you?" Vika shook her head and smiled modestly. She was very pleased by the attention paid to a small fish like her.

"Would you like to travel abroad?" Semyon asked.

"Oh, yes!" she said promptly.

"And what country would you like to visit?"

"I don't know, I guess any country is interesting." Vika was thrilled. "Why are you asking me?"

"Because that's what I'm thinking about," Semyon answered. "I want to reward you with a trip for your good progress in studies. But mind you, it's our secret, and nobody is to hear from you about it. Deal, Vika? I mean, nobody!"

"I promise!"

"And so that neither of us catches a bad cold," he said after a sneeze, "it's high time for us to go home, and tomorrow we'll start getting ready."

Vika was so overwhelmed by the unexpected talk that she hardly even noticed that they had already come to a bus stop. Semyon helped her onto the bus and she went home.

Chapter 22

THE NEXT MORNING Lena Somova called and said that she would take a taxi and pick up Vika right away.

"Go to the corner by your house," she offered. And several minutes later they arrived at one of the city hotels.

Vika didn't ask any questions, she walked proud and happy, felt privileged and important. Even if she was a small screw in that service machine, she was still connected with it, and that feeling raised her own opinion of herself greatly.

Talking merrily about some nonsense, they went upstairs and entered one of the rooms. A very nice suitcase stood there. Lena switched on the TV, put the suitcase on the bed, and opened it.

"Well, why are you staring there?" she asked Vika, laughing. "Come on, sit down next to me." They sat on the bed. "You and I are going abroad soon," said Somova quietly, "and these are our clothes." She put her hand on the open suitcase. "We're going to put them on and take them with us."

Vika screamed with joy and hugged Lena for a second.

"Try them on!" Lena took a pair of paper bags out of the suitcase.

Vika looked at the small heap of clothes with her mouth open, and carefully took them one by one, looking them over.

"Oh, Lena!" she delighted. "This is something...wow!" and taking the new dress, she ran to the bathroom to change. A bit later, Vika came out in the new dress, looking very ashamed.

"Magnificent!" Lena gave a whistle.

"But I won't wear it."

"Why?" Lena was at a loss. "You look beautiful! All the men will fall down looking at you!"

"No, I can't wear this," Vika blushed, glancing at the mirror.

"Why?" Lena smiled and turned the girl around. "You must be striking to divert attention. We're going for a walk, aren't we?"

"Lena, look at me!" Vika touched herself in the dress, and looked upset. "Everything is so tight-fitting, my shirt is open too low and my butt sticks out!"

Lena laughed, listening to her, and helped her put on sandals matching the color of the blouse. Vika glanced at the mirror again.

"In these clothes I look like..." she started in a breaking voice, "like...like...a prostitute! I won't go out like this. I'm embarrassed!"

"Ouch, Zotova, shame on you," joked Lena surprisingly. "These are very expensive and fashionable clothes, and you should be glad that you have them now. Don't panic," she said tenderly. "Everything fits your figure wonderfully. Let's put your hair down."

"I already look indecent!" said Vika and taking off the sandals.

"No, dear, you look just like you need to be," Lena patted her on the back. "Come on, try on the other clothes and let's choose what suits us best out of all of them."

Vika worriedly started trying on the rest of the clothes. When they were finished, Lena put aside the things she considered appropriate. After changing back into her clothes, Vika sat in the armchair looking worried, gazing at the heap of colorful clothes.

"You know, Lena," she said, "I like everything very, very much, but how can I wear it outside? My Mom will kill me for sure, and what will Sergei say?"

"Vika...these are for our journey," started Lena gently. "Do you understand? Nobody knows you over there, but you must feel very self-confident in these clothes...holy-moly Zotova," Lena laughed. "I understand you very well, but you're damn sexy in these things!"

Vika gave a start upon hearing this, and blushed.

"Okay," said Lena, and she put the chosen clothes in the paper bag and threw everything else back in the suitcase. "We'll leave them here, and we shall see when the time comes how you get used to them. Now let's go take a walk in the streets, and I'll explain to you your task."

Very soon Vika went home without having understood, in principle, what she would have to do.

Semyon Severov laughed when Somova told him about Vika's problem with the clothes.

"What can we do?" he thought it over. "We can't blow it."

"Vika's very shy and has never had fancy clothes."

"Walla! Now she has." Semyon breathed a sigh of relief, "I'll give you an officer as an escort and tomorrow you will walk with Zotova in her new dress around the city."

"Great!"

Vika wanted to go abroad very much and without choice, she agreed to these rehearsals. Very soon she felt a little more self-confident. She was flattered that people in the streets looked at her and boys turned back to shoot her a glance. Before the journey, Semyon met the girls in the same hotel room.

"Vika, I think you already know your task," he started looking at her. "You are to cause a diversion!"

"Yes, Lena has explained it to me," replied Vika.

"Go in the café smiling, but don't talk," Semyon continued, "Vika, you go first and, right away, without looking back at Lena, come up to the slot machines from one side, and start to look them over with curiosity and touch them lightly, bending forward."

He stood up, took off his jacket, and went to the TV set, swaying his butt a little bit like a woman. He made a curious and smiling face and, without bending his knees, as if looking for the TV buttons, bent forward a little. The girls burst out laughing watching him.

"Semyon, you're an actor!" blasted Vika.

"We're all actors in life," he smiled back. "Come on, show us how you can walk. Relax and go ahead!"

Vika stood up and started repeating after him. He corrected her and they practiced everything together, with her smiling, while being showered with compliments.

"Everything is great now," he said at last, satisfied with the result. "No pressure, feel as if you are on vacation. Be very relaxed and hang out next to the slot machines until Lena gets out on the street and you see her through the window. That's your task," he continued. "Tomorrow, you start from here and at the airport join your group of tourists. Good luck, girls!"

He looked through their clothes, choosing the ones Vika was supposed to wear on that day. Saying good-bye, he hugged them and left the room.

Chapter 23

THE NEXT DAY, Vika Zotova and Lena Somova met in the same hotel, changed, and started out to the airport.

"After all, Lena, would you please tell me where are we going?" Vika asked quietly in the taxi.

"South." answered Lena, and put her forefinger on her lips to signal no talking.

At the airport, they met their small group of tourists and, having joined them, laughed and chatted while waiting for the plane.

Now Vika knew where they were going, and began listening attentively to the discussion around her about that country.

"Lena, we're so lucky!" she whispered enthusiastically, embracing her. "Such an ancient country and all of a sudden we are flying there. It's amazing!"

"Great! I mean it," Lena echoed smiling. "We're lucky."

"But how will I talk there?" worried Vika.

"Don't be scared! You don't have to talk," Lena calmed her. "I know English and German, and I think that will be enough for us."

Registration for their flight was announced and after completing the process and checking their luggage, they set out on their journey. Several hours later, their plane was successfully approaching another country.

Vika was all eyes looking out of the airplane window and excited with what she saw. It was a very beautiful country with the highest domed mosques! Vika kept on pushing Lena and pointing to the window in unspeakable delight. Lena smiled, looking at her happy friend. "Soon we'll be walking over there."

At the airport, they quickly completed the formalities and went to the hotel. After they were shown their rooms they all gathered and were instructed once again on the rules of being abroad. They stayed with their group the whole evening and the following day spent their time walking and sightseeing.

Vika was awe-struck seeing the world in an entirely different view than in her country. People wore brightly colored clothes in a completely different style. Seeing the richness of the shop windows and no queues, Vika pulled her friend over, looking imploringly into her eyes.

"Come on, Lena! Let's go in, just for a minute," she moaned, pushing friend towards the next shop. "We aren't going to buy anything, we're just looking."

Lena laughed in response, "My dear buyer, we don't have money to go shopping. Besides, we'll have time before the departure, and we will have an opportunity to look in the shops."

The next day, they went out on the required route. Vika put on white slinky shorts, a nice turquoise little top, and matching sandals. With her hair down and a small white handbag, she felt excellent under the hot sun, catching the intense glances of men.

Talking happily, Lena and Vika stopped in small shops and chose some presents for their friends and family. Suddenly, Lena said with smile, "Now we'll cross the street and enter the café per our instructions."

Vika was startled and looked around in a slight panic.

"Look at me," Somova smiled and took girl by the hand. "Relax. Smile and don't forget what you have to do, okay?"

"Okay." Vika replied nervously. Her face just twitched with an imitation of a smile.

They went into the café and Vika looked around sensually and walked to the slot-machines, treading like a sly cat. She did everything just like Semyon taught her, maybe a bit more, and attracted everybody's attention.

And she succeeded! The few visitors inside immediately stared at her and embarrassed Vika with their whistles. But very soon she saw Lena through the window, in the street, with two drinks in paper cups in her hands. Vika hurriedly escaped from the café.

"Let's take a seat somewhere." Lena said, giving one of the cups to Vika.

They crossed the street, turned the corner and sat on a bench near a small shop. After drinking their juice and looking around, they walked further, winding through the narrow side streets of the city.

"Oh hell, Somova," whispered Vika nervously. "Is that all? Are we free now?"

"Yes, that's it." Lena sighed with relief and hugged Vika. "You're a good girl! Everything was just wonderful and clean."

"Wow, great!" screamed Vika. "And now we can spend all our money!"

"We have just enough money to buy a soft drink for each of us," Lena laughed, pulling Vika by the hand. "Let's just have a look at the shops."

"Please, Lena, don't be so serious all the time, let's pretend to be rich!" Vika was excited and shook her friend's hand, "We will be able to look at all of the expensive things. They're so interesting!"

Lena laughed, seeing that her partner was still nervous. "It's written on our faces that we're as poor as church mice."

"No it's not!" Vika rubbed her forehead absentmindedly and at the same moment they both burst out laughing.

Both felt the load lift from their minds. They relaxed after their stressful assignment, and walked and laughed checking out the small shops.

"Oh, Zotova, I have never been under such crazy attention of men like now!" said Lena.

"Me neither!"

"Look around...it's your fault! They're almost fainting looking at you."

"They're all so foolish," Vika confused. "I am terribly afraid of them."

"Did you sleep with Sergei?" Somova asked all of a sudden.

Vika raised her eyebrows. "Lena, that's a very embarrassing question! You shouldn't do that before the wedding," she answered in surprise, and her eyes started shining cunningly at once. "And you...with Anton?"

Lena laughed in replied, "Certainly, we did! I do love him, and we're getting married this autumn."

Almost jumping with curiosity, Vika looked around thievishly and asked in an undertone, "And how is it?"

"What?" Lena laughed again.

"When I kiss Sergei," said Vika with confusion, "I feel something hard in the lower part of his body," she stared wide eyed and blushed.

"Don't tell me, little chicken, you've never seen a naked guy! You've got two brothers."

"My God, Somova, are you crazy? They're my brothers!"

"Oh, sorry, you are right," agreed Lena. "That's all right, I can fix this problem. When we get back to the hotel, I'll show you."

"A-a-a...damn it!" Vika screamed, shrinking back from Lena. "H-h-how are you going to show it to me?"

Lena burst out laughing and nearly fell down. "I'll draw it! Don't be afraid," she eventually forced herself to say through her laughter.

As if a wave of joy had flooded them, they walked and made fun of everything, feeling absolutely happy.

"Oh, my friend, look...what a marvel!" Vika pointed to the shop window with fur coats, and they both froze looking at the splendor.

"Let's go in and have a look," suggested Lena.

"It's so wonderful!" Vika immediately agreed, "And we'll pretend as if we're rich and try the furs on as if choosing one, okay?"

"Are you again?"

"Please...please, just imagine," Vika whispered like a conspirator. "I want to try something on so badly!"

"Well, go ahead," Lena agreed, laughing, and they walked up to the door of the shop.

The door opened with the help of a smiling, small plump man, maybe the owner of the shop, who tenderly invited them in. They went in and froze, looking at the ocean of fur coats and hats of every sort and kind. Vika walked along the row with her mouth open in amazement, touching the soft silky fur of the coats, which attracted her eyes and her hand.

"Lena, it's impossible!" Vika said with awe. "What a beauty! I couldn't even imagine a coat like this!"

"May I try it on?" Lena asked the man, pointing at one of the fur coats.

"Sure! Sure!" He bowed smiling and helped her put on the fur.

"Where can I have a look at myself?" asked Lena.

"Oh, over here, ma'am," He took her to a small, open area behind the coats with three large mirrors forming an angle. Lena Somova stood motionless looking at her reflection in the mirrors, her cheek clinging to the soft collar.

"Vika, there's something about it!" she said in ecstasy.

The man also brought a fur coat for Vika. Looking her over, his eyes glistened and he put a fair-colored fur coat on her shoulders.

The girls enthusiastically turned in front of the mirrors, and the man brought more and more furs of every sort and kind, skillfully helping them try the coats on.

They had fun paying compliments to each other and failed to notice that the few customers had left, and that nobody else entered the shop. The only people there were those who appeared in the corner, sitting quietly in the armchairs and watching the girls joyfully pass through the rows.

The room became warm much too quickly. Maybe it was because Lena and Vika were trying on many coats. But all of the sudden they were feeling very hot, and beads of sweat glistened on Lena's forehead. A young assistant of the owner very politely brought out a tray with two opaque glasses filled with water.

"Oh, wow, such great service! Thank you very much," said Lena and gave one of the glasses to Vika, and took the other for herself. "We have to go," she said quietly, while drinking some of the water. "It's getting embarrassing now, especially since the owner is being so polite to us."

"Look, what a magnificent coat he has brought to me," Vika beamed, turning around in a long red fur. "It suits me so nicely, as if it were made for me!" she laughed and drank her water in one gulp.

Lena thanked the owner, took off the coat and looked at the price tag on Vika's fur after finishing her water.

"Zotova, it's probably better if I don't tell you the price," she started merrily, "because if we convert it to rubles, you'll fall down right here and will never, ever go to such a shop again. Oh, our poor rich baby," finished Lena sarcastically.

But Vika already felt as if she were going to collapse. Her head was spinning and her arms and legs became weak. "Oh dear, let's get out of here quickly, I feel very bad," she winced, taking off the fur coat.

"I don't feel well either. It must be a fur allergy," Lena replied, holding her throat. "We have to leave immediately."

They started to the exit, staggering a little. The owner seemed worried by their condition and offered them a seat to have a rest.

"No, no, thank you," Lena said, supporting Vika who felt very bad. Her face was completely pale and she was breathing heavily, and could barely keep her eyes open.

They almost made it to the door, but Lena had no more strength to hold up her sinking friend and they sat on the sofa, aided by the sympathetic owner.

Lena started suddenly and pulled Vika, who was fading in and out of consciousness. "Get up, get up quickly," she said as loud as she could, shaking her friend. "They have poisoned us here! We have to get quickly into the street!"

They both made an attempt to get up, but the smiling owner, who was kneeling on his knees in front of them, looked into their faces and pushed them back on the sofa.

"Come on, girls, everything will be fine..." he said, smiling in an obscene manner. Lena still tried to push him off, but her strength left her. She collapsed over Vika, who was already unconscious.

Chapter 24

FINISHING HIS WORKDAY, Anton Darenko was waiting for Lena's call, but the phone didn't ring. He looked at his watch and started in surprise — the girls should have been back by now. He dialed Lena's home number, but nobody answered; everybody was still at work. Then Anton dialed his home number, just in case, but Lena wasn't there either. *Well*, he thought, *the flight must be delayed*. He started to put everything in order on his desk before leaving the office.

Anton headed to the foyer and, while going downstairs to the exit, met some people with worried faces coming upstairs. Anton looked at them and stepped aside a little to make way for them and then went downstairs again.

Something tightened in his chest and a premonition crept into his soul. He stopped halfway and raised his head towards the people he had just passed. *Why don't I call the airport and find out?* he thought, and quickly went back to his office.

Anton dialed the right number at the airport, and asked for information about the flight. A woman's voice informed him of the time that the aircraft landed. He hung up receiver in confusion — the plane arrived on time. *Why hasn't Lena called me?*

Darenko became anxious, thinking about what he should do first, but he couldn't think of anything and decided to consult his boss and dialed his number. The secretary answered that Semyon Severov was holding a conference and would not see anybody that day.

As if in a cage, Anton darted about the office, chain-smoking and looking at the phone, still hoping that Lena would call. But the phone kept silent. Anton sat down at his desk and put his head in his hands.

"Lena, my darling, please come back," he whispered, refusing to believe the worst. "Please, please come back," tears started rolling down his face. "This can't be real! Everything is ready for our wedding!"

He stood up, lit up a cigarette and started pacing up and down the office again. Thoughts flashed furiously in his mind, *Maybe, they were just late for their flight or their plans changed!* He tried not to worry and decided to go home.

It wasn't until the next evening that his boss was able to talk with Darenko. Coming into Semyon's office, Anton immediately noticed that the chief's face looked drawn, with shadows under his eyes.

"Take a seat, Anton," Semyon offered wearily and pushed a pack of cigarettes towards him, "have a cigarette."

They started smoking and sat in silence for a few minutes. Then the chief sighed heavily, and sadly looked at his subordinate. "We live as if in a war, Anton." He took a deep breath, "You know it very well."

"Yes, sir."

"I cannot tell you anything now, because I don't know anything. According to the plan they were supposed to be back. What happened there? I can only guess. We'll try to find out and hope for the best."

"Me too..."

"Hang on, Anton!" Semyon rose, came up to Darenko, and patted his shoulder.

* * * * *

Two days later, Sergei Nilovski returned from his business trip and, after getting home, called Vika. Her brother Maxim picked up the receiver, greeted him quietly, and said that Vika wasn't home.

"Where is she?" Sergei asked merrily. "She's at her Granny's?"

There was suspicious silence in the receiver.

"Maxim, what happened?" he asked seriously this time. "Where is she?"

"I don't know," the reply was vague. "She was supposed to come back three days ago, but..."

Nilovski didn't let him finish.

"From where was she supposed to come back from?" he asked, feeling something was wrong.

"I don't know."

"Stay at home, I'm coming over." Sergei got nervous and went to Vika's home right away.

Maxim opened the door. He was home alone and started telling Sergei everything he knew when, in fact, he knew nothing.

"Vika said," Maxim continued slowly, "That she was going to work in your organization now and Semyon Severov sent her and Lena Somova on a business trip."

"What?" Sergei couldn't believe his ears. "You're talking nonsense! What kind of work? She has to learn and train more!"

He went to the phone and dialed the number of Semyon, but the secretary answered that the boss was not in. Sergei immediately dialed Anton's number and, having greeted him quickly, asked what he knew about it.

"We must meet," Anton said in a lifeless voice.

"Tell me what happened!"

"Go to my house right now and I'll come too. We'll talk over there."

Sergei threw the phone on the base and slowly turned to Maxim, who stood leaning on the wall and biting his lower lip to hold back the tears.

"They killed her, didn't they?" Maxim asked in a trembling voice.

"What???" Sergei shouted at him. He ran up, grabbing his shirt, "Don't you dare talk about her like that, do you hear me?!" he growled through his nostrils and darted out of the flat.

Sergei took a taxi and went to work. There he saw his friend walking to his car.

"I'll go to the chief!" Sergei said angrily, pushing Anton aside. "I believe he does know everything!"

"Don't go," Darenko stopped him sadly. "He also knows nothing and he's not there now."

Sergei faced Anton, peering tensely into his friend's dim eyes.

"Let's go to my home," Anton said quietly and they went to the car together. They drove silently, smoking the entire way.

When they got to the house, they slowly went upstairs to the apartment and switched on some quiet music. Anton sat in an armchair and Sergei on the sofa opposite him.

"Well, my friend," said Sergei slowly. "Come on, tell me."

Anton told him what he knew from Lena. That Semyon offered Vika a job to study and work for them. She was very glad and agreed. About a week later they were sent on a business trip.

"Why was everything done behind my back?" Sergei asked, dropping his head in his hands. "What does it mean she agreed to work?" he raised his wild-looking eyes to Darenko. "She's a child and has no idea of what her work consists of!"

He hit himself on the knees, jumped off the sofa, and started walking nervously about the room.

"Where did they go?" Sergei approached his friend very closely, and Anton told him.

"How many days have they been missing?"

Anton replied, sitting sorrowfully in the armchair.

"That's it!" Sergei looked at his friend, doomed, horrified, and moved back from him. "Do you understand that this is the end? They're in the Middle East!"

He ran up to Anton again, grabbed him by his shirt, and lifted him up from the armchair, shouting in his face, "Do you understand that they won't come back from there?!" Sergei threw his friend back in the armchair. "We have to do something!" he rushed around the room. "We have to call our people over there and start searching."

"Everything has been done and people were sent, too." Darenko answered quietly in a trembling voice. "We lost them."

"How could Semyon send Vika while I was away?" Sergei asked angrily, sitting down on the sofa.

"She has her Mom, and she gave consent too. What could you have changed?"

"I wouldn't let her go!"

"You wouldn't do anything. She couldn't listen to you, or would keep it from you. You knew she was going to work for us."

"Maybe she was going to eventually!" Nilovski replied, almost shouting, stressing 'maybe', "but not at that age!"

"Both girls were glad to go on the trip," finished Anton sadly.

Sergei was in a rage, trying to think of a way to help them. He rushed about the room, asking again and again about all the details of their departure and the part Vika was supposed to play there.

Sergei fell heavily down on the sofa when he learned about her diverting role. He dropped his head in his hands again, and shook his head.

"Vika, Vika," he whispered as if going mad. "My poor little girl...what did they do to you?"

A depressing silence fell. The two friends sat silent, deep in their thoughts, as if they had suddenly become orphans.

"Don't blame yourself, Sergei," said Anton. "You couldn't have changed anything. Not from here, anyway. There..." he sighed heavily, "I think it must have been Lena's mistake. She must have missed something or became distracted. It's her failure!"

"What's the difference now?" responded Sergei hoarsely. "I'd better go home." He slowly staggered out.

The next day everybody saw a change. Sergei Nilovski had turned grey overnight.

Chapter 25

VIKA ZOTOVA WAS coming to consciousness with difficulty. There was some noise in her head, as if an engine was running, or the noise of endless waves were rolling in her head. She didn't open her eyes yet, but her nose caught the slight scent of chloride lime, some medicine, and another rough, sweet smell.

She hardly opened her eyes and saw a round, smiling face at her side. She didn't know him. Vika moved her eyes, looking around and not having the slightest idea where she was, and she dozed off again.

Vika didn't know how long she had been in this condition, but little by little she regained consciousness and, waking up completely, saw a smiling man in white clothes in front of her again. No, she definitely didn't know him. Catching her eye, the man made a respectful bow and moved back, smiling in the same manner.

Vika looked around at the small room she was in — right in front of her there was three narrow arched windows. On one side of them were heavy curtains from one wall to the other, and near the curtains there stood small couches and tables. On the other side of her bed hung a huge, pretty rug and, again, thick curtains near the windows.

She lay buried in a big, soft wooden bed near which there was a small carved table or a bedside table of striking beauty — Vika could tell then what it was.

On the ceiling, from the wall above her head, not very high, there started a semi-circle above her bed, and there was a light, airy fabric with beautiful fringe along the edges hanging down to the floor. It dropped in small waves, half- covering Vika's bed on two sides.

Looking through this see-through material, Vika didn't notice that the same smiling man was coming up to her very quietly again, this time with a tray in his hands.

"Thank you," said Vika softly. "I don't want anything."

"Please, it is chicken broth," suddenly he said, ingratiating himself in broken Russian, "you need it." He opened the small cup a little bit.

Vika still felt sick, but the delicious smell of the broth tempted her and she agreed. Raising herself a little on the bed, she started sipping the hot liquid. She felt dizzy again and handed back the cup, not finishing it. Thanking the man for his concern, she fell down on the pillows.

"Where am I?" her voice was hardly audible.

"In a hospital."

"And who are you?"

"I'm the nurse," he answered, then took the tray and moved away from bed.

Vika lay there, trying to remember what had happened, but nothing came to her mind and she fell asleep again.

* * * * *

Later, she started waking up because somebody took her by the hand. Vika opened her eyes. Sitting on the bed near her was an elderly man wearing white clothes. He had a small, grey beard and whiskers. The same nurse was standing on the other side of Vika.

"Hello," said the grey-bearded man with a heavy accent. "I'm your doctor," he introduced himself, telling her his very long name. Vika blinked her eyes foolishly and understood that she would never in her life remember this name.

"Don't worry," he said merrily. "You can call me Doctor."

He smiled gently and stroked her hand.

"Hello, Doctor. Thank you," Vika said quietly and thought, *that's it, I must have died and I'm in heaven, and these are angels in white.* She decided to pinch herself. *No, it hurts,* thought Vika. *So, it's real, I'm alive...but what is this?*

Her hand felt her completely naked body under the blanket. Vika lowered her head, raised the blanket a little near her chin, and at the same moment wrapped herself tightly seeing her nakedness.

"Don't worry," said the doctor, kindly seeing her confusion. "Your clothes are on the bed."

"Thank you, Doctor," said Vika shyly. "What's wrong with me?"

"Poisoning, bad poisoning by spoiled food," he said mildly. "You're improving and we hope that you'll be completely well soon."

Vika strained herself, listening to the melodious but hoarse voice of the doctor, and understood almost nothing in his speech. Then the nurse came to the rescue with an interpretation.

"A very strange hospital..." she said, moving her eyes. "Am I alone here?"

"No, not alone," replied the doctor. "Everybody is kept separately so that infection cannot spread. Today you may sit up," he stroked Vika's hand. "But don't go anywhere — stay in your bed. The nurse will bring all you need and he will show you where to take care of yourself."

"Thank you, Doctor," said Vika quietly, feeling embarrassed because of such concern.

"To call the nurse use this bell," he showed Vika a small bell near her pillow. "Or just clap your hands."

Vika's eyebrows raised and she looked first at the nurse and then at the doctor, trying to hide her smile.

"I understand you," the doctor laughed. "But he's the only one who speaks Russian, and that's why he has been appointed to look after you and will always stay with you. There is also a teacher of our language receiving treatment here right now, and if you want," he looked into Vika's eyes, inquiring, "I can arrange with him for you to take lessons."

"Oh, Doctor," she became more surprised. "This certainly would be nice, but I hope...that I will not stay here for long...I am sorry...I don't know," she started in confusion. "Do I need it?"

"You'd better!" replied the doctor and tapped her gently on her hand. "I'll also help you with your study. I used to study in Russia a long time ago, and I studied your language too," he smiled, recalling his memories. "It's a very difficult language! I failed to understand your verbs and mixed everything up."

The doctor rose from her bed and bent over her a little, staring her in the face. "Take all the pills I prescribed for you," he pointed to the small table, "and eat fruit. Have some rest and get well!"

He said good-bye, turned around, and left the room without a sound.

Vika shifted her eyes to the nurse. "What's your name?"

"A-Ali," he replied pausing.

"My name's Vika Zotova," said she shyly. He smiled a little and started to hand her the clothes, demonstrating on himself how to put them on. She start laughing.

"I'll figure it out Ali, thank you," she pulled something peach colored with her hand. "Oh, it's so soft! In our hospitals they make you wear an old flannel gown and a thick, strangely-colored cotton nightdress."

He smiled silently in response and nodded his head. Vika thanked him and asked him to leave so that she could put on her clothes. The clothes fit her well and were very nice to the touch, but Vika still felt weak. After dressing, she lay down again and tried to jog her memory.

She recalled everything, how she came here with Lena Somova, and abruptly felt unwell. She remembered the fat, sweaty smiling face of the shop director and then, nothing. Her memory stopped there.

Suddenly, her instructions flashed in her mind. If something were to happen, call for our foreign consul right away. Vika rang the bell at once. At that same moment, the curtain was drawn aside and the nurse appeared.

"Ali, I forgot," she alarmed, "tell the doctor, please, that I need to contact my Russian consul. I have to report to my country about my sickness so that they won't worry about me."

"Fine, I'll inform the doctor about it." The nurse smiled, bowing slightly. "Will there be anything else?"

"I'm very sorry, Ali," she said shyly. "Could you show me where my toilet is?"

"Yes. Sure. The hospital is in the midst of repairs," he moved the curtain from the corner. "Here are our temporary facilities. I'll take you to the shower in the evening."

"Thank you very much, Ali," she smiled back. "I don't think I'll need anything else today. Thank you."

"When shall I serve the dinner?"

"A bit later, please, and just a little bit, I don't want anything right now."

"All right," he said, and left the room.

Vika looked around. *A strange hospital, very strange it's indeed,* she thought. *Maybe all hospitals are like this in the East? I read nothing about it, what a pity!* Vika thought, lying in bed, smiling.

Chapter 26

SERGEI NILOVSKI SLOWLY walked upstairs to Vika's apartment. He understood that he had to meet her relatives, but he was oppressed by enormous guilt and put off this meeting. Besides, he knew that Semyon Severov had already talked to them.

There was no news of Vika or Lena. Two weeks had lapsed since their disappearance. People were working diligently over there searching for them, but the girls' trail ended at the café.

Sergei stood near the door of her flat and thought, *How can I encourage and comfort her family when I myself feel absolutely devastated by grief?* He rang the door bell.

Maxim opened the door and invited Sergei in, looking sadly at him. Vika's mother came out of the room, greeted the guest, and offered some tea.

"No, thank you," refused Sergei decently. "I don't want any."

They came into the living room and were sitting silently, their eyes to the floor.

"I am very sorry..." started Sergei. "This is my fault."

Mother took a handkerchief out of her pocket and started sniffling. "Can anybody tell me where she is?"

"Somewhere in the East," Sergei answered and silence fell again.

Mother looked at him sadly, pulling herself together a little. "Don't blame yourself, Sergei, it's fate. You couldn't change any-thing," she said softly. "We all were glad when she was offered this work, and she was so happy going on that journey..." Mother started crying and dried her tears.

"Please, don't cry," Sergei clenched his teeth. "We hope that she will come back. People are searching for them."

"Forgive us, Sergei!"

"Why? It's you who should forgive me," he tried to calm her down. "I'll do my best to bring her back." He became choked up.

"Sergei, you can never enter the same river twice," Vika's mother said, coping with her tears. "The past is dead."

Sergei, grinding his teeth, "It doesn't matter to me what can happen over there," he said, slowly stressing 'what', "I only wish now that she comes back alive."

Heavy silence fell again.

"I am leaving for the Army soon," Maxim said all of a sudden.

Sergei looked at him. "Maybe it's better for now if you stay at home with your mother, she would feel better until your older brother Viktor comes back."

"Granny can come here to stay," he replied stubbornly. He seemed to have already talked about this with his mother. "All my friends are leaving this autumn, and I'm going too," Maxim went on. "It's sickening to stay here without Vika!" he dropped his eyes, biting his lower lip.

"Maybe you're right," Sergei agreed. "I'd like to go somewhere too, but you cannot escape from yourself."

"Well, you can go to that country and look for her, right?" asked Maxim, sniffling.

"They won't send me there," Sergei replied, rubbing his temples. "People are already working over there, but there is some hope, of course. It's the venomous East. They love beautiful women there, and beautiful horses, and their price may be the same..."

He sat, clasping his head in his hands.

"Forgive me," said Sergei once more. "If I have any information I'll tell you right away, and if she calls you or sends word of herself in some other way, please, let me know."

"All right, Sergei," replied mother.

"I'd better go," he said and stood up. "If you need something, call me. I'll be glad to help you. Please, don't forget, if Vika somehow sends word of herself, call me immediately, day or night."

"All right, Sergei," nodded mother again.

He said good-bye and went out of the flat.

Chapter 27

FOR A NUMBER of days Vika had taken two-hour lessons with a teacher, trying to understand and memorize those hiero-glyphs so that she would not be a disgrace to the Russian people for her stupidity.

Everyone here is very strange, Vika thought, walking slowly and holding a nurse's hand. *The doctor brings the teacher himself, but at the same time he tells me I should appear at the classes all covered up, so that nobody can see me. Who on Earth am I hiding from? Probably from the chief doctor,* she thought.

She grew noticeably stronger, but still sickness sometimes tortured her, and the doctor told her sympathetically that it was all due to her poisoning. She became quite friendly with the doctor. He was very nice to her and had even presented her with a little white fluffy kitten, which she now carried everywhere, afraid to leave it back in the room in case he should run away.

Vika looked down as she walked, thinking of the days she had spent here. She remembered the morning after the day she had asked for the Russian consul, and the doctor became upset, reproaching himself for his forgetfulness.

"How could I forget, Domali, to make a call to the embassy?" he smiled.

"But I'm not Domali," Vika uttered, confused.

"When we received you," said the doctor gently. "You had no documents with you, so we registered you by this name. It's a very beautiful name, and that's what we'll call you while you're here. We cannot obliterate entries in the registrar. You don't mind, do you?"

Vika was gazing at him in amazement, batting her eyes, say-ing nothing.

"And now you will tell us everything about yourself, and the nurse will write it down," the doctor went on, "so that we can send these papers to the embassy."

Vika started telling them about her family, when suddenly she remembered about Lena Somova.

"And where is the girl I was with at that time?" she asked.

"I am sorry, but I do not know anything about any other girl," the doctor answered perplexedly. "You came alone. She must have been directed to another hospital."

"Right, thank you," said Vika as she went on telling about herself. She spoke of where she studied, her mother's name, her address, and home telephone, hoping they would directly call there and inform her people at home so they would not worry.

"Well, not much of a biography, is it?" the doctor smiled when she finished. "And how did you manage to go abroad?"

"I was awarded a trip ticket for good progress in studies," answered Vika promptly.

"Yes, I remember something of the kind," the doctor laughed. "You can't just buy it in your country; you can only earn it as an award!"

"Why would you say that?" she shied away and stopped short, at a loss on how to object to the truth he uttered.

"Don't be upset," said the doctor gently. "I respect your country; it's very large and strong."

"Yes," affirmed Vika proudly, "it's large!"

She met with the doctor each day, and he spent a lot of time with her, frequently giving her compliments. She felt confounded by that and, seeing his vivid interest in her, continued to merrily communicate with him, thinking that he was interested in Russia.

The nurse interrupted Vika's thoughts, bringing her to the teacher's desk and carefully taking off the coverlet from her face. She was stifled under it and blushing. She waved the copybook at her face to cool herself, and handed the kitten to Ali.

"Be careful not to lose him," she said to him, and took her seat at the table in front of the teacher. And the nurse sat down beside at the same table, listening to everything and helping with the translation.

After classes they returned to her room the same way, and the doctor was already there. He took the coverlet off her face and embraced her, congratulating her on the progress in her studies. They were facing each other; the doctor was just a little taller than Vika, rather heavyset, with a small belly and very lively eyes.

"Well, how do you like the studies?"

"Hmmm..." Vika shyly picked her words, "it is quite difficult."

"Of course," he agreed. "But, you should have time for it. And, you hear this language all the time."

"I don't know," Vika was confused. "I'm trying. And what's going on with the embassy?"

The consul had come to see her at the hospital a few days after she had asked about him. He was very agreeable, but very strange — he hardly ever spoke any Russian, always needing help from the nurse. Unfortunately, for that matter, Vika had no idea what a consul should look like and was just very glad that at least somebody could inform her mom about her.

The consul had reassured her, telling her that the information would be transferred to Russia, and asked her to write her data on a sheet of paper. He took it and went to the door.

"May I ask you something, please," Vika began humbly, "why do I have to stay at this hospital? Wouldn't it be better to send me back home? I'm feeling quite well already."

"No, I'm sorry," the consul had gently replied. "You're better off staying here."

"How much longer will I have to be here?"

The man was obviously at a loss, so the doctor answered for him. "Three weeks are necessary."

"All right, thank you," Vika was content with the answer. Then he said good-bye to her and left with the doctor.

* * * * *

And now she was looking at the doctor, waiting for any kind of information from the embassy.

"That's what I have come to tell you, so you would not worry," said the doctor, smiling. "Just to tell you your people at home have been informed that you're safe and sound."

"Oh Doctor, thank you so much!" she hugged him happily and, humming a song, began to circle the room. But suddenly she stopped short, glancing at the bed.

"What is that?" she asked, staring.

"It's your new clothes," said the doctor, tenderly coming up to her and hugging her about the waist. "Now you may choose what to wear, and not just wear what they bring to you."

Vika gaped at the awesome attire lying in front of her.

"But, Doctor," she uttered, drawing in her breath. "This doesn't seem like a hospital in the least."

"It's everything as it should be," he answered, kissing her on the cheek. "And now, Domali, I want you to eat, have a rest, and in the evening I will take you on a little excursion around the hospital. You don't mind, do you?"

"No, I don't," she answered humbly, looking down.

"Is there anything wrong? What's up, Domali?" he asked, trying to lift her face up by the chin.

"I am very sorry, Doctor," she began, blushing, "but do you by chance have an ordinary shower here? This bath..." and Vika stopped short, quite embarrassed. The doctor laughed and embraced her.

"I'm so ashamed in these baths..." she said pursing her lips, tears in her eyes.

The doctor went on, laughing at her shyness, stroking her on the back.

"Don't feel ashamed, all of those massages are a part of the curing procedure," he uttered tenderly. "Relax and have a rest, and let the medical personnel take care of you."

I wish I could go home very soon! Vika thought, sitting on her bed when the doctor left. She was really awfully embarrassed by the evening bathing where she was taken by the nurse. It was a rather large, oblong, half-circle bath, but not slippery like the one at home and painted green. It was elevated and full of water rich in poignant flower aroma.

Vika had to step into the bath, and the two women standing on the two sides began to wash her. She would never agree to disrobe in their presence and asked them to leave, but they would stand motionless, looking down obediently, waiting for her to step in. And she would step in, confused and angry, never taking off the sheet she was wrapped up in.

She always became full of anger in those baths, after which she was carried carefully onto a special warm table, where her head was washed and her body was massaged, with some oils rubbed into her skin, and often she would fall asleep right there.

For some reason, all of her hair was removed from her body, after which she decided that it was done for the sake of disinfection. Experiencing all of this, Vika Zotova was awfully nervous and waited eagerly for the moment when she would be allowed to return home.

Chapter 28

THE AFTERNOON HOURS were dribbling along slowly, and after meals Vika would get into her bed taking the kitten with her. She felt very lonely. All her thoughts were about Sergei Nilovski. She was longing for him with all her heart, going to bed and waking up with his name.

She was having some foolish dreams with her running and running somewhere, and then wanting to get home and being unable to find her apartment. In her dream were a broken staircase and no matter how hard she tried to climb the steps, she could never reach her door.

Time seemed to have stopped. If she understood the doctor correctly, three weeks had to pass from the day she gained consciousness, so Vika was counting the days, thinking about how everybody would be happy to see her come back safely.

The kitten presented by the doctor became her only fun, and fulfilling his destiny, he was very funny and playful. Sitting in her bed, Vika was rolling a small ball brought by Ali, and the little cat was dashing after it with abandon, making shortcuts and falling flat with his belly on the ball.

Suddenly the kitty, changing the trajectory sharply, hit the ball with his paw, so that it rolled down to the floor under the curtain, where the cat ran after it. Vika quickly jumped up to the curtain and, looking towards the place where the kitten had disappeared, jerked open the curtain on the move, and at once she bumped into a fat man, knocking a small tray out of his hands.

"Oh, I am so sorry, please forgive me!" Vika was taken aback, casting fearful glances at the man. "I'll help you gather it all!" She began to pick up the fallen objects quickly. The man tried to stop her, saying something in his language, but she had already gathered everything and was handing him back the tray, smiling guiltily.

"Please forgive me. I didn't do it on purpose."

He was eyeing her silently, and at this moment, the nurse appeared with the kitten in his hands.

"Ali, thank you very much!" she took the cat from his hands and retired to her room as quickly as possible.

In the evening the doctor came and Vika told him about the incident.

"Please forgive me," she was saying apologetically. "I spilled something and broke some glass, but I really did it accidently, I didn't mean to."

The doctor smiled, looking at her upset countenance. "Well, you can't tie the kitten to the bed, can you? Don't be upset, just keep playing with him. And what name have you given him?"

"Prince!"

"The kitten is a prince?" the doctor laughed. "And, why is not a king?"

"He's little."

"Well, well, Domali, you've made me laugh," he said, hugging her and stroking the kitten in her hands. "Now entrust the little cat to Ali, and let's go have a look at our kingdom!"

The doctor opened the curtain and they set out along the narrow corridor. Possibly it was not so narrow, but there were boxes in the hallway along with hung curtains. The walls in some places were also covered tightly with cloth.

"We're making a renovation in the hospital," said the doctor. "So it's not very cozy now, but soon it will all shine anew!"

They entered a big room which looked like a large office. To the left were shelves packed with books all the way to the ceiling, and partially closed glass doors in carved wooden frames. On the right there were two enormous wardrobes with a man's portrait hanging between them. Below the picture there was a rather narrow little cabin with small doors connecting the two wardrobes, and in front there was a large dark-green leather chair next to a massive wooden table.

The room was richly decorated with all kinds of handiwork. There was a sofa and armchairs at the back of the room, as if to block the way to a large French window opening to a balcony. The floor was covered with a magnificent, vast, colorful carpet. Never in her lifetime had Vika seen anything half as beautiful. Back at home she also had a colorful floor cover, but it was just matted.

Vika froze on entering the room and stood gaping at the luxury.

"I think," she said, drawing her breath. "One can only see things like this in museums. How beautiful it is!"

"Come, let me show you the balcony," the doctor said with a pleased smile, and they went out to a large half-circle patio with many green plants, birds in cages, settees, and small tables. The balcony was covered with a roof, with vast open arches in front and on both sides.

Vika looked out from the balcony — hot dry air hit her face, and it seemed to her it was a different kind of air from what she had remembered during the days of her journey abroad.

She looked around — everything in her range of vision was enclosed in a long tall fence, with palms and other trees growing along it. Far away on the right there was a big wall between the house and the fence, as if to separate a part of the house.

"Well," the doctor said, coming up to Vika, "let's go on," and taking her by the waist, he opened the door out of the room.

They were walking and chatting cheerfully about what they had just seen, about their cultures, about ancient times, with Ali following in their wake like a shadow, interpreting everything thoroughly.

Having passed the corridor, they entered a large, cheerful room that was divided, as if it were in two parts with the least one being elevated two steps higher than the rest of the room, and separated by columns. The room was quite empty and had several doors and one large French window opening up to the balcony.

"What do you think, Domali, what would be the best color for this room?" the doctor asked, peering at her.

"I don't know."

"What colors do you think would best go in the bedroom?" he insisted, "What colors do you like, for instance?"

"Well...I'm not sure, various colors," she muttered shyly. "I like bright ones," and she pointed at her outfit. "But not too bright...and I dislike dark colors, they look sad, you know."

"I see," said the doctor, smiling tenderly. "Let's go on."

And they went out to the balcony, which was much smaller than the previous one and only had one large arch. It was a balcony with two rooms, and the second one was also quite empty. Vika looked out from the balcony.

"Oh, what a beautiful park!" she said in delight, looking down. "Can we go there?"

"We can," the doctor answered and they went out into the corridor again. Having gone a short distance, they began to go down a wide, spiral staircase. Downstairs they found themselves in a vast empty hall, with everything under construction. Passing it, they went out to the garden.

Vika gasped with the fresh air. She felt dizzy and stopped for a moment, rubbing her temples. The doctor embraced her cordially and took her to a garden house next to the small fountain.

"Now you see," he said sympathetically. "You're still weak and need some time to get stronger."

"Thank you."

She looked around — everything was abloom and breathing with peace! The day was coming to an end, and the long shadows of the trees were beginning to gradually cover the garden.

"Oh, may I come here again?" asked Vika, "It's so nice here!"

"Of course you may. I'll just show you another way, because there are people working here during the day." He took her by the hand and looked her in the eye attentively. "And please, you have a light cape, put it on for the walks, and cover your face with a thin veil."

"I must hide away from the chief doctor?" asked Vika naively, looking up at the doctor.

He drew his eyebrows together and paused for a second, smiling. Then one of his eyebrows lifted a little, and he uttered, looking at Vika intently, "Well done, my girl, how quickly you've guessed about the chief doctor!"

They sat for some more time in the garden, and then he saw her to her room and, kissing her on the cheek, said good-bye and left.

Vika took the kitten from Ali and got on the sofa. She was feeling a vague alarm and was very homesick and missing Sergei. Tears ran down her cheeks involuntarily, and crying, she fell down into the pillows.

Chapter 29

VIKA WAS ACTUALLY never alone. Breakfast was always followed by a visit from the doctor, who asked her how she was doing, a small examination, and an inquiry as to if she needed anything at the moment. But Vika felt she had more than enough attention and never asked for anything. The doctor usually went away fairly quickly and appeared again sometime after lunch, or in the evening.

During the day it was the nurse whom Vika spent her spare time with so she would not be melancholy. He asked lots of questions, but seemed to always be sad himself, and as if he was afraid of something. Lately, they'd spent quite a lot of time in the garden and had become good friends, discussing various matters.

After having her classes with the teacher in the morning, Vika and Ali went to the garden.

"You know, in our hospitals in Russia, you can always go out downtown," said Vika. "Let's go for a walk beyond the fence."

"You surely don't mean it!" Ali exclaimed in amazement. "The guards won't let us out."

Vika laughed. "In our hospitals, it is also very strict," she said cheerfully. "But sometimes one wants to break the regime just a little. Don't you ever break any rules or restrictions?" She looked at Ali inquisitively.

"I'm trying not to. Do you like studying at your school?" he asked all of a sudden.

"Well, it's certainly much more fun than sitting in this hospital, as if in a prison," she said, looking around to make sure nobody would hear. "But to tell you the truth, something is pleasant in my school, but something is not."

"Well, what isn't?"

"Too much need to study, the teachers are strict and not always fair," Vika answered spitefully. "You learn, give a good answer, and they say you could have done better and don't give you the highest mark. Another pupil goes to answer, and the teacher helps him, praises his answer, and gives him the highest mark."

"How can that be?" asked Ali.

"Because...the pupil's parents are high up in the service or sometimes work at a wholesale goods store," replied Vika. "You can't buy anything in the shops, everything is in short supply, so those parents have something the teacher is in need of. In return, the teacher just tells the pupil what he should learn and then asks him that exact thing at the lesson for the sake of a good mark."

"Well, how do you know that?" wondered Ali. "I don't think it's quite true to fact, I believe teachers are extremely decent people."

"I thought so, too. But I once happened to find a teacher's message to a girl telling her what she should learn for the next lesson."

"So, what did you do with the message?"

"I gave it to another teacher whom I believed to be very decent."

"Wow! What about her? What happened to the author of the message?"

"Nothing! Just nothing!" Vika replied, making a wry face as if with toothache. "Nothing whatsoever! Everything remained as it had been. I'm only too glad I have finished that school and I'm going to study at another one. Hopefully, there won't be anything like that there."

"There's nothing worse than injustice," Ali supported her, "But one should always hope for the better, and it's sure to come. Just look what luxury is surrounding you now," he smiled, waving his hand around the garden.

"What does that have to do with our conversation?" wondered Vika. "But then you're right, everything is so beautiful here."

"Just don't think that it is only you to whom things can happen," Ali went on, "everyone meets with some troubles in his life. Would you like me to tell you a story of a boy?"

"Yes, I'd love it! Tell me!"

"Just take it for a fairy tale," drawled Ali thoughtfully. "Okay?"

"Okay." She settled herself comfortably in the garden house.

"Then listen," the nurse began in a low voice. "It was very long ago. There was a boy living in the southern republic, and he was very happy he was in his large family. He had five brothers and sisters, and he was the oldest child in the family and went to school. His father worked as a driver and his mother stayed at home to look after the children and work about their garden. All the elder children helped her with it. In autumn and spring, pupils were taken out to the fields to gather the harvest. And everything was very good in the boy's life, and he was a very good pupil," Ali went on. "But when he was eleven, his father was the victim of an accident."

"Oh! What a pity," Vika sighed out sorrowfully.

"Yes..." the nurse affirmed. "The boy's father perished in the accident, and the family at once lost their means of existence. The boy's mother started a sewing business; as a matter of fact, she had always sewn for her family. So now, she began to sew day and night for other people, just to make her living."

"Couldn't anybody help her?" Vika asked with compassion. "What about the state?"

"The state paid a very small pension for the children," answered Ali. "The money was quite insufficient, so the eldest child in the family had to look for a job. He turned a penny wherever he was allowed to, and he was paid just a little money which he brought to his mother."

"And what about his studies?"

"First he tried to combine work with his studies," Ali answered in an undertone. "But then the boy appeared at school more and more seldom, and the next year he almost quit school, for he had to feed his younger brothers and sisters. It wasn't easy at all to find a job," Ali went on. "Very early in the morning, he would run to a special place in the town where there were already other people and poor children like him queuing for a job. A little later, other people would come and take those who wanted to go, to places where there was something to do. The boy had to work on equal terms with grown-ups, carrying heavy bricks, cleaning up animals' stables, moving heavy manure, as well as working all day long in the fields under the scorching sun. It was very hard for him, but he was glad to help his mother at least a little."

"Poor baby!" Vika exclaimed with a pity. "But why didn't their relatives help them?"

"Relatives did help as much as they could," answered Ali. "But they were all as poor as the boy's family. And then one day," he continued, "the four boys he was among were chosen to work somewhere in a field and driven away. They were traveling in a truck rather far, and were dropped near a large house, amid a garden. They were told to work in that garden and in a field. There was a lot of work to do, so they were left overnight. It had happened time and time again that the boy had to stay somewhere for a night to continue the work in the morning, so he didn't hesitate to stay this time as well. Before they went to bed at night they were given food to eat, and shown to the place where they were supposed to sleep. The boy went there to sleep together with the others, and from that moment, he didn't remember anything that happened."

"How is that?" her eyes get bigger. "Do you mean to say he died?"

"No, he did not die," answered Ali sadly. "He was as alive as could be, but when he regained consciousness, he found himself in another country, sold and bought by strange people, shouting angrily in an unknown language."

"And what happened to him after that?" Vika was dying to know.

"Somebody bought him..." answered the nurse with a sigh. "And he was taken away somewhere very, very far away together with some other people, until eventually they were dropped at some house. A few days later he was given something to drink and fell asleep. When he woke up, he had a pain in the lower part of his belly. He was ill for a long time, possibly because of the travel, or because something had been done to him — he didn't know. The boy often cried and missed his mom very much. But time went on, and he came to understand that he would never now be able to have his own family or children. He was a different kind of man now, and nothing could be done about that." Ali paused, but then, with a heavy sigh, continued his story. "Then the boy got well, and he was given a special job, a place to sleep, some clothes, and good food. And he soon got used to the other life."

"Do you mean he was adopted?" wondered Vika.

"No, nobody fostered him. He just appeared in another life. Perhaps not always kind and just, but that was his life now. What happened – such was his destiny."

"It's a very sad story," Vika sighed, "the poor and unfortunate boy!"

"I don't know," said Ali thoughtfully. "The boy was growing, and he wasn't hungry at all. And what would he have seen back at home? But he was just missing his mom very much and sorry he couldn't give her any help."

"I'm missing my mom, too," Vika said sadly, looking around the garden. "But it is just a little wait now before I can see her," she concluded with certainty and joy.

"Yes, of course," started the nurse and he changed the topic quickly, "And have you ever swam in a sea or an ocean?"

"No, never!" she replied, smiling. "I have never even seen such a mass of water. But we do have the Black Sea, and I think when I finish school, maybe I'll go there to have a rest, and why are you asking me? Have you seen an ocean?"

"Yes, lots of times," answered Ali proudly. "The doctor frequently goes for business trips and takes us along."

"He's a very kind doctor," Vika confirmed. "And, very, attentive."

"Yes. He's nice, you're mighty lucky. Only do not make him angry."

"I'm trying to be good," she answered cheerfully. "Back at home we also have very nice and kind doctors. I've stayed at a hospital several times. They are rather particular, they can hug you sometimes," Vika smiled at her recollections. "But they would never kiss you on the cheek!"

"I think they must be concerned about getting an infection," Ali assured her.

"And there are too many people at the hospital, they just cannot kiss everybody," Vika affirmed, laughing. "Perhaps I'll also go to study to be a doctor after school, I do like it! Think about this, how everybody would love and respect you!" she bowed playfully to all sides.

"You would make a very beautiful doctor," said Ali smiling.

"Oh, thank you! But I'm afraid I won't be able to, it takes so much studying, and I have no patience, I will probably change my mind."

"And that's right!" assured Ali. "It's men that rule the world, and a woman shouldn't study too much, she needs to be beautiful, stay at home and love her husband."

"That's silly!" laughed Vika. "All people are equal! A woman, like a man, has a right to study and work," she concluded proudly. Then, on second thought, she went on with doubt, "Well, maybe here in your country men are very rich, so women do not have to work. But I think it's very boring to sit at home."

"It isn't boring at all," Ali shone with a smile. "When you have children, and are with the man who you must love."

"Oh please, Ali!" Vika laughed at his reasoning. "Don't you see, you don't marry a man unless you love him," she started to explain. "So why 'must you love' him? You just love and that's all! And if the people stop loving each other, then they divorce and don't live together."

"That is not so!" the nurse argued calmly. "It's the man who is to determine a woman's destiny, and she must love him. It's according to the Koran!"

"We have no Koran, Ali," answered Vika. "We don't seem to have any religion at all, and we're okay...as alive as ever!"

"What do you mean no Koran? What are you speaking about?" Ali was sincerely amazed. "Half of Russia is Muslim, and you're saying you have no Koran. So, you don't know your own country in the least."

Vika eyed the nurse thoughtfully.

"You are right..." she uttered slowly, "of course, you're right. And I have a lot of friends of various nationalities, and they're very, very remarkable friends! And our way of life is absolutely the same. And they love our motherland the same as me, and live according to the same laws. Girls study, fall in love, marry, and if necessary, get divorced. And what does it all have to do with religion when it's just a normal life?!"

"Life should go in accordance with the written religious laws," answered Ali. "And the Muslim religion is the most correct and strong!"

Vika gave a heavy sigh.

"Ali," she began gently, "why should I start to argue with you? Of course you are right! Those are the rules of your country, and I can't discuss them...probably, that law, you need here. I don't know," she was confused. "I love my country, and I like living in accordance to its laws, and we have equal rights in everything. Sometimes even a woman can kick her husband at home," she smiled, remembering the noisy family of her neighbors.

Ali also smiled at what he had heard.

"Can we have something to eat now?" Vika asked shyly. "I'm very hungry for some reason. May I have a little snack just now?"

"Certainly," said the nurse, getting up. "What would you like to have?"

"I would like a piece of fish, if I could," she answered timidly, heading towards the building. "I like fish."

"That's good," he smiled tenderly and accompanied her to her room. Very soon he brought some food.

Vika never got hungry in her room. On the little table, there was a large vase of fruit, as well as all kinds of sweets and dried fruit. Everything was always remarkably fresh and fragrant. It was just the water she did not like here, it was absolutely unpleasant, tasteless, and had an odor. Vika could not force herself to drink it, so she ate a lot of fruit.

Chapter 30

WHEN ALONE, VIKA Zotova began to think more and more often about her talks with the doctor and Ali. Again and again she replayed in her mind everything she had heard, and she had a feeling that some window was opening a little bit for her, and she started to see the same picture, but this time through other eyes. Vika lay in her bed and recalled her recent talk with the doctor.

"Domali, tell me about your plans and dreams," the doctor spoke, sitting opposite Vika.

"I don't have big plans," replied she gingerly. "I have not thought seriously yet about what I'll do in the future. Now the main thing is to get well and finish school."

"A good plan," said the doctor. "Two more years of schooling is not so quick. But for you, I think it will not be hard."

"Why do you think that?"

"Your language teacher told me that you catch on very quickly," the doctor said, "and I see how you try to say things in my language. I like that very much, thank you. I also speak English and can teach you, if you wish of course."

"No-o-o," uttered Vika, rolling her eyes. "Thanks a lot, but for now I just won't be able to study any more languages...thank you!"

The doctor laughed through his beard, seeing her fright.

"Nobody will make you do anything," he said. "Don't worry. This is only if you wish."

"Thank you, Doctor, but in my country, no foreign language is required, in fact, everybody speaks Russian. That is unless of course you want to acquire a profession where proficiency in some other language is also required."

"And the best way of all is to learn everything from childhood," supported her doctor.

"Yes," Vika did not deny this. "There are special schools where the foreign language is taught from the first year."

"That's it," he confirmed. "That's what I'm telling you about. The earlier you start to learn, the better! Knowledge gives people the opportunity to go higher in life."

"All people are equal in our country," replied Vika humbly, "and my mom says that it's not important where you work, the main thing is to work honestly and not be lazy."

The doctor's beard concealed his smile.

"If somebody has healthy ambitions, it's not bad at all," he went on softly. "One should always strive for light in one's life and take a position in society. It'll bring respect and fortune to you!" He looked carefully at Vika. "But a woman doesn't need to learn a lot, she can receive everything in a moment," he went on subtly. "All she has to do is to find a man of high position and immediately he'll raise her up to his level."

"I've never thought about that," said Vika quietly. "It's too early for me to think about getting married. I'd like to acquire a profession."

"I don't know what is early for such business," the doctor pronounced laconically. "But I know quite well what is too late. And Allah alone knows, when you'll be thinking about that," he said with delicate irony. "But I know for sure that the main thing for a woman is to have a successful marriage."

They talked for a long while and Vika heard some things for the first time. Something seemed funny to her, something — very clever, or completely unacceptable in the society she lived in.

* * * * *

Vika got up from her bed and stretched a little bit. *I've not done any exercises for such a long time,* she thought. *As soon as I arrive home, I'll go in for sports.* Vika stood beside her bed, holding on to it, and started to do some exercises. The doctor entered the room and caught her doing it.

"Oh-ho-ho!" he laughed. "I think things are on the mend and you feel perfectly healthy!"

Vika became confused and stopped her exercises. The doctor came up to her and embraced her.

"Don't be shy! It's excellent when you are strong and active," he patted her slightly on her back. "Have you been engaged in sports?"

"I trained at the circus studio for several years."

"Now I see why your balance is so good," the doctor said, stepping back a little bit and looking at her with admiration.

"Oh, no," blushed Vika. "My Granny always told me that I walk so straight as if I've swallowed a bar."

The doctor burst out laughing.

"Domali, that's not so! I don't know who of your relatives has swallowed a bar, but you should be proud of your figure and not feel so shy about it!" And he came up to her again and embraced her.

"I don't want you to get bored," the doctor went on. "Very soon we'll finish with the repair of a small swimming pool downstairs and you'll be able to swim there."

"Oh, thank you, Doctor. But I don't have a swimming suit."

"That's not a problem! You'll have everything. And tomorrow, Ali will bring you some women's magazines. Maybe looking at the pictures will at least make you feel better."

"Thank you, Doctor."

"How do you feel about going to the balcony now? We can sit there, talk, and listen to the birds singing."

"OK!"

As they walked, the nurse followed them, helping with the translation.

"You see," the doctor pointed to Ali, "this is what I've been talking about, his knowledge of the Russian language helped him take a higher position and not have to work as hard as others, he is appointed to only look after you."

"Oh, Doctor," Vika was bewildered. "I don't want to be a bother to anybody, and I'm so sorry. If it's necessary, he may go and work with others. I won't stay long here, and I can sit alone."

The doctor stopped, moving a lock of hair off her face, and stared at her.

"You will never be alone," he said tenderly but firmly. "I don't want you to get bored. I like your infectious laughter very much, and I want to hear it all the time."

He hugged her and gave her a peck on the cheek.

"I've told you about knowledge," he went on blandly, making her sit down in an arm-chair opposite him. "Because I already know you a little bit and can say that the time will come and you'll want to learn another language to speak and read."

Vika, lost in her thoughts, was looking directly at the doctor.

"I've heard this before," she said sadly, recalling Sergei Nilovski.

"I think the person who told you this wished only the best for you. Do you have a hobby?" he suddenly asked.

Vika looked at him perplexedly.

"Something you like to do in your free time?" the doctor began to explain.

Vika batted her eyes, recalling what she used to do. "Well, I sew a little bit for myself..." she said, confused. "I knit. But I don't think I like it, it's just something I need to do," she hesitated, then asked, "What hobby do you have?"

"I have many hobbies," the doctor smiled. "I like to do many things, for example, I would love to ride horses. I love and know how to shoot, and have a good collection of ancient arms. But most of all, I'm carried away by one hobby, which captivates the whole world!" He looked at Vika, smiling slyly. "Can you guess what is it?"

"No, I don't know..."

"Don't be shy," said the doctor cheerfully. "Tell me, what do you think everybody likes?"

"Oh, I'm ashamed to say," Vika was embarrassed with her thoughts. "But I think everybody likes to eat and sleep."

The doctor burst out laughing.

"Yes, that's true," he said. "But the main hobby of mankind is to make money and have money! And how settled you are in your life depends on the quantity."

Vika looked at the doctor with admiration.

"I like to surprise you," he smiled. "You're absolutely from another world. I do not presume to judge whether that world is right or wrong, but for sure, it's upside down!"

The doctor told Vika many interesting things, and she listened silently and wondered at his knowledge. For some reason, she thought that Middle-Eastern people were rather ignorant, unable to read or write, and now she saw a very educated man.

And, as if reading her thoughts, he said suddenly, "But I think, Domali, you don't have the idea that all people are the same and they all have one aspiration," he looked seriously into her eyes. "All people are different and many, very many, are content with very little, making no efforts to do anything and not even dreaming of more. Have you ever seen camels?" he asked unexpectedly.

"Yes, in a zoo."

"Let's go tomorrow to ride them. What do you think?"

"May we?" Vika was surprised. "Will the guards let us?"

"You'll hide in the car and we'll drive out," he pronounced conspiratorially. "And now I'd like to take you to a small concert to show you how our women dance."

Vika opened her eyes widely, looking astonished at the doctor, and he continued, "You'll have to cover yourself so the chief doctor won't see you," he grinned with his eyes. "We'll be sitting on cushions on a small dais. You'll seat yourself cozily," he went on. "The concert won't be long, but you should sit quietly and don't show yourself, okay?!"

"Okay!" replied Vika joyfully.

The doctor told something to Ali, and he left, but came back very quickly, having fetched a dark, hooded, ling cape. Two men brought a closed palanquin. Vika, after putting on the thick cloth and covering her face, seated herself inside the beautifully decorated palanquin, and two men lifted it up and carried her somewhere. In a short while, she was helped out and asked to sit down carefully as the doctor told her. Then the doctor came with some people and sat down in front of her.

Vika felt a little suffocated and she could not see very well through the dense gauze, but she was able to notice that this room was richly decorated with columns. The floor was shiny, with a beautiful, round ornament in the middle.

A large chandelier was sparkling and shimmering with crystal drops from above. Small, shiny oil-lamps were flickering on the walls all around, exhaling a heady, rough smell throughout the room.

The concert was not very long, and Vika had already seen such belly dances at home on TV: nearly-nude women, in transparent attire with much jewelry, dancing, wriggling, and shaking their hips as if they were separate from the body.

When Vika was brought back to her room and the doctor left, she took off her outer clothing, tied a gauzy scarf on her butt, and tried to dance as those women.

There was something similar in her movements, but her hips were absolutely uncontrollable, and they did not move like the hips of those dancers, no matter how hard she tried.

After practicing a little, Vika laughed at herself and decided to take a bath. *Now I know exactly,* she thought, *what I'll do when I'm at home. I'll go to the modern dance studio, so as not to be so clumsy, and maybe I'll even persuade Sergei to go with me.*

Chapter 31

THE NEXT MORNING Vika woke up in a wonderful mood. *A few more days,* she thought, *and, I'll go home!* She smiled, got up from her bed, and walked to the dressing room, humming something.

After freshening up quickly, she tried to dance once again. It was funny and she was cheered up even more. The breakfast was brought in, Vika having finished it rather quickly, and was playing with the kitty. Soon the doctor entered the room as energetically as the wind.

"Good morning, Domali," he greeted and hugged Vika, who had risen to her feet from the floor.

"Good morning, Doctor!"

"How are you today?" he said, making himself comfortable in the armchair. "I see, wonderful! Did you like yesterday's dances?"

"Yes, of course," she answered, sitting again on the floor. "I've seen something like that on TV once."

"Would you like to learn it?" the doctor asked, smiling, seeing her playful mood.

"Oh, Doctor, I'll never learn to dance like that. I tried yesterday already."

The doctor laughed, looking at her.

"I think that won't be hard for you at all! Tomorrow evening I'll bring a teacher for you and we'll see. And right now, let's get ready, we are going to ride camels."

She jumped up from the floor happily. "And what about Prince?"

"Leave him here! Don't worry, he won't disappear!"

Vika gazed thoughtfully at her clothes, not knowing what to put on for such an occasion. The doctor came up and picked out some suitable clothes.

"Put on this light mackintosh as well," he said, throwing the chosen clothes on the bed. "And gather your hair on top."

"All right," Vika replied, and ran to the dressing room to pin her hair on top of her head and change her outfit.

The doctor was sitting on her bed, when, humming, she flitted out before him, ready for the journey. He looked at her rapturously with his dark brown, bright eyes. "You're gorgeous!"

He got up from the bed and took her by the hand. "This wide scarf is just amazing on your slender waist!"

He twisted her around, showering her with compliments.

"Domali, you look very beautiful with your hair gathered," he said, examining her neck and face. "Your ears are small but nice, and are not pierced for some reason. Why?"

"I don't know..." said Vika, blushing.

"Well, this can be corrected," he hugged her, "and now let's go!"

* * * * *

The palanquin was brought into the room. Vika got inside, and was taken to the car. She sat down in the back seat and looked around.

The car was large and nice; the rear windows were draped densely. There was a curtain in an arch fringed along the edges behind the front seats from above, and nobody could see who was sitting in the back seat from the street.

A large driver with a small, black beard got into the car. Ali took the front seat. He asked Vika to lie down on the seat in the pillows, and they set out.

In a short while, Vika fell asleep, and woke up when they were in a fenced yard near a large house. Dry, hot air puffed into her face.

Vika smiled at the doctor, getting out of another car, and looked at his outfit with surprise — there was a large piece of fabric on his head as a headscarf supported by two rings. The doctor noticed her changed look at once.

"They will also tie a scarf on your head now," he said, smiling. "And your small nose will also be covered tightly, so you won't choke on the sand."

"Ah-ah...clear," Vika chattered lively. They entered the house, at the back of which was a large, metal hangar. Light brown buildings, in which animals were kept, apparently, were on both sides of the house.

Soon after a short break, they went out to a small yard from the side entrance and began to seat themselves on camels. Vika stood on a porch, not daring to come closer.

"I'm afraid of them," said she quietly to the doctor. "They will throw me down!"

"Don't be scared. You'll have a gentle animal and the seat is quite comfortable," he assured her. "It won't throw you down, unless you jump yourself."

They came up to a peacefully lying camel, covered with a large bright rug with tassels, and a seat as beautiful as a throne, which was rather spacious and with low sides. It was covered from above with an embroidered baldachin with delicate frills on edges made as an arch, and the hangings, pursed up from below, fell along its small, carved columns.

"If you want," said the doctor, "you may loosen the curtains below and close your seat from any side if you wish. But I'd like to see you!"

"Thank you," Vika pronounced shyly, touching the throne. "I like it so much."

"I'm glad and I'd like to assure you that the journey won't be long and tiresome," the doctor said, looking how she was helped to take her seat inside. "And I think it'll be interesting for you!"

"Oh, sure!"

Vika was lost in the soft pillows of the throne, and the doctor only saw her happy eyes, because her head and face were tightly covered with a headscarf.

"Domali, are you comfortable?"

"Yes, very much. But I cannot control the camel."

"You don't have to do that, it'll follow another animal. Only when it gets up and down, hold the sides, just in case," he took Vika by her hand, looking fondly into her eyes. "Don't tremble, relax. And put on sun glasses. Don't worry, I'm close! Okay?!"

"Okay," said an excited Vika. The doctor mounted the camel prepared for him, and the people who helped them started to make the animals get up.

Vika, having curled her legs up, grabbed hold of the sides so as not to fall out, and froze, waiting for the camel to get up. Large gates opened up and their group moved slowly to the exit, where horse riders were already waiting for them.

Low, gray and yellow looking mountains with rare shrubs and thorny plants extended from both sides, and the group moved among them, going afar.

"Domali, don't hold the sides so tightly," the doctor said softly, riding a camel near Vika. "Put on glasses or a veil, covering your eyes from the sun."

"Uh-huh..." Vika nodded her head.

"Real sand will start behind the mountains," said the doctor. "I'm sure it will surprise you!"

"Of course," she looked around. "But frankly speaking, I can't imagine the mountains of sand."

And she soon saw them. Like a sea, the desert lay vast before her eyes. The smooth tops of sand hills seemed like waves running one after another. There were light yellow sand drifts, with no end to them as far as she could see. Far away the sand seemed to be transparently-white and the sky was also colorless. The unsteady line of the horizon was bleeding into one color and then fading away into the infinity.

A part of their group, mounted on camels, had ridden ahead quickly, but Vika and doctor with the rest of the people, were moving rather slowly. Vika was riding between the doctor and the nurse. The doctor was telling funny stories about camels, and Vika was chiming in with stories from her own life. They were laughing merrily as the road along, using hand gestures to aid them in the explanations.

Soon Vika felt sand on her teeth.

"How can sand get into my mouth through a lot of layers of fabric?" she asked.

"This is very fine sand," the doctor answered. "It's like dust and it gets through everything."

The rest of the way they traveled in silence, speaking when required.

In about two hours they came upon a small oasis. The oasis was dotted with palm-trees of various heights from short to very tall. Surrounded by a group of trees was located a tabernacle. Vika could see people had set up small campsites and they were already cooking something on the fire.

They dismounted and Vika, in light sandals, first stepped on the hot sand. She sat down and took it in her hands, sifting it between her fingers; it really was partially like dust and very sticky. Vika began to shake it off her hands, but it appeared to be impossible to remove. The small particles of sand had covered them all over like flour. Again she grabbed the warm sand with her hands and built a little pyramid out of it.

"It is amazing!" she said in delight to the doctor. "Can I climb up that hill?" She pointed to the nearest small sand hill.

"Sure," the doctor replied and Vika ran up it.

"There's no way to catch up with you," the doctor laughed marching quickly in her wake. The mounted men also rode up the hill on both sides of them from a considerable distance.

Vika and the doctor reached the top and stopped on it to catch their breath. Vika circled about for a while and jumped on the top.

"I can't believe I'm looking at all this!" she laughed, "We have hills of snow, you have hills of white-hot sand, let's be friends and exchange!"

"Let's do that," he answered in laughter catching up her merry-making.

"Now can we glide down the hill?"

"Of course, we can!" the doctor exclaimed, grabbed her by the hand and, holding up their clothes, they dropped down on their butts and slipped down, laughing.

Having helped each other up, they walked to the tabernacle, shaking off the sand. Their faces and heads were still wrapped up, but the sand was everywhere and they were spitting, trying to rinse their mouths while taking off their capes. Others assisted them in washing their hands and faces, and they entered the tabernacle to eat and have a rest.

"Thank you for such a wonderful excursion!" said Vika timidly. "I've heard somewhere that doctors abroad were rich people, but I certainly could never have imagined just how rich. And now I see this tabernacle, these people, these camels, horses and everything..." she paused for a moment, "thank you, doctor, for the great attention, I will never forget it!"

"You're welcome," he answered tenderly. "I want very much that you never forget it, and that you like it."

"Thank you! I do like it very much!"

The meantime, after having a rest, they set out for the return trip, and having done it all over again, she found herself back in her room.

"Doctor, I'd like to express my tremendous gratitude to you again for the trip!"

"My pleasure, darling!" he smiled, hugging her good-bye. "See you tomorrow, Domali!" And he left.

Vika felt great fatigue, and she was quite unwilling to think about the things that seemed strange to her that day. She summoned the nurse and asking him about the bath made up her mind to think it all over the next morning after she got a good night's rest.

Chapter 32

TIME WAS APPROACHING for Vika's day of discharge. In the morning, she went to have foreign language classes. A teacher of dances came in the afternoon, when she had already had dinner and relaxed.

Vika sat down on the sofa, while waiting for her, looking through the magazines brought by Ali a long time ago. She could not help but a smile as she remembered the doctor bringing the dance teacher to see her one evening.

* * * * *

He sat down in the armchair, keeping an eye on their actions. Three of them, Vika, Ali and the teacher, were standing in the middle of a room. The teacher was a middle-aged woman, a little bit fat and short. Vika was standing in front of her in a tight T-shirt and in loose, light trousers.

The woman looked her over from head to toe, gave her a friendly smile, and then showed her how to lower her pants down on her hips. Feeling embarrassed, Vika lowered them as shown, exposing her waist and a part of her belly. Ali was translating everything the woman was saying without interfering.

The women stood opposite each other and the teacher started to slowly show the motion of the dance. Vika began to move her thighs like the teacher, who quickened the pace and then stopped, seeing that Vika was lagging behind. They tried to repeat the motion from the very beginning.

Vika was laughing at her awkwardness, trying hard to imitate the movements. Then the woman showed her how to move her body and shoulders. But Vika's dance was constrained. The doctor sat smiling, watching the process.

The teacher asked Vika to come up to the wall and stand against it with her back and butt. Then she showed her how it was necessary to step aside from the wall and lean the body in different directions shaking her shoulders a little, without moving her butt from the wall. Vika tried to do her best to perform all this, but her body was uncoordinated. She repeated the movements more than once, but her body wouldn't obey, as if it were not hers. Vika burst out laughing, stepping aside from the wall.

They stood behind one another. The teacher slowly started to move her body in the rhythm of the dance, gradually quickening the pace. Vika's whole body strained, her knees bent, she followed the woman with all her body shaking and trembling as though she were paralyzed. She raised her hands and twirled only her fingers.

Roaring with laughter, Vika sat down on the floor. Everybody burst into laughter.

"I have never seen anything like this," the doctor clapped, wiping the tears. "But don't feel upset, you'll master it little by little."

And since that evening, Vika had started to study dancing. She made progress in it, though sometimes she wasn't quite up to the mark. Nevertheless, it wasn't boring, and it broke the monotony of her life.

Today, having had a lesson, Vika and Ali went out for a walk in the park. They were wandering along the alleys lined with palm trees.

"I'm leaving rather soon," Vika said with joy. "I wonder how it will be, shall I go to the embassy to be sent home, or will the consul come here again to take me back?"

She glanced at the sad nurse, walking with her.

"Ali," Vika touched him by the sleeve, "don't be so upset! Everything will be all right!"

She was looking at him with sympathy to divert his depression. "You're a very good friend and I promise to remember you, and to send you letters."

"That's good," said Ali quietly, looking down.

"I've missed a lot of classes at school," smiled Vika. "And it won't be easy for me to catch up with the class!"

"Probably," agreed the nurse, biting his lip.

"Do you know Ali, when I will be discharged?" asked Vika. "Will it be tomorrow or next Monday?"

And she again looked into the eyes of a nurse.

"Ali, please don't be so upset!" Vika begged, shaking his sleeve. "Just think how delighted my mom will be to see me!"

She picked up a small flower and began dancing cheerfully along the alley, going to the fountain.

"As I see it," she glanced at the bright hospital building, "the redecoration is already over, and rather soon you'll have new patients here! And you'll have more work to do," said Vika cheerfully, feeling the fountain water with her hand.

"It's possible," he replied, sitting on the bench.

"Maybe you have fallen ill?" Vika took a seat next to him. "You're so silent today. What are you thinking about?"

"About you," he uttered, depressed. "I want you to understand me. I wish that we were friends."

"No doubt! I'll write to you, if it's possible."

"Things do happen in life..." he continued in a confused tone. "Life is the most priceless thing and it's worth taking care of. Because only the living can hope and try to change things."

"I have no idea what you're talking about," Vika blinked in a silly way.

"You're a clever girl," the nurse went on slowly, "and I want you to be strong too."

"Do you think that I'm not strong?" she looked at him. "I'm stronger than most of my classmates," said Vika proudly. "Do you know how many times I can pull myself up? Let's go, I'll show it to you!" And she rose, looking around for a place to show her strength.

"I believe you, I believe," said Ali quickly. "That's good. It will probably help you somehow."

"Stop that, Ali," she went to the fountain, ignoring him. "I don't understand you today. Don't be so upset! Have a look, what fine weather we're having. It's so warm!" she embraced herself, smiling. "And the doctor told me that tomorrow we're going to have a horse ride. So don't be so upset and get ready!"

But the next day, there was a problem with the horse ride. A black, very tall, beautiful horse was brought to Vika. It was squinting at her with his plum-colored eyes, trying to turn his head on a very tall neck to look at her. Vika was looking at this miracle in horror. And when the horse snorted quietly, striking a hoof against the ground, she jumped back.

"Oh no, thank you! I'm afraid of him!"

"Don't be scared," the doctor tried to cheer her up, "The horse is very clever and obedient."

"Sorry," Vika was very confused and stepped back, "but I have never before in my life ridden a horse, and I have never seen such a tall one!"

The doctor grinned and said in a soft voice, "But you aren't going to ride a donkey!" He was smiling tenderly at her. "All right, we'll bring you a smaller horse."

And another horse was brought at once.

"But it's almost the same," uttered Vika in tears. "I can't. I'm sorry, I'm afraid. A camel will be enough for me."

The doctor giggled and embraced her.

"Don't be upset, Domali," he said with sympathy. "You're right. You need to do things one step at a time. Today, you will just watch the races, they're rather exciting."

"Thank you, Doctor," smiled Vika. And she was accompanied to the place, from where she could observe the races.

Vika felt very uncomfortable and ashamed because of her cowardice, though the doctor had not displayed his discontent. On returning to her room, she finally calmed down, thinking, *what's the use of all these horses?* She would be going home in a day or two!

Chapter 33

ON SATURDAY, AFTER dinner, the clouds covered the sky, and late at night it began to thunderstorm, a very rare thing in these places.

Vika went to bed earlier than usual, in order to speed up the time of her discharge from the hospital. But just after the midnight, she awoke. She could not understand what had made her wake up, whether it was the night dream or the dry peals of thunder.

She lay in bed, trying to make sense of her dream. It was as if she was on the bank of a river or a lake, and Sergei Nilovski swam away from the bank. She was shouting to him, "Come back! Come back!" and running along the bank, looking for help. At that time, Sergei was swimming further and further away. So she awoke feeling as if she were waving her hands and shouting.

Vika silently rose from her bed and looked out the windows, the bottom level of which was just on her chin. She looked at the tops of the trees and at the sky.

"Oh, goodness," she said in a low voice, "I want go home so much!"

Then she looked at the bright flash of lightning.

"Sergei, where are you?" Vika whispered as if she were praying. "I want to be with you," and she burst into tears, leaning against the wall.

Only at dawn she did regain consciousness, squatting in tears next to the wall. Vika stood up to go to her bed.

In the morning, she woke up late. It was still cloudy outside, as though it was drizzling, and she had a headache. Vika got up, dressed, and had breakfast.

On Sunday, the doctor usually came by at noon, and that day he didn't change his routine. "Good afternoon, Domali," he came in, as always, a little bit unexpectedly. "How did you sleep today?"

"Rather well," Vika smiled.

"The noise of the thunderstorm interfered with your sleep," said the doctor with sympathy, looking at her. "It occurs rarely here and it will be over soon."

Vika looked out of the window with sorrow.

"But you have some time to relax today," he went on. "You should go out and breathe in some fresh air. It will help you to feel better!"

"Thank you, Doctor," said Vika. "I'm very grateful to you for everything."

"You're welcome," he embraced her. "I'm sorry, but I should go. I have a lot of work to do," and, staying for just a short time, he said good-bye and left the room.

After his departure, Vika laid down on the sofa and fell asleep among the cushions. By the evening, the weather had become better. Vika and the nurse went out into the garden. It was very warm and stuffy.

"In my home, it usually becomes cool after rain," said Vika, walking along a damp path.

"And it rains a little bit more often than it does here." added Ali.

"With snow," laughed Vika. "Yes, it's true. Indeed," she said, as though trying to convince him. "This month sometimes it has already snowed."

They came inside the garden house and sat in silence for some time, looking at the fresh greenery.

"I had a dream today," said Vika quietly.

"What was it about?'

"Something troubling," she answered. Ali looked at her.

"And were you crying at night?" he asked sadly.

"I want to go home, Ali!"

They sat silently, looking down, finding neither the words nor the subject for conversation, and soon she asked permission to go back to her room.

"I think you need a hot bath," said the nurse, seeing her melancholy mood.

"That's good," she answered indifferently.

Having had a bath, Vika slept the whole night and the whole morning of the next day. It was almost noon when she awoke, and she looked around, lying in bed, surprised that nobody had woken her so far. She took a hand bell and rang it. At the same time, Ali entered the room holding the kitten in his hands.

"Good morning," he smiling and gave Prince to Vika. "How well have you been sleeping?"

"Very well," she answered cheerfully, stretching herself. "And where is the doctor?"

"Shall I bring breakfast right now or a little bit later?"

"Please, right now," Vika answered, skittishly playing with the kitten, and Ali left the room.

* * * * *

She rose, feeling wonderful, and quickly changed her clothes and tidied herself up. Breakfast, as always, was big — choose whatever you like or you may eat everything! Hot tea, coffee and juices were served as well.

Vika was finishing ate when Ali appeared again.

"Shall I bring anything else?" he asked obligingly.

"Oh, no, thank you. Can you leave a glass of juice here? I'm so thirsty today."

"Certainly," Ali said as he stood looking at the dark sky out of the window.

"And where is Doctor?" asked Vika, having made herself comfortable on the sofa.

"He has left on a business trip."

"But he told me nothing about it yesterday," she said, bewildered. "Has there been an emergency?"

Ali walked around the room, rubbing his temples and not knowing what to answer. He sat down on the edge of Vika's bed, rested his elbow on its back and looked down on the floor guiltily.

"Ali, I don't know how long I've been staying here, but two days ago, according to my calculations, I was to be discharged,"

Vika said slowly, looking at him. "And why has Doctor left without discharging me...why hasn't told me anything?"

"Because he isn't a doctor," the nurse whispered.

"What?" Vika raised her eyebrows. "And who is he?"

"It's n-not important at-t all," Ali stammered.

Vika lowered her legs from the sofa and stared at the nurse with round eyes, blinking frequently.

"What are you talking about?" she asked. "What a silly joke, Ali? You've recently spoken that we are friends. Be honest. What's the matter? Why have I not been taken to the embassy?"

Ali looked at her in silence.

"Domali," he said in a trembling voice, as he rose from the bed and started to walk around her. "You see...Domali," he started stammering.

Vika sat on the sofa with her eyes fixed on him. She felt that something was wrong, but didn't understand at all what it was.

"Go ahead, Ali, speak out," she said calmly.

"You're in a harem."

"In what harem?"

"In a real one," he answered in a hardly audible voice.

"What are you talking about? What is this?" she said in surprise, coming up to him. "What harems? They're only in fairy tales! That's all in the past! We live in the twentieth century and people fly into space nowadays!"

He pressed to the back of the bed, keeping silent, not knowing what to say. Vika, slowly holding her breath, was looking at him, slightly stepping back.

"I want to go out," she tried to breathe deeply.

"Please, stay here now."

"Say that I'm dreaming!" she raised her voice, not believing what was going on. The nurse kept silent. His chubby face was perplexed, and he had tears in his eyes.

"Ali, you're telling lies. All this isn't true! You're the liar!" Vika jumped from him and made her way out in the direction of the blinds, from where everyone appeared. "I want nothing!" she shouted, crying. "Do you hear me? I want nothing! I want to go home!" she drew aside the blind and ran through the corridor.

Suddenly, a huge, swarthy man with a dagger on a belt emerged in front of her. "Stop!" he stretched out his hand.

"Ah-a-a..." Vika rounded her eyes with horror. Looking at that hand in silence she instinctively moved back from the man. And at that moment, someone behind her stopped her gently by the shoulders.

She screamed out and ran back towards her room. She felt sick and at the point of vomiting, rushed into the lavatory. Ali prevented her from closing the door.

Vika was shivering and throwing up. She cried, wiping her face with a towel, and then rushed to the bed, having pushed the nurse away. He sat down next to her and, silently sobbing, wiped his tears with a fist. Suddenly Vika sat up, still shuddering. "Believe me, Ali, that fence..." she pointing at the window, "it's not a barrier for me! I can easily jump over it and go to the embassy. Please, help me!"

"The guards are everywhere. Which embassy?" he asked almost in a whisper.

"My embassy!" she shouted, jumping out of the bed.

"You're in a completely different country..." he said in a low voice. "And you don't have any documents."

"How can that be? I had a passport with me! And if all else fails, it's just necessary to go to the police, and they will deliver you to the embassy!" shouted Vika.

Ali sat motionless and whispered, "It's possible to convince our police to do anything, and if you went there, they would just deliver you back here."

Vika jumped up to Ali. "It is not true! I saw the consul come here," she nervously waved her arm around the room. "We have to find him!"

"He's not the consul," mumbled Ali. "He's the doctor's friend!"

Vika looked at the nurse in confusion, and with sudden horror. "This one is not a consul. That one is not a doctor," she began sharply, stretching her hands to the right and to the left. "This is not a hospital and the country is different! Do you realize what are you saying?" Vika choked out the words with emotion. "And who are you then?" He was sitting silently on the bed, with his eyes on the floor. And at that moment, Vika screamed, jumped away from him, and covered her mouth with her hand.

"A-a-a...you're...you're that boy..." she said slowly in a trembling voice, removing her hand from the face. "You're that boy...whom you told me about."

Paralyzed in horror, Vika's body started to shiver. She went slowly towards the sofa, as if she were going crazy, and sat down quietly.

Chapter 34

MUZAPHAR HAD BEEN far from his place for several days, settling his business. During one of these days, after dinner, he lay down on the sofa to have a rest, and involuntarily thought about Domali. Tonight his friend was going to arrive here by plane. And he smiled, having recollected how he persuaded him to be the Russian consul for Domali.

"I can't," his friend had said then. "I actually don't know Russian at all. And what I knew, I completely forgot. Can you imagine how many years have passed by?" he laughed, "go figure this picture, the consul of the country has forgotten his native language!"

"Ridiculous, certainly," answered Muzaphar. "But I don't have any choice at all. And I think that she's too young and could hardly even imagine what a real consul should look like. She may think that he has been living in this country for such a long time that he's forgotten the language!"

Both of them burst out laughing.

"All right," the friend agreed. "But I don't understand your plan. Tell me about her."

"Do you remember a doctor Svetlana from Russia? That woman, who refused to come here with me?" Muzaphar said with a frown.

"Well, how can I forget your Russian love?" his friend smiled. "And why have you brought up the facts from your youth?"

"Domali is Svetlana's copy," Muzaphar uttered proudly. "Seeing her, I thought that my heart would stop beating!"

"So, maybe she is her daughter?"

"No. I've already found out everything about her," said Muzaphar. "And they are not even relatives."

"Surprisingly!" the friend exclaimed. "And where did you take her from?"

"Do you remember I recently flew on a business trip to our neighbors? I invited you to join me, but you refused," explained Muzaphar. "And so once, walking down the street, I saw her. Whether you believe it or not, I almost fell down!"

"I believe you," the friend confirmed. "And what was she doing there?"

"They were tourists," continued Muzaphar. "Together with another girl, who was her senior, they were walking and doing some shopping there. They were so cheerful and carefree! All the passers-by were staring at them."

"I can hardly imagine their parents having allowed them to go alone?" the friend said in surprise.

"Well, don't you remember the Union?" it was Muzaphar's turn now to be surprised. "Girls there go everywhere on their own, and without being accompanied by anybody."

"That's quiet right," nodded the friend. "And what happened afterwards?"

"We were together with my security guard, Baker by name," continued Muzaphar.

"Oh, how huge he is!" the friend inserted with delight.

"And so, we were going behind them. And I realized that I could not let her get away," said Muzaphar. "And I didn't know what to do, as it was broad daylight with crowds of people everywhere!"

Muzaphar, half-lying on the sofa, smiled and scratched his beard, having recollected that exciting moment, and again resumed his reminiscences.

"Well, do say what you thought up then," his friend insisted impatiently.

"And nothing came to mind," Muzaphar answered frankly. "I decided to find the hotel where she was staying and to steal her during the night from there. But thanks to Allah, I had good luck, and everything took place in its own way and rather soon."

His friend was listening to Muzaphar's story with great interest, without interrupting him.

"They came into a fur shop and began to try on fur coats," continued Muzaphar. "The only thing I had to do was to pay the owner of the shop for his help and that's all! We took away Domali, and the second girl was left to him. Nobody was offended!"

"That's great!" the friend said in delight. "Certainly, I shall go with you as the Russian consul. You have intrigued me and I want to see her as soon as possible!"

Reminiscences about Domali always caused Muzaphar to smile. He rose from the sofa and walked inside. Since the time he saw her, he couldn't stop thinking about her. And the more he communicated with her, the more he loved her and thanked Allah for such a great gift.

Muzaphar looked at his watch, expecting a phone call from his friend in order to have supper together. Their fathers used to be friends, and they were also friends, helping each other in urgent situations and having common business interests. Muzaphar was grateful to his friend, as he had superbly played the part of the Russian consul.

That day he arrived in an expensive suit, a white shirt and a tie, with a black folder under his arm.

"Well, do I look like Russian?" his friend asked, smiling. "Here, I have found a Russian dictionary and brushed up on some Russian words. So take me to her at once until the words have slipped out of my memory and I have sweated in these clothes."

Muzaphar smiled, having recollected how wonderfully it had passed, and they sighed with relief, leaving her room.

"She is very lovely," said his friend cunningly and looked at Muzaphar. "Well, you know me! How much?"

"Thank you very much for your help!" answered Muzaphar. "But I wouldn't sell her."

"Why do you need what you already had?" the friend persisted. "How much?"

"Don't become angry, but I won't sell her," said Muzaphar softly.

"I shall give you a very good sum," his friend didn't stop.

"Oh! No! No! No! I want to teach her languages and to take her everywhere with me as a European woman," Muzaphar spoke with a smile. "Well, just imagine that my youth has returned!"

"That's right," his friend grinned, finishing the deal. "And how did the idea of the hospital dawn in your head?"

"It was also Svetlana, who was a doctor, which made me think of it," Muzaphar responded. "I won't repeat again what happened once. I think you remember that girl who rushed at me with a knife?"

"Of course, I remember."

"It's necessary for Domali to have some time to get acquainted with me, to get used to me and to fall in love with me," continued Muzaphar. "And here is the situation that I thought of, a hospital is the best variant. Nothing seems suspicious for Domali, because in her country, education and medical care are free of charge. Svetlana told me about it then," Muzaphar explained to his friend willingly. "And they also stay in hospitals for a long time, until they recover completely!"

"Oh, wow, I didn't know!" his friend continued in surprise. "You have arranged everything in a clever way. Well, let's wait for the results."

The telephone rang, having interrupted Muzaphar's reminiscences. He took the receiver and heard his friend's voice.

Chapter 35

VIKA'S HEART JUMPED and thoughts like hurricanes filled her mind. She understood now that she and Lena Somova had been stolen, simply stolen. She wasn't in a hospital with the diagnosis of a stomach illness. They had been given something — they had been poisoned by these men!

Suddenly she remembered everything: those glasses with water, that shop, and even the people she saw from the corner of her eyes, they were sitting at that time in the corner of the store. Who were they? thought Vika. *Maybe all this was somehow connected with our task? Could I have said anything? But what could I have told? I knew absolutely nothing!* she rushed in guesses. *Oh no...he stole me, because I looked vulgar and defiant! But why does he treat me so well then?* Vika sat, with her head clasped in her hands, and feverishly searched for the answers to her questions. *What does he want from me?* she thought. *I know that my country would never leave its citizens in a situation like this. Maybe he will release me, if he is paid?*

She looked up at Ali. He sat motionless and it seemed that he was hardly breathing.

"Ali," Vika called in a low voice. He started and turned his head. "Please, help me," she looked at him with a slight hope in her eyes. "It's necessary to inform our embassy and they will offer him money for me!"

"He won't agree," said Ali in a whisper.

"Why won't he agree? This is money!" Vika rose from the sofa. "And what does he want then?"

"He loves you."

"Wha-at?" Vika's eyebrows moved upwards. "Have you gone crazy? He's an old man! What kind of love are you talking about? He's too old for love."

"Well, he isn't really so old," Ali exclaimed in surprise. "He's over fifty, but he's still a very strong man."

"Over fifty - that's like a hundred!" Vika blurted out with mockery. "He should better take care of his grandchildren!"

"He loves you," repeated Ali once again, not finding any more powerful arguments. "I don't remember him ever being as happy as he now."

"Shut up! Shut up!" Vika waved her hands. "If he doesn't need any money, it means that he's rich," she said in a loud voice, nervously moving up and down the room. "It means that he can buy any woman. Is that so?"

"Yes, it is," confirmed Ali.

"And if it is so," Vika said abruptly, "why has he chosen me? I'm far from being a beauty and I am not going to marry him."

"I don't think that he can marry you," said Ali softly, rising from the bed. "You're not a Muslim, and besides that, he has wives."

"Oh my God!" Vika uplifted her hands and stopped in the middle of the room. "If he has wives, how can he think of another woman?"

"He loves you," Ali repeated once more, like a wind-up toy.

"No, no, no!" screamed Vika. "I want to go home! I have a fiancée there!"

"Uh...no!" cried Ali in a terrified voice, as he jumped up to her, looking around. "Never," he hissed, "you hear? Never, any-where, speak about it! You can't even imagine what could happen to you if you were not a virgin."

Vika's eyes became big and round.

"What?!" she said in a trembling voice, backing away from him. "How can you speak about that? How do you know about me?"

He was silent. And thus she understood why she had regained consciousness absolutely naked — she had been completely exam-ined.

"I hate this!" Vika cried out and started rushing around inside the room. But she stopped just once to face Ali. "I'll kill him!"

Ali shuddered and straightened up.

"Never say that!" he said slowly and severely. "You don't think that you'll die at once, as soon as you do any harm to him. It's terrible for me to imagine what would happen to you."

Vika looked at him angrily.

"I shouldn't show this to you," he continued. "But now my destiny depends upon your behavior," he gave her a long raincoat and covered her head with a big hood. "Let's go!"

Vika saw nothing and he, taking her by the hand, led her along the corridors. Then they began to go downstairs, and again they went along a corridor. Then the iron door clanked. The smell of dampness spread from below. Ali, holding Vika firmly, began to help her go up the steep staircase. Then again, they went along the corridor.

It seemed to Vika that there would be no end to this road, but suddenly they stopped and stood standing for some time without moving.

"Please," Ali whispered in her ear. "Say nothing," and he cautiously raised the hood from her face.

It was semi-darkness around them. Vika began to blink her eyes, she squinted them, trying hard to see something. At last her eyes focused in the darkness, and she saw directly in front of her an iron door with a latticed window. She involuntarily stepped forward, examining what was there in the depth of the window, but Ali held her tightly by the hand, not allowing her to move.

With great pressure Vika peered through the window. At last she saw something shaggy there. It was a woman, and she was also looking at them. Then the woman cried wildly and waved her hands to them. Vika shuddered and stepped back, continuing to look through the window, as if under hypnosis. Ali carefully lowered the hood on her face and pulled her by the hand.

When they returned to the room, he helped her take off the raincoat, and seated her on the sofa.

"Who is she?" Vika asked, in a voice trembling with shock.

"That is the woman who wanted to kill her master," said Ali. Vika was silent.

"Don't be angry with me," he started timidly. "It's not my fault that you have appeared here...it's your destiny. And still, it's possible to say that you're one of the lucky ones. Muzaphar-al-Tamim is a very good person."

Vika looked up at him with her eyes full of tears.

"Don't I have any way out?" she asked. He shook his head.

"He loves you," said Ali in a half voice. "He placed you on his territory, not trusting anybody. He gave some of his guards to you and had this part of the house redecorated for you. And all this is for you." Ali gazed at her. Vika sat with her eyes on the floor, and his words seemed to echo in her scattered brain.

"You only should remain the same as when he saw you the first time," Ali continued cautiously, looking at her insane condition. "Be like an actress," he begged. "And in due course, you will grow fond of the owner."

"It's so easy to be an actor..." Vika croaked in a hardly audible voice. "But this is my real life..."

"You should agree that this life is not so bad...the only thing you have to do is ring the hand bell, or clap your hands."

"Yes...certainly..." she responded slowly. On the point of fainting, she echoed his words, "clap one's hands...or ring the hand bell..."

"You need to go to sleep," said Ali, looking at her anxiously.

He stood up and left the room. He returned very quickly with a glass of water and gave it to Vika.

"Y-yes..." she said in a low voice glancing inside the glass. "The same glass of water was the beginning of everything."

"Please, drink. You should have some sleep."

She looked at Ali as if doomed and drank the water.

Chapter 36

VIKA DIDN'T KNOW how much time she had been sleeping. But, having just awakened, and without even opening her eyes yet, she felt dizzy and her head hurt. Vika recollected everything that had happened, and she was seized with hopelessness. She opened her eyes a crack and saw Ali sitting beside her on a chair.

"That's good," he said, smiling up at her. "That's very good. It's necessary to get up. Just look — the sun is shining outside," he got up, pointing at the window.

"I don't want anything..." Vika whispered. "I wish to die."

"What do you want? Why do you want it?" Ali looked at her. "You're very young. Your life is only beginning. Almost everything is ahead of you!"

"I don't want it," Vika repeated and turned away from him.

He stood near her bed and could not find any words to cheer her up.

"You know..." started Ali in a low voice, kneeling down in front of her. "I too, don't want to go back to where I was working before you appeared. And I also don't want any punishment because of you." He held his breath. "Please, don't ruin this for either of us. I shall do everything possible to make your life easier. Please, think about it, and don't do anything in a temper."

Vika slowly turned her head to him; there were tears running down his face.

"Find something good in your position," he continued, sobbing. "Just look, aren't you lucky?" He put his hand on his chest. "I'm here, I'm your friend, and I can speak your language to you. And then we'll see what we can do. It's important that you aren't lonely and that you're loved!"

He wiped the tears with a sleeve and continued kneeling in front of her.

Vika looked at him attentively. *Maybe he is right,* she thought. *Maybe everything will somehow be arranged? Maybe I can find some way out from this situation. Maybe...,* hope flashed through her brain.

"Ali," she said in a low voice. "Please, stand up."

He stood up, still sniffling.

"Forgive me, Ali," Vika said hoarsely. "You felt much more terrible here than I, and you were alone." Ali began to cry again. "Don't cry," she whispered. "Now I understand the sense of your words 'to be strong'. Only I don't know how to be strong when you feel completely crushed..."

Covering herself with a blanket from head to toe, she lay motionless for some time, and then slowly sat up in her bed.

"Will you bring me some tea, please?" Vika asked quietly. "Also, let's go for a walk."

Ali began to smile and left the room quickly. Vika rose from her bed slowly, as if she were very sick, and went to the toilet room to tidy herself up. *Well,* she thought, combing her hair. *Maybe something can be changed, I haven't talked to the doctor yet!* Suddenly she stopped.

"No, he isn't a doctor," she said to herself in the mirror. "My God, let me remember his name! What's his name?"

She rubbed her forehead, straining her memory. A month ago he introduced himself, but it was a long foreign name. It had slipped her memory.

Vika looked down and, deep in thought, suddenly recollected Sergei Nilovski. She even felt his presence, heard his voice! She remembered all his lessons and she felt abruptly that something had changed inside her mind.

"I must survive," she whispered, slowly lifting her head. "I'll be very attentive and I will remember everything!"

Vika looked at the mirror — different, serious eyes looked back at her!

"Ali," she shouted, and he immediately appeared in the door way. "Ali, what is the doctor's name..." she stammered. "What's your master's name?"

Ali looked at her, frequently blinking.

"Have you forgotten his name?" Vika asked in a soft way. And he said the doctor's long name.

"But nobody addresses him like this," he uttered in confusion. "It's necessary for you to address him only as Muzaphar-al-Tamim."

"Thank you, Ali," she answered, bowing. "Muzaphar-al Tamim." Vika tried to remember his name. She repeated it and went to drink the tea. Sitting on the sofa, she thoughtfully looked into her glass, sipping the hot liquid.

"As far as I understand, Ali, you have all the medicines here to make a person become unconscious," she said in undertones. "And I'm having a splitting headache now. Can you bring any medicines to me?"

"I have already put it in the tea," answered Ali.

Vika stopped drinking and stared at her cup. "Are you my friend?" she looked up at him seriously. He nodded. "Let's make a deal, Ali. You will tell me when you put something into my food. Settled?"

"Okay," answered Ali timidly and soon they went for a walk in the garden.

Chapter 37

MUZAPHAR RETURNED SEVERAL days later. Having learned that Vika had seen the prisoner, he became very upset and shouted at Ali for not having found any other way to convince Vika to be obedient. But at the same time, Muzaphar himself had given him the order if Vika wouldn't calm down.

"How is she now?" he asked Ali after a while. It was obvious that he didn't wish to have any complications.

"She is okay," he answered with quivering lips.

"What does that mean, 'okay'?" Muzaphar imitated his high voice.

What could Ali answer — he was afraid of his owner! He was so afraid of him that he was ready to strangle this Russian girl for the sake of his own life. He didn't want his life to become worse.

"She is waiting for you, sir," Ali answered, bowing with respect.

"Go away," Muzaphar told him. Ali disappeared immediately.

Vika was sitting on the sofa, looking through magazines when Muzaphar entered the room. She lifted her eyes and smiled timidly at him. She put aside the magazines and went forward.

He rushed towards Vika, strongly embraced her and stood there for some time, having suppressed his excitement. Then he stepped aside a bit to look at her face.

"Oh Allah, thank you!" he uttered in a trembling voice, and Vika saw his eyes full of tears. He pressed her to himself again.

"Why are we standing here?" he said suddenly. "It's your house! Let's go. I'll show you your rooms."

"And what is this room for?" Vika asked shyly.

"It's not a room," Muzaphar smiled. "This is part of a large hall and everything will be put in order here."

He took her by the hand and led her quickly along the corridor. There were a few people still working. They smiled and bowed when Vika and Muzaphar approached them.

A beautiful, carved wooden door swung open in front of Vika and she stood, taken aback. It was the same room with the columns she had already seen, but now it was absolutely different.

Luxury that Vika could not even imagine struck her eyes. Behind the columns, on the platform, there was a beautiful bed; it looked like a real throne.

Upwards a soft light radiated from a low dome of the ceiling. The walls were partially draped with fabric. The room sparkled of new furniture and ornaments.

Vika examined the surroundings, motionless. Muzaphar felt happy, seeing her amazed face. He embraced her by the shoulders and led her to the balcony, which was richly decorated as well. Then they entered another room as beautiful as the previous one.

"And this is your new wardrobe," Muzaphar said, drawing the curtain off a large mirror. "This door," he pointed, "connects these two rooms with a corridor where your own bathroom is."

He smiled, embraced Vika, and kissed her on the lips. Vika felt ashamed, as if she were put in boiling water. She turned red. And a terrible feeling of betrayal towards Sergei pulled hard on her. She stood in front of Muzaphar with lowered eyes.

"Don't be afraid of me, Domali," he said gently. "Settle down in the mansion, it's yours. Check out everything. If any doors are closed, it means that redecoration is still taking place. I'm sorry, for now the noise may sometimes be loud, but rather soon everything will be over."

"Thank you, Doc..." Vika started the phrase and paused, having reddened more at that. "Thank you, Muzaphar-al-Tamim," she tried to regain her composure, "but I need nothing."

He stared into her eyes. "Well, let's sit down and have a talk."

He carried her away to the sofa and placed himself in the armchair opposite her. He looked at her face without saying a word. Shivering with fear, Vika looked down, afraid to look up.

"What would you like, Domali?" Muzaphar asked in undertones.

"I want to go home," Vika whispered. Muzaphar cleared his throat a bit and began thinking.

"Each girl," he started slowly, "she stays with her parents only for a short period of time until she becomes a grown-up. And then she leaves her parents' house for the house of a man and remains there forever. And I think, Domali, that you have a very good house right now where you can live and be proud of it."

Vika didn't know how to answer. She remembered too well that prisoner, and she was very frightened of saying something wrong. She kept silent, unable to stop shivering.

"Well, why are you so quiet? Speak out, don't be afraid. What do you want?"

"I'm missing my mom very much," Vika said in a trembling voice. Muzaphar gave a deep sigh, looking at her.

"Well, my pretty girl," his voice sounded like a song. "Don't you understand that I won't let you go?"

He stopped talking again, deep in thought. "But I wish to hear your happy laughter," said Muzaphar. "And believe me, I understand your affection for your mother."

He stared straight at Vika, who was slouching by this time.

"You're a smart girl and you can advise me what I should do in this situation."

Vika felt like she was almost about to die, shivering with fear. She suddenly realized that the door had slammed and that she had no way back anymore.

"Don't be silent, Domali, I like very much to listen to your soft voice," Muzaphar said quietly. "It's just when you try to pronounce our words. It's very cheerful. So, what about your mother?"

"I miss her," Vika squeezed out in a whisper.

"Well...we'll bring your mom here."

Vika slowly raised her eyes.

"Unfortunately, not tomorrow," he added at once. "But I promise you, it will be soon. And you, I think, understand that she won't return home either."

Vika looked at Muzaphar with fright, frequently blinking her eyes. He was very serious. She moved her gaze down and slowly shook her head.

"So, as far as I understand, your mom will stay at home?" Muzaphar sighed with relief.

"Yes..." nodded Vika in shocked.

"Then what else?"

"Can I have my real name?"

"No, Domali," he said confidently. "This is your new life and your new name. Anything else?"

"No, thanks," Vika shrunk, just on the point of bursting into tears.

"Then come up to me," he smiled and stretched his hands towards her. She stood up slowly and stepped to him.

"Come to me girl," he repeated tenderly once again, pulling her to his lap. "Don't change anything, Domali. Do you hear me? Do change nothing," he finished slowly and, having pressed her to himself, he kissed her slightly on her lips.

"Well! Well!" Muzaphar said skittishly a few moments later. "Stand up! I want to show you something."

He rose and clapped his hands. At that same moment, someone entered the room. Muzaphar told him something. He left the room for a moment and then appeared again, holding a big book in his hands.

"I have found and bought a dictionary for you. Now I will not be the only one with a dictionary," he patted his pocket where he always held a small Russian dictionary. "Now you will find words and read their translation."

Muzaphar stood, watching with pride how she was being handed the dictionary. Vika took it, opened it at once, and saw familiar letters.

"Thank you, Doctor," she said and was immediately taken aback, so she began to apologize, "Forgive me, please, I'm used to addressing you like that."

"Nothing terrible," answered Muzaphar, embracing Vika again. "Time is necessary for everything. I'm glad that we have understood each other," he stepped aside. That's all. It's time I went away and you settle here, have a rest, and learn our language."

Muzaphar looked at Vika, smiling, and she gave back a tearful smile.

"Oh, I might have forgotten," he said, already in the doorway. "Ali is at your disposal. And he'll show you your new servants. Let them take care of you," Muzaphar said loudly, closing the door behind him.

Vika remained alone. But now she was sure that she was being watched by Muzaphar's people. She looked around, not able to contain her stress anymore, and she ran to the bed and snuck under the blanket, sobbing in hopelessness.

Chapter 38

SEVERAL HOURS HAD passed before Vika came somewhat to her senses. She rose from the bed with melancholy and went through the rooms. She carefully touched the stuff around the room, afraid to break anything.

Ali turned up accompanied by some women. "This is your servant, she will always be with you," he introduced her to Vika.

"What is your name?" Vika asked sadly.

"She doesn't speak Russian."

"What kind of a servant is she if she doesn't understand anything?"

"On the contrary, it's good," Ali answered politely. "You will have to learn the language. Don't be upset, please, I'll always help you with the translation."

"What's your name?" Vika repeated in the woman's native language.

"Intesar," the woman bowed.

"O-kay," Vika said slowly, examining the woman.

The woman was middle aged, olive skinned with very black hair. Everything about her was big: her black eyes, her nose, cheekbones and hands. She faced Vika, strong and broad.

"But I don't need any servant," she fixed her eyes on Ali. "Can I give her back?"

"No," the answer followed. "It's your master's decision, and she will always be with you."

"Well...thanks," Vika moved into another room. Ali followed her.

"Please, don't suffer too much because of Intesar," Ali pleaded. "She's a good worker, trained to do a lot of things, and she will help you." Vika shook her head without a word.

After that, Intesar followed Vika like a shadow. Not one, but now she had two shadows, the second was Ali! Vika could not do anything without his translations. Gradually she got used to their constant presence and did not refuse their obliging help anymore.

* * * * *

Several days went by in the same way. Muzaphar visited Vika frequently and they spent a lot of time together, walking in the garden and indoors. Vika was busy learning the language and dancing more persistently, understanding that she should do it, but still hoping in the back of her mind that maybe Muzaphar would feel sorry for her and would let her go home. She took pains to look like the same cheerful girl he had known her before, so as not to make him angry.

But one morning Intesar said that Vika would have a special day without any classes, according to the master's order. Vika blinked in doubt, lying in bed, thinking why. *We're sure to go somewhere,* she thought. *I should get up quickly and tidy myself up.*

She lay in bed for a bit longer, stretching and thinking about her life. Then she got up and went into her bathroom, looking at Intesar angrily — even here she did not leave her alone.

Vika came up to the mirror, and bending her head, looked down at the dressing table. *Oh, my God!* she thought. *Who can gather strength to look merry and careless?* She examined the things on the table in sorrow and looked into the mirror.

"Well," she said in a soft voice. "Smile, Vika! Probably it's likely to help...make an effort and sing something patriotic." Vika fell to thinking. "I don't know...hmm-m, let it be the anthem of the Soviet Union!" This idea cheered her up a bit and she began singing the anthem.

Having tided herself up with the help of Intesar, Vika had breakfast and went out to the balcony. Muzaphar turned up there in no time. He came in smiling with a steady step, wearing loose clothes, and happily embraced and kissed Vika. Ali was trotting after him with a small box in his hand.

"Today we're having a special day," Muzaphar said solemnly. "And I want to give you a present." He clicked his fingers and Ali came up, bowing to him, holding a velvet box in front of him.

"Open it," Muzaphar said to him and Ali immediately obeyed. Delightful jewelry caught Vika's eyes.

"That's for you, Domali!" Muzaphar looked at her piercingly.

"What is it?"

"These are gold, diamonds and rubies," Muzaphar chuckled with pride.

"So amazing! So beautiful!" Vika breathed out excitedly. She stood, unable to touch anything or examine the contents.

"Is this all mine?" she lifted her eyes to Muzaphar.

"Everything is for you. That is my present."

"It's very, very beautiful stuff!" Vika exclaimed. "Thanks a lot!" She clung to him a bit. "But I don't know how to, or where to wear it?"

"This is a ring. And these are earrings," Muzaphar pointed at the jewelry. "Take it easy. Intesar will explain the rest to you and she'll help you put them on.

"What an amazing ring!" Vika picked it up out of the box.

Taking it, she looked at her fingers, thinking where she should put it. She tried the ring on her middle finger. It was massive, but her size.

The big red stone was looking at her, twinkling and playing with its various color scheme, framed by a few rows of diamonds. Vika put her hand aside and looked at this splendor. The ring was rather heavy, and Vika had never seen such a beauty in her life.

"This is a miracle!" she twittered in a whisper. "And for what a reason have you presented me with such riches?" she smiled skittishly and squinted her eyes at Muzaphar slightly.

"We're going to get married today," he answered happily, embracing Vika. "And you'll have an opportunity to wear it all!"

Her smile became stiff and she dropped her eyes down.

"Tonight we're having a kind of ceremony," Muzaphar continued gently. "So have a rest and get ready," he kissed her on the cheek. "And it's high time for me to go. See you later, my dear! See you soon!"

He embraced her heartily once again and left the room.

Vika sat down in the armchair with her eyes fixed steadily on her fingers and the ring. The tears fooled her eyes. Intesar took the box away from Ali and made him leave the place. She came up to Vika, and kneeling down beside her, gave her a handkerchief to wipe the tears. Intesar stood there silently, understanding that she could do nothing to help.

"I don't want to," whispered Vika. "I don't want anybody!" She burst into tears and then went slowly towards her bed.

"My God! Why? What for?" she was crying bitterly. "Sergei, take me away from here, please, take me away! Mommy, please, helps me!" Vika fell down on her bed, hiding herself under the blanket and sobbing inconsolably.

Chapter 39

THE NEXT MORNING was the beginning of a completely different life for her. Upon waking, Vika figured out that she was already alone in bed. Muzaphar had gone away.

She was afraid to move and to touch herself, as it seemed to her, she was now very dirty. Vika still felt his hands, lips, breath on her...she still felt him inside her.

That's it! the thought burned her up. *I'm a dirty woman! Nothing can be changed now!* Tears were rolling down from her eyes. "Why didn't I just die?" she sobbed in torment. "How can I live after that? I can't be with Sergei anymore! I'm dirty, dirty, dirty!" She hid under the blanket and closed her mouth, afraid of her own loud voice.

Some time passed before she calmed down a little bit. She wanted to take a bath immediately to wash off the traces of the previous night.

"Intesar," she called indistinctly. "I want to take a bath!"

"The bath is ready, my madam," Intesar replied softly and obligingly.

She helped Vika to rise, covered her with a soft dressing gown, and accompanied her to the bathroom. Some food and drinks were brought there for her. She was given a massage with some oils rubbed into her skin. This brought her back to life.

Gradually, Vika felt better, she wouldn't want to die anymore, and she sat before the mirror gloomily, letting Intesar dry and fix her hair.

Vika's face looked quiet, but different thoughts furiously rushed about inside her head. Ali approached noiselessly, bringing her hot tea. Vika looked inside the cup and fixed her eyes angrily on Ali. "What have you put inside?"

"Nothing, my madam," he shuddered, his eyes wincing.

"Put some poison in it next time," she began to drink her tea.

Ali faced her, not knowing how to begin the conversation.

"Don't change yourself, please," he started to say in a low voice. "All women go through this, and the whole world is engaged in it."

"My God, what a horrible world!" hissed Vika.

Ali knelt down beside her and glanced into her face with great anxiety. She continued slowly to sip her tea, looking at him maliciously.

"You should be very happy now," he said, faltering and squinting at the hot cup of tea in her hand. "You see, forgive me, please, but nothing must be changed," he looked around furtively. "Otherwise, he will send you to live with his other women and they will make your life hell."

Vika fixed her eyes on him. He was obviously very nervous, saying all this, and his face was twitching all over. Vika stopped drinking her tea, having understood the horror of his words.

"Muzaphar will be doing with me everything he wants, and I must have a happy face?" she said in an undertone, as she shrugged from a cold spasm that ran over her back. She became silent, looking tensely at Ali.

"What do I have to do?" she asked, depressed.

"Please, keep his love for you, and this will save your position."

"And yours as well," she echoed, turning her eyes off him.

Vika's life had changed from this day and she changed too, because she felt the weakness of her position. There was no real wedding, she understood that already. It was just a beautiful, solemn ceremony, perhaps, especially for her.

Now that Muzaphar was in her life, he visited her constantly, sometimes several times a day, and lavished gifts upon her. He played with her happily, caressed and made love to her where and when he wished.

Vika did not like it at all and she felt awfully embarrassed, but Muzaphar was even more excited with that. Laughing, he twirled her around the room and showered her with kisses, paying generous compliments.

Intesar taught Vika with all her efforts and available means what to do in bed with a man to delight him. But Vika turned red from many things she heard from Intesar, and she refused some things categorically.

The New Year was over and the summer was coming. Muzaphar treated Vika as fondly as before and she returned his affection. He made new documents for her, which she had never seen, and now took her on all his trips, together with Intesar and Ali.

The thought of escape did not leave Vika's head, but the possibility had not come yet, and she began to do her best to show that she loved Muzaphar and that she was happy and wanted to change nothing. He covered her with jewelry as heavy as a New Year tree and was very happy, spending all his free time with her.

Chapter 40

THE POLICE SERVICES were doing their utmost to find Vika Zotova and Lena Somova. More than six months had passed when in one of brothels, Lena was found. They had to pay money and resort to a trick to get her out of there.

She was barely recognizable, and when she was brought to her motherland, Anton Darenko cried upon seeing her. Slim as she had always been, she actually now looked like a skeleton drawn on yellow skin. Her front teeth were knocked out, her eyes were black and blue all around, and her whole face was covered with cyanotic bruises. Dirty and shaggy hair was sticking up in bunches on her head. She was not able to understand anything very well, because she was trembling with drug intoxication. She was sent to a private clinic, and the doctors started to cure and nurse her back to health.

After Sergei Nilovski saw Lena, he could not find any rest, nor get a night's sleep, imagining Vika in her place. He kept asking the doctors about the girl's condition, and when it became a bit normalized, with the boss's permission, he visited Lena in order to get at least a slight hint about where Vika might be.

Everything he heard from Lena was already known to him from the transcripts of her interrogations, so he didn't learn anything new. Vika's trail had disappeared.

It was with a heavy heart that he went to Vika's mom, just to somehow support her and give her hope, telling her that Lena had been found. Vika's mom listened attentively, although Sergei gave no information about Lena's condition or where she had been found.

"I understand," said Sergei. "I'm unable to help you in your grief, but now we have at least some hope that Vika will also be found."

"Thank you, Sergei," Vika's mom replied sadly, "thank you for your support. But you know, life is going on," her voice quivered, and there was a moment's pause, "please don't get stuck in this spot; go ahead and find yourself a bride. It's too late to look for a remedy now."

"I don't need anybody," Sergei answered slowly, and both were silent for a while.

"And where is Maxim?" Sergei asked a little later.

"In the army," Vika's mom replied quietly, "My elder son, Viktor, will return from the army this fall."

"This is good...we know each other."

They talked a little more, and then Sergei began to leave.

"I will let you know everything I can find out about Vika," he said in his good-bye. "And please, if by chance you find a trace of her, do tell me as well."

"All right, Sergei." Vika's mom returned his good-bye, and Sergei was off.

Very soon Anton Darenko was sent on a lengthy mission abroad, and during that time, Lena Somova was brought to court as the senior of the mission she went on with Vika. She was found guilty and convicted.

At the same time, Sergei Nilovski asked to go out of the country too, on a long business trip for himself. Before the departure, he dropped in to say good-bye to Vika's mom. He told her about further events in Lena Somova's life.

"I absolutely disagree with their decision," Sergei went on, upset, "but nobody asks me, and Lena will have to do her time."

Vika's mom was shocked with what she had heard.

"What for?" she asked.

"It's up to them, they know best," Nilovski replied ruefully, pointing upwards.

"I feel very guilty before you," Sergei added after a pause. "Forgive me please, but with Vika it's quite a different story. I only wish her to be found alive."

"Oh Sergei, Sergei," Vika's mother sighed deeply. "It's destiny, don't blame yourself and go on your important mission with a light heart."

"I'll call you from there," he said at parting, "and give you my telephone number. Call me if you come to know anything!"

"All the best to you, Sergei," she replied, "I wish you good luck!"

Sergei Nilovski left the house and went on his journey.

Chapter 41

IT SEEMED THAT all of a sudden Vika's birthday snuck up on her. Muzaphar presented her with an amazingly beautiful necklace made of gold, diamonds and sixteen large emeralds.

"Please, put it on now," Muzaphar said, bringing the gift to her room in the morning. "Today is your birthday, and I want you to be the most beautiful all day long!"

Vika was still in her nightgown when Intesar helped her to put on the gems. Vika headed to the mirror.

"Ohhh!" was all she could utter, touching carefully the blazing wealth on her neck. "Thank you so much," Vika said happily, kissing Muzaphar as he came up to her. He hugged her and turned her back to the mirror.

"Look at your eyes," said Muzaphar, smiling. "Aren't they shining the same green light as the gems? And the sixteen emeralds are your sixteen years." He kissed her gently on her ear.

"Thank your so much!" said Vika once more, smiling modestly. He turned her to face him and, covering her with kisses, carried her back to the bed.

They spent almost all day together, and the next morning, rode off to the desert again on camels. Vika had already learned to easily manage the animal, controlling it with a long, thin stick and shouting to it, "Hut, Hut!" so that it would move quicker. She was moving quicker than the caravan, barely maintaining equilibrium in her seat.

"I think," laughed Muzaphar, "it is high time you should be fixed to your seat with ropes, so you don't fall out and break your neck!"

"Catch me," replied Vika joyfully and gave her camel another whipping, trying to escape from Muzaphar.

Vika could not help laughing loudly when the camel that was carrying her jolted like a bag of potatoes, grunting at the fast pace.

Muzaphar never failed to catch up with her, enjoying himself heartily as he watched her laughing her head off.

"Of course, it's not a horse...not half as quick," he laughed. "On a horse you have to hold on to the animal with your hands and legs while on the run. But then, on a camel you may cross the desert much more easily. And, although they are not very quick, camels are more reliable."

Vika had also already mastered horse riding, but was still afraid of a horse's might, and she usually rode very slowly, never quite feeling at ease with it.

* * * * *

A few days after her birthday, they left for another country on Muzaphar's business. And when they returned, Vika was feeling exhausted and worn out. She had always been airsick, but this time the sickness continued for a number of hours, and the nausea persisted.

Having taken a bath, Vika settled comfortably on the balcony, looking sadly at the setting sun. Ali was standing behind her, and the complacent Intesar was circling nearby, asking every minute whether she should bring her anything else.

"Ali, sit down, please," said Vika, showing him to the nearby sofa. He took his seat shyly, trying to hide his happy face.

"What makes you so joyful?"

"You also have no reason to be sad now," he uttered. Intesar settled on the floor at her feet, and Vika saw her modest smile.

"Why on earth are you all so happy?" asked Vika, smiling. "Have I missed a holiday?"

They were exchanging glances, not daring to say anything. They had already learned to love Vika. The girl treated them as her equal, never shouting, never humiliating, and always sharing something tasty.

"Go ahead, Ali, tell me your secret," Vika urged, burning with impatience.

"Well, it isn't for sure yet," he began, stumbling. "But possibly, it will be so."

"What will be so?" enquired Vika.

"You will have a baby!"

"What baby? Which baby?"

"Your baby!"

"How can that be? If I don't want it, how on earth can it appear?"

"Yes." Ali confirmed, happily jerking his head. Vika stole a couple of glances around.

"But Muzaphar is not young," she whispered. "What children can he have at this age?"

"Domali, please!" Ali was scared, and he also looked around. "He's not old at all, but..." he stumbled a little, "it's been a long time since he had children. All of his children are grown up."

Vika was sitting, stunned with the news, batting her eyelashes in dismay.

"How can such things happen?" she asked in a low voice. "That you should know, and I should not know of some baby? And why should I need a baby now?"

"Didn't your mom speak to you, even about that?" Ali stared at her.

"About what?"

"Well...each woman," he began timidly, "each month, has her women's troubles."

"Oh, God! What are you talking about, Ali?" she interrupted him shyly. "It's absolutely unimportant and is certainly none of your business!"

"What do you mean 'unimportant'?" he argued, amazed. "It's very much more than important, it's your watch! If you are well, then everything is well, and they keep coming regularly."

"Then I'm sick!" she replied. "And I will have to be cured!"

Ali stopped, not knowing what to answer, and Vika was lost in her thoughts, trying to remember when she had last had her 'women's troubles'. She had never watched their regularity and, straining her memory hard, never remembered when exactly she had had them.

Vika stood up and paced the balcony nervously. Ali also stood up, watching her perplexedly.

"What can I do about it now?" she asked as she approached him.

"You should thank Allah for such a great gift," Ali uttered. "And just wait happily for the child to appear."

Vika stepped back from him, frightened and frozen, looking straight in his face. She understood immediately that she couldn't discuss anything with him anymore.

The discovery pressed her down. *How can I run away now, with a child?* Vika thought, gazing perplexedly at her absolutely flat belly. *Perhaps it's not really so, and everything may still go right?!* Vika sank slowly into an armchair.

Ali came up to her and kneeled at her feet.

"You're so happy madam!" he said in a low voice. "You have everything as it is, and now you're going to have a baby."

"What do I have, Ali?" Vika looked at him sadly. "I'm like a prisoner. Why should I need all this if I cannot have my own life? I cannot go out anywhere...who am I here?" Tears ran down her cheeks.

"Oh, no," Ali was trying to soothe her. "You live like a queen, Muzaphar-al-Tamim takes you everywhere, and you travel to many countries!"

"What do I see there?" Vika sniffed. "I'm tired of sitting alone with you in hotel rooms, not even going out to eat!"

"Please, stop crying, Domali," Ali whispered, looking around in fear, "I cannot even imagine what would happen if Muzaphar-al-Tamim thinks you do not want his baby."

"Yes, certainly...I understand," Vika agreed, rubbing away her tears.

The next morning Muzaphar rushed into her room and, taking her in his arms, began to circle with her around the room.

"Thank you, my little girl, thank you!" he exclaimed, "I'm the happiest man on earth! You will soon bless me with a baby!"

He put her on her bed, covering her with kisses.

"You can't imagine, Domali, how much joy you have brought into my life," he went on, breathless with happiness. "And now we'll be waiting together for the little one to appear."

Vika was smiling in return.

After that news, she had a bodyguard appointed to look after her. Muzaphar stopped all sexual intercourse with her, but was as gentle as ever, taking her along on almost all of his trips.

Chapter 42

DEEP DESPAIR SEIZED Vika for the first time after the news of her pregnancy. She would still stare with some hope at her flat belly in the mornings, but it had already been three months of horrible sickness and vomiting which had become only too frequent.

Her brain was working feverishly, pondering over what was to be done now, with the time having become so restricted. And the tiny hope for escape has narrowed now to almost extinguishing, leaving actually no gleam of light whatsoever.

Ali and Intesar were bustling near Vika happily, trying to entertain her and never leaving her alone. Only when Vika was vomiting in a toilet was she by herself for a moment.

In the beginning, Intesar had tried to help Vika when she was sick, but the sight of Vika vomiting made Intesar feel sick also, and she had to run out. Vika, noticing Intesar's reactions, would sometimes run to the toilet and make herself vomit on purpose, thinking that someday this tactic might come in handy for her.

But in the countries they were visiting and in the hotels they stayed in, there were no toilets in the hallways at all, or they were without windows, so Vika's hopes were melting rapidly, while her belly was beginning to slowly grow.

Muzaphar had forbidden her to exercise, while trying to fulfill her wishes. Vika smiled humbly and never asked for anything. So, he himself began to offer her advice. "I've read somewhere," he said once, "that if a pregnant woman contemplates beautiful things and takes joy in life, she is sure to have a healthy and handsome baby!"

Muzaphar was sitting with Vika on the balcony and watching her with a smile. "Soon the Christian New Year is coming," he went on, "and I would like to take you to Europe again. What would you say to that?"

"That would be wonderful!" Vika chirped, embracing him lightly.

"We have already been to France with you," Muzaphar reminded her. "And now we'll go to Germany, I have some business there, too. But you will have time to see the decorated streets and Christmas trees. They're very beautiful decorated, I like them," he smiled.

"Oh, how nice it is of you to think of taking me," Vika exclaimed, kissing him on the cheek. "The New Year is my best-loved holiday! It's always snowy, so much fun, and it smells of fir-tree with oranges!"

"How can a fir-tree smell of oranges?" Muzaphar laughed.

"In my homeland," Vika began to explain, "Santa Claus always brings sweets and oranges. As a matter of fact, normally it is almost impossible to buy this fruit – only for the New Year."

"Then I should also, like your Santa Claus, present you with oranges for this holiday!" said Muzaphar smiling.

"Oh, thanks! I've already had almost too much of them here," Vika laughed in return. "And before long I am going to be like an orange myself!" She pointed merrily at her slightly rounded belly.

"Well, then, it's a deal, we're going!" Muzaphar concluded, laughing together with her and standing up in front of the sofa. "And what kind of a present would you like to get from your Santa Claus?"

"I don't know," she answered modestly. "I have everything, and this trip will be a present in itself. Only, may I take just a short walk in the streets there?"

"All right," Muzaphar embraced Vika tenderly. "We shall see about it."

* * * * *

Closer to Christmas, they went to Germany. Vika had never taken much jewelry with her on her trips, because she never had anywhere to wear it. The only thing she never took off was a large ring, the first gift from Muzaphar, with a ruby and diamonds.

Having arrived at the hotel, which was situated in an antique building, they settled in on the third floor, as Muzaphar said, so that one could see the New Year street from the window. But he did not let Vika go for a walk there.

"Look at it from the window," Muzaphar said on the second day of their arrival. "You can see absolutely everything."

"But didn't you promise that I could walk on the snow?" pulling her courage together, Vika ventured to remind him gently.

"There is practically no snow here," he answered. But, after a little pause, he relented, "All right. Tomorrow after lunch go out and walk next to the hotel."

She always had Ali and Intesar around her in her rooms, as well as a guard, ever since she had become pregnant. Silent as a rock, he was invariably by the door.

The next day after lunch, as had been promised, they began to get ready for a walk. Vika put on an absolutely white dress and a red fox-fur coat on top of it, just covering her knees. Muzaphar had presented it to her early last year.

Accompanied by the three people, Vika left her room, and at once saw the toilet. She immediately began to cough gently pretending as if she were sick, and just a few steps before the toilet, she suddenly recalled.

"Oh, Intesar, you'll have to go back," Vika said, upset, "I left my handbag behind. We'll wait for you here."

Intesar, casting a glance at the guard, went back to the room and was almost at its door, when Vika felt suddenly sick, and covering her mouth with her hand, hardly restricting the vomiting, she headed to the toilet. Coming in, she saw at once a small, narrow window and pressed the door harder behind herself. She did not have even a moment to think.

In an instant, Vika jumped up to the window and tried to open it — it opened! Jumping up on the windowsill, she squeezed outside, and in a moment, she appeared on a small ledge extending along the building.

Pressing her back to the wall and not looking down, Vika moved quickly to the corner where the drainpipe was running. Reaching the corner, she seized the drainpipe and began sliding down, chafing her skin until it was bleeding.

The ground floor of the building was covered with a small roof. Vika jumped down on it, hastily seeking a place to go down. Finding nothing suitable, she instantly grasped the edge of the roof, turned over, and hung for a moment then jumped down to the asphalt, slightly twisting her leg.

She ran through a small, narrow space between the buildings, and then Vika rushed out into the street, crossed it, and disappeared behind the corner of another building, where she saw moving cars.

Chapter 43

HEINRICH SCHULTZ WAS returning home from visiting his friends Vanessa and Hans. Always after visiting their hospitable house, he couldn't help feeling sad.

He had been friends with Hans from youth, both had fiancés whom they married as young men. Vanessa somehow quickly gave birth to children with Hans, and their home was now bustling and ringing with children's voices.

But Heinrich's wife did not want to have kids, devoting herself to her work, and often leaving on business trips. At first, Heinrich was very insistent about having at least one, but all his persuasions failed. And soon he, like his wife, gave all of himself to studying and working, and continuing his father's business, and with time, he stopped worrying about children. Only in the rare minutes when he met his friends and saw their younger generation did he think about what ages his children might have been by then.

After eight years, the family life of the Schultz's was, in fact, rare meetings at the breakfast table and boring weekends spent together. They still went to a concert occasionally, or visited an exhibition, or went to see their friends, but their love had long ago died out, and both could not help the feeling of loneliness they had while they were together. Gradually, they spent less and less time together, and in the long run, somehow very quietly, without troubles or tears, after almost ten years of married life, they parted.

And it was the second decade, now, that Heinrich was alone, having not found anybody, and for that matter, wondering whether he should marry once more. His business was a success. He loved order and comfort in his life, which was the object of earnest care on the part of his housekeeper, Greta.

Pondering on his life, Heinrich quietly drove around a corner. Suddenly, a red and white blurred figure jumped in front of his car...he started and hit the brakes. In front of him, there was a young girl's face, frightened to death.

Heinrich stopped short and, as if in shock, somehow opened the door of his car when the girl began to pull on the front door handle.

"Please, please, help me!" Vika cried to him in German, jumping into the car and falling down on the floor. "Hurry up, go away from here! Hurry! Hurry! Leave!"

And he, as if under hypnosis, looked into the wild green eyes of the girl, and gunned his car away. He dodged around the streets as if he were in a real chase. He kept glancing into the rear view mirror. Nobody was chasing him.

"Where are we going?" Schultz asked finally, almost arriving at his house.

"Please, anywhere, hide me," Vika was looking up at him with a prayer in her eyes. "I will explain everything to you later!"

He opened the automatic gate of his house and, crossing a small lawn, drove into the garage sideways. From there a narrow path led to the house.

When all the doors closed behind the car, Heinrich switched off the motor and looked attentively at Vika. Her hair had loosened and was lying in waves on the fox-fur coat. The face was very pretty, but looked extremely scared. Heinrich's eyes traveled to her hands.

"My God!" he exclaimed, "You're covered in blood!"

He left the car and quickly, almost running, went around it to open the door on Vika's side. She began to crawl out with great difficulty from the narrow space of the front seat.

Eventually getting out, Vika faced Heinrich, still breathing unevenly and looking around like with a haunting expression. They lingered for an instant, facing each other, and then Heinrich, saying nothing, took her by the sleeve of her coat and pulled her to the house.

Greta backed away from the door, upon seeing the entering guest, with an absolutely bloodless face.

"Good afternoon," uttered Vika faintly.

"Please, help her to wash herself," said Heinrich, pushing her slightly to his housekeeper. Greta greeted her dryly and took Vika to the bathroom, leaving her alone there.

Vika was shaking from the escape she had just been through. She still could hardly believe in her new-found freedom, and could practically not feel her own body. Looking at her clothes, torn and stained with blood, Vika took off her fur-coat and turned on the water to wash her hands and the blood off her clothes. And only now, dipping her hands into the water, did she feel the ache jerking them away.

Vika gazed with horror at her cut hands with stripped-off skin and half-broken nails. She still couldn't stop trembling, and, overcoming the pain, she began to wash her hands and face.

After a few moments, limping slightly on the hurt leg, Vika emerged slowly from the bathroom, pulling the coat over her shoulders. Greta offered politely to hang the fox-fur coat in the wardrobe and left the room. Heinrich, casting a surprised look at Vika's Eastern dress, came nearer to her.

"Show me your hands," he said and looked at them. "Greta, please bring the first-aid kit and help her treat and bandage the wounds."

When everything was finished, Vika was invited to the dining-room.

"Please, don't tell anybody about me," she said with tears in her eyes. "I will leave your house very quickly."

Heinrich was watching her attentively with his dark-grey eyes and, sitting her down on a chair, poured a glass of wine for her and for him, waiting for Greta to cook something to eat.

With the first sip of wine, Vika felt the warmth at once and grew a little calmer. Heinrich went up to the window and looked out. He was tall and slim, with a thick grey mass of hair.

"Thank you very much," Vika said in excitement, "You have saved my life!"

He uttered no word, and turned to face her silently.

"Thank you, frau," she said to Greta, who had put dinner in front of her.

"What kind of accent do you have?" asked Heinrich, "What country are you from?"

"From the Soviet Union," Vika answered in a low voice, and there fell a silence over the room.

They quietly finished dinner, and then they proceeded to the sitting room. Heinrich lit the fire in the fireplace, and offered Vika a place to sit down, in one of the armchairs, and placed himself facing her. He gazed back and forth attentively and sadly at the fire and at Vika. Soon Greta came back from the kitchen, and also settled herself nearby. They were all silent for some time.

"Very well, now," Heinrich finally said, turning to Vika, "try to tell us what has happened to you."

Vika was looking at them and was at a loss of where to begin. Pausing to recall all of the German that she had ever studied at school, Vika stumbling and crying, related to them the story of her tourist journey, up to the moment when Heinrich had stopped in front of her in his car.

At the end of Vika's story, there was again silence in the room, except for the wood crackling in the fireplace and the restrained sobs of Greta. Heinrich was watching Vika attentively, listening to her, and when she finished, he transferred his gaze back to the fire, sitting and pondering for a long time.

"Why on earth," he began in a dull, slow voice, "right when we're in such tense relations with the Soviets, would a Russian appear in my house?"

Vika shrank all over with his words.

"And she's even not just a Russian," he went on, gazing now at Vika. "She's a woman who has also run away from a harem."

He sucked on his cigarette and, placed one leg across the other, and stared at Vika with cold eyes.

"Please, don't tell anybody about me," she said, crying, "Muzaphar will certainly search for me...he has his people everywhere. Possibly, he will even turn to the police. But I will call home to my mother, and she will help me," Vika was urging in despair, "and I will leave you very soon."

"Well then," ordered Heinrich in a military tone, "no calls from my home telephone. Greta has a car, and she'll take you downtown, and there you will call from a post office. No mentioning of my address or my name, anywhere."

He rose up from the armchair, bid everybody good night, and left the room. Vika sat shrinking and watched him leave in fear. Greta came up to her quietly and put her hand on her shoulder.

"Come on, girl, I'll show you to your room," she said compassionately and took Vika to her bedroom.

Chapter 44

IN THE MORNING, Vika woke up in the dim light of the coming dawn and peered into the contours around her. She just could not make out where she was, and didn't recognize this room she was in.

Yesterday night, possibly because of the stress she had been through or due to the wine she had drunk, Vika changed into the pajamas Greta had brought her, dropped down on the bed, and fell asleep instantly.

Now she was lying down, feeling all her body aching with pain, and something in her belly turning around and grumbling. She touched her belly and remembered everything at once...Vika quickly sat up on her bed, looking around and listening to the sounds indoors. Everything was absolutely silent.

She stood up and started searching for a switch to turn on the light in the room. Stumbling noisily on a chair, Vika finally found the switch.

A mild light filled the small room, as the window was drawn tightly with a curtain. It was rather cool and Vika, searching with her eyes for her clothes and not finding them, went back to her bed. And, wrapping herself up in her blanket, just sat there thinking of Sergei Nilovski.

Her thoughts were interrupted by a light knock on the door. Vika called back immediately, and Greta entered the room.

"Good morning, Vika!"

"Good morning, frau!"

"I have mended your torn clothes," said Greta, handing the attire to Vika. "They're very beautiful clothes," she went on. "Only you'd better not go out in them here."

"Thank you so much, madam! But it's dangerous for me to go out in any clothes now. And I have not been out for such a long time." Vika uttered sadly, taking her clothes. "Thank you very much," she repeated again.

"Christmas is coming this evening," Greta smiled slightly. "So please, get up, fix yourself up, and come to the kitchen to have breakfast, I'll be waiting for you there."

Vika looked at the closing door. *Oh, my God,* she thought, *might I not be dreaming about it all? Might it be for real that I'm free? No matter what happens next. Thank you, Lord, for helping me get away!* Wondering at herself, bowing her head down, Vika began to pray all of a sudden. "Thank you, God, for these people you have sent to me, and help me, please, to get home."

Vika got up and, quickly fixing herself up, set off to look for the kitchen. She crossed a rather large sitting-room where they had been sitting the night before, and saw a half-circle staircase going from the big entrance door of the sitting-room, along the wall, to the second floor. Passing the large hall, Vika appeared in the dining-room from which there was a small door to the kitchen.

"Come in, don't be shy," she heard Greta's voice call her. "I've already prepared everything, so we're just about to eat."

She entered the room and saw Greta, bustling, laying the dishes on the table next to the window. Greta was a thin, petite woman, with short grey hair and a kind face with small wrinkles. *She must be the same age as my granny,* she thought, smiling.

"Come on in, Vika, sit down at the table and let's have breakfast."

Greta put down a kettle with hot water on a trivet and took her seat facing her guest. "Let us say our prayers," she proposed in a low voice, putting her hands together.

Vika was listening to a foreign prayer, repeating the words in her mind.

"Amen," finished Greta.

"Amen," Vika echoed at once, and they started with their breakfast.

"Are you baptized?" asked Greta after a pause.

"Yes."

"And what is your confession?"

"Christian."

"Oh, poor child!" Greta uttered with sympathy, "With a Christian belief, and to find yourself in a Muslim country." She said more prayers. "So, what Christian confession have you been baptized in?"

"I don't know, frau," Vika muttered shyly, finishing her breakfast. "I was a little girl when I was baptized, and it was my granny who taught me everything," and Vika showed Greta the way the fingers were to be put together to pray.

"Oh, I think it is the Old Orthodox Christianity," Greta was surprised. "If I'm not mistaken, it was changed in Russia a long, long time ago. The old believers suffered great repression and ran away in all directions. Oh God, forgive me," Greta concluded, crossing herself.

"Oh, frau," Vika said delightedly, "you know the history of religion so well! I would have thought we were of the same belief, but yours is quite another way of crossing your chest."

"Because we're of the Catholic religion," Greta answered, "but God is one, child, and our rules are almost the same." She prayed once more on finishing her breakfast.

Having removed the dishes, they settled down at the table to discuss Christmas, when Greta saw the gates open and Heinrich's car drive in.

"May I go to my room?" Vika asked, looking at the approaching car.

"Yes, certainly."

Vika thanked Greta again for the breakfast, and retired quickly to the room allotted to her. Entering it, she sat down quietly on a chair, took a magazine from the table, and began to look it through.

In a short while, in his overcoat, without knocking or saying hello, Heinrich entered the room and put a newspaper in front of Vika. And he himself proceeded to the window and stared outside. Greta also came to the door.

Vika was looking back and forth at each of them with frightened eyes. Greta came in silently and, taking the newspaper, sat down on the bed and began to turn it over and over, trying to find something. Suddenly, she stopped and started reading something closely. Then, promptly upon finishing, she looked up, her face full of surprise and alarm.

"God, what can we do now?" Greta gasped under her breath.

"May I see this newspaper?" Vika stood up and approached the woman.

Taking it, she saw at once her photo that had been made for her new passport. And beneath it, Vika read that someone had kidnapped the pregnant wife of a guest of the country, and the latter was offering big money for her return.

Vika put down the paper and slowly sat down on a chair. There was a tense silence hanging in the room, with only the small clock ticking on the wall.

"It was a very good Christmas present I've received this year!" Heinrich grumbled and turned around to face the room, "and plus a pregnant one!"

Vika was sitting, looking down. "Please, don't give me back to him! I'm not a wife of his, and I'll soon leave you."

"Too bad if not now!" Heinrich retorted sharp. Vika rose slowly.

"I'm sorry, I will go now," she rose slowly and headed for the door. "Thank you for everything."

"You're welcome," he said squeamishly and turned back to the window.

"Please give me my coat," Vika turned to Greta, and together they went out to the corridor, where Vika had her fox-fur coat.

"Thank you," she uttered to Greta, slightly bending her head forward and turning to the exit.

Taking a deep breath of the cold air, Vika stepped outside and slowly, holding on to the banister, began to go down the steps. The door closed behind her back.

She had already moved from the stairs onto the asphalt path, a little powdered with snow, when the door of the house opened again, and Greta appeared on the porch. She called out to Vika and hastily began to climb down the steps after her.

"Why, my God, what am I doing?" Greta whispered, nearing Vika, "God, forgive me! On a Christmas day, I've turned a human being out into the streets." She pulled Vika by her sleeve back into the house. "Hurry! Hurry!" said Greta, while pushing her up the stairs, looking around in fear. "God, let nobody see us!" She brought Vika back into the house, and closed the door behind her.

Vika stood still, leaning on the wall with her back, tears running down her face. Heinrich left the sitting room and stopped, staring coldly at the two women.

"Forgive me, Heinrich," Greta said to him humbly, "but it will be a great sin to drive anybody outside on a day like this."

He gazed at her blankly, keeping silent.

"She's quite a young girl," his housekeeper went on, pityingly pointing with her hand to Vika, "and moreover, as it appears, she's going to have a baby."

Greta paused to take a breath and pull her thoughts together.

"Aren't we Christians?" she said angrily, "How can we give her back to a Muslim, knowing that he has stolen her and she's not a wife of his? So God must have deemed it proper to have her come to this house," Greta finished, gasping.

Heinrich kept silent, moving his eyes from Vika to Greta.

"I'll think of a way to help her," the housekeeper said, calming down a little. "We'll go to a post office after the holidays, and Vika will call her home. She'll be helped with her documents and will be off."

"All right," Heinrich answered after a little pause. "But you must understand that nobody is to know of her presence in my house. She's a relative of yours, if anything."

"Yes, certainly, thank you," Greta looked at Heinrich gratefully. She had been working in this house her entire life, knew well the master's nature, and understood him even without words.

Heinrich looked at Vika from top to toe once more, and left the corridor.

"I'm very appreciative of you, frau," Vika said in a low voice.

"It's all right, my child, cheer up," answered Greta with sympathy. "We shall think of something."

She helped Vika out of her coat and took her back to the guest room.

"I'll go cook dinner and you have a rest," said Greta. "You've had enough troubles, better have a sleep," and she left the room, closing the door behind her quietly.

Chapter 45

AFTER A WHILE, Greta came back to Vika's room and invited her to have a snack, adding that she was cooking special meals for the Christmas dinner party.

"Thank you, frau," replied Vika politely, "but I'm not hungry at all."

"Come on, eat as much as you can," Greta insisted, "you may not be hungry, but the baby does need nutrition. He's not guilty of anything and should be born healthy."

Vika followed Greta obediently and after the meal, began to help her with dinner.

"Look at the pies I've already made," Greta said, taking Vika to the fridge and showing her three round pie shells filled with crème layers.

"I like baked things very much," said Vika. "And how are you going to decorate it?"

"Well, I'm not," Greta grinned. "Why should we need any decoration — it's just the two of us, it's good just as it is." But she broke off, looking at Vika, "it's not two people, but three already," she corrected herself. "And not even three, but four," Greta concluded, gazing at Vika's belly with a smile.

Vika looked down shyly. "If there is nothing else to do at the moment, I can make crème or decorate the cake somehow," proposed Vika.

"Go on, you're welcome to," Greta agreed readily, taking out the necessary ingredients.

And Vika started working, telling Greta that in her motherland, Christmas is not an official holiday and is not celebrated as merrily as the New Year.

"It's because religion is forbidden in your country," Greta replied. "And how far along are you?" she asked abruptly, pointing at Vika's belly.

"I don't know for sure, probably something around five months."

"Oh, then he must be moving already," Greta brightened up.

"Who?"

"The baby."

"How can he be moving inside?" Vika said at a loss. "He must be very little."

"That's true and it's just the small ones who move." Greta grinned, "you must listen to him attentively."

Vika had almost finished with the cake decoration and stood still, staring at Greta, whose eyes were wide open with astonishment. And just at that moment, Heinrich entered the kitchen and stood at the door, contemplating about the women. Vika lowering her head, concentrated on the cake decoration again.

Schultz proceeded to the fridge, took something out, and left the kitchen in silence. In a moment, he was back, standing again at the door, peering at Vika. She was at a loss of how to hide from his gaze. Hurrying to finish with the tart, she handed it to Greta.

"Oh, how beautiful!" the woman exclaimed, taking it. "I love this decoration so much, and the clock in the middle!"

Greta brought the cake closer to Heinrich.

"Look how nice it is," she said, and the man shifted his eyes to the tart.

"Yes, pretty," he agreed.

"M-maybe there's something else to do?" Vika asked, stumbling over the words, looking out of the corner of her eye at Heinrich, who was still standing at the doorway.

"Just a moment, we'll find something," Greta responded, obviously unwilling to let Vika go.

"You know what I'm thinking," Heinrich ventured ponderously, "It's a Christian holiday, and everybody seems to be Christian here, so why should Vika stay clad in a Muslim dress?"

Vika looked at him with fear. "I don't have anything else to wear."

"Something should be done about it, Greta," he shifted his eyes to his housekeeper.

"You're certainly right, Heinrich," the woman looked at Vika. "But it's going to be very difficult to find her something to wear at the moment."

"And you just try to," he finished, leaving the kitchen.

"Let's go and look for something," Greta said to Vika.

Having looked through everything that Vika could wear, at least to some extent, they stopped at a pair of Heinrich's trousers, almost new, but already a bit small for him, and a warm, checkered shirt he had never liked nor worn.

When she had changed clothes, Vika came back to the kitchen, where they were both sitting. They immediately stopped their quiet talk and froze, looking at Vika. Heinrich sniffed and pursed his lips, eyeing her in surprise. In this disguise, Vika looked like a slim teenager with a braid plait behind her shoulder.

"It's better like this, I think," he said.

"Yes, of course, thank you," answered Vika. She really felt quite different having changed clothes. It was as if she had gotten rid of something.

But a deep nostalgia suddenly flooded over her, and even before appearing to them in the kitchen, the tears started, as she remembered Sergei and her mom. And if there had been an opportunity, she would have set out to them now on foot; it was just her condition that hindered her, and the total absence of documents.

They enjoyed Christmas dinner together around the decorated table with candles, and Vika even received a little present.

Having had a drink of wine, they began talking about their countries.

"What TV programs do you like?" Heinrich asked her.

"Various," Vika answered, half-ready that there was a catch involved on his part.

"And what kinds do you have in your country?" he insisted.

"We have three channels with all kinds of programs on them."

"Only three channels?" he was amazed. "It sounds 'Cro-Magnon' to me."

"Why is that?" she uttered, insulted. "We read a lot of books. We have theaters, picture galleries, a classical ballet, music, and singers."

"And pensioners as the leaders of the country," went on Heinrich, in tune with her, but in a mocking tone.

Vika pursed her lips, and broke off looking at him. She was too aloof from politics, actually didn't quite understand them, and was absolutely happy about the world she had once lived in.

"And what kind of music do you like?" asked Heinrich, again in a milder tone.

"All kinds."

"Get specific, Vika, what kinds?" Schultz insisted, "Pop, rock, jazz...?"

Vika's eyebrows went up in surprise. "I'm not a musician and honestly, I've never heard those words before. I do like classics though."

Now it was Heinrich's turn to show surprise on his face. "Classics? Amazing! And, what is about opera?"

"No, I don't like opera," she confessed frankly, "but I do sometimes watch operettas. Better to say I did," Vika stumbled a little.

"And what singers do you know or like?"

"Well," she paused to think, "Alla Pugachova, Bulat Okudzhava, and Eduard Hill."

"And foreign ones?" he interrupted Vika with a grin.

"Dean Rid, Joe Dassin," straining her memory she answered slowly, "Luciano Pavarotti."

"Well, let it be," Heinrich interrupted again, "perhaps you're not that much Cro-Magnon after all, but strange you surely are."

"I don't know..." Vika answered timidly, "May I go out for a walk in the backyard?"

"You may," Heinrich said, "only please don't switch on the light."

She went out into the fresh air in the dark. *What happiness it is,* Vika thought, *just to go out for a walk like this!* A thin layer of snow was crisping under her feet, and pondering, she slowly moved away from the house.

The yard was surrounded by a high fence, and there was a small park arranged inside with neat paths. There was a white gazebo in a corner, under the trees, also white with snow, with each twig clad in tender, snowy garment. Against the dark sky, the trees looked like fairy-tale imagery carved in lace.

Vika entered the garden house and, clearing the snow off a part of the bench, sat down on it, rolling a snowball in her hands. She felt quite peaceful, and looking out from the garden house, peered into the diamond bed of stars in the sky. *Somewhere there, in the motherland, the same stars are shining for Sergei Nilovski!* she thought melancholically. *But, how far away it all is! Completely in another life...and, I am completely different now.*

Everything was still and quiet in the park. But quite near, from behind the fence, street noises could be heard. A few search-lights were chasing each other in the sky, and from time to time, closer or a bit farther away, colorful fireworks could be seen.

Suddenly there was a crack, as if somebody had stepped on a dry, frozen twig. Vika started, looked around. Everything was tranquil and white, as if under a light veil, and Vika could not see the entrance of the house behind the bushes. She shuddered with a slight chill and, after a minute standing up silently, began to move slowly towards the house.

Vika jumped at seeing somebody walking on her side through the bush. She peered harder and guessed that it was Greta who had come out to look for her.

"Are you all right?" the woman asked in a low voice, coming closer to Vika.

"Yes, thank you, frau. It's been so long since I have seen anything like this," Vika smiled. "The air is so fresh here and everything is so clean!"

"Yes, it's beautiful here," Greta agreed. "But we better go home, who knows what can happen here at night," and they entered the house.

Taking off her coat and thanking Greta for the wonderful evening, Vika made towards her room quietly.

"Why don't you want to watch TV?" Heinrich asked her, sitting at the fireplace. "Do sit down and watch a fairly interesting, funny program," he almost ordered her.

"Thank you," murmured Vika and sat down on the sofa in front of the TV set. She had almost forgotten what it looked like and stared at the screen with pleasure.

Soon Greta came, covered Vika with a warm plaid blanket, and settled nearby, also wrapping herself in a warm cloth. It was rather cold in the house and the radiators were just warm enough to heat themselves.

Chapter 46

AFTER TWO DAYS, Greta took Vika to the post office to call Russia. Vika put on Heinrich's old hooded coat hiding her hair under a kerchief wrapping her head.

"Let's go to another town," Greta proposed, obviously nervous.

"Thank you so much. I was also going to suggest to you that we go to another town, because Muzaphar has his people everywhere, and I'm not safe anywhere," said Vika.

"And would you please also put the hood on your head."

"Okay," Vika put her hood on obediently and lowered her head until they reached the post office. She was shivering and her teeth were chattering, either from cold or from fear.

Greta, stopping in one of the narrow streets, began to explain to Vika how to go to the post office. "Go to the end of this block and turn to the right," she pointed. "There will be a post office at the corner of the house. I'll be waiting for you in the car. Here, take the money," and Greta held out the marks.

Vika got out of the car and walked ahead quickly, lowering her head and not looking around till she entered the post office.

Very few clients were inside, some sitting on the chairs along the windows, some filling in the lines bending over the desk, and there were two people standing in the line to the wicket. Vika did not dare go up and order the call. The automatic dial booth was occupied, and she was reading posters, waiting till it was empty.

Vika needed the code for Russia, and she was slowly looking through the information on the walls when, finally, almost by the window she saw a small slip of paper with codes of countries. Vika quickly found what she needed and stepped aside.

The waiting time was dragging very slowly, and one more man was ahead of her. So as not to attract attention to herself, she sat down quietly on the last chair, and waited without looking up.

Thoughts raged in her head like a whirlwind. Vika was repeating again and again what she had to tell her mother, and what she had to ask her about. She couldn't help quivering at the thought that she would soon hear her mom's voice.

Finally it was her turn, and she entered the booth. Reading the rules with difficulty, Vika dialed the necessary numbers. There was an interrupted dial tone in the receiver and the contact failed. Again, with trembling hands, she began dialing her home number. She heard a ring tone in the receiver and then somebody answered.

"Hello?" Vika heard mom's voice. "Hello?"

"Mama!" she gasped, almost in a whisper. "Mama...it's...me!"

"You're alive?" came back her mother's failing voice after a pause. "Where are you?"

"I'm already in Germany, Mom," Vika said, and insidious tears ran down her face. "Help me, mummy, I need documents, I have nothing. I want go home," Vika sniffled, choking with tears.

"What are you talking about? What do you mean home?" her mother whispered, frightened. "Stay there and don't show up here."

"Are you all right, Mom? I need the documents...I want to go home!"

"I'm telling you, do not return!" said her mother nervously. "You know, Lena Somova was found, brought back, and put in a jail for ten years."

"What for?" Vika asked.

"She knows what for," her mother half-whispered, "for treason."

Vika was listening to her in shock and almost at once forgot everything she had wanted to ask about.

"Mummy, I say, mummy," she shouted into the receiver stifling with tears. "Please call Sergei Nilovski. He'll be able to help me."

"What?" her mother retorted. "Don't ruin his life and career, or those of your brothers! Their lives are in order, and your popping up will ruin everything for everybody. Stay where you are and don't come here," her mother finished sharply.

"Mom, what is it you are saying? What do you mean stay here?" Vika was choking with sobs into the receiver. "I have neither money...nor documents...and I am...Mom...I have..." she just couldn't pronounce the words about her pregnancy.

"I'm very glad you're alive, but please don't call anymore," Vika heard. "The telephone may be tapped, and I don't want the disgrace," and her mother hung up.

Vika, unable to make sense of it, was staring blankly at the receiver in her hand and blinking her eyes, and was quivering all over. She left the booth slowly and, seeing nothing in front of her, like in a fog, headed to the exit. Something was thumping dully in her temples, and when she came out into the street, she just walked aimlessly.

Suddenly, somebody took her by the sleeve and pulled her in the opposite direction. It was Greta. She brought Vika back to the car and, after settling her in, began to drive out of the city.

She very carefully moved the car to the narrow labyrinth of streets, looking around every minute. Finally, having made sure nobody was following them, she went to the highway, heading to her town.

"Let me off," Vika howled suddenly when they were passing another bridge. "Please let me go out."

"No!" Greta snapped dryly.

"I don't want...to go...anywhere," Vika was choking with words, sobbing spasmodically. "Please let me off here."

But Greta did not even so much as attempt to put on the brakes. She drove steadily ahead, casting frequent glances into the rear view mirror. And Vika broke into tears, unable to hold in her stress anymore. Greta, looking at her, also began to sniffle.

They drove off the highway into a town, and stopped at a shop parking lot.

"Don't cry, Vika," Greta patted the girl's hand. "Please, calm down. I don't know what it was your mother told you, but it means this is how God would have it. I'll tell you my own life story sometime later." She was looking warm-heartedly at the blubbering Vika.

"Things will straighten out somehow," Greta tried to soothe her. "It's very seldom in life that everything goes the way you would like it to. You should wait, it doesn't all happen so quickly. And with some time, it will all go right."

"Nothing will ever go right!" Vika answered hopelessly, "Never, ever! Please forgive me, thank you for everything, but I will have to go away from you."

"Where to?"

"Don't know," Vika still cried. "Anywhere. But I can't wear out my welcome anymore, thank you for everything you've done for me. And let Heinrich know, I'm very grateful to him for having taken me in. He's saved my life." And taking the handle, she opened the door.

"Wait, Vika, wait!" Greta prevented her from going, and she was desperately looking for a reason not to let Vika go just now.

Greta was unaware yet of the underlying cause of such a desperate reaction on Vika's part, but she did understand when she had come into the post office and heard Vika shout and cry into the receiver, that something had happened. And the thing that had happened must have been very serious for Vika to have left the telephone booth blindly. *Probably*, Greta had thought at the time, *waiting for her documents is going to take some more time.*

"Look here, Vika," Greta began once more, watching her getting out of the car. And then all of a sudden Greta found what she could say, "You must return that coat to Heinrich, and take your fox-fur coat."

Vika paused for a moment, brooding, and got back into the car, shutting the door.

"There's a good girl," Greta patted her on the hand amicably. "Now wait for me here, I'll drop into the shop and buy something."

She left quickly and returned in a while with two big packages in her hands. Stopping a few steps from the car, she looked at its front part and smiled.

"I'm an old conspirator," said Greta, handing the packages to Vika. "Please, give me the plastic scraper blade under your seat." She went to the front of the car, and then to the back to do something. Laughing, she came back and sat down in her seat. "I almost forgot," said Greta. "We're lucky the police didn't stop us."

Vika gazed at her in amazement.

"Back there, when we were leaving our house," the woman explained, "I plastered the license plates with wet snow and dirt...just in case, you know. And so, we have been driving, as it were, without any numbers." They laughed and drove carefully out of the parking lot and homeward.

Chapter 47

HAVING RETURNED FROM the post office, they entered the house.

"Go and have a rest in your room," Greta said to Vika. "I'll cook something to eat and we shall talk."

Vika retired to her room and thrashed about it like an animal at bay. She couldn't make herself believe what she had heard from her mother. *How could a thing like that have happened to Lena?* Vika thought. *What am I to do now?*

She was seized by despair at the thought that she would never again see Sergei Nilovski. Mother had said she just couldn't see him, that she should avoid ruining his career and life. "And what's going to happen to my life now?" whispered Vika.

If I cannot go back home anymore, thoughts were racing through her mind, *cannot see Sergei, then why should I need this life at all?* She fell down on the bed crying.

"I don't want to live, I don't want to," Vika was sobbing into the pillow. "I want to see Sergei, just to see him, I don't need anything from him. Dear mummy, what on earth am I to do now?"

Greta entered the room noiselessly and sat down on the bed by Vika's side, putting her hand on the girl's shoulder. Vika started and turned her head to Greta.

"Please forgive me, frau! But everything that's going on is just unbearable."

"Here, drink some water," Greta handed her a glass of water. "And please calm down."

Vika sat up, took the glass, and looked at the water, then shifted her eyes to Greta and back to the glass again.

"I wish I could just drink this water," she said in a low voice, "and go to sleep, and wake up already at home, in my own bed. And think it was all just a dream."

All of a sudden Vika again felt everything turn upside down inside her belly.

"But, it's not a dream!" she said ruefully, looking up at Greta. "It's all absolutely real!" Her eyes filled with tears. They were silent for some time.

"Whatever happens, Vika, life must go on."

"Wha-a-at for?" inquired the girl hopelessly.

"For the sake of the living."

"What if one doesn't want to? What if everything is lost?"

"One should pluck up one's courage, one should think of the future," Greta persisted.

"There's no future for me. There's nothing left!"

"What do you mean nothing?" wondered Greta. "There is very much left! Very soon there is going to be a child and he's what you should think about."

"Yes, you're right," echoed Vika. "Of course, I have to consider him before anything else." Vika looked up at Greta, obviously pondering something. "I need a doctor," she said firmly. "Really, I need one."

"What's up, girl? What are you driving at?" Greta was alarmed. "Just dismiss the idea from your mind. God has given you this baby. Don't you burden your soul with such a sin, oh my Lord, the child is already so big."

Vika gazed at her silently.

"I say, Vika, you can't do this," Greta began nervously, "You just simply can't. Don't you see? It's a live human being already."

Vika was gazing at Greta with an air of detachment, thinking to herself.

"Do you want me to tell you a few things about my life?" without an answer, the woman began her story.

"I was born at the beginning of this century," Greta started in an undertone. "The time was far from easy, with the hunger and cold. And during the first war with Russia, my parents perished, and I, just a little girl, remained alone. I don't remember that time very well," she went on ponderously. "I was too small and often ill. I was outside with no home, and was freezing cold all over. And it was just then that I was picked up by Heinrich's grandparents. They had already growing grandchildren, but still they had the mercy to adopt another child, to nurse and raise me."

Vika was listening attentively to the housekeeper's story, try-ing to find in it something in common with her own life.

"Well, then," Greta went on, "I was growing up, learning at school, helping about the house. And when Heinrich was born, I was already a teenager. And he was a very weak child, so I was attending to him all the time. In a few years I got married, but God didn't let us have children," Greta remarked sadly. "And then Hitler took power, and my husband was taken to the army soon. And he perished somewhere at the Russian front...and I just remained to work in this family. We also had a hell of a time during the second war...and I also saw columns of Russian captive soldiers — almost all of them quite young they were and bare boned."

Greta paused to cope with the painful memories and to draw her breath.

"I only cannot understand," she continued, "why Russians put up the wall to divide Berlin. Well, what can't be cured must be endured, and anyway, life had to be arranged somehow in a new way," she became silent again.

"You must hate Russians," considered Vika. "Then why should you help me?"

"No child, no! It was nothing of the kind," Greta blurted out. "It was not Russians who began the wars with us, but we did. So why should I hate you? And we are all equal in God's eyes."

"It ought to be so..." Vika agreed hesitantly, lost in thought. "That's something I can never understand, why have we always had wars between us? Perhaps somebody around us needs it? What do you think? We're so much alike," Vika went on, "And our cultures are very close. Okay, leave out the cultures, kings in Russia were Germans!"

"Well, history is like that..." Greta replied in an undertone with a deep sigh. Silence filled the room again.

"So, Vika, I was just going to tell you this," Greta returned to her story, "I was dreaming of a little baby all my life, but God didn't grant me such a joy. And neither have I had a chance to nurse Heinrich's children...everything is in God's will," she crossed her chest sadly. "And you're lucky, you will have a child!" Greta smiled weakly. "It doesn't matter now who the father is, it's going to be your own child, and it will beguile your life. You'll have something to live for."

"Maybe it's really so," Vika uttered slowly. "But what can I hope for without documents or money?"

"For God's help and mercy," answered Greta.

"My granny told me," Vika put in, "'God helps him who helps himself.' And I do need a doctor."

"Vika, you cannot visit a doctor having no documents, and once you're in no need of this child to such an extent, just leave it with us, and we shall raise the little one."

"What are you talking about?" Vika looked at her, at a loss, and added, "I have no way out at all!"

"Why?" said Greta cheerfully, rising up from the bed. "There is a way out — to the kitchen! And we will now go and eat something. Otherwise, it's only beastly ideas that can occur on an empty stomach."

And off they went to the kitchen. After eating and washing the dishes, they sat down at the window and talked about the little differences in cooking in their respective countries. Suddenly Greta started.

"Oh, I've forgotten all about it," she stood up and headed to the corridor. "You know, I've bought something necessary for you," she handed to Vika one of the packages taken from the shop.

"Oh why, you didn't have to..." Vika was embarrassed, "I don't need anything!"

"Come on, take it out! Don't be shy," Greta encouraged her. "I just hope everything will fit you."

And Vika began to produce table socks, white handkerchiefs, warm pantyhose, shampoo and all kinds of other vials and little cans she had no idea of the intended use of.

"Oh, thank you very much," Vika was ill at ease. "But I have no money at all to pay you back."

"You needn't," smiled Greta, "It's a New Year present to you from your Santa Claus!"

"Thank you," Vika repeated again.

"And now grab it all and go to your room to have a rest," Greta said mildly, "We shall think of something later on."

Chapter 48

VIKA WAS STANDING in reverie at the window, and saw Heinrich Schultz's car drive into the yard at twilight. Then he entered the house, but Vika heard nothing for some more time. Vika, without switching on the light, was walking up and down the room, thinking of her mother. She was so much in need of her aid and advice at the moment.

She doesn't love me, Vika thought. *Oh no, it can't be so, it really isn't! I'm her daughter after all. She must be just very much ashamed of me.* Vika was pacing restlessly in the room, unable to find the answer to the question, or what she needed to do now.

And all of a sudden she heard muffled voices, probably from the sitting room. Vika sat down on the bed and was listening hard to the voices. She could not make out any words. In a while, Greta knocked on her door.

"Vika, will you come out please?" she called in a low voice, "Heinrich wants to talk to you."

Vika stood up and moved slowly to the sitting room, stopping at the doorway. Heinrich sat at the fireplace smoking a cigarette. He turned his face to Vika. She was at a loss as to where to hide from his penetrating eyes.

"Not talking, eh?" he said, without even so much as greeting her. "Come on in, sit down, go ahead and speak up!"

Vika was casting downward glances from him to Greta, then, looking down at the floor, she remained stuck in her place.

"Come on, come on," Greta said coming up to her, "please, sit down by the fire."

She took Vika to the armchair facing Heinrich and seated her down there, remaining in the room as well, and settling down nearby.

Schultz kept eyeing Vika silently and smoking.

"Did you have a talk with your mom today?" he asked slowly.

"Yes," Vika hung her head very low.

"What did she say?" Heinrich went on. But Vika kept silent.

"Why are you secretive again? She has told you something, hasn't she?"

"Yes."

"What was it?"

"She said I can't come back now," Vika began in a low voice. "She said that, because I did not return on time together with the tourist group, I will be convicted as a traitor and put in jail. And she is not going to do anything for me because she doesn't want to mess up my brothers' careers and lives."

"Your brothers' careers and lives? Uh," Schultz interrupted her, "what about your career and life?"

"Nothing," Vika felt embarrassed. "She said, stay where you are."

"That's a bunch of crap!" Heinrich uttered with derision. "That's how much your mother needs you then," he sniffed and turned away towards the fire.

"Neither do I need any problems," he said in a short while. "And I'm not going to keep you in my house."

"I understand," Vika said hopelessly. "I will go away now." She rose up from the armchair.

"Where on earth are you going to go this late at night?" Greta took up the ball suddenly.

"It's just much better at night," Schultz snapped roughly. "No one is going to see her here. And it would be better if you took her away somewhere out of the town."

"Please, take me away," Vika implored, turning to Greta.

"I say, are we human beings or God-forsaken creatures from below?" Greta exclaimed in dismay. "She's only a child. How can one push out a pregnant girl in the winter? And, do it at night?" she yelled.

"All right," said Heinrich. "Tomorrow let there be no trace of her here."

"Thank you for everything," Vika said gently, standing up. "Please, don't worry, I will leave now. And you needn't take me away anywhere."

And making a little bow, she headed to her room.

"No!" Greta blocked her way. "I won't let you go," and she forced Vika down on the sofa.

"So what are you doing, Heinrich?" the housekeeper flared up. "You attend church, don't you? How come you're deaf to another one's pain?" Greta was almost choking on the words. "You're all alone, aren't you? And you're driving her away, not even trying to help."

"I have helped her already!" he snapped back. "Risking, putting myself in harm."

"It was God's will to have thrown down this child in front of your car," Greta answered excitedly, almost huskily.

Vika rose from the sofa.

"I pray, please, don't quarrel," she said, stumbling. "You shouldn't fight because of me. I'm really very grateful to you, Heinrich, for your having stopped at that moment and taken me away from there. And there's nothing else I need, thank you, and I'll just go away. Will you please, frau, give me my clothes?"

"Oh, Lord!" Greta cried out with tears. "Suppose you go now, how do you think I can go on living with that?"

"Forgive me," Vika whispered, heading to her room. Greta followed directly after her.

"Never despair, girl, never despair!" she held Vika, "we'll figure out something tomorrow." And she left the room.

Vika was really very much afraid to go out at night in such an unfamiliar town. She stood at the window and started crying silently, looking into the pure, starlit sky.

Right above her head, high in the sky, a round, white moon was shining. And she recalled that far-off moon back in the mountains, where she had spent time together with Sergei Nilovski. *Perhaps, Sergei, you're watching the same moon now,* Vika thought. *But there is nothing you can do for me. I have died for everybody, including you.*

For a long time, Vika stood by the window, swallowing her tears. Then Greta came in bringing her a small supper.

"Thank you, I don't feel like eating," she refused, and she went to bed.

At night she had nightmares, and again there was the dream she had had once, with her looking for her apartment and unable to find it...there were all the flats in the house, and there were neighbors talking to her, but there was no such thing as her own flat, and the number was non-existent.

She woke up in the morning feeling perplexed. Where was her home? Vika stayed in bed for some more time, putting her thoughts more or less in order, then got up and, not finding her own clothes, began to dress in what was there.

No matter how big this house was, including the garden, Vika couldn't feel either richness or satisfaction here. It was always cold, with everything spent in a meager and scanty way.

Vika headed to the kitchen, hearing some noise from there.

"Good morning, frau."

"Good morning, Vika! Come on in," she called back. "Sit down, we're going to have breakfast just now."

Vika took her place humbly at the table near the window. "I'm sorry," she said, "I couldn't find my clothes. I should change, I think."

"Let's eat first, and then you'll change," Greta answered, putting the breakfast on the table.

They ate quickly and cleaned everything up.

"I was thinking for a long time yesterday," Greta began slowly. "You cannot go anywhere like this. And mind you, you are being looked for. Neither will I burden my soul with such a sin — to turn you out to wander. No way," the housekeeper said firmly, looking at Vika.

"As far as it is within my power," she went on, "I will help you. Today I have already called my sister-in-law, she's lonely too, and we're great friends."

Vika was gazing at the little slim woman in amazement.

"I have told her about you in a nutshell," Greta continued. "And I've just asked her to shelter you for a short time, until I have found something else. She's a very nice woman and believe me, she is able to keep secrets."

"Thank you so much!" said Vika gratefully.

"And now, let's get ready to go," Greta smiled, taking Vika by the elbow. "And you must know this little girl, you're not alone, I will not leave you!" Then they went to get ready to go.

Greta put in front of Vika her washed and ironed attire. "You'd better not wear this now," she said. "It's so noticeable, you know. Just remain in what you're wearing now, and take it with you. Turn your coat inside-out, and put it on."

Vika smiled, imagining how she looked in such an outfit, and did everything as she was told to. Greta gave her a small, old bag and Vika put her sparse belongings in it.

"I'm ready," Vika said finally.

"That's good." Greta cheered her up, "I've already piled up some things for you there in the car, so you can make use of it all. You'll have to make things yourself, sewing or knitting, and I'll be there very soon to help you."

"Thank you very much!" Vika looked at Greta with wet eyes.

And just at that moment, the front door opened and Schultz appeared in the doorway. He shut the door and stood there panting, looking from one woman to the other.

"We're already going," muttered Vika, scared, and bent down to take the bag.

"What's happened to you, Heinrich?" Greta was alarmed. "Has something happened at your work? Why have you come back?"

He was standing in silence, without a word. Vika's blood ran cold. *He has called the police*, she thought, *or Muzaphar*. She was overcome with a cold sweat, a nervous chill. She fell heavily back against the wall, dropping her bag.

"We have to talk," he said, passing through the corridor and taking off his coat. Both the women were watching him, at a loss as to what to do.

"Where were you going?" Schultz looked at Greta.

"I was going to take her to another town, to a friend of mine," she answered timidly.

"Yes...in another town — that would be much better," Heinrich said in reverie, rocking on his feet from heel to toe. "Probably, this is where she's being searched for."

"Well, they're not beasts, are they?" said Greta. "They will forget about Vika with time. He has a lot of wives even without her, and, for that matter, she's not a wife to him at all."

"And the child?" Schultz asked, peering at Greta.

"What do you mean the child?" the housekeeper confused. "The child is to live with his own fortune. Things happen in this life, you know."

And they were silent, looking straight in the eye of one another. Vika, listening to them talk, realized that nobody had called anyone, and her breathing became easier. There was a heavy silence hanging in the room, and Heinrich paced back and forth, pondering something and casting short glances at the women.

"We'd better be going," Vika murmured, moving off the wall.

"Yes, we must go," Greta echoed, and they headed to the side door.

"Wait!" Schultz said all of a sudden. "How much time do you need to make some documents?" He looked at Vika.

"I don't know...but I'm certainly going to do everything as quickly as possible."

"All right," Heinrich said. "Live here until you've made the documents. And try to," he shifted his eyes to Greta, "be sure that she is seen by nobody."

Vika, dumbfounded, looked at Heinrich, blinking her eyes foolishly.

"Thank you, Heinrich," said Greta. "I knew all along you were kind-hearted and a real Christian!" She pulled Vika by the sleeve.

"What's that disguise on her?" Schultz sniffed, looking at Vika. "What have you done to her coat?"

"We've just turned it inside-out," Greta smiling, "so as not to attract attention."

"Conspirators," Heinrich grinned and left the house.

"That's good now," Greta gave a sigh of relief, helping Vika out of the coat. "It will be much easier for us here and later on we'll think of something."

She lifted the bag and started pushing Vika slightly to her room.

Chapter 49

THUS VIKA REMAINED in Heinrich's house. She was very grateful to them and helped Greta with everything. Heinrich told his housekeeper to buy some inexpensive but necessary clothes and footwear for Vika to wear while she was expecting. And when it all was brought in by Greta, he inspected everything and calculated the sum spent on the purchases.

As a present on her own part, Greta bought a black wig for Vika and some cosmetics with black Indian beauty spots. And when they left to go somewhere, Vika would always camouflage herself under Greta's keen guidance putting on the wig and placing beauty spots on her face. The two of them made great friends.

Nevertheless, Vika appeared only in crowded places and generally moved about with her head lowered. In a short time, she became noticeably rounder in shape and was unable to conceal her small belly.

Having no opportunity to work, Vika was in desperate need of money, and once she ventured with a suggestion to Greta, "I'm very sorry, frau, but I do need at least a little money. Could you please offer my fox-fur coat for sail at a shop? I don't wear it anyway."

"Oh, Vika, I don't want to sell such a beautiful thing," the woman exclaimed. "But you're right, you'd better get rid of it. I just don't want to leave my telephone number and address at the shop."

"What can we do?" asked Vika.

"I'll call my sister-in-law and ask her if she can help us," Greta said thoughtfully, "and we shall offer the coat for sale in another town, as far away as possible."

So they did, and very soon the fox-fur coat was sold. Greta went and got the money. They bought some necessary things for the child and for Vika.

Spring came. The sun was getting warmer and the night was retreating, making the daytime longer. The garden around the house was becoming alive, filled with birds' songs and the smell of the warm ground. In the evenings, Vika would walk there and always sat down in the garden house, brooding and feeling homesick.

She wanted so much to at least hear the voice of Sergei Nilovski, and once, coming across a post office with Greta, she called him at his apartment. Vika heard the husky voice of an elderly woman in the receiver, probably it was his mother, and saying nothing, Vika hung up.

The future scared her, and with a fluttering heart, she felt the clear sensation of a new life moving inside her. Now what could she give this baby? Vika was overcome by disappointment, and unable to find even a single answer to her questions, she just waited. *What will be, will be!* she thought.

Heinrich did not take any part in her life, with their communication restricted to a few phrases once in a while. When he was at home, Vika tried to stay in her room. But once, he called her to the sitting room.

"How are you coming along?" he asked, pointing to her belly. "When will the time come?"

"I don't know," Vika answered, embarrassed.

"I've been thinking a lot about the matter," Heinrich said thoughtfully, "and I would not in the least like to turn my home into a hospital, but I can't see another way out."

He was silent for a moment, puffing at his cigarette.

"Are you feeling well?" he asked.

"Yes, I am."

"I have friends," Heinrich went on unhurriedly, "they're old and true friends. They have two grown-up children, and the wife is a doctor. Her name is Vanessa. I have told them about you."

Schultz was speaking slowly, obviously ill at ease.

"The problem is, she is not a children's doctor, nor even a women's one," Heinrich went on, "but she agreed to examine you and help you deliver the child. I'll bring her here tomorrow by three o'clock."

"Thank you," replied Vika timidly.

And the next day she was examined by Doctor Vanessa who was content that there was nothing abnormal, based on a visual examination. Together they tried to determine and calculate the time for delivery, and Vanessa was absorbed in reading the few books on the subject that she brought with her. Vika could help her a little. Finally they determined the time would come in about a month.

"I'm so afraid," said Vika nervously.

"So am I," the doctor remarked. "But we will do it and everything is going to be all right if you listen to me. Don't worry. I will leave you one of my books. It's about getting ready for, and what to expect during labor. Just read it and don't be nervous. You're young and healthy, so everything is going to be all right!"

"Thank you, Doctor," said Vika by the end, and Heinrich quickly took Vanessa away. Vika, after opening the book and seeing the pictures, was scared by the events ahead of her even more!

Chapter 50

THREE WEEKS HAD passed since the doctor's visit. Late at night, Vika felt a heavy pressure in her belly, and a kind of uneasiness seized her. She was restless, visiting the toilet from time to time, and unable to sleep.

It was past midnight already, and Greta silently entered her room. "Why aren't you asleep?"

"I'm trying to," answered Vika weakly, "but as soon as I start to fall asleep, my stomach begins to ache."

"It means the labor is beginning," Greta concluded, trying to keep cool, but looking rather nervous.

"Oh no, don't say so," Vika was frightened. "It's still a week away."

"Of course, it would be better to wait for another week," Greta confirmed. "Especially since today is the first of April."

They made all the necessary preparations, and followed the procedures as they were described in the book, and started waiting. Greta switched on more light in the room and began to pray.

"You need to pray, too," she looked at Vika.

"My grandma said that religion appears when people are born and when they die."

"You see, it's really your time!"

Vika paced up and down the room, tortured by the pains seizing her, which also prevented Greta from going to wake up Heinrich for him to fetch the doctor.

"I'm so ashamed of bothering people in the night," Vika explained, "it's after three o'clock in the morning and it wouldn't be good to wake someone up before the work day. Just wait a little while longer."

Vika was suffering the pain, uttering no sound. Greta feverishly read the book on obstetrics, which she had already read a number of times, and watched the clock and Vika's condition.

Closer to six o'clock, noticing the shortened intervals between Vika's fits of pain, Greta, without saying a word, went to wake up Heinrich. He jumped up immediately, put on his jumpsuit and started off for the doctor.

They were back in somewhat more than an hour. Vika felt horrible by that time. The doctor examined her and gave her some injections and something to drink.

"It's all going to be all right," the doctor smiled, "Just you do as I tell you to."

Greta was pacing nearby, very nervous, doing her utmost to cheer the girl up. And Vika was gritting her teeth to control the pain, and thinking that she was now on the verge of dying, and that something was irrepressibly tearing her whole body apart. The pain was unbearable, and she thought that at any second, she was going to die.

Vika listened to the doctor and silently did everything she was told. Time seemed to have stopped for her in her overall anguish, and just when it was more than she could bear, something suddenly happened, and she instantly felt relief. Vika saw the smiling face of the housekeeper.

"It's a girl!" Greta said mirthfully with tears in her eyes.

"Congratulations!" the doctor smiled, wiping perspiration from her own face and attending to the baby, who started crying very loudly.

When everything was finished, Vika was changed into a clean nightgown and given her baby. It was the first time Vika glanced at her child. A white, pug-nosed little face, with curly dark hair, was squinting at her.

"It's a very nice girl, and with a good weight, too," Vanessa said, smiling and taking the child away from Vika. "She's going to look very much like you."

"Thank you, Doctor," Vika answered in a weak voice. "Thank you very much."

"Well done, girl," Vanessa remarked approvingly, and gave Vika another injection. "Now you must have a good sleep. Tomorrow I'll come to examine you both. Good luck!" And having swaddled the child, she left the room.

"Thank you so much," Vika muttered to Greta, almost inaudibly while the latter was fixing her blanket. "I thought I was going to die."

"I thought I was going to die, too, watching you," Greta responded with a smile. "But, we've done it. Congratulations! Now you go to sleep, and I'll put the baby to bed. Don't worry, just sleep." And she left the room following the doctor.

* * * * *

Vanessa was standing in the sitting room with the child in her arms, facing Heinrich Schultz. Until he heard the girl's cry, Heinrich had been pacing the rooms nervously, putting more wood in the fireplace and puffing on another cigarette.

Already he hated the child, who had caused so many problems and so much stress. And then, Vanessa was holding the little wrap in front of him, Heinrich was captivated for a moment by the face of the sleeping child. When the baby suddenly smiled a little in her sleep, he smiled back at her.

"It's a girl," said Vanessa, "A nice, large one. Want to hold her?" she eyed Heinrich attentively.

"No, I don't think I want...I could drop her," he answered uncertainly.

"Then just sit down in an armchair, and I will hand her to you." Vanessa smiled, handing the child to Heinrich. He took the girl, peering hard into her little face.

"She will look very much like Vika," Vanessa said gently, taking the mug of coffee Greta had brought her. "It's good the child is a girl, they'll be like two girlfriends. How old is Vika now?"

"Sixteen," Greta answered, taking the baby from Heinrich.

"Oh, poor little child," Vanessa uttered compassionately, settling herself in an armchair by the fire. "She still has growing up to do, and here you are, with her child. By the way, with a daughter, she will quickly grow up."

They sat for some more time by the fireplace, drinking coffee and talking. Then Heinrich took her home, and when he came back, he freshened up and headed out to work.

Chapter 51

VIKA SLEPT FOR almost twenty hours and woke up the next morning. Looking around the room, she did not find the baby, so she got up slowly, slipped into her gown, and went out to the corridor and headed for Greta's room.

The child slept, sunk into a soft pillow in a large chair drawn up to Greta's bed. Vika came up and bent slightly over to look at the girl's sweet little face, so infinitely close and already dear to her. At that moment, Greta entered the room.

"Good morning, frau," Vika smiled, and then she cast a suspicious glance at Greta. "Is there anything to worry about?"

"Good morning, Vika," answered Greta. "Only worrying about our little girl," she glanced tenderly at the child.

Vika also shifted her eyes to her daughter, but squinted at Greta again. The woman seemed to have become somewhat fresher, more alert, changed into new clothes, and her face had taken on a look of major importance.

Greta had put a soft blanket on a table in her room, thus arranging a swaddling-spot for the baby.

"I've already given her water," Greta said tenderly, taking the girl in her hands and putting her on the table, "she needs to be fed soon."

"With what?" asked Vika.

"With your breast," Greta said as she piled up the swaddling clothes. Vika shifted her eyes to her small breast, then eyed Greta in surprise.

"Don't worry," Greta patted her back sympathetically. "The doctor said the quantity of milk doesn't depend on the size of the breast, and you should suckle the child anyway."

"Oh, look at her," Vika exclaimed joyfully, pointing at the girl's face. "She's smiling at me!"

"Yesterday she smiled at me too," Heinrich said, entering the room. His voice startled Vika.

"Good morning," he said, nearing the child.

"Good morning," Vika answered, and at that moment, the girl began to wake up.

"That's a good girl, get up now," Greta chirped tenderly as she unwrapped the tightly rolled towel containing the child.

Vika was gazing at the little girl in amazement. She had never seen such small babies. Having gotten rid of the swaddling clothes, the baby girl stretched her little limbs to her belly, then yawned and farted. Vika laughed on seeing it.

"She's acting like a real human being," Vika said in merry surprise, cautiously touching the girl's tiny fingers.

"She is a real human being!" Greta uttered proudly, "Even though she's a very small one." And, stroking the child tenderly, she wrapped it up tightly in clean diapers.

"Let your baby breastfeed," she gave the little wrap to the new mom. Vika took the girl into her hands with a thrill and, pressing daughter to her bosom, retired with the baby to her room.

It was really wise of Mother Nature to have endowed womankind with everything necessary to give life and nourish a new life. This must be the very essence of being a woman. So Vika was breastfeeding her daughter, holding the baby in her arms.

Little by little, everything settled down and resumed its natural course. Against Greta's insistent reluctance, Vika took the girl to her own room and constantly attended to her on her own.

But Greta would use any opportunity to grudgingly take the child to her, washing her together with Vika, and trying to spend as much time as possible with her.

Before the baby was born they had both been discussing baby names. Vika had been inventing all kinds of intricate names for a girl, while Greta had only been offering traditional ones.

But when the baby girl was born, Vika studied her closely for almost a month, trying to guess what name would suit her best. The child was very active and restless, and Vika saw that none of the long names she had invented would do. So, on second thought, she gave her the traditional Russia's name of Maria.

"Maria! Sweetheart!" She was calling her daughter's name while playing with her, and massaging her as Vanessa had taught her to do. Vika would tell her Russian fairy tales, nursery rhymes and sing her the lullabies she could remember from her own childhood, or those she composed herself. Greta liked the name too, and was giving all her time to the child's upbringing, noticing each little change in her.

Heinrich did not take any part in the fuss over the girl, casting just occasional glances at her. A bed along with some other children's things, were brought to them by Vanessa, who visited them from time to time to inquire about the baby.

Vika could not help pondering as to what to do next. And having regained her senses to some extent, she returned to the thoughts about a way to make the documents for herself and now also for her daughter. She had no idea whatsoever who to address on the matter.

Sergei, Sergei, Vika was thinking ruefully, *how I need your advice and help now. Why haven't you ever tipped me on whom to turn to in such a case?* She would often cry, longing for her home and for Sergei Nilovski.

* * * * *

Maria was growing rapidly as a strong and clever girl. By the end of the summer, they could already leave the child with Heinrich for a short time, so they could go where they needed to go.

Vika decided to find some Russians and turn to them for help. But no matter how long she spent with Greta walking around shops, cafés and streets, Vika never heard her native language. All different tongues seemed to be spoken around her, but not Russian.

"Probably, we'll have to go to Berlin," Vika proposed one day.

"Oh yes, go ahead," Greta answered her with fear, holding the child in her arms. "You'll be taken there by our police and put in jail for illegally staying in the country without documents, then passed over to your authorities for them to put you in jail, too."

"So what on earth am I to do now?" Vika asked, sinking helplessly down on a chair. "Please, let's go to a post office, I want to call my mom once more."

A few days later they set off for the post office and Vika, entering the telephone booth, dialed Nilovski's home number first. The same old woman's voice answered. Vika hung up the receiver silently, and started dialing her own home number. After a few long buzzes, she heard her mom's voice.

"Hello. Hello."

"Mom! Hello, Mom!" Vika said, "It's me!"

There was a short pause in the receiver, then it was hung up on the other end. Vika dialed her number once more, but there were long buzzes with nobody picking up the receiver. Again and again she dialed her number, but no one wanted to talk to her.

Vika gazed at the silent telephone, at a loss, then left the booth and turned slowly to the exit.

"Hi," somebody greeted her with her native language and blocked her way. She looked up and saw the unfamiliar face of an elderly man.

"I don't know you," Vika answered in Russian, and moved to pass him. But at the same moment she stopped short, turning to him.

"Hello," she said. The man smiled at her.

"What fair winds bring a Russian girl here?" he asked affably.

"Just a windfall," Vika answered, peering into his face.

"Should we go out to talk?" the man offered, and they left the post office.

"Let's drop into that café over there," he pointed to a café across the street. "We'll have coffee and get acquainted."

They crossed the street, bought a cup of coffee, and went out and settled down at a small table outside.

"What is your name?" Vika asked, smiling.

"Andrei," the man answered. "What's yours?"

"Kathy," Vika lied, afraid of telling her real name. "And what are you doing here?"

"Working and living," Andrei answered with a smile. "Now what are you doing here?"

"I'm solving some problems," Vika answered, reasonably understanding that she should not trust the first person she meets. But hearing her native tongue spoken, she could hardly stop from bursting into tears and telling him her bitter story. But there was something in his countenance and behavior that set her on alert, so she was trying hard to keep her distance while talking to him.

"What problems may obsess a beautiful girl like you?" he asked playfully. "Could I possibly help any?"

Greta slowly passed near their table, listening attentively to their conversation, and Vika made no sign they knew each other.

"I don't know," Vika answered his question, "it's all very serious...but perhaps you might know somebody who can help me."

She was biting her lip, at a loss as to how to act.

For a number of months Vika had tried in vain to find some Russians, and here she chanced to find somebody, and now he was sitting by her side. A total stranger, alien to Vika, and she had nothing to do but to turn to him for help.

"What kind of problem is it?" he asked sympathetically, bending nearer.

"It's somebody...needing documents," Vika said uncertainly.

"What kind of documents?" Andrei asked in a low voice.

"A passport."

"For what country?" he went on, taking her hand.

"This one," Vika answered, pulling her hand away awkwardly, "and make it as real as possible."

"Certainly!" agreed Andrei gently. "But it will cost somebody a lot."

"Just how much?" she asked impatiently.

"I'm not sure," he answered, almost touching Vika's face. "I will inquire and tell you the next time."

"All right," she said, backing off a little. "Where shall I find you?"

"And where do you live, young lady?"

"Far from here..." Vika thinking feverishly of what to say. "Shall we say, meet at this café?"

"When?"

"When are you going to find everything out?"

"Well, probably...in two days or so," he said. "Let's then meet here in three days, okay?"

They settled on a time of the next meeting and parted. Vika went down several narrow streets, looking around to see if she had been followed, and finally came to Greta's car.

"Who is this man?" Greta asked, driving out from the road-side.

"A Russian," Vika answered unhappily. "I have no idea who he is, but he's promised to help me."

"Very strange," said Greta thoughtfully, "I would not trust anybody if I were you."

"Neither would I," Vika agreed, "but I have no choice and please, let us drop by a jewelry store."

Greta looked at her in surprise.

"I'd like to find something out," said Vika. And they stopped in a small jewelry shop.

"Greta, what a piece of luck that you have such a small car! You can't even move in a normal car along those narrow streets, to say nothing of parking. You're a very skillful driver!"

"Thank you, honey," Greta answered, and they went to the shop.

Vika needed money, so she decided to sell the ring she was always wearing with the jewels turned inside. Peering into the showcase slowly, she was looking for something of the same kind, to have an idea of how much it might cost.

Rings with diamonds were very expensive, but she could not find anything like her bulky ring. Vika turned the ring on her hand so she could see the jewels better, to make it easier to compare, when the salesman came up to her.

"What a beautiful ring you have!" he said with delight.

"Thank you," answered Vika modestly.

"Anything I can help you with?"

"Prices," she answered frankly. "How much do you think I could ask for my ring?"

"I'm afraid I cannot tell you the price offhand," he uttered, and smiled. "I should first take a closer look at your ring."

Vika stretched her hand out to him. The salesman examined the ring.

"Let's go and see it in the light," he proposed, and they retired to the desk where he switched on a bright light, taking out a magnifying lens.

The diamonds in the ring gave a blinding blaze under the rays of light, with all the colors of the spectrum. Having examined the ring, the salesman named his price.

"But that seems to be a very low price indeed," Vika said in confusion, taking back her hand. "You don't even have a comparable ring, and your prices are much higher."

"I'm sorry," said the Eastern-type salesman, "but the rings we have are new."

"Thanks," Vika turned to go.

"Just a moment," the salesman tried to stop her politely, and raised the price a little.

"Thanks, I'll think it over."

He almost followed them out, raising the price once more.

"Thanks," she repeated once more, having already determined the approximate price the ring was worth.

On returning home, they told everything to Heinrich Schultz. He was rather surprised at Vika's recklessness, but he also considered it to essentially be the only way out. Therefore, he approved of the venture, warning again that neither his name, nor address should be mentioned anywhere. Greta told him about the ring and the sum offered to Vika for it.

"I could take the ring from you as pawn," Heinrich said, after some thinking, "and give you the last sum the salesman named. When you start working, you will return the money to me and take your ring back."

"Thank you," Vika agreed and, taking the ring off, handed it to Schultz.

Chapter 52

AFTER THREE DAYS, at the appointed time, Vika was sitting at the same café, talking to the Russian Andrei.

"You're looking great!" he said, sitting down at her table.

"So are you, thanks," Vika answered, greeting him.

"How is this person who's in need of documents?" he asked playfully, moving closer to Vika.

"I think, not bad. Is there a hope that the passport can be made?"

"It's far from easy," he said in a low voice, glancing around. "But I've met with the right people and they've promised me to help you."

"Oh, that's wonderful!" gasped Vika happily. "And how much is it going to cost?"

Andrei named the sum. Her eyes rounded with amazement.

"It's very expensive," Vika said, drawing her breath. "I haven't got so much money!"

He looked at her very attentively, and took her tenderly by the hand.

"We could settle it for a smaller sum," he ventured insinuatingly, with his eyes glazing over.

"How can it be done if they're demanding a certain amount of money for the passport?"

"I can help you," he was stroking her hand tenderly. "It's true, if we become close friends."

Vika took away her hand carefully, and was lost in thought for a while, examining the coffee cup.

"When do you need the money?" she asked, reckoning she could borrow the missing sum from Heinrich.

"I could help you," Andrei offered once more, looking at Vika.

"Thank you," she answered shyly, having caught his hints. "I could give you a part of the sum now and the rest of it when the passport is ready."

"Well, okay," Andrei agreed promptly, and handed her a sheet of paper. "Write down the information to be registered in the passport."

Vika took the paper and wrote the name and date of birth she had invented for herself. As for the child, she decided to register her in the passport and make her daughter's documents later on, as she was short of money now.

Andrei took the paper, read the written data, and put out his hand to take the money, casting cautious glances all around. Vika handed him the money and he, without even counting it, put it in his pocket.

"Well, well," Andrei said, "you've paid, let's say, the larger part of the sum, so there's just a trifle left and the passport will be ready."

"When?"

"In a week, I think," Andrei answered, and took her by the hand again. "You just think once more, darling, about my proposal, I could help you with the rest of the sum." He raised her hand to his lips. "We could settle the question right now," he whispered, squinting his eyes as he spoke.

"I'll think it over," replied Vika shyly. "When are we meeting again?"

"In a week, my darling. Same time, same place." He smiled and, saying good-bye, left quickly.

* * * * *

Greta was watching their meeting out of a window from the post office.

"I don't like him," she said, puckering her face in disgust as they got into the car. "He's sort of repugnant!"

"Neither do I like him," Vika sighed thoughtfully. "But if he makes my passport, I won't care a fig what his muzzle looks like."

Greta grinned and looked at Vika suspiciously.

"Why are you nervous?" she asked. "Everything is as good as done."

"I was short of money."

"How can that be?" Greta exclaimed. "You had a real great sum, didn't you?"

Vika told her how much Andrei was demanding for the document.

"O-oh...he's a damn thief, he is!" Greta was indignant, "Demanding such a huge sum from a poor girl like you!"

"I have no choice," Vika sighed. "Neither have I the missing sum."

"But you've given him your money, haven't you?" Greta said uneasily. "So, you must be hoping for something?"

"For Heinrich," said Vika. "I will try to ask him to lend me the necessary sum."

"To ask and to get are two quite different things," Greta answered perplexedly, and for the rest of the way they kept silent, each deep in her own thoughts.

Schultz listened to them without interrupting.

"It's very bold of you to be so sure I'm going to give you the rest of the sum," he told Vika coldly and a bit contemptuously. "You're already indebted to me."

"Yes, thank you," Vika said. "Only what kind of indebtedness is it, once you have my ring in pawn?"

He eyed her silently for a long while.

"I will think your request over," Heinrich said, "but if I do give it to you, you will give me a voucher."

"All right," replied Vika.

For a number of days Vika waited in suspense, wondering whether Heinrich would or would not give her the money. But just a day before the appointed date, Heinrich put a sheet of paper in front of Vika.

"Write the voucher," he said dryly. And Vika wrote everything he dictated. He read it and, folding the sheet, put it into his pocket and produced the money.

"Don't give him the money until you have taken the passport and checked it," he said.

"Thank you very much!"

And the next day she set out with Greta to that town, to the appointed place. But Andrei didn't come. Vika spent more than an hour at the café, casting glances here and there, but he still didn't turn up. She got up and walked on the pavement along the building, but he was nowhere to be seen. He had disappeared!

Looking around at a loss, Vika strolled to the car, but stopping at the corner, she kept peering into people's faces. *Perhaps he was delayed?* This flashed in her mind and she came back to the café, ordered another cup of coffee, and went out to the table.

For a long time she sat at the table, dumbfounded by what had happened, looking blankly in front of her. Greta came up slowly. "Let's go to the car," she said in a low voice.

They got into the car and went home. Vika cried the entire way, burying her face in her hands.

On seeing them from the porch of the house, Heinrich understood everything at once.

"I knew you were a stark fool!" he said contemptuously to Vika. She ran sobbing to her room. In a few minutes, Greta entered looking very upset.

"Now listen to me, Vika," she began in an undertone, "many kinds of things can happen in life. So what's to be done now?"

"Why do they happen in my life?" Vika asked, crying. "Why am I so unlucky?"

"Everybody has a different fate," Greta uttered sadly, "and the game is not up to you."

"The game is over," said Vika hopelessly. "There is no more money. And there never will be!"

"Now forget it," Greta was soothing her. "Return the borrowed sum to Heinrich, take your voucher back, and forget all about that Russian guy."

Vika was looking at Greta, wiping off her tears.

"I don't think you're crying about the jewelry you've lost for now, are you?" Greta continued in an undertone. "Just make believe there never was a ring."

"Perhaps I'm exactly very sorry that I didn't put on all the gold I had then," Vika said ruefully. "I would have something to sell now that would provide me the money I need."

"Why? So you can give it to a crook like that?" Greta added in the same tone as Vika.

"How could I have been so trusting?" Vika burst out crying again.

"Stop crying," Greta took her by the hand. "Stop it! And stop blaming yourself! Even wild animals in a sad pickle come out and turn to people for help...knowing that a man can kill them," Greta gave a heavy sigh. "So let's just suppose you've made an attempt of coming out to people. Calm down and don't cry. You still have to nurse your child."

"Thank you for everything," Vika whispered, hugging Greta.

In the evening Vika gave the money back to Heinrich, and he returned the voucher to her.

"You should be glad you're still alive," he said crossly, after counting the money. "He must be one of your traitors who has remained here ever since the Second War."

Vika started and looked at Schultz in fear.

"This Russian," he continued, "could have invited you somewhere to give him the money and killed you there. You must understand that you got off easy," he finished, and retired to his room.

And in the morning Vika realized that, because of the stress, her milk had vanished. But they had long since started to give little Maria additional feedings, sharing from their own table with her, so it was not hard for her to do without her mother's milk.

Chapter 53

VIKA HAD ALWAYS helped Greta around the house, but ever since Maria appeared, all the housework fell upon Vika's shoulders. Greta didn't have to call in anybody now to clean the house, Vika was in charge of it all. Only once a year, Greta hired somebody to wash the windows, and there was worker in the garden.

Vika was busy as a bee day in and day out, dusting, cooking, cleaning the kitchen, washing, and ironing. In rare minutes of repose, she took her child from Greta to retire with the girl to the back yard's gazebo.

The girl was growing strong and at eight months, she began to walk by herself. Vika was happy to see the first steps of her daughter.

"Well done, my little girl," she twirled about and laughing with her. "You're just doing everything to make things easier for me," she tossed Maria up and the girl burst out laughing.

"My little sweetie," Vika said tenderly, pressing her daughter to herself. "I love you so much, my little flower, and I promise to you that I'll do everything to make your life better. I'll do my best for you."

Maria looked serious, straight into her mom's eyes, as if understanding the meaning of what was said.

"And now you, my dolly," Vika went on, kissing her daughter, "please do your best for me. We haven't got money for disposable diapers," and she unfolded her empty palm in front of Maria, "so, let's get used to the pot and not soil the pants."

From that day on, the girl quickly got used to the pot. Remembering the talk with her mom, she would show everybody her little fists, then unfold them, look at her empty palms, and say, "Money goo-goo."

Vika really did not have any money at all. Everything Maria needed badly she had to ask from Heinrich, and he would send Greta on a shopping mission, cutting down everything in half.

Vika became very thin, giving every piece of herself to her daughter, and shabby, still wearing the things she had during her pregnancy. The bulk of Maria's clothes had been brought by Vanessa.

Christmas and New Year were nearing. Vika felt absolutely worn out and depressed, having no opportunity to buy anything herself.

"What would you think, Greta," Vika began cautiously one day, "if suppose I went out to clean other houses as I'm cleaning yours, would they pay me money? Could I save a certain sum?"

"No," Greta answered, gazing suspiciously at Vika. "You would have to pay for housing, for food, for a baby-sitter for Maria, for everything."

"How much did you pay the people that came to clean your house?"

"That money would not be enough for you to live on," Greta answered. "And you'd better look attentively at Heinrich, he likes you."

"What do you mean?" Vika smiled nervously. "He likes me so much that he almost starves me to death."

"Well, you should not say so," Greta said, offended. "It isn't bad at all to be able to value money."

"You know, frau, I have not had a single minute when I didn't think about my situation," Vika uttered in an undertone. "So I will certainly think of some way out. As for Heinrich...he doesn't need anybody."

"I know him better, darling," said Greta. "And I've talked with him about you more than once. He told me you could count on his help if you did find serious people to make your documents."

Vika was eyeing Greta in silence. "How can one live together with somebody without love?"

"Besides, you did live with Muzaphar, didn't you?!" Greta answered bitingly.

"But he did love me!" Vika protested, "And Heinrich despises me."

"Then why on earth did you run away from there?" Greta asked caustically, then seeing tears in Vika's eyes, changed her tone promptly. "Let us not quarrel over trifles! You just think about what I've told you."

Vika didn't say anything and retired to her room. *What else can I do?* she thought, looking at her daughter who was sleeping peacefully. *I've already called Nilovski at home, but he's never answered the phone yet, so he must be absent.* Vika started crying, sitting down on the bed.

"Sergei, Sergei, I want to see you so much," she said aloud. "I need your help!"

Her daughter rolled a little in her sleep, hearing her mom's voice, and Vika moved closer to her, stroking her gently on the back.

"And so...I must find a way out even disgusting as it may be," Vika wiped her tears. "I probably must try this chance, too. He's not that terrible a man. It's just that he hates me so much," Vika shuddered, imagining Heinrich's face with a squeamish look.

But on viewing all the pros and cons, she began from that day on to smile playfully at him, and sit at the fireplace beside him in the evenings. He appreciated her endeavors so much that he even bought a sweater for her as a Christmas present and some fruit for Maria.

"Well, can't you see what I told you?" Greta smiled, nudging Vika's rib jokingly. "Didn't I tell you he likes you? Be affable with him and he'll do his best for you."

"Uh-huh," Vika mumbled, pursing her lips.

She had already seen all Schultz's shrewdness and frigidity of demeanor with her. But desperately being in need of help, Vika decided not to retreat, and when he told her he would give her money for the documents, she began sharing his bedroom with him.

Greta was happy to have settled Heinrich's life so smartly, but Vika suffered each time she went to bed with him. Heinrich was showing total indifference to her, and the rare sex they had would finish in him pecking her cheek and crawling back to his half of the bed. As for the money, it was as bad as ever — Vika did not have any! And she was feeling now much more done in.

"You aren't looking happy at all," Greta said to her at breakfast one day. "Why aren't you eating?"

"Thanks, frau," said Vika downheartedly, "but I don't want to."

"You should eat something or else you won't be strong enough to do your work."

"It's impossible, eating the same food every morning," Vika said, almost crying. "The child needs vitamins, eggs, fish, cottage cheese, and not only a piece of bread and tasteless porridge."

"I do buy those products sometimes," Greta said, taking offense. "We can't spend all the money for food."

"One can't spend it for food, can't spend it for clothes," Vika grumbled slowly, "what can one spend it for? It's cold in this house, and I'm dressed like a beggar, always making things over for Maria. I'm penniless," Vika stopped short.

"Your life isn't bad at all," Greta said quietly. "Just stop worrying and proceed with the documents."

"But you're driving everywhere with me, don't you see I cannot find anyone?" Vika gasped. "I have no idea where I can turn. Possibly Heinrich could address the powers officially and ask for the documents for me?!"

"Are you all right?" Greta was scared. "Do you mean to bring him to destruction? Don't you even dare ask for it! He'll never do a thing like that."

"Very well," Vika said slowly. "Then we'll have to do it on our own."

But all her endeavors were fruitless so far. Greta was helping as much as she could, and even began to lend Vika her car to go to another town to do the search.

"Just don't let the police get you," Greta said, handing her the car keys. "Or else I'll have to say you have stolen it from me."

"Thank you, frau," answered Vika, "I'll be very careful. But you need to be a real trickster to avoid a meeting with the police here. They're so numerous...they're everywhere, like an army cantoned in the town."

"So, just try to avoid new problems," Greta instructed her.

Time was passing, and the right people did not come along, and Vika called her mom again. But for some reason, nobody answered the phone, and after a pause, a voice said that the number was not in service. Vika dialed Sergei's number again, but every time the same woman's voice answered her call, and she would hang up the receiver without uttering a word.

Chapter 54

IN THE SUMMER, Greta decided to restore the house, to make some refurbishments, to paint, glue, and replace little things everywhere. She called in some workers from outside for the major work, but most of the painting and doing up, fell on Vika.

Day in and out she was working around the house, choking with the smell of the paint and falling off her feet with exhaustion. Little by little, the house was taking on a fresh look, and by the end of the summer, it was finished. But somehow Vika could not recover from her fatigue; she felt unwell and took to more frequent walks with Maria in the park behind the house.

One day, while sitting in the garden house, she bent down to her daughter playing on the floor and felt that it was somehow difficult for her to bend, as if something were hindering her. She touched her stomach. *Seems like there's nothing to get fatter with,* Vika thought, *I should practice morning exercises.* But suddenly she felt an obvious movement inside her body.

"Oh no, not this!" she uttered aloud in horror, and put her hand on her stomach again. The movement repeated.

Vika began to recall feverishly when she had had her last period. And she figured out that it had been sometime late in the spring.

"I am so stupid!" Vika exclaimed angrily, jumping up from the bench. "How could I have been so busy that I didn't even notice it? Those damned repairs!"

She couldn't calm down, pacing the garden house, tortured by questions.

"Something should be done, immediately!" she stopped short in her pacing, "Children are out of the question," Vika picked up Maria and rushed into the house with her.

"Schu-ultz!" she shouted right from the porch. "I need to talk to you," and without putting down her daughter, she dashed up the staircase. Greta, frightened, looked out of the kitchen.

Heinrich Schultz was at the desk in his office. He pouted at Vika, who had just run in.

"You must be crazy to behave like that," he uttered, looking at her with contempt.

"I am crazy!" Vika put down her daughter. "I am pregnant!"

"I knew all along you were unpredictable," he sneered turning off the table.

"But I don't need that child, either," Vika said sharply, and faltered. "I need a doctor! Now! Do you understand?"

Heinrich was sitting and examining Vika in silence.

"I never thought," he began slowly, "that my child would be from a Russian."

"No child whatsoever!" she uttered, and coming up to his table, put the telephone closer to him. "Call, please, call Vanessa now!"

"She's not a women's doctor," he pushed the telephone away, "I've already told you."

"But she might recommend a doctor to turn to," Vika said firmly, pushing the telephone closer to him again.

"I'll think it over," Heinrich said dryly, looking at Vika angrily.

"It is urgent!" She took Maria and left the room. From that day, she moved back into her room again.

Days passed, but Heinrich did not seek a doctor, nor did he call Vanessa. Greta moved around the house, smiling, trying to do part of the housework herself again.

"Why don't you want to help me?" Vika asked Heinrich a few days later. "You don't want the child either!"

"Why not?" He answered unexpectedly, in a quiet voice. "I'm not that young now, and I will only be happy to see my own child."

"What?" Vika half-whispered in horror. "And what about me? What am I to do with two children?"

"Don't worry," he said sympathetically. "You better not be nervous now. It's a sin to have an abortion."

"What about to have children with no future, isn't that a sin?" Vika almost shouted. "What can I offer them? How are they to live having no documents?"

She choked with emotions, helpless, hardly able to keep herself in check.

"Listen to me, Heinrich," Vika said as quietly as possible, pulling herself together. "You know I'm not in a position now to have another child. I ask you, please, help me with the doctor. Give me the money for the abortion."

"No, Vika, I won't take a sin like that on myself," he answered calmly. "Plus, we have everything the baby needs."

Vika backed off and went to her room without saying another word. She had heard or read somewhere that lifting heavy things may result in miscarriage.

And Vika moved all the furniture in the house lifting it on one side and on another. But the child persisted in developing and in the winter, aided again by Vanessa, Vika gave birth to a boy.

Schultz was very glad, glancing at the child, but never moved a finger to make any documents for him. Vika named the boy Stanislaw.

* * * * *

Heinrich watched begrudgingly how she was treating his son, not even hiding his detest for Vika, and one day he said that he should hire a nurse for the boy, a real German woman, so that Vika would not affect him badly with her communist behavior.

"Why? How can you say a thing like that?" Vika said, taking offense and holding the child in her arms. "Stanislaw is my son, isn't he?"

"You've got a daughter," he interrupted sharply. "Now raise her so that she won't be like you."

"Heinrich, what's wrong with you?" Vika asked in anguish, "Why have you become so cross with me? What for?"

"I haven't become cross!" he said dryly. "I've always been like that. But something has changed with the birth of my son. And I want to have order in everything. Tell Maria, that Muslim girl, not to touch him with her dirty hands."

Vika stood up from the chair.

"Well, firstly," she uttered distinctly and slowly, "my daughter is not a Muslim! She isn't baptized at all. And secondly, Maria is a sister to your son."

"That's the horror of it!" Heinrich said angrily and left the room. Vika was standing with Stanislaw in her arms, panting.

"I wouldn't talk to him like that," Greta said apprehensively in an undertone, casting glances at the door. "Don't make him angry, be kinder to him. Who are you here? Did you forget that?"

Vika Zotova silently turned her face to Greta, waiting for her to say something else.

"You should understand, Vika," Greta went on instructively, "that it is preferable for you to be yielding now, so that he should not choose to call the police." Greta moved closer to Vika and almost whispered, "They would arrest you and leave the children here. Do you understand? He will foster them and all the problems with documents for the children will be solved."

Vika was watching Greta with an unchanged face. She had already thought about it, but on hearing things like that from Greta, understood instantly that those were Heinrich's words. Without saying a word Vika took the children and went to her room.

The fat is in the fire, it's high time to run! she thought. The horror of the whole reality was pressing her hard. *My Lord, I should have run away from here a long time ago...home...to Russia! No matter what happens...even if I'm imprisoned, I'll serve the term and quit, but my children will have documents there.*

Vika unfolded the map and began studying it, as she had done quite a number of times before, at a loss as to where she should run. *Well, was it in vain after all that I was shown that cave,* she thought hopelessly. *I should find it. No matter what happens, I should reach our border and cross it somewhere!* Vika was scared and gave way to tears.

"Sergei, Sergei..." she said aloud. "Help me! How much I need your help now."

The children cuddled silently to their mother, wiping her tears, looking at her sadly, not knowing how to help. Vika pressed them to her bosom.

"Now, please grow kids. My son, please, grow up as quickly as possible," she whispered, "you'll have to walk on your own feet and eat everything that adults eat."

From that day, Vika changed her behavior cardinally. She chirruped merrily with the people in the house, doing her regular work. Sometimes she would jokingly hug and peck Heinrich on the cheek, paying no attention to his turning away squeamishly, and if possible, she would steal small sums of money, saving it for her escape.

Chapter 55

TIME WAS PASSING. Heinrich Schultz watched in amazement as the merry Vika played with the children, and had no suspicions whatsoever about her intentions. Stanislaw was growing without giving Vika any troubles. He was growing into a strong and very quiet boy. Maria played with him with pleasure mixing Russian and German words, as Vika spoke to her only in Russian and Greta German. But when Heinrich came, the girl would draw apprehensively apart from Stanislaw, hiding behind her mother, for he did not let her play with her brother.

Vika retained outward calmness, pitying her daughter and showing no sign of her displeasure. She was waiting. And the children, as if anticipating something important, were growing obedient and became bosom friends.

Stanislaw began to walk when he was ten months old, and by the summer, he could already run freely. Greta often gave Vika her car for going out on business, but never let her travel by herself with both children.

Vika was waiting for a handy occasion, as she had actually chosen her route. But Greta was unyielding. She always left Stanislaw at home or got grudgingly into the car together with the children. Time was moving on, and Vika already began to worry seriously.

But one morning Greta was really out of sorts and could hardly walk to the kitchen to have breakfast.

"Oh, I do feel somewhat crooked and shaky," she complained to Vika. "Probably it's going to rain. This headache, too…" Greta rubbed her temples.

"Take these pills to relieve the headache," Vika passed her a glass of water and the pills. "Please, go to bed to relax and we'll take a drive to a park, so as not to make noise."

"You can walk behind the house as well," Greta grumbled discontentedly, but did not insist. She took the pills and retired to her room.

Vika glanced at the children.

"Maria," she said embracing her little daughter, "you have always been a good girl, so do help mummy now, will you?"

"I will!"

"Now quickly finish your breakfast and finish feeding Stanislaw. I'll go get ready. We must do everything very quickly now. Do you see what I mean?"

"Yes, Mom, I see," Maria answered with her mouth full of food.

Vika gave her a peck and almost running to her room. She had long ago stored everything necessary for the journey, so taking a blanket and some pillows, she carried it all down to the car and came back to the kitchen again.

Maria was finishing eating and scolding her brother for lingering. Vika smiled on hearing her and, coming up, tapped them approvingly on the heads.

"You're the best children in the world, you really are!" she said tenderly. "And the best team, too! Come on, little Stanislaw, finish it quickly and off we go."

Checking the cupboards in the kitchen Vika found some food to eat on the way and carried them to the car. She returned and took the children to her room to change clothes.

When they were quite ready, Vika looked around once more, lest she had forgotten anything of importance.

"Well, kids, let's now sit down for a moment before we go," she suggested in an undertone, "and say a prayer, so God will help us to get home. Repeat after me, my girl."

Vika began to say a short prayer. Maria repeated as best as she could, mangling the words and adding an invention of her own. Vika grinned as she was listening to her daughter and, upon finishing, squatted in front of the children. The kids were sitting like two little sparrows looking at their mother attentively.

"You're my little darlings," Vika said nervously, taking each of them by the hand. "Listen to me attentively." She looked seriously into the eyes of both. "Now you must be very obedient! No crying! If I say 'hush,' it means you must be silent and not utter a sound. Got it?" Vika said this strictly and they, casting glances at each other, nodded in agreement.

"Starting with this minute you're to be grown ups! It is very important!" she continued, pressing the kids to her bosom for a moment. "And now—off we go!" Vika got to her feet and, looking around once more, took the children out of the house quickly.

She placed them on the rear seat and showed them how to move the back seat and hide in the luggage trunk. There, she had arranged a comfortable sleeping berth for them. Once more Vika checked the money and Greta's passport she had taken, just to be on the safe side. She had also prepared some glue and her own photo to stick on it later on, saying, "God bless!" she headed off.

* * * * *

Vika quickly drove out of the town to the highway and headed to the south of the country. In a few hours she was driving up to the first border. She trembled with the thought that it might be her last one.

At the last station where they stopped for a few minutes to buy gasoline and put themselves in order, Vika hid the children in the luggage compartment, and was at a loss as to whether she should put on the wig or just go as she was. Pausing to think for a while, she decided not to camouflage herself. She just put on a little makeup and loosened her hair and set forth to the border.

Vika slowed down her speed, as she saw the cars in a line, slowly driving up to the check-point. Vika was following a truck. She had the jitters. Driving by men in military uniform, Vika smiled modestly at them. Having stopped the truck ahead of her, they let her pass. And again, she headed along the course she had planned.

In a few hours, Vika crossed the narrow band, another country's territory and, after a short stop to have a rest, she rode on nearing a border once more. The vehicles were stopped randomly and Vika was lucky again to pass this part of the way without trouble.

After going through several hours of nervous stress, she gave a sigh of relief and tears poured from her eyes. She had to quickly find a cheap hotel before it got dark, and then in the morning, go as far as possible to the south of the country.

The kids left their hiding place and were chirruping merrily in the rear seat, casting glances at their mother.

"Thank you, my sweet little friends," Vika said, sobbing. "You behaved wonderfully! Well done!" and she stroked them tenderly.

Vika settled in for the night in a small inn near the highway. It smelt of rot and mice, but she was happy putting the children to bed by her side. She had made the first step homeward and had done so much for this moment. *It's long since I called Sergei,* she thought, going to sleep. *I should call him tomorrow.*

Chapter 56

GRETA WOKE UP after lunch and stayed in bed for some time, listening for sounds. It was too quiet in the house.

She stood up and went to the children's room. When she looked around, she immediately saw that some things were missing. Awareness slowly crept in and she lagged to the kitchen, examining everything around her.

She searched cases and found that some food items were gone. She sat, doomed, on a chair and stared out the window, still hoping for something.

Greta sat at the window for a long time, deep in her thoughts. At last she realized that Vika had run away, she started to cry. She loved the children with all her heart, and had already taken a fancy to Vika. She liked that young girl, because Vika was light-hearted, easy-going, and diligent.

Greta did everything she could to keep Vika with her and lighten her old age. And now she moved in tears around the place, looking in corners, as if she could find them there. But the house was empty.

In the evening, Heinrich Schultz came home from his work. After his greeting, he stole a look at Greta and began to go upstairs. But something in her appearance surprised him and he stopped, suspiciously peering at his housekeeper's reddened eyes.

"What's the matter?" he asked. "Where's Vika?"

"She went to the park with the children," Greta answered in a low voice.

"What does that mean, with the children?" Heinrich said slowly, going downstairs. "I told you, you must go with them or leave Stanislaw at home."

"I felt so bad in the morning and stayed in my room," Greta answered guiltily.

"When did they go?" he got nervous, making for Vika's room.

"In the m-morning," Greta wiped her tears.

"In the morning? And you didn't call me the whole day?"

"I thought they would come back."

Heinrich began to rush around the rooms, panting and banging doors.

"I'm calling the police!" he blurted out, making for the telephone.

"And what will you tell them?"

"That my child has been kidnapped!" Heinrich cried.

"What child?" Greta stopped him. "You have no documents for this boy."

"This is my son!" he shouted angrily, and froze at the telephone, without lifting the receiver.

"I'll kill her!" he turned to Greta, "The moment she comes back I'll throw her out and immediately call the police."

Greta started to cry quietly.

"You can't call the police when she comes back," she said in a low voice. "Then you'll be asked how she turned up at your place and why you didn't report her to the authorities for such a long time."

"I told you we should have thrown her away a long time ago," Heinrich threateningly moved closer to her.

Greta looked straight into his eyes, wiping her tears and pursing her lips. He stepped back, blinking, and started to pace the room, cursing at Vika.

"Why do you hate her so much?" Greta asked. "She is such a nice girl, and everything was in your hands."

"Don't tell me anything about her," he shook his fists. "The little Eastern bitch! If I had called that Muslim at the very beginning, I would at least have his money! And now she has kidnapped my son!"

Schultz was beyond himself, rushing up and down the house, and every second looking towards the gate.

"He is her son, too," Greta sighed deeply. "Indeed, you're right, we should have called the police immediately, and maybe she would be happier now."

"What are you talking about?" he stopped and looked at Greta.

"We both know..." she said quietly, "and this is my sin, that I didn't tell her anything. Though she loves her motherland, she may wish in such circumstances to stay here forever. But I knew, when she became free she would not stay at your place, because you treated her badly."

"And you think," Heinrich hissed angrily, "that after picking her up in the street I should give her my credit card and keys to the safe?"

"Then you should have called the police," said Greta firmly, "but not take advantage of her and have a child!"

"You blame me?" asked Heinrich, sniffing scornfully and turning away from her as he stared out the window.

"Call the police," he said quietly some time later. "I can't just wait around, doing nothing. Call and tell them that your car has been stolen. Maybe they can find her like that." He turned to Greta, short of breath.

"We can't call the police for them to come to our place," Greta said sadly. "Tomorrow in the morning you'll drive me to a shop, and I will call from there, and say that my car was stolen from a parking lot."

"But they may not find Vika!" Heinrich raising his eyes to her, filled with horror. "And I may never see my son again," he clutched his head with his hands. "I lost my child..." Heinrich croaked. "I lost my dear boy..."

Heinrich staggered to the second floor, stumbling as if he was blind. Nobody slept in the house that night. And in the morning, on his way to the office, he took Greta to a shop. She reported that her car was stolen.

After some time, she was paid the total insurance amount, and it seemed that everything sorted itself out. But there was no peace in their house. Heinrich and Greta felt deserted and guilty.

Schultz kept listening to the news, hoping to hear something about Vika and thoroughly read the gutter press, peering at the photos. But there was nothing about Vika. *How could I find her?* he thought, sitting regularly with the paper. *Do I need to run an advertisement for Vika's disappearance? But maybe her name is not Vika...what have I done? Where is my baby son?*

He sobbed, feeling at last the whole weight of his loss. And Greta cried, moving quietly around the house, and sometimes she heard the merry voices of children and Vika's laughter.

Chapter 57

VIKA WAS AWAKENED early the next morning by noisy swearing outside the window. She opened her eyes and for a long time couldn't comprehend where she was. With great effort, she collected her thoughts and remembered everything. She quietly stood up and pushed aside the curtain, trying to see the arguing people.

Two people, a man and a woman, were getting into a car, waving their hands and yelling something at each other. Vika smiled, watching the scene and looking at the part of the street she could see.

Small buildings, painted in different colours with crackled and peeled-off paint here and there, stood snuggled to each other, with only a few narrow passes between them.

A great amount of bright signs were heaped along the whole length of the street, advertising various shops and bars, showing their names. A clothes line was drawn from the second floor of the neighbouring building across the street to an opposite building, and drying clothes hung on it.

Vika smiled and again lay down in the bed with the children. She gently and thoughtfully looked at her children's faces. They resembled each other in some way and both looked like their mother. Vika cuddled them to herself and kissed each on their cheeks. Maria woke up at once. She always slept lightly. Widely opening her brown eyes, she looked at her mom.

"Good morning, Mommy," she chattered, stretching herself sweetly. "Let's get up?"

"Okay," Vika smiled back, and they got up, leaving Stanislaw still sleeping.

Vika checked her food supplies and, leaving a part of them for breakfast, packed the rest.

"We have to eat quickly and drive further," she told Maria.

"Where?" the girl asked, seating herself on her mother's lap.

"Now only to the south," answered Vika quietly, "and then we go home, to Russia. We're Russian! But don't tell anybody about it, okay?!"

"Okay," the girl answered, delighted.

"And now wake up your little brother and let's have breakfast," Vika pushed Maria lightly. She jumped from her mother's lap and merrily ran to the bed.

"Stanislaw, Stanislaw, wake up quickly, we go to Russia!" cried Maria.

Vika laughed and decided it would be better not to tell them about her future plans.

In an hour they were already on the road, going further to the south of the country. The sun shone brightly as in summer and a light warm wind blew in the open windows of the car. The road went through mountains and villages, curving smoothly and nearing the coast.

Vika breathed in the obvious smell of the sea, and driving a little further, she saw a beautiful panorama in front of her. For the first time in her life she saw the sea and came to a standstill at the sight of the wide expanse.

The endless azure surface of the water went far away and merged with a horizon of nearly the same colour. Boats of different sizes quickly moved close to the shore, and giant ships were seen in the distance, though it was not quite clear whether they stood in one place or continued their route on the expanse of sea.

The sea was on one side of the road, coming closer from time to time and then moving away from the road, winding in the mountains. In some places the green abundance covered the mountains like a terry carpet, but often bare rocks frozen on slopes in their movement towards the sea, came close to the roadside or hung over it. And there were small cottages among this variety and elegance of nature.

Vika occasionally looked around, trying to drive the car carefully. She kept going hot and cold at the sight of a police patrol, but nobody ever stopped her. She safely arrived at a large port city that evening. Her plan was to find a Russian ship and ask a captain to take her with the children to Russia, and there she would come up with something.

Vika found a small hotel to settle in that she could afford with her money close to the sea port, if only one could call it a hotel. It was more like on old, small building. She planned to stay there for a short period, as her money and food supply didn't let her stay long. Vika was determined to implement her plan quickly.

The next day after breakfast she went to see the city and the port. It was very noisy in the streets, full of many idly walking people.

Vika was impressed with the smiles and hospitality of the people. For the first time in several years she heard a lot of compliments on her part. She was captured by the general movement, and she felt herself already a part of that diverse crowd, and merrily walked with the children in the direction of the port.

Vika saw many ships and boats under different flags, but none of them was under the red flag of her country. She walked along the embankment, listening to multilingual speech, but didn't hear a single Russian word. And after looking at the ships, she understood that they were all passenger ships. Unfortunately, Vika didn't know where to look for cargo vessels.

Realizing that her plan was not in the least an easy one, Vika became upset and sadly went to one of cafés to get lunch for the children. She was met by a kind, smiling cook, who right there in the street, fried and cooked something on the fire. And while Vika was studying the menu, he already managed to talk with her children and ask about their names.

Quickly choosing something for the children, Vika sat at one of the tables, as far as possible from the cook. She was obviously served more food than she ordered and additionally was given a glass, in which a waiter began to pour wine.

Vika got scared, seeing what he was doing.

"Many thanks, but I didn't order wine," she said in German, covering the glass with her hand. The waiter smiled kindly, pointing to the side.

"It's from him," he said. And Vika looked in that direction. The cook merrily waved to her. She decently smiled back, slightly bowing her head gratefully.

"Thanks," she repeated again, shifting her gaze to the waiter and not removing her hand from the glass. "Thank you, but no wine for me."

He smiled confusedly and went away, taking the wine with him.

Vika fed the children, without taking her eyes off the port, thinking about what to do next. *Probably, this is a small port,* she thought. *Maybe the Russian ships don't arrive here. Maybe I need to go further south.*

Upset by such unexpected circumstances, Vika returned to the hotel and decided to drive further in the morning. Counting her money again, she decided not to visit any more cafés, but limited herself to buying food in small shops.

The next day Vika went to another town and, after straying for a long time in its streets, at last found a port and a cheap hotel.

She remembered how, long ago, she was surprised at the narrowness of the streets she was seeing now. Everything was situated so closely that it seemed there was no space for people or vehicles.

Cars at night, well as during the daytime, stood on pavements, closely pressed to the houses' walls near their owners' windows. But Vika was afraid to park Greta's car close to her hotel, leaving it always somewhere in the neighbouring street and reaching the hotel on foot.

Chapter 58

FOR TWO DAYS Vika Zotova went to the port, where she hoped to find her countrymen, but fortune didn't smile on her. And seeing her money vanishing, she began to look for a job.

She grew very thin and looked like a beggar in her old jeans. Nobody was in a hurry to employ such a worker. But finally, she was lucky and got a night job with scanty wages — cleaning a corner restaurant.

The owner frightfully pestered her, asking her to go to bed with him. Vika firmly refused, and at the end of the week, he paid her only half of the amount agreed upon. Vika was upset and came back to her hotel on the verge of tears. Answering the sympathetic questions of the front desk lady, she told her the reason behind her low spirits.

"Calm down. Stop crying." The lady took the telephone and looked for the number she needed. "I know of a restaurant, not so far away...recently, they talked about how a cleaning lady was needed." She found the telephone number and called. After a short conversation, she gave Vika directions to the place, and Vika immediately went to the given address.

Vika was greeted amiably and shown her work. The restaurant was much larger than the previous one, and was run by an elderly pair.

"You may start already, this evening," the woman said, smiling. "Don't worry, you're not alone, we always have two people to do the cleaning at night."

"Thank you," Vika answered modestly. The hostess looked at her attentively.

"Let's go and I'll show you the fridge, in which we leave food for you," and she pulled Vika's sleeve.

Vika looked with surprise at the hostess, because at her previous work, all the cupboards and refrigerators were locked. From that night on, she did not starve and could even always bring something to the children.

* * * * *

Driving around the town, Vika found a beautiful square with a small fountain, quite close to her hotel, and she began to go there sometimes with the children for a walk.

She did not feel lonely with her children. It always seemed to her that in some short time she would go home. But all the same, she was afraid to be in a strange town and she was not pleased with the compliments of gentlemen, as men in her close circle always wanted to go to bed with her.

Drunken sailors, scrambling out of numerous beer bar basements, would say things to her, trying to entice her. Running home from her work at night, Vika understood that she lived in a very dangerous district. And after hearing another brawl and fight of the neighbours, she moved to another hotel, which was a littler better and closer to her work.

The next day, she had a short rest after her work and went to the port with the children. Vika was walking a new way, and thought about Sergei Nilovski and her life here. Suddenly she saw a post office right in front of her.

She stopped in thought, wondering whether or not to spend her scanty income on useless telephone calls. And at that time, a gentleman opened the door, smiling, and invited them to come in.

Vika hesitantly went in and saw at once a vacant booth. *Well,* she thought, *let me try once more to get through to somebody, since the door is open and there is a vacant telephone...maybe this time I'll be lucky?* And she dialled Sergei's home number.

"Hello," Vika heard his voice in the receiver. "Hello."

She immediately was at a loss...stopped breathing, and opened her mouth like a fish, without uttering a sound.

"Hello," Nilovski repeated again, patiently waiting for an answer.

"Sergei..." Vika could only say in a faint voice. The receiver went silent for a second.

"Where are you?"

Vika named the town and the country.

"Stay there, I'll find you," he said quickly and hung up the receiver.

Vika vacantly looked at the silent telephone, and tears began slowly to flow from her eyes. She didn't believe what had happened, and still heard the voice of Sergei in her head.

Wiping her tears, she slowly came out of the booth, and a gentleman came to her and started to ask something.

"Sorry, I don't understand you," Vika answered in German.

"Are you okay? Do you need any help?" he repeated at once in German.

"No, thank you, now I'm fine!"

Vika went into the street, still unable to come to her senses, and absentmindedly went back to the hotel again. *Sergei, how could you find me in such a big town?* she thought suddenly with fear. And she immediately remembered, how he told her once what to do if you got lost in a foreign town.

Vika thought a little and ran to the front desk to ask where the main town square was located. The lady took a small map and started to show a whole list of squares.

"Oh, so many!" Vika was confused. "Thank you. I think I'll never find them."

Without hesitation, she at once took her children and drove in the car to check which square looked more like the main one.

In the evening, Vika was completely at a loss and unable to define the main square. The nearest one, with the fountain, seemed not quite so bad to her. She decided to drive around the town once more and in the morning, would choose where to wait for Sergei.

But in the morning, when she came to the parking lot, Vika saw an empty place. She came to a standstill, not knowing what to think — was the car stolen or taken by the police? Vika anxiously looked around and went back to the hotel.

The theft determined the choice of the meeting place and, after grieving a little over the car, Vika started to go every day by noon to the nearest square. The children merrily played near the fountain, frightening numerous pigeons away, and Vika nervously looked around, afraid to miss Sergei.

But days passed, and he still did not come, and she cried in despair, returning to the hotel and beginning to realize that maybe Nilovski would never come.

Chapter 59

VIKA CONTINUED HER night work and at noon invariably went with the children to the square. Her wish to get some sleep took over and, standing near the fountain, she sadly stared in the water. Then one day, she heard a quiet voice behind her, "Hello."

Vika startled and slowly turned towards the voice, still not believing what she had heard. In front of her stood Sergei Nilovski! She had no strength to say anything and looked at him, opening her eyes wide and holding her breath. He abruptly clasped her to himself, seeing that her eyes were filling with tears.

For some time they stood embraced and silent, coping with overflowing feelings.

"We must go away," said Sergei quietly and, at that moment, the children ran to them, and put their arms around their mother's legs.

He looked down at the children. "Whose children are these?"

"Mine," Vika breathed out.

Some confusion emerged. Sergei looked at the children in unhappy surprise.

"Let's go away," he said, getting control of himself. "Where do you live?"

"Not far from here."

"Okay, come on," Sergei put his arms around Vika's shoulders.

When they went into Vika's room, he embraced her again and started to kiss her, running one hand through her hair.

"I imagined our meeting so many times," Sergei whispered, controlling his tears with difficulty. "Let me just look at you," and he cautiously pushed her away from him. Vika cried.

"No, this is not a dream," he again pressed her to himself. "My girl is with me. Please, do not disappear from my life again," he became silent, swallowing tears.

"Thank you Sergei," Vika whispered.

"What for?"

"That you haven't forgotten me and you came."

"I would come to the world's end for you," Sergei pressed her to himself again. "I need nobody but you. Thank you for surviving. I must apologize to you, forgive me."

"Come on, Nilovski, what happened — happened. It's not in our power to change the past. Don't blame yourself. I survived only because I thought about you...believed that I would see you again," tears choked her and she buried herself in his chest, having no strength to continue talking.

The children sat on the bed, quietly cuddled up to each other, and watched the scene. Stanislaw looked blank and at last, started crying, too.

"Well...that's it, enough," Sergei said, as gratefully as he could, and he looked at the children. "It's the end of the water kingdom. Let's get acquainted," he took Vika's hand and went to the children.

"What's your name?" he gave his hand to the girl.

"Maria," she answered uncertainly, looking at her mother.

"And your name?" Sergei turned his eyes to the boy.

"His name is Stanislaw," the sister answered for him.

"They're good children!" said Sergei, squatting down in front of them and gently cuddling them to himself.

"Forgive me, Sergei," Vika said quietly, close to him. He pressed his finger to his lips.

"Ts-s-s...say nothing. We'll talk later."

He stood up and, taking her by her shoulders, looked into her eyes.

"Nothing happened, do you hear me? No-thing," Sergei said under his breath. "Forget everything! I'm happy that you are alive."

He sighed deeply, pressed her to himself and looked around the room.

"I'm short of time," he said a little bit later. "I've been here for three days already, and we must decide what to do now."

They sat on the bed.

"First," Sergei said, "right now we need to move to a normal hotel. Come on, Vika, get ready. Second," he was obviously nervous, biting his lip. "What documents do you have? Show them to me."

"Nothing," Vika said faintly. "Only a passport, that is not mine."

"And for the children?"

"No documents for them, either."

"Well..." Sergei rubbed his temples. "I've provided a passport for you, but I knew nothing about the children. And any transfer with them is a big problem."

Vika stopped packing her bag and worriedly looked at Sergei.

"Tell me how to arrange for documents," she said quietly. "I'll stay here to prepare them, and you go home. I'll come when they're ready."

"No! I won't leave you here alone. We'll think of something."

"I had a plan, Sergei," she said sadly. "To find a Russian ship and ask them to take me...or to find a ship of the country, where that cave is, do you remember it? And ask to take me with them."

"My girl, you can't even imagine how dangerous it is for a lady with absolutely no rights, to be alone on a ship where only men are. And have you thought about the children?"

"Indeed, I thought about them," Vika sobbed. "I want them to lead a normal life."

"We have to think it over quickly," Sergei said in a low voice. "For now, get ready, let's go to another hotel."

She quickly threw her few things into her bag and looked around the room.

"We're ready," and she took Stanislaw into her arms. Sergei picked up the bag and they went out.

"I'll rent a car," said Sergei.

"Wait a moment," Vika stopped him when they were passing the restaurant where she worked. "I need to drop in and get my wages."

"Did you work here?"

"Yes, I had no money at all," Vika said shyly, and went inside the building.

* * * * *

They settled in a decent hotel as a man and wife under the assumed names and documents which Sergei Nilovski had. Entering the room, he attentively looked Vika over.

"You won't manage the trip," he said sadly. "You have become so thin. And the children..."

"Don't be afraid, Sergei," Vika smiled shyly. "The children are well-behaved and I'm strong."

"I know," he drew her to himself. "Now let's go to a shop and buy you some proper clothes and things we all need."

"Maybe we shouldn't spend money? I'll manage with what I have. Everything is so expensive here!"

"My Victoria...I'll begrudge nothing for you. Let's go!"

They went shopping, leaving the children to play in the room. Sergei himself chose things for Vika, even underclothes, as she firmly refused to buy anything for herself.

"Try this on," he gave her a green tracksuit. "You may use it on the trip."

When Vika put on the tracksuit, she went out to show it to Sergei.

"Of course we will take this tracksuit," he said, looking at her. "You're a real beauty in it!"

"Oh, Nilovski, the tracksuit is beautiful, not me," she laughed, and he went to choose toys for the children.

When they bought everything they needed, they came back to the hotel and then Sergei left them and drove away. Some time later he came back, smiling.

"That's all," he said. "I have agreed and the day after tomorrow, we set out to sea and go to another country."

And he named it.

"But it's not at all what we need," Vika was surprised.

"Now that's not important," said Sergei. "We simply must start to go closer to our border. And there we'll quickly go to the cave. It is very dangerous," he said seriously. "But I have absolutely no time to get the documents ready, and with the children, we can hardly choose another way."

Vika was under quite a strain while she listened to him. Mentally she prepared herself for the crossing, but now, with the cave obviously so close, she was terrified with memories.

"Relax," said Sergei and embraced his girlfriend. "It won't be soon, maybe by that time something different will turn up. And now we go out to eat."

He came to the children, sat on the floor near them, and embraced both of them.

"Well, young people, how are you?"

"Fine," Maria answered glibly. But Stanislaw, very stiff, quietly began to move aside, cautiously casting sidelong looks at him. Sergei laughed and took him in his lap.

"No, my friend, now you'll be with me," he said, embracing the boy and looking attentively at the child's face. "Well, you have your mom's green eyes!"

Vika sat with them on the floor and Sergei embraced her too.

"Everything will be fine, Vika," he said comfortingly. "We have to put up with this a bit longer and everything will be sorted out!"

"Thank you, dear," Vika smiled gratefully, putting her head on his shoulder.

Chapter 60

THIS WAS THEIR first night. They came back to the hotel after the restaurant, bathed the children, and then Vika put them to bed, while Sergei went to shower.

He was in bed already when Vika, having put the children to bed, went to the bathroom. Upon walking out in a light nightgown, Vika was dumb struck, looking at the room.

There was a bottle of champagne, and chocolate and fruit on the small table. A flickering candle light was spread around the room. Sergei came up, took her in his arms, circled her around the room, and began kissing her.

"I love you, Sergei," whispered Vika. "I never new how much I loved you!"

He covered her lips with his kiss. Then, looking into her eyes, pronounced quietly, "You're my life, Victoria! I love you more than life!" he kissed her again and sat her on the bed, and opened the bottle of champagne.

"Let's have a drink, my dear," he said, giving a glass of champagne to her, and taking the second one for himself. "Let's drink to our meeting!"

They touched their glasses and took a sip, eating chocolate.

"Let's drink some more," Sergei filled the glasses again. "Let's drink to our love," he kneeled down next to Vika. "I was close to death without you then," he breathed out, looking into her eyes. "I was living only with the hope that I would find you."

"Me too," she said quietly. "I love you, Sergei!"

"I love you, Vika!" Sergei echoed, and the glasses clinked together.

"To our love!" they said together and finished drinking champagne.

That was their night - nothing similar had Vika had in her life. She was drowning in his love and caresses...his voice, his hands, his lips, his body...she was dying of happiness! He was her entire world! Her universe!

But the night seemed to be too short for them, and like a fast bird, it was getting to be morning...and they fell asleep only at dawn, snuggling each other.

The children woke them up in the morning. Nilovski did not allow Vika to get up and ordered breakfast to their room.

"Let's forget all out troubles," he said tenderly to her, serving coffee. "Let these days be happy for us." Vika smiled at him shyly, in return feeling infinitely happy.

By lunchtime they set out to look for the children's park that Sergei had noticed not far from there. And having found it, they entertained themselves there till night, enjoying swings and merry-go-rounds together with the kids. They were happy to see each other, and forgetting everything else, kept kissing again and again.

Returning to the hotel, they had dinner and Vika put the kids to bed. Then she and Sergei went down to the café.

"It's our last night over here," Sergei said, handing a glass of wine to Vika. "Tomorrow night we will use a boat to get to the ship. And further on we'll have to move pretty quickly. We won't have another rest until we're in Russia."

Vika was looking at Sergei happily.

"Let's drink, Victoria, to our lucky way back home!" Clinking their glasses together, they tasted the wine.

The café was mildly lit and was gradually filling with people. Near their table there was a small statue with a fountain decorated with flowers all around. Beautiful, tranquil music could be heard and they were drinking wine, talking, and gazing at passers-by.

"I have a kind of sneaking fear, Sergei," Vika uttered in an undertone, "as if something is going to happen..."

"We'll be doing our utmost so that nothing happens," he answered gently, hugging her.

"What if they put me in jail there?"

"They won't," Sergei answered with diffidence. "They oughtn't...I will fight for you." He fell silent, lost in thought. "And should something of the kind happen," he was biting his lip nervously, "we will be waiting for you — the kids and me."

There hung a silence. Vika was slowly sipping her remaining wine.

"What a beautiful night," she said sadly. "Look at how many people are here, and all of them are doing whatever they want to. They're happy...shall we perhaps stay here? We'll make our documents and start living like everybody else."

Sergei gave a heavy sigh.

"No way," he replied, also in a low voice. "Firstly, we may be found at any moment. Secondly, who are we here? What are you going to do here? Thirdly," he continued melancholically, "there is no place, Victoria, better and dearer to you than your own country. In a foreign land, nobody really needs you; while at home—the walls at home are your friends, your comfort, and you're helping hands. Weren't you homesick, missing Russia?"

"Oh, very, very much!" Vika sighed deeply.

"So that's why we are going to make our way home." He kissed her. "And there, if everything is all right, we'll send the children to a kindergarten, you will go to college, and life will straighten out."

Sergei Nilovski called up the waiter and ordered more wine and snacks. They were sitting and talking for a long time, and it was only after midnight that they returned to the hotel. The wine was making them dizzy, and all through the rest of the night, they were lost in their love, never letting go of each other. And it was only at early dawn that they dropped into a short sleep.

* * * * *

A part of the day was spent merrily with the kids, relaxing and getting ready for the trip. After lunch, they went for a walk, bought some food, then came back to the hotel and went to bed, in order to set out at night.

In total darkness, they made their way in a boat to the right ship and got aboard noiselessly. They were being waited for there and were taken somewhere very deep down in the boat.

"Don't worry," Sergei said soothingly, closing the cabin door behind him. "It may perhaps be noisy here, but the way is not very long, and we shall have to suffer through it."

He looked at his watch and started examining the room, opening another door.

"Now, the countdown has started," he said gently. "There is water and a toilet here, and we have enough food. We will relax and hide until we get to the appointed place."

More than two days they spent aboard the ship, and finally the time came to leave the ship at night. They reached the shore easily in a tiny boat, scooping out the water that swamped inside again and again. And in utter darkness they groped in the wake of their guide to the next stop. There they found a small café, where they ate and waited for morning.

Vika's head still hummed from the horrible noise of the motors back at the ship. She kept praising the children time and time again for their having not cried or grizzled throughout the whole way. And they were sitting, probably also a little deafened by the noise, looking at their mom with sleepy eyes.

Sergei Nilovski set out to look for a vehicle and soon, just before daylight, he returned driving a small car.

"We'll drive as far as we can from here," he said, helping everybody in. "And there, at the sea coast, we'll stop at a hotel and relax till tomorrow. I even think we may have a chance to swim in the sea."

"Wow...that would be great!" Vika hugged him. "I've never bathed in a sea."

"You're very young, baby, and everything is ahead for you," Sergei kissed her and they set off quickly.

The children fell asleep instantly, nestling in the rear seat, and Vika was nodding off, sleep pulling on her eyelids.

"You go to sleep," he offered her. "There's a long way to go, so you'd better relax."

"And you?"

"Later," he answered, fairly alert, and she yawned and dropped off to sleep at once.

In a few hours, Vika was woken up by the noise of a door opening in the car. Opening her eyes, she saw Sergei servicing the car with gasoline. Yawning and stretching herself, she got out to join him.

"Is it still a long way to drive?" Vika asked, coming up.

"I think, about three or four hours."

"Let me drive," she offered. "And you can have some sleep. Just tell me where I should drive to."

"So, you still haven't forgotten how to drive, have you?" Sergei said in surprise.

"I've had some experience here."

"That would help me a lot," he embraced her. "I'm really very sleepy. Just drive very carefully, so the police don't stop us."

"I've got some sensation with this kind of driving," Vika smiled, and they got inside the car. He showed her the route on the map. It seemed to be quite near, but the road was very twisty and a part of it ran through the mountains.

Vika made herself comfortable in the driver's seat and reached for the ignition key. But there was no key! She examined the panel closely and shifted her eyes to Sergei.

"I couldn't find the leasing office quickly enough," he was explaining defensively, connecting some conductors to start the car. "It will be returned to the owner, we'll do nothing to it, just don't stop the motor anymore."

Vika tittered changing gears and driving out of the servicing point.

"The thief is in grief — he's robbed by a thief," she said laughing. "I'll tell you sometime later about how I took somebody's car to drive and then it was stolen from me."

Sergei glanced at Vika in delight. "Do tell me all about it sometime," he smiled wearily. Vika drove out to the highway and he fell fast asleep.

Vika was driving steadily along a rather narrow way running sometimes in the hills covered with a thin wood and sometimes down in a plane, among grey stones and sparse shrubbery. Passing by settlements and casting occasional glances around, Vika could see three- or five-story brown buildings. But mainly there were just two-story houses, often painted white.

In about four hours she drove up to the appointed place and woke up Sergei. He changed back to the driver's seat and drove a few circles around the narrow streets of the small settlement, choosing the hotel. He loaded everybody out at the corner, took the car a considerable distance away and came back on foot.

They were accommodated in a very nice little inn with a red roof, almost at the shoreline. Looking out of the window, Vika saw the smooth, blue surface of the swimming pool situated at the side of the building.

"Sergei, look, isn't it fantastic!" she exclaimed. "May we bathe here?"

"Yes, certainly," he came up to her. "We'll just have to buy swimming suits first, and then we may go to the water."

After meals and shopping for some necessary things, they headed to the swimming pool. There was a special shallow section for children, and grown-ups could enjoy swimming in the large area of the deep pool. Sergei requested a woman from the personnel to look after the children, and after some swimming in the pool, Vika and he went to the seashore.

They were running, laughing, and chasing each other, and just from the run, quite close to the shore, they splashed down into the water. The bottom was covered with small but sharp pebbles, and only in some places was there sand.

It wasn't very comfortable to walk barefooted on the bottom, and one had to be careful not to step on an urchin. But they were larking about in the transparent waters of the sea, forgetting everything.

And the water was really crystalline, steel, shiny, and quite unusual. Even when they had swum far away from the shore, they could see each pebble on the bottom. Vika scooped some water into her palm and started examining it.

"Just look at it, Sergei, it seems as if there are tiny glassy particles suspended in it!"

"I think they must be some kind of seed shrimps or seaweeds," he swam up to Vika. "We should read somewhere about it."

"But you don't feel them at all," Vika was delighted, "The water is all brilliant under the sunrays...and it's so easy to swim!"

"That's because the water is very salty," smiled Sergei.

"Awfully salty," she agreed.

"People here wash their throats with it, to keep healthy!"

"Yuck!" Vika stuck out her tongue, laughing. "Everybody is washing, pissing, and then drinking."

"Not drinking," Sergei splashed some water towards her jokingly, "just gargling their throats. Now, a really dirty place is the far East. Huts are situated there just on the water, it's terribly muddy, stinky, and is used simultaneously as a toilet, a laundry, a bath, and then they use the same water for drinking."

"That's awful, Nilovski," Vika splashed water at him and swam towards the shore.

In the evening, Sergei went away to settle plans on getting further away, and came back rather late at night.

"If nothing goes wrong," he uttered apprehensively, "then tomorrow night we'll take a small fishing boat and cross to another country. I'll have to clear up some details about it tomorrow before we go."

The children, tired after their busy day, were fast asleep on the sofa in the large room.

"Let's go to the bar," Sergei offered, hugging Vika. And pressing her to his chest, he began to kiss her. Vika, kissing him in return, threw her arms around his neck, and he swooped her up in his arms, and carried her to the bed in the room.

It was almost midnight when they went down to the bar, and they spent a few hours there enjoying wine, kisses, and occasionally dancing slow dances.

Chapter 61

THE NEXT NIGHT, lying on the bottom of a cockleshell, they were crossing to another country. Vika was only troubled lest the children would fall ill, contracting some infection, as her store of medicines was meager. But the children were strong, and the weather was still warm the entire way.

Having rolled and pitched on the waves in the dark waste of waters, they moored to a shore and, stepping on slippery stones, made their way to the land. Then they made part of the way following a guide through prickly shrubs and straying among rocks, and went out to a small coppice. They got to a settlement, and then got on a bench, and by the morning, they had reached a small village.

There they took a taxi and drove to a larger town where they could rent a car. Starting from that moment, they were driving almost continually day and night, with short stops, and taking turns at the wheel.

In the morning, Sergei stopped at a small inn.

"Here we'll stop and have a rest," he said, helping everybody out. "We'll have a decent meal, a good sleep, and at dawn, we'll be on the move again."

All of the next day they drove and drove with only short rests, following the intended route. Late at night, they were all exhausted by the time they arrived at the target place and settled in for the night in another hotel.

On the way, Sergei and Vika had talked about everything, considerately avoiding sore points. Vika was already aware of all the news of her motherland. The country's leader she had grown up with had died, succeeded in the office by another pensioner. The deficit of everything remained the same, with possibly the problem of food shortages having worsened.

"Why aren't we buying them from these countries?" Vika wondered. "They have full stocks of everything here."

"It's not profitable for us," Sergei answered. "We must develop our own industry."

"Then why doesn't it develop?"

"There are many reasons for that, and first of all, there are lots of enemies around us who don't want us to be well-off."

"These countries don't look very rich, either," remarked Vika. "And the people don't earn too much money, but somehow they do have everything. Well, it's beyond me."

"Of course, it's hard for you to understand at the moment," agreed Sergei. "We live under another system."

"And that's why," Vika interrupted him merrily, "I'll have to again rinse my hair with vinegar after washing."

They burst out laughing.

There was nothing better than just sitting this way, side by side with Sergei, chatting light-heartedly about everything. He had always been her idol, her dream. And she loved to listen to him, enjoying his voice and seeing his face. They were infinitely happy to have found each other and it seemed to them that they had never been apart those long years. Nor did they feel anything had happened in that period.

"Tomorrow morning," said Sergei thoughtfully, "we'll come to a forest, and we will go through it to the foothills."

"But we are already in the mountains, aren't we?"

"Yes, we are," he agreed. He continued, "By evening, we will come to a small cemetery where we're going to have a rest before nightfall."

"Why a cemetery?" Vika was startled. "Have you already been there?"

"Yes," Sergei answered, hugging her. "I think to avoid someone finding us, we should be in places that are normally avoided by people."

"I'm afraid of the cemetery."

"You should be afraid of people who are alive, not dead," he soothed her.

Sergei produced from a bag a backpack, hooks, ropes, a flashlight, and boots for everybody he had bought beforehand and put aside, everything he considered to be needed on the way.

"Must we really just throw out all the rest?" Vika wondered, examining the heap of things he had put away as unneeded.

"We will only take warm clothes," confirmed Sergei. "And the rest of it is to be thrown away."

Vika was sincerely upset, fingering such important and almost new clothes and toys she was going to have to part with now.

"May I take any of them?" she asked timidly.

"Yes, you may, but they will be heavy to carry."

Finally, having decided about the luggage, they went to sleep.

* * * * *

Getting up early in the morning, before dawn, they quickly reached the small forest, and when the sun rose, they were already far away. Sergei was leading them along a path he knew well, carrying his backpack and Stanislaw. Vika was carrying a tightly-bound blanket and holding Maria by the hand, sometimes taking her in her arms.

"What do you think, Nilovski..." Vika tried to start talking.

"Hush," he whispered, "tcc...try not to step on dry twigs, listen closely to the sounds."

With small rest halts, they came to a small river.

"We must walk in it upstream," Sergei said, taking off his boots.

"But the water is probably cold," Vika was gazing at him in wonder. "And there are stones all over!"

"That's why I have told you to take your sandals. Roll up your pants as high as you can, put on your sandals and go! Remember, my baby," he went on tenderly, "in the mountains, under no circumstance, let out a sound. Mind the echo!"

They changed their clothes. Sergei, taking Maria in his arms, was the first to step into the water. Wincing, he moved ahead. Vika snatched up Stanislaw and started after him.

"Ugh..." she could only gasp, catching her breath in the icy water.

"Don't stop, come on," Sergei said, looking back. And resisting the opposite flow of water up to their knees, they pushed on, hardly able to keep their balance on the stones.

Having made a rather long way upstream, they crossed the river. Vika was showering with sweat, and her feet were red with cold.

"Well done, girl," Sergei praised her. "I was very afraid lest you should fall."

"So was I," Vika confessed frankly, shuffling off her sandals.

They had a little rest and started cutting their way among the hills and shrubs. Totally exhausted, they reached the small cemetery Nilovski had mentioned.

Looking around, he found a comfortable place to have a rest amongst the bushes and short growing trees, in a small wallow at a rock. They cleared a spot, spread the blanket out, ate, and fell down to relax.

In a while, Vika woke up and opened her eyes. Sergei's eyes were watching her.

"Why aren't you sleeping?" she asked, half-whispering, embracing him.

"I've had a nap," he answered in an undertone. "Don't want anymore."

Vika glanced at the kids, they were snoring peacefully under the blanket.

"It's getting cool up here," Sergei said, pressing Vika against him. "Soon it's going to be much colder."

"I hope we don't catch a cold!"

"I only wish we get home safe," Sergei said anxiously, "and there we could cure ourselves."

"Suppose we are captured here?"

"It shouldn't happen, not for the world," he answered seriously. "We would be put in different jails, and most probably for a lifetime, without even going into the matter. As for the children, they would be sent somewhere or sold."

Vika looked at him with horror, and carefully, slowly began to look around.

"That's why I'm telling you, 'Hush!'," he drew her to his chest. "Though the route is reliable, you should look out and be careful, just in case."

"Couldn't we have used another way?"

"There are lots of ways," Sergei answered. "But everything needs time. And, with such young children with us, too, this is only way right now."

"Oh, Sergei, Sergei," she sighed deeply, pressing against him. "How are we to move in the cave?"

"We'll throw away the backpack and everything we don't need," he began to explain. "I'll tie Stanislaw to my chest, we'll take Maria by both hands and make our way slowly."

They fell silent watching the sunset, and each thinking to themselves. Then Vika looked at him seriously, at a loss on how to touch on the topic she was anxious about.

"Sergei, have you seen Lena?" she uttered timidly.

"I have," he said.

"Why was she put in prison for such a long term?"

"She made a mess of the operation and let the group get lost," Sergei answered slowly, and then glanced at Vika suspiciously. "And how do you know about her?"

"I was...I..." she couldn't make up her mind to tell him. "You know...I called home, and called you, too."

He sat up with a jerk beside her.

"So it was you who phoned and said nothing? My mom told me about it."

"Yes," Vika nodded and fell silent.

"Can you tell me more about it now?" Sergei took her hand and looked her in the eye. "Did your mother tell you about Lena?"

"Yes."

"When did you talk to her?" Sergei asked nervously.

"Before the New Year," Vika looked down, "the next year after Lena and I were lost and I was brought to Germany."

"What? Where?" He jumped up to his feet and immediately dropped down on his knees before her. "What are you talking about?" he whispered, taking her by the shoulders. "What did your mom tell you?"

"She told me," Vika began tentatively, "that I should sit still over there and not ruin anybody's life...or career."

Nilovski hit his knee with his fist.

"I know when it was," he said angrily. "They moved out of their apartment shortly after that."

Vika's jaw dropped in amazement.

"And w-where did they go to?" she asked, stumbling over her words with apprehension.

"Somewhere up north," Sergei said between his teeth. "What fucking sort of career do your brothers need?"

"She was worried about yours as well."

"I can take care of myself," he jabbed himself in the chest with his finger nervously, puffing his nostrils. "How could she have done such a thing?"

He stopped short, drawing his breath and collecting his wits.

"When was Maria born?" he asked, and Vika named the date.

"Damn it," Sergei cursed, once more beating himself on the knees. "You called your mother when you were pregnant...when I was working in Eastern Germany."

It was as if somebody hit Vika, she started and sat straight, eyeing Sergei in shock.

"You don't say so! See? You don't say...we were very close at hand," she burst into tears, falling down on the blanket.

He was sitting clasping his head between his hands, unable to find soothing words for her.

"You should have told everything to my mom," Sergei uttered perplexedly.

Vika stopped crying and, wiping her face, sat next to him.

"Possibly, everything might have gone another way," she said quietly. "But," Vika fell silent, shrugging her shoulders. Sergei embraced her, and they were sitting, watching the sunset until it grew utterly dark.

Chapter 62

IT WAS WELL after midnight when they started noiselessly uphill. They moved fairly quickly throughout the night, following the winding paths and going up higher and higher.

Sergei was carrying the backpack and the sleeping Stanislaw, while Vika and Maria were marching in their wake, trying hard not to lag behind. From time to time, Vika had to carry her overtired daughter, panting at the steep, rising slope.

Having walked for some time, Sergei stopped for a little rest halt to have everybody change into warm clothes and throw down into a precipice everything they did not need. It was becoming unbearably cold; their breath was steaming and their hands freezing.

"Come on now, let's go," Sergei hustled them, glancing at the slightly whitening sky. "We must be there before dawn. Please, keep looking back, there are beasts of all kinds ranging here."

And Vika, snatching Maria, marched again following him in single file. Her teeth chattered with fear. She kept casting haunted glances around, she thought she heard some sounds beside her, and she looked away in horror from close abysses.

The barely-noticeable path was sometimes becoming so narrow they had to squeeze their way forward, and the small pebbles tumbling from under their boots were flying down noiselessly.

Vika kept catching her breath with the fear of stumbling, and her arms grew numb, heavy with her daughter who was holding on to her neck, too tired to walk on her own.

Sergei was hurrying. He was constantly looking back at Vika and hissing at her if she chanced to stumble or make noise. It was dawning gradually and it felt like the sun was going to rise in a short while. But all of a sudden it became hazy.

"This is good," Sergei stopped for a moment, panting. "Doesn't matter if its haze or clouds...the main thing is that we're almost there."

Vika couldn't answer a word, leaning against a rock, wheezing.

"When we're up...at the patch," he whispered, gulping down saliva, "then we'll have a rest...come on!"

Vika started after him again, hardly able to move her legs and afraid to change the position of the numbed arms holding her daughter. She felt a hammering in her head, a thickening in her ears and the taste of blood in her mouth.

Suddenly the haze began retreating downwards, and they found themselves at a brightly lit slope. Wind blew in blasts. And when it seemed to Vika that she was unable to take another step, Sergei stopped and, pressing his back to the wall, looked up.

A brow of the rock in front of them formed here, as it were, a small corner, and the rock they were pressed against was growing a bit wider upwards and was partially hanging over the path.

They carefully placed the woken up children in the corner, and Sergei put the backpack in front of them.

"Sit still now...and don't get up," he said huskily to the children, panting, and pressed his back against the rock, kneading his numbed hands.

"I'll go...and look out around the corner," he said, glancing up again, "Just to be sure...we're exactly there."

Sergei pushed off the rock and moved slowly around the corner along the narrow path. Vika followed him. Turning around the rock, she saw him stop about seven yards away from her, and moving off the rock, he looked around.

"Yes," he said, turning to come back to her. "This is exactly the right place."

Sergei made a step towards her...and suddenly something thumped, cracked, and the stone he was standing on abruptly fell down into the dark abyss, together with him.

"A-a-ah..." Vika gasped, and dropped down on her hands and knees, looking at the place where he once stood...and, as if under hypnosis, she started crawling to it.

Abutting with her hands against the very edge, Vika looked down, trembling, unable to understand or feel anything...one more inch would bring her down...following him.

How much time had passed, Vika did not know...all of a sudden a huge eagle flew quite near her and waved his wings, making a circle. A chilling blast of wind from the abyss blew Vika in the face; she started, backed off, and at once heard some squeaking.

"Sergei..." Vika gasped, choking, shocked, and edged off the collapse, eyeing in horror the eagle hovering nearby.

She crawled around the corner and saw her children there.

"Do-ogs," the girl was whimpering, looking at her mother.

"What dogs?" she shook her head with pain, blocking her ears. But suddenly she could hear the barking of dogs as well.

"Dogs...dogs," she started rushing about on her knees, pulling the children up and then seating them back again, obviously at a loss as to what to do.

She opened the backpack mechanically and dumped everything out of it. Ropes and hooks fell right at her feet. She took a hook and, staggering, began casting it up, then pulled on the rope, hoping the iron hook would claw against something. But it flew rattling and clanking back down, almost hitting her.

Again and again Vika threw up the hook and pulled on the rope. Finally it stuck in something, and Vika, making sure the rope held strong, turned to the children. Her breath came in pants through her open mouth, and she couldn't see how she could lift them.

Kneeling, Vika was touching with her trembling hands the children and the ropes. Then she picked up her son and began tying him up to her bosom, binding herself up together with him. Then she tied her daughter to the end of the loose rope hanging down from the stone.

The children were whimpering and trembling with fear and cold. Vika shouted at them, threw everything they did not need into the abyss and, seizing the rope, began clambering up. She was too weak to cover this short distance, but still, when she was up at the brow, she desperately seized the rope, trying to flop over on the rock. But she could not, hindered by the child at her breast.

Vika went down again and feverishly began to untie her son. At some point, she could hear again the far-off barking of dogs, and was casting glances at the path, making haste in her movements.

She tied up Stanislaw to her back and again, grunting and moaning, began her climb. With great difficulty, stripping her hands to blood, she finally managed to fling herself over to the stone and she directly began pulling on the other rope lifting her daughter.

Without pausing for a moment, Vika tied her son again to her bosom, released the hook off the rock and bound herself and her daughter with that rope. She took Maria by the hand and pulled her to the narrow opening of the cave...but stopping abruptly at the entrance, sat down facing the girl.

"Listen to me," mother whispered, looking crazily at her daughter. "You must go very slowly pressing to the wall with your butt." And she pressed her daughter to the wall. "Like this! Or else you'll die!"

The girl, pressing her trembling lips, was looking at her mom in horror.

"Got it?" Vika insisted pressing the girl's back to the wall again. "Like this!" And standing up, she began squeezing into the cave.

Stopping on the ledge, Vika shined the flashlight on the wall and, verifying the direction, set forth directly, pressing Maria's back to the wall once more.

* * * * *

A whole eternity seemed to have passed before they reached the exit at the other side. And putting her daughter up onto a stone, sideways, with the son tied up to her bosom, Vika began crawling out.

As soon as she was in the open air, she untied herself from Maria, fastened the hook to a rock, rebound her son to her back, lowered down her daughter first, and then climbed down from the stone by herself.

She grabbed Stanislaw, took her daughter by the hand, and paced down quickly, almost running, making out the path in the light haze.

Vika had utterly forgotten where she had to go from here. She continued to just walk down, along the barely visible path. The mist was clearing away, and quite near, she saw a vertical cliff and at the foot was their camp from long ago. Stumbling, she quickened her pace as if somebody was waiting for her there.

Coming out to the site, Vika did not see anybody...but again she heard the dogs barking, quite clearly now. She shook her head, looking around like a hunted-down animal, and ran to a big boulder, hoping to hide on it.

Stepping on a small rock, Vika pushed up Maria and handed Stanislaw to her, but she herself had neither the strength nor the time to take a running jump onto the boulder. Two huge dogs were careening straight for her...Vika squatted, crouching and howling, and covered her head with her arms.

The dogs dashed up to her, but did not touch her. They stopped short, almost nosing her, and were growling and barking, baring their teeth angrily. But all of a sudden the dogs calmed down and Vika heard an old man's voice soothing them. Lifting her head, she saw an old man nearing her with a walking stick.

"Grandpa..." Vika trembling, recognizing him as the same David's grandpa, in whose house they had lodged back then.

He came up closer, squinting to see her better.

"Grandpa...it's me...Vika," she said as loudly as she could. "We stayed here with you once...with a group."

"I remember," he answered, having made her out clearly, "Sergei's fiancé."

She shifted her eyes slowly towards the mountains from which she had come. Up above, on the boulder, the children burst into tears.

"O-oh, I see you have company with you," Grandpa said in surprise, looking at Vika suspiciously. "Now let's take them off there and move on."

As if in a daze, Vika took the children off with difficulty, still staring at the mountains in the distance.

"Let's go, darlings, let's go," Grandpa was pushing Vika ahead, seeing her condition and beginning to understand that something horrible must have happened. And the whole of the company plodded along.

Chapter 63

VIKA WAS WALKING in the wake of Grandpa, stumbling and looking back again and again. The old man was leading Maria by the hand, and at times would glance anxiously at Vika who led Stanislaw. She was shaking and staggering as if drunk, she was even too weak to take her son in her arms, and the child kept glancing at his mother with fear and walked by himself, without even asking her to pick him up.

In the evening they reached Grandpa's house. He invited everybody in, but Vika shook her head and sat down on the stones, gazing vacantly ahead.

Grandpa, having fed the children, put them to bed and prepared a bed for Vika, and then came out to join her.

"I have put the children to bed," he said, sitting down quietly beside her and offering her a mug with some brew. "Here you are, have a drink."

"Thank you," Vika answered almost inaudibly, refusing the drink.

"And I was just out gathering roots, you know?" he said in a gentle voice. "It was really a piece of luck for you today, you know...I had almost finished with it."

He was looking at her worriedly, anxious to find something to distract her with.

"I still have your little curtains hanging there...you know," he said cheerfully. "The ones you sewed when you were here with Sergei."

"Sergei..." echoed Vika. "Sergei..." she repeated, and breathing faster, turned her head to Grandpa. "He's...he's...there," panting, she pointed to the mountains, trying to say something, but choking on the words, and she flopped down on the ground, somewhat in a state of shock.

Grandpa carried her home with great difficulty, where for two days he watched her as she tossed and turned in a state of mental anguish and oblivion, constantly calling for Sergei.

Her hair became tangled, and because of the stress, it began to fall out in tufts. The old man cut her hair around the wound that was on one side of her head. He kept putting a cold compress on her forehead, and trying to make her drink some of his brews. The children sat in a corner, quiet as mice, occasionally coming up to their mother.

Late during the second night, Vika came to her senses and opened her eyes, looking around her. Grandpa was sitting by the fire with the children, telling them something and putting sticks in a row in front of him. Vika called him, barely audible.

"That's better now, that's better," he got up fussing and came over to her. "It's really better this way, honey. Now I'll make you some hot brew, you know...and tomorrow you'll be flying about like a bird," he helped the eager children up to her bed and went back to the stove, picking out some of the herbs hanging on the walls.

Vika was looking at the children, wearily suffering the pain that pressed her head like a vice. Her ears were ringing, her mouth was dry. She shut her eyes for a while. Grandpa quickly brought her a mug of some warm, dark brew.

"There is drink for you," he said melodiously, bringing the mug to her lips. Vika drank it all and dropped off to sleep.

She woke in the morning hearing Grandpa leave the house, and sat up slowly. She felt weak all over and sick. She was unable to stay sitting up and lay down again.

Grandpa returned and started making the fire.

"Good morning," Vika said very quietly.

"Hello, honey," he responded eagerly, heading to her, and he put his palm on her forehead.

"Well, that's better, you know," he said, smiling slightly, and returned to the stove. "Now we'll cook some chicken, it's about time you ate something, you know."

During the day, Vika drank some brew and clear chicken soup, and by the evening she felt much better. The kids, getting more cheerful as well, were playing with each other and tailing Grandpa around the yard.

After two days, Grandpa began getting ready to go some-where early in the morning.

"I'll go to see David, my grandson, you know," he said. "Something ought to be done."

And after breakfast he left quickly, and the children remained with their mother. Vika could already get up and walk slowly, but the awful depression was crushing her, and looking at her children blankly, she cried endlessly.

* * * * *

Grandpa returned by the evening carrying a sack full of clothes and food supplies. And the next day, by lunchtime, David came on horseback bringing more things for Vika and the children.

Vika, seeing David, burst into tears at once. He came up and hugged her, recognizing her with difficulty. He saw a very lean, yellow-skinned, weary woman wrapped in a shawl, livid rings under her eyes.

They went outside and, stopping some distance from the house, sat down on the stones, and Vika, for the first time in her life, crying, told him the whole truth from the very beginning up to the moment of Sergei's death. She remembered nothing after that—nothing at all—even in fragments.

Sighing heavily, David took her hand.

"Poor little girl," he said in a low voice, stroking her hand and looking far away. "Poor Nilovski! How unhappy you guys have been," he fell silent, unable to say anything else.

"Sergei cannot be returned now," he said ruefully after a while. "We'll think of something for you, don't you worry. And what's up with your head? As far as I remember, you used to have beautiful hair."

Vika took off her shawl.

"Yeah," David said thoughtfully. "You're lucky there are no mirrors here. Now, let me shave you."

"Thank you, but I don't want anything," Vika said listlessly, pulling on her shawl. "I don't even want to live...so why should I care about a trifling thing like hair."

David looked at her attentively.

"Why don't you try to think about your future and yourself," he said gently. "You have children and you'll have to take care of them."

"The government will take better care of them," Vika forced the words out slowly.

"You see, I have four children," said David. "And I would never entrust them to the government."

"I don't want to live without Sergei," she burst into tears again. "I don't have even a hope now to see him ever again."

David stood up and started pacing back and forth near her.

"I do understand you very well," he said compassionately. "It's a terrible and irretrievable loss. And to tell you the truth...I can hardly believe it," he fell silent, sniffling and rubbing his temples. Then, recovering his thoughts and spirit, he went on slowly, "What's happened can never be corrected, and most probably one just ought to try and stop thinking about it." He paused, looking at Vika. "Time does cure all kinds of injuries. Well...at least it scabs them over."

Vika looked up at him, her eyes full of anguish.

"I feel so bad," she whispered. He sat down by her side again and took her hand.

"You just live here for a while, read the children the books I have brought," David said. "Get a little stronger...and I'll think of a way to help you. The documents, too, need to be made some-how...we can find a way out of this," he put his arm around her shoulders. "And now come on, just let me shave your head, so the hair grows out evenly afterwards."

They returned to the house. David shaved Vika, which made the kids merry indeed. Then he dawdled around with them, playing and showing them the books and toys he had brought for them. They had dinner together and by the evening he left.

In a couple of weeks Vika grew noticeably stronger from the fresh air, but a heavy heart still burdened her, and thoughts of Sergei Nilovski persisted, making her cry constantly.

One day David came again, bringing their documents.

"It's been a long time since this settlement has been smashed away by mud torrents," he began to explain in a temperate manner. He held out to Vika a thin notebook with something written in it. "These people seem to have no relatives anywhere...nobody has ever inquired about them or sought them. We shall now carefully fill in your passport preserving your date of birth, including the year," he said, producing the clean blank documents. "We'll also fill them in for the children, preserving their dates of birth. I will finish it all later on. As for the place of birth for you, it will be this settlement."

Vika shifted her eyes to the notebook in anguish, opening it.

"Dana, Elizabeth, Arthur," she read slowly and looked up at David. "Who are they? They have such strange names."

"Well, we don't have much choice, do we?" he explained. "So just read and memorize your biography," David said, smiling, pointing to the notebook. "And let's go, I'll take your photo for the passport."

Vika took off her shawl — thin hair was just showing on her head.

"Well, well," David said thoughtfully. "What on earth shall we do?"

"Why, just take her picture with the shawl on," Grandpa advised. And Vika put on her shawl.

Having made the pictures and talked for a while, David had dinner and, taking the passport with him, he was about to leave again. "Oh, yes, Vika, look here," he was already standing in the doorway. "Of course, you better remain here...near us, I have a very nice wife. She could help you with everything. But people are always nosey, and they will keep asking questions. And, God forbid, some distant relative of this family should show up," said David. "Therefore, you will have to go to Russia and get lost somewhere else. What would be the best place? I don't even know...that all must be thought over, too. And you should just try to get the children used to their new names."

And saying good-bye, he left, promising to come back in a few days.

Chapter 64

IT WAS VERY painful, indeed, to call her children by alien names. It took Vika a long time to explain to them that, in a new country, they needed new names.

Maria, laughing and frequently speaking German, was calling Stanislaw by his new name 'Arthur.' The boy wailed and tried to fight her, thinking she was calling him funny names. Nobody reacted to their new names. Almost two weeks later, David came to fetch them.

"You'll have to leave," he said sadly. "It will soon get snowy and it's very cold in the mountains."

Vika cried as she parted with Grandpa, kissing him and thanking him for everything. She mounted a horse and tied Maria in front of her. David mounted another horse, taking Stanislaw with him and fastening Vika's things behind him, they set off. Having ridden off a ways, Vika turned around and waved her hand to Grandpa, looking in anguish at the mountains around her.

They reached the lowlands fairly quickly. Down below, a car was waiting for them with a bag in the trunk.

"My wife has gathered a few things here for you," David said, pointing to the trunk. "And there are food supplies in the bag."

"Thank you so much," Vika said in a low voice, beginning to put her luggage together.

"And this is for you, also from my wife," David handed her a small black handbag. "There you will find all your documents, the tickets, and money."

He produced more money from his pocket.

"This is for you for the time being," and he held out the money to Vika. "Divide it into parts, wrap it up, and hide it wherever women usually do."

"And where do women usually hide such things?" she asked shyly.

"Well," David tittered, "a part of it you fasten to the inner side of your bra, and another part to the inner side of your panties."

He gave her two handkerchiefs with pins and while in the car, she quickly managed all the manipulations with the money.

"Thank you very much," she said again, getting out of the car. "How am I to repay you for all you've done for me?"

"Just live," he embraced her. "And bring up your children. Now get back in and let's get moving, or else you'll miss your plane." They got into the car and started off. Vika, looking out of the window sorrowfully, began sniffling and wiping away her tears. He tried to soothe her as best he could.

"Don't you worry," said David. "I've put my coordinates into your bag, so as soon as you settle down, please call me at once. We'll keep helping you as much as we can," he patted Vika on the hand.

"And where am I flying to?"

"To the Urals, in central Russia," he smiled. "My wife and I decided that people live a bit better off there, and we think it's fairly easy to find a job there. And there, in the small town, I have some friends. I have jotted down their address, so you may turn to them, mentioning me, if you want to."

"Oh, thank you."

"My God, I've almost forgotten!" added David. "My wife is a doctor, and she has put all kinds of medicines in the trunk you might need, and written notes on what and how each is to be taken. What if you fall ill on arriving...it must be cold there already."

"Thank you," Vika said melancholically, as if she didn't even hear what he was telling her.

"Yes, as soon as you arrive, stop at a hotel at once, and then begin to search for a job somewhere in a kindergarten, and find some lodging to rent. Okay?"

"Okay," Vika echoed.

"And just don't forget to call me sometimes, will you? Don't disappear," David insisted. "And I'll tell you what to do next."

All the way to the airport David was trying to lighten Vika's mood, distracting her with talking. But she kept looking back at the mountains, wiping away the unending tears.

Having reached the airport, David drove into a parking lot, stopped the motor, and turned to face her.

"You know, Victoria," David said, seeing her depressed condition, "you must get strong enough now to wake up to life. You're obliged now to think of your children."

He took her hands and shook them gently.

"Why have you come all this horrible way?" he demanded sharply. "You must be courageous now and raise your children! Can't you see?" he looked her straight in the eyes. "Don't let them perish," David insisted. "Can you hear me? Have mercy on the little ones, they have nobody but you with them! And they are not to blame for anything!"

Vika was looking at him attentively with her wet eyes.

"You know what?" he said with pain in his voice. "Just don't you look behind anymore. Yes, just like this, go on living without looking back. Just keep doing something," David said, nervous with his helplessness. "Go to study, spend more time with your children! Go further and further away from this period, and if the reminiscences begin choking you again, you just switch over to something else, so that you don't get bogged down in the past. Don't blame yourself for anything — it's just your destiny. And start your life anew. Only don't tell anybody anything, ever — it's going to be easier that way."

David was watching Vika, seeing how much she needed support now, but he could do nothing else for her at the moment. He had already done what he could, and more than that.

"Thank you for everything," Vika said in an undertone, and they got out of the car, heading to the airport building.

David helped her to register her tickets and the luggage. They went to the gate where the boarding took place. When it was Vika's turn, David hugged her good-bye.

"Well, this is it," he said. "I wish you good luck and happiness with all my heart!"

"Thank you for everything," Vika answered, and started walking slowly inside the hall.

It was with a heavy heart that David watched her go, unable to find anything that could soothe and encourage her at that moment. As if pressed down by a burden, Vika moved away from him, her head bent, her hands holding those of the children.

Maria was springing joyfully beside her mom, swinging her free hand. But unexpectedly, she turned back and, smiling, waved her hand to David cheerfully. David also smiled and waved to her in return. And suddenly he felt encouraged. *Why, certainly!* he thought. *Vika will pluck up her courage, she will for sure! Her children will help her to!*

Summary

Just one mistake can change a young girl's life forever.

This story is a lesson in life for Vika Zotova, as she grows up in the Soviet Union prior to Glasnost. For an innocent, fourteen-year-old girl, that truth becomes all too real when she meets Sergei Nilovski, a KGB officer who becomes the first love of her life. Before their relationship can full mature, terror strikes. She is laughing and joking one minute, only to wake up days after, as slave in a foreign land. And, her young mind is continuously thinking about ways to escape.

Biography

NINA GUEST

NINA GUEST is a published author in Russia. Her first book, *Don't Disappear, Part I*, is not only a Russian best seller; it has been adapted to a successful, long running Television Mini-Series. And, the publishing house can hardly keep *Part II of Don't Disappear* on Russian bookshelves. Nina's Russian culture largely influences her writing. She writes fiction and non-fiction, comedy, poetry, and movie scripts. Some of her works reveal life as it really was in pre-glasnost, Communist Russia, as well as currently within the Russian Federation. Look for *Don't Disappear, Part II*, and a new comedy on US bookshelves within the near future.

LaVergne, TN USA
15 September 2010
197167LV00002B/38/P